PRAISE FOR *THE BIRDWOMAN'S PALATE*

"When history and climate change threaten to overpower us, we need books like Laksmi Pamuntjak's *The Birdwoman's Palate* to remind us that it is through love, culture, and sharing the good things nature has to offer we will find solace and the solutions for moving forward. It is a well-told tale that brings us closer, over time and space, in the hour of need."

—Sjón, author of *The Whispering Muse* and *Moonstone*: *The Boy Who Never Was*

"A beautifully written novel: humane, humble, passionate, and ripe with culinary interactions . . . A fitting tribute from the author of Indonesia's first independent good food guide."

—William Wongso, Indonesian culinary guru

"The novel has an aura of a dream, too, a little shimmery—it's in the idiom of twenty-first-century text speak, and yet, as I was reading, I thought of Dutch still lifes, with their artfully perfect fruit, flowers, fish, and meat, reminding us of mortality and decay amid beauty. *The Birdwoman's Palate* for me is an incitement to take time to savor the present from the endless protocols that mask and organize human frailty."

—Margaret Cohen, author of *The Novel and the Sea*, professor, and Guggenheim Fellow

"Who better to write a book about a culinary tour through Indonesia than Laksmi Pamuntjak, whose passion and knowledge of the local cuisine is unsurpassed. I still remember when she took us around Jakarta on a local food tour eighteen years ago. This book brings me back to the street satays and sit-down feasts we experienced together."

—Jean-Georges Vongerichten, award-winning chef, restaurateur, and author of *Home Cooking with Jean-Georges*

Praise for Laksmi Pamuntjak's
The Question of Red

"This magnificent, heart-wrenching novel is more than a long overdue look at Indonesia's genocidal past. It is a poetic reflection on the traumas that divide a society and the emotional as well as political complexities in addressing and thus healing them."

—Ilija Trojanow, author of *The Lamentations of Zeno, The Collector of Worlds, Along the Ganges, Mumbai to Mecca: A Pilgrimage to the Holy Sites of Islam*

"[*The Question of Red*] signals Laksmi Pamuntjak's bravery and scope as a writer and may yet prove to be a landmark work of Southeast Asian writing."

—Tash Aw, author of *The Harmony Silk Factory*, winner of the Commonwealth Writers' Prize for Best First Book

"Great literature lights our way and helps us to understand distant worlds; the best books make us part of those worlds—with all their horror, as well as their resplendence and intelligence. That's the kind of literature that Laksmi Pamuntjak writes."

—José Eduardo Agualusa, author of *A General Theory of Oblivion*, shortlisted for the Man Booker International Prize

"An absolute must-read . . . it holds so many important lessons about Indonesia."

—*Die Zeit* (Germany)

"In *The Question of Red*, Laksmi Pamuntjak masterfully weaves a web of narratives dealing with a dark, bloody chapter of Indonesia's history, the 1965–66 anti-communist purge—a topic that remains controversial to this day. It is more than a love story or a historical novel; it is also an erudite reflection of the stunning amalgam of what Indonesia is: a Muslim-majority country influenced by both the modern West and its Hindu heritage."

—Yenni Kwok, journalist for *Time* and the *New York Times*

"One of Asia's greatest modern love stories! It is never easy to combine personal tragedy and love with a political holocaust, but Pamuntjak writes with such enormous confidence, emotional maturity, and beauty that she has no problem merging the two. This novel, translated by herself into English, unquestionably places Indonesian fiction on the map of the twenty-first century and Pamuntjak as one of its principal writers."

—Ahmed Rashid, author of *Pakistan on the Brink: The Future of America, Pakistan, and Afghanistan*, longtime contributor to the *New York Review of Books*

"Perfectly and poignantly captures the dizzying unsteadiness of a traumatized world poised between normalcy and catastrophe."

—*Frankfurter Allgemeine Zeitung*, upon naming *The Question of Red* to the Top 8 Books of the 2015 Frankfurt Book Fair

"With this novel, Laksmi Pamuntjak establishes herself firmly as one of the most eloquent writers of Indonesian history, intertwining scenes of great tension and reckless passion with sections of great historical interest . . . It needs a skillful pen to take on the Mahabharata and to rewrite Indonesia's recent history."

—Saskia Wieringa, author of *Lubang Buaya*, writing in the *Jakarta Globe*

"This is a richly textured, multilayered novel—an intricate weave of erased histories, living memories, and formative myths of war and peace . . . With passion and exemplary commitment, Pamuntjak brings to life a forgotten era of turbulence, with its casualties, its victims, and its perpetrators. I was immersed in the novel's world for a week, and when I emerged I was spellbound for days."

—Aamer Hussein, author of *The Cloud Messenger* and
Another Gulmohar Tree

"Laksmi Pamuntjak's luminous imagination has brought us a seminal work of Southeast Asian literature. *The Question of Red* explores with urgent context and brilliant writing one of the world's least known but most brutal political mass murders of the twentieth century. This profound meditation on memory and forgetting deserves a worldwide audience."

—Margaret Scott Rauch, Indonesia scholar, adjunct assistant
professor of public administration, New York University

"What makes [*The Question of Red*] not merely a historical epic or a common love story is the stylishness of its prose, the psychological depth of its characters, its reflexivity and erudition, and the meticulous research that lies at its heart, which breathes life to the setting and all the life situations and existential dilemmas it encompasses."

—*Kompas* (Indonesia)

"This novel will join the pantheon of the all-time greats in Indonesian literature."

—Goenawan Mohamad, essayist, poet, founding editor of
Tempo magazine

"The best [Indonesian] novel since *The Earth of Mankind* tetralogy."

—J. B. Kristanto, journalist and literary critic

"One of a few novels that stresses the sense of anxiety plaguing us in Indonesia these days: the anxiety that the terrifying 'events of 1965' will be lost, stripped from collective memory. We do not want to return to brutality."

—*Tempo*

THE
BIRDWOMAN'S
PALATE

THE
BIRDWOMAN'S
PALATE

LAKSMI PAMUNTJAK

*Translated by Tiffany Tsao
and revised by the author*

Text copyright © 2014 by Laksmi Pamuntjak
Translated © 2018 by Tiffany Tsao and Laksmi Pamuntjak
All rights reserved.

Previously published as *Aruna & Lidahnya* in Indonesia in 2014 by Gramedia Pustaka Utama. Revised and edited by the author for this edition. Translated from Indonesian by Tiffany Tsao and revised by the author. First published in English by AmazonCrossing in 2018.

Published by AmazonCrossing, Seattle

www.apub.com

Amazon, the Amazon logo, and AmazonCrossing are trademarks of Amazon.com, Inc., or its affiliates.

ISBN-13: 9781542048354 (paperback)
ISBN-10: 1542048354 (paperback)
ISBN-13: 9781503937345 (hardcover)
ISBN-10: 1503937348 (hardcover)

Cover design by David Drummond

Printed in the United States of America

A Culinary Map of Indonesia
Cities visited in the novel, with key local dishes named below

Madura

Bangkalan
Nasi Bebek Sinjay
Nasi Petis

Pamekasan
Soto Madura
Kikil Kokot

Sampang

Banda Aceh
Rujak Aceh
Sate Matang
Ayam Tangkap

Medan
Kari Bihun
Bihun Bebek
Medan-style Kwetiau Goreng

Parapat
Naniura

Singkawang
Bubur Babi
Kwetiau Goreng

Pontianak
Bakmi Kepiting
Pengkang
Lek Tau Suan

Palembang
Pempek
Pindang Patin
Es Kacang Merah

Jakarta

Surabaya
Rujak Soto
Botok Pakis
Sate Klopo

Mataram
Ayam Taliwang
Beberuk

Lombok

1

Virus

In my dream, I watch as Koh Copin is gunned down, shot dead just as he's ladling broth into a bowl of noodles. He crumples immediately, tumbling face-first into the pot of steaming stock, and Cik Lani and her two flunkies drag his lifeless body away from the stove and lay him down on the restaurant floor. His head and face are garnished with strands of yellow egg noodles, vermicelli, and bits of leafy greens. His eyes look funny—wide open and bulging, as though in surprise, like the eyes of a grouper when it realizes it's taken the bait. His nose, thankfully not his strongest feature, is all mashed up like an overcooked wonton.

I scream. Or maybe not. But I do feel a rush of sadness because Koh Copin is no longer the King of Noodles—and this, after he reluctantly sullied his menu by adding liang *tea and assorted fishballs, both of which he thought profoundly un-Chinese. I remember him saying, "When I die, a thousand years from now, Copin's Noodles will be the top noodle joint in town."*

Now look at him. He can't even compete with Awat's Noodle House across the road.

Something comes over me. I watch myself step momentarily into the scene and touch Cik Lani's arm. She's staring at her husband's body—sallow, slack, his T-shirt covering only half of his paunch. Everything seems sadder and so much more exposed under the neon light. I smell urine. The entire restaurant smells of it. Wet paper towels are scattered on the floor, as if they can salvage what's left of the noodle man.

"You can't let them get away with it," I tell Cik Lani. "Awat's kids must have been behind this. You have to avenge your husband before they figure out how to make a better fishball."

"Are you nuts?" says Cik Lani, her voice hoarse.

For a split second, she looks blank.

Suddenly, she stands up and walks outside. I watch her cross the busy street with long, manly strides, the steps of a crusader, paying the chaotic traffic no mind. When she reaches Awat's Noodle House, she calmly takes out a gun and starts shooting everybody inside the restaurant: the old grandma in charge of making black bean sambal, the young woman behind the cash register, a pair of servers wrapping fishcakes in banana leaves, two of Koh Awat's nephews who are preparing Bangka-style noodles at the food cart out front, a customer reaching into a glass jar at the counter for some prawn crackers, three oblivious diners slurping up their tofu and fishcake noodle soup.

Silence. The kind you read about in thrillers and murder accounts. The eerie calm between the act itself and the realization of what's happened. It's over too fast, and why on earth is it so hot? The air fills with the rank fumes of gun smoke and vinegar, and another, more nauseating smell—fear, sweat? I can't tell.

For an instant I don't know whether to applaud or call the police, but before I can do or say anything, I find myself in a high-end Japanese res-taurant, the kind that only serves multicourse omakase *and thrives quietly on word of mouth.*

Before me lies a piece of toro sushi, singular and luminous. From its iridescence and its milk-fed-veal-like pinkness, I know it must be a Tuesday, or a Friday, and I smile because I've barely hit thirty-five and am about to taste that impossible cliché—the taste of heaven.

When I look up, the sushi master chef is staring back at me. It's Koh Copin.

"Now this is what I call real magic," I say, genuinely impressed. "Not only did you rise from the dead, you also had the good sense to bring a piece of heaven with you. YOU ROCK!"

November 2012

"You're late," says the woman when the elevator doors open. "Did you just wake up?"

Yes, and I'm regretting it already.

"They're in the meeting room." Her tone is curt, as if I've done her some personal wrong.

I slip in next to her halfheartedly, though I could have just taken the stairs—the building is only two stories high. I recognize the woman, but in my frazzled state I'm hesitant about making small talk. From the corner of my eye, I see that her smooth brow is now furrowed again—as though she's deciding on the proper course of action. I wonder: Do I stay quiet? Do I come right out and tell her, "Shut up. I don't even know your name. You have no right to ask me anything"? And how on earth does she know I'm late because I overslept?

I rack my brain trying to remember her name. Nina—that's it. From R&D. Fifteen years of service and passed up for promotion at least a half dozen times. Figures—bitter, shriveled, reduced to dissecting the habits of others. (Story of my life, too, but that's for another time.)

I smile at her, twice in fact, but I refuse to say anything. Now, there's no way that I can slip away to the cafeteria to grab a quick breakfast. I avert my eyes from the mirror in the elevator. I don't really want to know what I look like.

But before I tell you about my two lives—food and avian politics—one heaven, the other earth, I should explain that I am what people in my business call an epidemiologist. It's the glorified term for an outbreak expert. It's a taxing business, outbreaks, and you can't be at it all the time. When there's a real outbreak, it's doomsday. When there's none (which is usually the case), your entire life is pointless. *You* are pointless. So these days I only consult on epidemiological matters. It's more dignified that way. You only get to work when you know you're being useful.

The conference room I'm heading to is one of many at the Directorate of Outbreak Control and Infrastructure Rehabilitation. Even by Indonesian standards, this is an excessively long name, so the bureaucrats have, for their own benefit, helpfully shortened it to DOCIR. (I'm sure it's for our benefit, too. After all, we're an acronym-obsessed country for a reason. So we play along.) DOCIR is part of the Ministry of Social Wellness and Fitness—which I'll simply refer to as "the Ministry" from here on out, even though it also goes by the moniker SoWeFit.

Anyway, the Ministry is headquartered on Jalan Perwira in East Jakarta, which is all very fitting because *perwira* means high-ranking official, and, well, you get the gist.

I should also explain that I'm not a staff member for this august, if slightly anxious, institution. Technically, I'm not a staff member anywhere, but for the past six years DOCIR has been working with OneWorld, a small but kick-ass NGO based in South Jakarta that I consult for. Of all the NGOs that have solicited my services, OneWorld is the only one that hasn't written me off. They seem to value my expertise. In fact, they even seem to *like* me—especially since 2005, when avian flu took the world by storm.

❦

Let me explain further, since many of you may be too young, blissfully unaware, or willfully ignorant to remember what happened back then.

In 2005, the Indonesian government, ever the panicky establishment, formed a special consortium (with, of course, the requisite lengthy title: the Avian Flu Action Coordination Committee, or AFACC). As often happens, state-endorsed overreaction stirred up nationwide panic, and soon people were scrambling to get rid of their pet chickens, ducks, and other birds, fearing contamination. It is worth noting that there was at this time a conspicuous upsurge in the production of homemade *abon ayam*—dry-fried shredded chicken. Simply to die for when sprinkled over rice or toast.

In retrospect, I wouldn't be too bitter about any of this if it hadn't affected my favorite aunt, who runs an organic farm in West Java. One day, her aviary, for years a source of pride and sustenance, suddenly disappeared, just like that. Four turkeys, three Bangkok chickens, at least a dozen pigeons.

"Really?" I asked. She's rational, fearless, her own woman. *Surely this is only temporary,* I reasoned silently. But when I pressed her further, the possibility that she—of all people!—was turning into the multitude began to flicker in my head; for there she was, shrugging indifferently, saying it was time to "pare down," to "consolidate," as though she'd just gotten rid of some old clothes.

You have to understand. This woman *loved* birds—both the feeding and the eating of them. I still remember how she'd adopt stray chickens in order to keep them off the streets. And how we'd take weekend trips to Chinatown to gorge ourselves on roast duck. She also supplied me with the only recipes for *confit de canard* and duck *a l'orange* that were actually any good and that kept my penny-pinching friends from OneWorld happy whenever they came to my place with a hankering for Western cuisine.

In short, this whole avian flu mess had proven very disruptive: to my colleagues, my kitchen, my confit de canard, my aunt's *character*, goddammit, and also, to a certain extent, my entire life.

The meeting room on the second floor of Building C is uncharacteristically full, with well-groomed people in starched shirts standing around, trying not to look like idiots. They're waiting for someone to take charge and tell them why they're here. Their collective breath reeks of heavy breakfasts—fried rice, most likely, or steamed rice with last night's leftovers. And still they've managed to arrive on time. Bastards.

I dither at the door, toying with the idea of leaving.

To be honest, these meetings bore me to tears. And every time the media covers a new case, the Ministry acts like it's been hit by a tornado and calls everyone together.

The case that caused the most panic? Another corruption case, thank you very much: an exposé of corrupt management in the avian flu vaccine factory outside Jakarta. Apparently, a Ministry official, quite a big gun, was involved. The police, the Finance Audit Board, and the Anti-Corruption Committee immediately started a finger-pointing contest. They investigated, declared their undying support for each other, denounced each other, then went back to declaring undying support. The Ministry shook like an old car whenever they pulled a new stunt.

I heard the case did a number on the minister: high fever, shortness of breath, coughing, vomiting, and drastic loss of appetite, not to mention headaches, diarrhea, and a sore throat.

I'm not sure what caused the minister to be so distressed, much less—what's the word?—frail. Perhaps people began accusing the Ministry of exaggerating the national threat posed by avian flu. But that's just my guess. A number of experts also insist that the government is going about it all wrong. Rather than storming onto individuals' farms and slaughtering their fowls, they should focus on monitoring industrial breeding farms instead. They say it's in those factory farms, both foreign-owned and local, that the malady truly began.

Of course, the bureaucrats have their own opinions. I was once privy to a debate between bureaucrat T and my friend A, a health reporter. We were both invited by said bureaucrat to a restaurant in Krekot Bunder, famed for its fish head curry and fried paddy squab.

A: Word is that this whole avian flu thing has been blown out of proportion on purpose, secretly funded by certain, um, "agencies" in the US. Their real objective is to make Indonesia a case study.

Bureaucrat T: Nah.

A: And that it's been further exaggerated by international businesses trying to make billions of rupiah in profit from selling vaccines.

Bureaucrat T: Nah.

A: Not to mention played up by corrupt government officials trying to get their hands on national budget funds to "help alleviate the crisis," all in the service of lining their own pockets, of course.

Bureaucrat T: Bullshit.

And right before my eyes, my friend A went stone silent, just like that, clearly not wanting to press the matter further. Really! What a wimp. I was so disappointed in him, partly because he turned out to be not that much of a reporter after all. Worse still, in a fit of anxiety and shame, he proceeded to devour all the curry, leaving nothing behind, only thorns and gills and what looked alarmingly like an eye. His mother obviously didn't teach him good manners. And to cap it all off, there was bureaucrat T, leering lecherously at me over his avocado smoothie, drizzled with gooey chocolate and condensed milk and served in a ridiculously tall glass. *Wanna leave?* his eyes asked.

Then again, what if A in all his novice ineptitude was right about clamming up? For the facts of the matter were, and remain, puzzling: the minister, instead of burrowing into a hole and letting things blow over, made a miraculous recovery and demanded that the production of new vaccines—ones for humans—be resumed.

Do I have my own take on this? Damn right I do: we have no need for such a vaccine because there's no evidence of the virus spreading through human-to-human contact. None. Besides, before such a project can go forward, all kinds of things need to happen first: an official endorsement from the proper authorities, further investigation by parliament working committees, blah blah blah. The red tape stretches a mile long.

But I never said a word, not now, not then, and not even a few months ago when I bumped into bureaucrat T during one of those interminable meetings at the Ministry. Why rock the boat? Why rock anything? And so it is that OneWorld keeps getting brought in, kept in the loop, and cooped up in laborious meetings like this one. Or rather, why *I* keep getting brought in, looped, and cooped.

So here I am once again, late for work and hungry as fuck.

*

I enter the meeting room and feel all eyes on me. Everybody looks genuinely perturbed. Maybe they'll let me have my breakfast after all.

"Morning, Aruna. How are you?" someone says.

How are you? I feel slightly terrorized, as if everyone in the room is actually part of me, but disguised as other people, and they're all ganging up on me because they know me better than I know myself. I try to focus on the person who's just asked me the question: a woman, middle-aged, someone I then realize is from the Ministry's Directorate

General of Empowerment. Just another bureaucrat to deal with. I don't remember her name.

"Have you had breakfast, dear? Here, have a cream puff." She gestures to a box of baked goods someone has brought in.

I feign a smile while sidling quickly to the corner by the window, as far away from the round table as possible. Before she can say anything else, I ask, "Where's Irma?"

"Still with the reporters. There's been another case of avian flu."

"Really. Where?" I keep a businesslike tone—the one I keep for strangers and my mother.

"In some village in Bogor. Gorowong, I think. A boy, four years old."

"Okay. Well. That's probably why she isn't here."

Irma Shihab is the go-to person at DOCIR and hence a key member of the Ministry's staff. She's the one tasked with talking to the media and international institutions like the Global Health Institute. She also gets to step up to the plate whenever there's a crisis to be averted. Funnily enough, these crises always seem to occur when the head of DOCIR decides to take a long coffee break in some five-star establishment and doesn't even bother coming back to the office.

I like Irma. She has a lovely smile and a kind face. She's also the only person I actually enjoy talking to in this bureaucratic snake pit. I like that she knows where to eat, and more impressively, she knows where to eat in the more obscure parts of Chinatown, which is where most good food is. Also, though she doesn't eat pork, she never bats an eye when she sees her work colleagues supping on the forbidden meat.

"Don't you fear the fires of hell?" I asked her once.

"What does that have to do with anything?" she said. "I may not eat pork myself, but far be it from me to prevent a hungry woman like you from noshing on her noodles."

"Noodles," she called them, barely even blinking, though in truth you almost couldn't see the noodles for the *char siew*—those glistening slices of barbequed pork, so richly lacquered it was borderline obscene. I remember wanting to say something equally profound about her faith, a reciprocal gesture, but she said what she said with such earnestness. It was the same attitude she had about her job, her family, her favorite niece and nephew, her modest but tasteful art collection. For a brief moment, I thought I was in love with her.

In contrast, my dislike for this other woman—this overfamiliar, cream-puff-proffering bureaucrat—is growing by the minute. But I have to play nice, so I ask mundane questions in a bored-sounding voice: where the case has been referred to, when the epidemiology test was conducted, whether the lab results are available, and so on. She seems to pick up my veiled recalcitrance and replies in the same dismissive tone.

As soon as the case was diagnosed, she says, the patient was brought to Hospital X, pronto, and within twenty-four hours the patient's house and surrounding area were combed. Every conceivable spot, no stone left unturned. There's a muted sadism in the way she stresses the words "spot" and "stone." She reminds me of the principal at my primary school—a nun who had a reputation for welcoming every stray cat that came her way with open arms; yet, before my time, she'd also belted a whole generation of students for the slightest misdeed.

Suddenly I realize something isn't quite right.

"Wait," I say. "Why wasn't I told?"

"How would I know?" the woman snaps. "Why didn't *you* know already? Bogor's practically next door."

I consider her answer for a while. It's petty and unprofessional, but since no one in her position is paid to be anything other than petty and unprofessional, I let it go. She doesn't seem to be the right person to ask anyway. My instinct tells me that the government rushed in—no surprise there—to put a lid on the investigation before the big, bad media machine had a chance to weigh in. Not that I don't understand, or even occasionally approve of this impulse. In most cases, the media always messes up things anyway: an incident is blown out of proportion, and everybody goes apeshit. And the government is the last institution to know how to handle everybody going apeshit.

But I'm still unappeased. Why didn't the Ministry call us over? Is it possible that they've stopped trusting us? Is it possible that this is a special meeting to axe us OneWorld consultants and appoint someone else?

The woman stares at me, unable to mask her disdain. I blink an imaginary dust particle from my eye and shove a hand into my bag, pretending to look for something. Suddenly, she perks herself up and joins the consultants from the Global Health Institute, who orbit the round table like vultures.

As usual, they own the space. I've forgotten the name of the American with eyes like raisins stuck on a snowman's face. He looks like a rodent and talks all the time. One thing's for sure, his underling, Katrin—from Flores, and drop-dead gorgeous—is completely smitten with him: her mouth hangs open as she takes in every word he says.

More people are taking their seats at the table. Along with the mouseman and the beauty queen from the Global Health Institute, there are twelve people from SoWeFit, aka the Ministry—including three DOCIR officials and their secretary, the dislikable cream-puff profferer, and that Nina woman from R&D. Also in attendance are two officials from another ministry—the Ministry of Agriculture—and a bunch of people I don't know: academic types, from their distracted gazes, and assorted individuals from the private sector.

There's a lull, and I find myself glad that Leon isn't here. He's a consultant, too, but for the Global Health Institute. Two months ago, he ratted me out to my boss at OneWorld when he caught me stuffing my face with chicken wings during an out-of-town work assignment when everyone else was dealing with dead chicken of a different kind. Granted, I was guilty as charged, but that doesn't mean he's not a jerk. He *is* a jerk who thinks he's God's gift to women. So, okay, he *is* very good-looking. But I'm glad he's not here for another reason. I don't think I could handle the sight of him drooling all over Katrin like a stupid teenage boy.

It's 9:42. More cream puffs and some *lemper*—little rice dumplings stuffed with chicken—are offered to me. This time by Tam. He's a lecturer in veterinary medicine at the Agriculture Institute in Bandung and, like me, a consultant for the Ministry—someone I actually *don't* particularly dislike (though that's not saying much). I'm momentarily seized by the urge to say something hackneyed like "*Et tu,* Tam?" But he's sharp. He sees my situation quite clearly.

"All alone, huh?"

Damn Tam.

"Yup, just me."

"Hmm."

I know he really wants to say something. His eyes dart this way and that. I quickly look down at my BlackBerry. I'm just about to start a round of Doodle Jump, the only game I have any semblance of competence in, when Tam begins squawking like one of my aunt's late birds.

"I've said it a thousand times. We can't blame SoWeFit for everything. The responsibility also lies with those dipshits at the Ministry of Livestock. They should have come up with an effective vaccine for the birds long ago. But why bother when you can create a vaccine that's both useless and expensive?" He pauses. "Still, joking aside—"

"You call that a joke?" I ask.

He ignores me.

"How many times have I said that veterinarians are the first line of defense? As long as we're still being sidelined, this is exactly where we'll always be—stuck in perpetual stasis. Holding our useless meetings, issuing useless statements to the press, swapping out useless consultants."

I try to ignore the possible jab.

"Okay, okay. But what are you saying that we don't already know? We all know the Ministry of Livestock has been co-opted." I deliberately linger on that word, "co-opted," such a sterling example of almost half a century of bubble-headed bureaucratese. "The culture of corruption pervades vaccine production. But what do you expect? The people who work there are mostly party people."

Culture of corruption. There's more superlative gibberish for you.

"A very *particular* party," says Tam ominously.

"Yes, yes. Of course," I say impatiently. "What's new, though? Why kick up a fuss now? We've been working for a long time with SoWeFit, you and I. Six fucking years. Being too outspoken will just get us fired."

He shrugs. "Whatever."

"Hey," I say, "six years isn't bad in exchange for some ass-licking."

He stops talking. Despite myself, I realize I'm angry at him, as if he were responsible for my imagined precariousness.

When Irma finally enters the meeting room at five minutes to ten, she looks tense. With her are six people: a foreign consultant whose face I've been seeing a lot in DOCIR internal meetings, a DOCIR director who oversees avian flu, and four others I've never met.

It's when I realize that the four others are the heads, respectively, of the Directorate General of Animal Contagious Diseases, the Directorate General of Outbreak Management, the Directorate General of Zoonotic Diseases, and the Directorate General of National Surveillance that I know this is not just some routine meeting. It's a full-blown emergency.

Two and a half hours after the meeting wraps up, Irma and I are sitting at a restaurant at the corner of Jalan Salemba Raya. I'm not quite sure why we've ended up here, rather than, say, one of the local Arab joints, which are still pretty decent even if they don't hold a candle to the glorious gems in Little Arabia in the Condet Pejaten area, the ones that do goat and biryanis because they were born for it. Or why not the Padang food stall in front of the Salemba prison that is always packed to the gills? When Irma walks ahead of me into the restaurant, I notice her usually flat stomach is looking a tad paunchier than usual. Terrible. Not the paunch, but my noticing it and feeling a little smug, as though we're in the same league to begin with.

"You must want somewhere quiet," I offer, trying to make sense of her choice while noticing too that her arm muscles are taut from all that early morning Bikram Yoga she does. That's right. Early morning. Bikram Yoga. Packed like sardines in an airless room, at 105 fucking degrees. I'd rather die.

I check her out again. Not bad for forty-four. Not bad for any age.

"No," she says, laughing with surprising lightness. "I just want someplace with healthy food."

I sit there, trying not to hate myself too much.

We study the menu: *Sayur Asam, Karedok, Rrujak Buah*—tamarind vegetable soup, blanched vegetables in spicy peanut sauce, spicy fruit salad. I watch as Irma's eyes linger briefly over *Lontong Sayur*, a Medanese dish: rice cakes drenched in a coconut-cream-based vegetable curry. While she hesitates—lontong sayur may have vegetables, but it's far from virtuous—I quickly place an order for *Kol Nenek*, a rare find, not just in Jakarta, but also in its home province, Central Java, in whose cuisine this restaurant purports to specialize. I try to explain to Irma that this delicacy isn't as terrible as it sounds, because I know what she's thinking: Doesn't "kol nenek" mean, of all things, "Grandma's cabbage," and is there anything more homely and harmless than that? But nothing could be further from the truth. The dish actually consists of tiny boiled snails swimming in a pungent pool of fermented soybean gravy.

Irma isn't interested. She seems preoccupied.

I, on the other hand, am pleased as punch. The details flood back to me. Right after the meeting she grabbed me by the arm and whispered in my ear, huskily, urgently, like a secret lover: "Let's escape. Lunch. Just the two of us."

This, I should stress, doesn't happen very often. Everywhere she goes, people trail after her like the tail of a comet. It's no secret that she's likely going to be the next head of DOCIR—and the first woman, too. She's used to living on borrowed time and a hell of a lot of stress. Whereas I—I am a world champion of petty disaster. My feelings, if they count as feelings at all, are too minor league for the likes of her. Yet today she wants to escape, to have lunch, just the two of us. On one of her worst days.

As we wait for our food, I try to give her time to absorb all that has taken place during the meeting. She looks at me with her clear brown eyes—so sincere, so troubled, so beautiful.

"It isn't as if it's, like, easy." She sighs. "I mean, this whole thing."

I nod.

"If we say these recent cases aren't cause enough for concern—that there are still no known cases of avian flu spreading through human-to-human contact—people will think we're being passive and incompetent. I mean, I'm not saying it isn't true: people in Indonesia have been getting infected with avian flu since 2005. But as long as the biomedical industry in this country has an interest in pushing homegrown vaccine production, they'll keep stirring the shit and causing public panic."

I nod sympathetically. "And producing the wrong kind of vaccines, to boot."

I'd like to think that any self-respecting epidemiologist should know, unequivocally, that what the world needs is a vaccine that will be administered to poultry, not humans. Which is why it really gets my goat whenever I'm so much as reminded of those odious lowlifes who've been clamoring for the latter. They keep droning on about the threat posed by the deadly virus, putting the screws on those equally stupid and self-serving parliamentarians to pour megabucks into their projects. And all the while, they deny the real facts of the matter: that their urgency is misplaced and the process of contagion even more complex than hepatitis.

"The thing is"—Irma's voice suddenly turns grave—"these new cases need to be investigated thoroughly."

At this point, I'm only half listening. My mind is still full of high schoolish anxieties—why does Irma feel the sudden need to talk to little old me? I decide she doesn't trust her colleagues, and therefore she must be feeling desperately alone. Someone like Irma doesn't enjoy being alone, doesn't know how to be alone. After all, she's not me.

"And I mean thoroughly," Irma continues. With a pencil, she circles a few words on a document in front of her. "Look," she says. "Eight cities: Banda Aceh, Medan, Palembang, Pontianak, Singkawang, Bangkalan, Surabaya, Mataram. What do you think is the common thread?"

I see no common thread, or any thread for that matter. Like all the experts in the meeting room barely an hour ago, I don't understand how, in a mere seven days, symptoms of acute pneumonia consistent with those of avian flu have been phoned in from eight separate cities. Eight cities spread out across the archipelago. Eight cities never before afflicted by avian flu.

I tell her I'm as baffled as she is, especially since each of the eight cities has only one patient. One. Which doesn't make it an outbreak. Not technically, anyway.

Irma says, "You remember what that expert from Bali said, when hundreds of ducks died recently in several regencies in Java? 'The government is ill equipped.'" Irma's quoting from memory. "'Ill equipped and clueless. They should have cleared out the infected farms and shut down all avian traffic in the area. But as usual they were too slow.'" Then, as a note to self, she adds, "One can only hope—"

"But what we all feared has already happened," I say curtly, for there's really no other way to say it. "The virus has mutated. There's a new variant."

Indeed, barely two weeks ago, the Ministry announced the discovery of a new strain of avian flu in the district of Brebes that is now afflicting cities and regencies all over the archipelago.

An uneasy quiet intrudes. Irma seems reluctant to delve deeper into this other matter. I catch something flashing in her eyes, a new purpose.

She plants her fork into the sculpturelike mound of blanched vegetables the waiter sets before her.

I continue, emboldened. "Stopping the virus should really be a cooperative effort. It's not just the Ministry's job. Especially when it comes to raising public awareness on the importance of adopting preventive measures. Still. As long as efforts to contain animal-borne diseases aren't made an integral part of the nationwide health system, our work, including the work of NGOs like OneWorld, will always be stalled. But you know this. You know this as well as I do. I mean, as if working with regional authorities who do whatever they goddamn feel isn't enough of a headache."

"You always blame decentralization."

"For good reasons, too."

Irma seems deflated. But before I can speak any more of my mind, she regains her ground and steers us back to the mission at hand.

"We need to start an investigation in these eight cities as soon as possible. Before the press catches a whiff of it, and we're all toast."

I pause. "All right."

Irma's fork is still staked upright, a proud cross, incongruous religion-wise, atop the scruffy pile of water spinach, bean sprouts, and cucumber. I watch the prawn crackers wilting slowly in the murky peanut river and feel a pang of grief for their sorry fate.

And for Irma, too, because all of a sudden she looks like someone who's trying to recall something crucial—something that could even save her life, but that she can't remember.

But instead of wallowing in whatever it is, I hear her say, "You think you can manage that? Eight cities in two weeks?"

I smile and nod. Despite myself I'm moved; for in this, a rare vulnerable moment, Irma is still putting on a brave front, still trying to stick to the matter at hand.

"I've talked to your supervisors. Diva told me your hundred and fifty days with OneWorld are almost up. You're on your . . . hundred and forty-eighth day, if I'm not mistaken?"

I nod again. One hundred and fifty days is the maximum an independent consultant in Indonesia is legally allowed to work for and be paid by a single firm.

"DOCIR still has some funds left for this project. So why don't you work directly for me? How does that sound? Two weeks at your usual per diem."

It seems to be an invitation for me to negotiate. It crosses my mind that I should increase my rate by 10 percent. But before I can reply, I hear someone's shrill, vulturish screech: "There she is! Told you she'd be hiding out here."

The wind blows, bringing with it the roar of car engines and a blast of sweltering heat, along with the screecher and four other Ministry vultures. As if on cue, they take their positions around the table, wholly uninvited, feeling wholly entitled.

I only see it for a nanosecond: the shock in Irma's eyes. And then, as she does on TV, she morphs back into the public Irma: devastatingly immaculate, like her pearly white, all-too-even smile.

And just like that, I'm sidelined once more. I, Aruna, nothing but a lowly consultant in their eyes—statusless, birdwoman, nerd. But I don't care, have never cared, because now I'm free to enter the world of scents and spices.

And so, slowly, I lick the finger I've just dipped in the snail gravy. I taste heat, a hint of piscine, cloying sweetness. The snails, born and bred in rice paddies, are minuscule, each no bigger than the upper segment of a pinkie. They're long and lean, unlike the rotund green snails I once tasted in a restaurant in Bogor. I scoop one up with my spoon, pucker my lips, and suck, deep and strong. Then, as soon as its stubborn little body peeks out from its shell, I slurp it up whole, and lo! I've managed to savor kol nenek in all its glory. Without the aid of a toothpick!

2

BONO

One night I dream about my friend Bono. It's a scene from his childhood, and he's like a character in a movie: someone outside himself, someone unreal, an actor playing a role. In the opening shot, he's standing on a beach, savoring the salt breeze—or so I imagine.

All of a sudden, he turns away and walks toward a voice calling him from the main road. Something in his gaze changes, reminding me of a frightened deer.

He enters a restaurant—one of the many along the street. I don't see who is calling him.

A few minutes later I, too, go into the restaurant, and I see him sitting at a table with a middle-aged couple. The woman tries to stroke Bono's hand, but, gently, he brushes her fingers away. He seems tense and keeps his gaze lowered.

In front of him is a bowl of piping hot soto. *I can't see what kind, and it takes me a few seconds before I realize that Bono is being subjected to some sort of test administered by the man.*

"Come on, concentrate," says the man, his expression fierceness itself.

With great effort, Bono takes a spoonful of soto, *then a second, and a third.*

"What do you taste?"

"C-c-candlenut. And t-t-turmeric."

"And? What else?"

"L-lemongrass? And kaffir lime leaf?"

"Which one? Lemongrass or kaffir lime leaf? Don't be wishy-washy."

"L-l-lemon . . . lemongrass . . . or . . . or both. Yes. Both."

"Are you sure?"

Bono doesn't answer. He seems to be having difficulty breathing.

"Are you positive?"

"Yes, sir. Both."

"So, what kind of soto do you think this? What is its provenance?"

Bono pauses again. I can see his heart beating wildly in his chest.

"Ma-Ma-Madura?"

"Which part of Madura?"

Again Bono hesitates.

The man ignores the woman's attempts to intervene.

"I—I don't know, Father. Bangkalan? Sumenep, perhaps . . . yes, Sumenep."

"Think. What color is it?"

"Ye-ye-yellow, Father."

"You've really forgotten? Isn't soto from Sumenep white?"

"In that case, this must be Bangkalan-style soto. Th-the broth . . . it's ye-ye-yellow. And it hasn't . . . hasn't been made with t-t-tripe. A-a-also it hasn't been served with any p-p-potato fritters."

For a moment, the man regards his child with a wild fury, as if he wants to beat him for not being smart enough, for stuttering like an imbecile—in short, for not being worthy of being his child. With an irritated flourish, he draws the bowl away from Bono and toward himself. Child and mother look on as the man slurps the soup demonstratively, down to the last dregs.

Then, as if this last gesture isn't brutal enough, the man asks the waiter to bring them an assortment of banana-leaf-wrapped bundles, all kinds of pepes *and its close relative,* botok. *He unwraps a botok, exposing its moist, grated coconut flesh, and holds it out to Bono.*

"*Go on. Try it.*"

Bono does as he's told.

"*What kind of botok do you think this is?*"

"*Vegetable, Father.*"

The man pounds the table with his fist. "*Vegetable, meat, fish,*" *he hisses.* "*How dare you speak in such generalities. It shows you're just like everyone else. That you can't be bothered to use your brain. That you're too lazy to think.*"

Bono nibbles a spoonful, then a second, and a third. "*Fiddlehead?*" *he asks in a whisper.*

In an instant, something changes in the father's expression. There's a sort of cautious anticipation in the depths of his gaze, mingled, perhaps, with hope—joy, even. And I know that Bono sees it, and that for a few seconds he allows himself to hope as he's never hoped before.

"*Do you like it?*"

"*Ye-ye-yes, sir, I like it.*"

"*Why? Explain.*"

But for some reason Bono doesn't speak, as if there's something balled in his throat he's trying to keep down.

At long last, he replies. "*Be-be-cause it tastes good?*"

One second passes, then two. And then, with an expression of utter disgust, the man stands up, tosses a few bills at the cashier, and leaves.

When Bono emerges from the restaurant, a cigarette between his fingers, I run up to him. His mother is nowhere to be seen.

"*Hey,*" *I say.*

"*Hey,*" *he says.*

"*So that's fear, eh? Makes you lose your tongue?*"

Strangely, he seems relaxed.

"*Not necessarily,*" *he says calmly.*

He isn't stuttering anymore. He isn't the same Bono as the Bono in the restaurant.

*"Fiddlehead botok—*botok pakis. *I know the taste intimately," Bono continues. "One nibble and my mind begins parsing out each distinct sensation: sweet, spicy, salty, sticky, the spices, the fibers. I assign them adjectives, I assign them colors, I weave each sensation into a swell of verbal music until each and every aspect of the dish has been translated into a magician's litany that binds us all under its spell. Believe it or not, in that respect, I am him. I am my father."*

"Why didn't you point that out to him back there in the restaurant?" I ask. "I thought his affirmation meant the world to you."

"I didn't want him to think we were alike, because that would mean that he was someone worthy of respect, of emulation. And that would mean I had lost. It would have meant Mother had lost. My father is dead to me."

He takes a long drag on his cigarette.

"And furthermore, tasting food is an act of pleasure," he says nonchalantly. "And writing about that pleasure is an artistic gesture. But at the end of it all, the highest art, the truest art, finds its expression in satiating the hunger of others. That's why I became a chef."

❦

I knew Bono long before he became famous. I knew him when he still went by his baptismal name, Johannes.

I was working for an advocacy group at the time; he was employed at a PR firm. We met while working together on a project that gave us many opportunities to observe each other quietly, from afar. We were around the same age—me twenty-eight, him twenty-five—and neither of us was much of a talker. I'd just finished my master's degree program in Thailand, and he'd just finished his in America.

He wasn't a looker, not by any stretch of the imagination. He wasn't exactly fat, but he had a double chin and was in poor shape. He had a crew cut—and I hated crew cuts. His lips were fleshy and protruding and perpetually moist and pink as if he were wearing lip gloss or had just finished a heavy make-out session with someone. His complexion was unusually pasty for his age. His glasses were too thick.

But something made me feel comfortable around him: he was like a person who wore the wrong clothes or the wrong color, who had the wrong hairstyle or the wrong name; it was like there was something about him that was always pleasingly out of place. I visited his office once and saw he had images of food plastered all over the walls: ads for oatmeal and Bear Brand milk, scenes of Dick and Jane messing around in the kitchen, and classical-style sketches of French cuisine—the kind artists sell along the length of the Seine in Paris. There were artsy black-and-white photos of all kinds, too: a pretty woman taking a bite of marbled steak, a child in a café trying to catch the waiter's attention by spilling his milk all over the table, an old woman tottering down a country lane with a baguette tucked under her armpit, and a dog with a twinkle in its eye as it carried in its mouth an apple snatched from a market stall. Cartoonish posters were interspersed throughout, with headings and sentences like "Say Cheez," "The Zen of Sataying," and "What Alice Told Her Gardener."

One evening, at dinner in a restaurant with other co-workers, I was struck by how similar our senses of taste were. Or, more specifically, how we didn't order food the same way other people did. Since then, whenever we went out to eat with co-workers and friends, I took note of how he would read the menu. At certain restaurants he didn't so much as glance at one, but at other restaurants he would pore over descriptions with great fervor, as if each and every word were of great significance and had the power to transform his worldview.

He also ordered dishes with the instinct of a seasoned food lover. In some places, his strategy was fairly orthodox: "What's the point of trying the Wagyu steak? If they're selling it for this cheap, the steak can't be all that good." Or, "Better to stick with the tried-and-true at this Thai restaurant. Safest to order the classics. Mango salad, pomelo salad, green beef curry, red duck curry, basil chicken stir-fry . . ."

But in other places, he chose to assume a more passive role—a tourist from another planet: "An izakaya like this isn't the place to order sushi or sashimi. Order a number of dishes from the specials pasted on the wall, even if you can't read the Japanese. If you're uneasy about what you may be ordering, just tell the waiter to bring a selection of chicken, tofu, eggplant, root vegetables, whatever's most popular with the regulars. They'll all be very different from each other, but chances are they'll be tasty."

There were also times he'd order dishes that sounded positively mundane, but delicious when well executed: for example, a *poulet rôti*, say, in a French restaurant. "Only a really solid chef can make a good roast chicken," he'd say.

At other times he'd take the opportunity to order something exceptionally unusual: like a small, primo portion of angel-hair pasta smothered in caviar at a super-pricey Italian restaurant I'd been dodging all week because I feared I couldn't afford it. Turned out I was bowled over for life. And even though the portion was super-small and the price outrageously expensive, the dish was simply exquisite: so fragrant, so clean tasting, yet highlighting so distinctly the flavors of garlic and the little roe capsules bursting against the tongue. For the first time, I understood that certain kinds of beauty could only come in small packages.

"How do you do it? How do you always order the right thing?" asked one of our co-workers who had an unfortunate knack for always ordering the wrong thing. "I mean, how do you know which roast chicken at which restaurant is good? How is it possible to have a sixth sense about such things? How do you know what to order?"

Bono being Bono, he just smiled.

But I knew what his answer would be: he never ordered the wrong thing because he was a tireless patron of dining out. After all, instinct doesn't fall from the sky or seize you like a *jin*, directing your five senses to the right choice without fail. Instinct is born of experience.

But that fateful day came: Bono and I completed the project we'd been working on together, and I knew that my twice-weekly visits to his office were at an end, unless I was willing to visit anyway and give him the impression that I was interested in him. And I was definitely not interested.

That night, all of us gathered in a restaurant for an end-of-project celebration thrown by his PR firm. He sat opposite me. We ignored each other, as though tacitly acknowledging that our chapter was about to close, yet also agreeing that we were not going to get all sentimental about it.

Suddenly, my neighbor—a woman in her forties—began complaining about how difficult it was to serve traditional Indonesian cuisine to the important guests she entertained in her home. She was an utter bore, a poseur. She was also the wife of the big boss—an Englishman.

"The thing is, I *want* to serve Indonesian food. In fact, I *long* to serve Indonesian food," the woman said. "But my husband always forces me to serve the food in our Royal Copenhagen Flora Danica. And even though I comply with his wishes, he's never satisfied. 'It's not elegant enough,' he says. So then I ask what isn't *elegant enough*? 'The food,' my husband says. *The food* isn't elegant enough."

Not surprisingly, everyone around the table began whispering. A lot of us didn't know what a Royal Copenhagen Flora Danica was. The official flower of Denmark? A type of flower having something to do with the gorgeous race car driver Danica Patrick?

Addressing us as if we'd come from another planet, the woman went on to explain that it was tableware, the best and most prestigious porcelain tableware in the world—much higher in quality and much more expensive than mere Wedgwood. By this time the general incredulity had given way to plain disgust. I was especially irritated at her husband's dismissal of Indonesian cuisine. "Not elegant enough!" What gave him, Mr. Snooty Englishman, any right to pooh-pooh the cuisine of an entire archipelago?

The woman sighed. "The main problem probably lies with our cook. The food tastes fine, but its presentation is really just—how do I say this?—not beautiful enough. Or interesting enough. What's the point of having exquisite dishes if the food itself looks so . . . uninspiring."

A cough was heard from the across the table.

"But nowadays," a respectful voice ventured, "most Westerners know how to handle spicy food. Some even prefer it that way."

"I know. But that's not really my point." Now the woman looked a bit embarrassed. She knew she had made a faux pas and would now be forced to cover it up somehow.

Suddenly, from across the table, Bono's voice boomed, rich and confident. "Here's my take, for what it's worth. Buy your favorite pickled vegetable dish from whatever place you deem best. And if possible, buy a variety that uses clear spicy sauce, not peanut sauce. Peanut sauce is stunning if you know how to make it and can guarantee it'll be a hit. But in most cases it's just messy. Arrange the pickles on a round platter with a single slice of freshwater scampi or lobster, grilled flaming red. Do the same with *rendang*: buy the beef curry from your favorite Padang-style restaurant, and don't buy one that's too spicy. To hell with charges of authenticity. You can't expect Western palates to appreciate a flavor fully if the first impression is of overwhelming heat. Anyway. Serve it on an elegant platter, sprinkled with slivers of fried onions, and top it all off with a single enormous red chili, sliced lengthwise.

"Then find a good lamb curry and decorate it with coriander leaves. Buy some skewers of sweet Balinese-style *Sate Bali*, or perhaps *Sate Buntel*—the main thing, as with the pickled vegetables, is to avoid drenching them in thick peanut sauce and *kecap*. Prepare pickles, fried onions, shrimp-paste sambal, mango sambal, and sweet sambal in beautiful little bowls. Last, but not least, don't forget to fry up some fresh prawn crackers and *melinjo* crisps and serve them in one of those quaint oversized glass jars."

The boss's wife fell silent. And there he was, Bono, *my* Bono, looking around proudly, such a performer, such a beautiful show-off, as if the other guests were showering him with wild applause.

Later, when he went out for a smoke, I followed him.

"Well, so much for your job," I said. Like Bono, I never saw the point of making small talk. Certainly not with him.

"I don't really like working in this industry anyway," he said airily. "In August, I'm heading back to the States to study again."

"You *are* a true chef, aren't you?"

"And you," he said. "You're welcome to correct me if I'm wrong. But you're not really an outbreak expert. You're a person who finds joy in doing whatever, as long as it involves food."

Four years later, when he returned from New York, he wasn't the same person—the guy with the thick glasses and a middle name that people loved to make fun of because they couldn't help it. He'd become more than Johannes Bonafide Natalegawa; he was a *brand*. Like Rihanna. Like Shakira. And like them, he knew how to market himself, and at the right moment, too. Within a few months of his arrival in Jakarta, he built up his reputation as a personal chef. At the time, Jakarta high society had wearied of dining out. Restaurant standards were becoming more inconsistent. "Fine dining" was less "fine" by the day. The traffic was getting worse. Increasingly, people longed for privacy, and also exclusivity—dining experiences beyond the spending capacity of the hoi polloi.

Bono met their needs.

After graduating from the Culinary Institute of America, he worked at two famous kitchens in New York. That was in 2010. As with all the other ambitious young kids who dreamed of becoming chefs, he knew that tossing salad in a world-class restaurant would help his career far more than learning how to make lobster thermidor in a middling establishment.

Getting work at a prestigious restaurant certainly didn't mean financial success; a lot of kids took up positions as *stagiaire*—unpaid apprentices. But competition was fierce, and Bono was all too aware he was one of the lucky ones, even though it meant pushing himself to work harder and longer so that he could catch the attention of whatever god ruled the kitchen of whatever restaurant he worked in. The chance to meet those deities in person—Daniel Boulud, Dan Barber, Jean-Georges Vongerichten, David Chang—wasn't something that just fell into your lap.

The first kitchen Bono worked in operated according to a system very different from the traditional French *brigade de cuisine*. He didn't have the opportunity to rotate through different stations and tasks. The emphasis was on specialization. All the kitchen staff had to hone their skills in specific areas: plucking poultry, whipping up sauces, and shaping fluffy white steamed buns until they were blue in the face, until they were considered masters of their craft. Bono's fate was to be the master of slicing onions and peeling potatoes. And he worked at it around the clock, like a man possessed.

But he was diligent and he was patient, and the opportunity to speak face-to-face with David fucking Chang himself finally came, after he'd spent five months and six days working himself to the bone at Momofuku Ssäm Bar.

Their interaction was brief. But on the strength of those few words, Bono's heart blossomed, just so, like the heart of an artichoke.

After two years working for David Chang at Momofuku and Andrew Carmellini at Locanda Verde, followed by six months at Jason

Atherton's Pollen Street Social in London—peeling vegetables, frying eggs, sautéing carrots, grilling steak, perfecting the art of browning butter—only then did Bono feel that it was time to return to the motherland.

Why return? Three reasons, he said. First, the competition in New York and London was too steep. Second, if you wanted to survive as a chef in a city like New York or London, you basically had to reconcile yourself to a life of slavery, of abuse, at the hands of a godlike *maha*-chef for at least two years—the minimum amount of time required to improve your abilities, train your palate, deepen your knowledge, heighten your perception. Bono was willing. He was willing all right. But he was also young and hungry, and he didn't want to waste any more time. Third, and perhaps most compelling, it would be much easier to become a culinary superstar in Jakarta.

Furthermore, his years in New York and London had done much for him.

He could converse with ease about the latest trends, from molecular gastronomy and new experiments in winemaking to the philosophies behind the raw- and slow-food movements. He knew how to play up his international credentials while simultaneously reminding his audience about his local roots. He knew when to mention his experiences dining at Noma in Copenhagen and El Celler de Can Roca in Spain and when to sing the praises of local fare—a bowl of Pontianak-style shredded-crab noodles or Ternate's signature *rica-rica* chicken.

He knew which aspects of his personal life were appropriate for sharing with an Indonesian audience—definitely not squabbles with other young chefs or drunken episodes at *gele* parties or one-night stands with near-strangers. In Indonesia, he spoke passionately, as though he meant it, about the importance of family, about treasured memories and valuable life lessons.

Life in New York had also made him a skilled storyteller. At the end of the day, in that city, everybody had to know how to tell his or her story, because life was stranger, larger, fiercer than fiction. To succeed, you couldn't just float along like a leaf in a lake; you had to swim across the sea. And everyone had to be able to tell stories about small triumphs, coolly, humbly, as if other, more impressive, more meaningful triumphs lay ahead that would carry them still farther to distant shores of success.

He knew how to tell stories in a down-to-earth manner—of his three-month trip to Italy with Andrew Carmellini to deepen his knowledge in the arts of making pasta, bread, cheese, and prosciutto, and how they went truffle hunting in Alba. And also how to mention his many brunches at Prune, where Gabrielle Hamilton herself would be weaving in and out of the weekend crowd, as if he, too, was part of her world.

And most importantly, he knew how to navigate the ins and outs of Jakarta high society. In fact, he was impressively canny this way. He could assess personalities almost instinctively. He knew when to put on airs and when to affect humility, when to act outrageous and outraged, when to act conservatively. He knew when to be himself and when not to be himself, something I never could get the hang of. And for all this, I had to take my hat off to him.

But I only really became aware of the depth and breadth of his self-education when I'd been invited to a dinner party at the house of a young architect who specialized in restaurant design. The architect was completely besotted with Bono and had begged him to put together a special menu for his friends.

That night, I saw how much Bono had changed. He looked tall and commanding in his white chef's uniform. His team comprised five people: two to help him in the kitchen, two to wait on the long table—beautifully set for eighteen guests—and a sommelier. They were practically kids, but they moved with intense speed, energy, agility. Kids used to hard work and being in competition with those around them, who'd made their own way in the world and, in doing so, relied on their self-discipline, knowledge, or social skills to ensure their success. Kids who were strong, smart, hungry.

I waited a few minutes before waving at him from a distance. He was standing behind the island in the open kitchen. When he saw me, he darted over to greet me: "Run! Oh, Run! I'm so happy you could make it."

And then he embraced me tightly, almost gratefully—something he'd never done in our whole history together.

The rest of the night was like a dream.

DINNER

Hosted by Aditya Bari

December 5, 2011

Jala in a roasted squid consommé

(inspired by Jason Atherton's signature

dish at Pollen Street Social, with slight

modifications)

Quail, cereal, bread, and tea

Burrata, scallions, and truffle

Spaghetti—black

Duck *agrodolce*

Olive oil torte and poached pears

Ice cream and sorbet

Courtesy of Chef Bono

3

CAULIFLOWER AND SQUID

I have this recurring dream. I am sitting in an open-air kitchen the size of a soccer field, watching my grandmother in her backyard. A battalion of ravenous turkeys trails after her. The clay pot she carries contains not bird feed, but rose and jasmine petals—the flowers of the dead. "It's for the spirits," she says. "Help me spread them around the yard."

My grandmother cuts an impressive figure. Although she's eighty-seven, her stride is quick and sure, her spine is straight and strong, and like her son—my father—in his older years, she likes to wear a plain, unpatterned kimono. To this day I've never fully understood their relationship—between my father, who rarely spoke, and his mother, so brave, so tough.

My mother would always say that the similarities between them didn't stop at their habit of wearing kimonos. "They both love chili, garlic, and everything to do with birds. Their temperament and thought processes are the same too—linear, unbending, stubborn, easily angered, self-centered."

But the only characteristic my dream reveals of my grandmother is her excessive love for her turkeys.

I remember my father and his own birds: how his eyes would light up when he'd talk to his beloved parakeet, how his lips would coo soundlessly when he'd stroke his little magpie-robin. For a brief moment, in the contortions of his face, one caught a glimpse of the likeness between mother and son.

"But turkeys need food, and spirits won't show themselves as long as we're here," I protest, feeling a little sorry for the turkeys, who are being forced to eat flowers.

My grandmother shakes her head. "Just scatter them around," she says. "You'll see. Those turkeys will want for nothing."

It scares me to imagine the yard filled with spirits. You can't order what kind of spirits you want. What if they had gaping wounds in their backs like the dreaded sundel bolong? What if they were violent, or smelly, or evil? What if they were allergic to poultry? What if they stole the turkey eggs, so large and tasty, and devoured them all—I mean, how could anyone resist? Or even worse, what if they slaughtered all the turkeys, destroying my grandmother's source of income?

Still, I'm even more frightened of what my grandmother will do if I disobey.

I begin scattering the flowers on the grass. Five minutes later my grandmother and I go inside the house. The turkeys don't follow us for some reason, but they also show no interest in the flower petals blanketing the ground. Instead, they mill around near their coop, as if waiting for something—instructions from above, perhaps, or rain, or music.

My grandmother busies herself in the kitchen. I make as if I'm working on my homework, but actually I peer through the window at the backyard shrouded in darkness and the beating of wings.

Night falls.

Not a sound. Not even the wind blowing or the frogs croaking or the crickets chirping.

In the morning, through the layer of dew on the window glass, I see that the yard is green and spotless. The turkeys are in their coop. Not a single flower petal remains.

"What happened?" I ask my grandmother, who is busy making breakfast.

"What do you think?" she asks in return.

What is it that dictates perception? Why do we see something one way and not another? Perhaps it is this that they call the "mind's eye"—the eye that perceives the grass is green because the color green calms the heart, that perceives the ocean is blue because the ocean is where we set sail our hopes and dreams, that perceives blood is red because the color red will prepare us for the dead body we may discover next.

But the yard is, really and truly, immaculate.

"It's impossible. The turkeys couldn't have eaten all those petals," I half whisper.

"They didn't," says my grandmother. "The spirits were happy we took the trouble to pay our respects to them. In return, they transformed our offering into food for the turkeys. If you don't believe me, go look inside the coop. All the turkeys are fast asleep because they're so full and content."

It was decided that I would leave in three days' time, on Sunday. The decision was made at a meeting between my bosses and my colleagues, who arranged my travel schedule. The office needed one and a half more days—Friday and Saturday—to book flights and hotels, to contact the Ministry branch offices in each location, and to arrange travel funds.

And now I return to my apartment on Jalan Pangeran Antasari. It's around nine o'clock.

Bono is bustling about in the kitchen, absorbed in a culinary experiment of some sort. He's recently stopped his work as a personal chef to take up the position of head chef at Siria. It's the hottest, most innovative restaurant in Jakarta at the moment—and he almost never has time to rest. Today is the first day of his two-week leave. Without him saying a word, I know that he's transferred a fair amount of ingredients from the restaurant's kitchen to my apartment: all kinds of meats and fish, creams and sauces, soup stocks, and several bottles of expensive wine. Not so much as to be conspicuous, but enough, at any rate, to play around with. He acts as if he owns the place—*my* place. He doesn't even bother to greet me when I come in.

Still, I'm happy to see him. I'm always happy when he's in the apartment, cooking, watching DVDs, sometimes crashing on the sofa for a night or two, which he often does on weekends especially. We're like an older sister and younger brother. Or a pair of twins. What's that term he once used? "Twin solitudes," which sounds much more fitting and much more appropriate than "soul mates." We know how to lead our own separate lives, and because we aren't romantically involved, we rarely use silence as evidence of something lacking or an excuse to pick a fight. And when food appears, simmering in woks, adorning platters, filling the apartment, there will be only good conversation.

I lean in and study the wok's contents. Fried rice and . . . what is that? "Leftover steak from the restaurant?"

"Wagyu," he says, not bothering to look up. "And a bit of leftover green sambal from the *itik lado mudo* I found in your fridge. It'll be delish. I promise."

A friend of mine who's crazy about Padang food has just sent me a duck curry smothered in green chili from Batusangkar. As usual, Bono has rooted through the contents of my refrigerator and found something that set his brain going. And also as usual, he hasn't asked permission. But I never protest, because I get to enjoy the results. Wagyu-beef-fried rice. Foie gras noodles. Spicy stir-fried bitter beans atop a sliver of fried tuna belly.

And now he begins to pontificate: "Don't you find it ironic that these days the combinations of such words—'fried rice' and 'Wagyu,' 'noodles' and 'foie gras'—make so-called seasoned diners raise their eyebrows and titter because they willfully, deliberately misunderstand them, taking them for 'fusion' of the most uncreative kind? Like, huh? As if true creativity consisted only of combining a minimum of ten elements, all unconventional, all incompatible! Or else they regard such dishes as prime examples of fusion in confusion, as if the mere act of combining anything from the 'West' with anything from the 'East' were somehow risible in itself. I can't *stand* such people." Then he adds, as if somehow I were the object of his frustration, "You've been living in Indonesia for too long."

Why is it suddenly about me? But it's something he tells me all the time.

He continues. "We're back to the thick-skin thing again, baby. If the general public continues to hold two views that are just plain wrong, then why should we give in to either of them? What's important is that *we* know why we're doing what we're doing."

There are a lot of things I love about Bono—this is one of them. And even though I'm sure he'll reach a point one day when he'll tread too hard on my toes, I still love him for it.

A few minutes later, we're sitting at the dining table, a plate of steaming hot fried rice in front of each of us. It's already Thursday and, for all his self-centeredness, he knows I need something to help me relax. He opens a bottle of chilled Riesling from the Clare Valley in South Australia—a Grosset Polish Hill 2010, one of his favorites.

He speaks a bit about his day, filling me in on the latest details of his ongoing rivalry with his sous chef—a former employee of a very famous and well-respected restaurant in Jakarta, but whom Bono considers rather superficial. And it isn't just because he hasn't done an apprenticeship abroad, he adds hastily.

"I know, I know," he continues, with a shrug. "All chefs—even the best of the best—can learn a lot from their team. Not just from their sous chefs, but from the other members, too. One can always benefit from the culinary knowledge of others."

"So what's the problem?"

"The problem," he says sharply, as if annoyed that I of all people should be asking him this, "is that when he's working for me, his main task is not to show off his creativity! And certainly not in front of

Jonas, Tanya, and Michael, for fuck's sake! The three most sophisticated gourmets in this fucking country—well, if you don't count fucking Nadezhda—who just happen to be our big bosses! His main task should be to put *my* creativity into execution—*my* ideas about a dish and its creation, springing from *my* vast stores of knowledge about spices and the culinary arts. It's his fucking job to carry out those ideas and perfect them!"

For a moment, I say nothing. What should I say to this dazzling but exasperating person, with his double chin, his glossy bee-stung lips, his arcade of battle-mongering scowls and grimaces that seem to hold a private dialogue with him? I know my duty as a friend is to stand by him and love him, however large his ego has grown. But maybe what Bono really needs is a girlfriend. Still, the second I think about it, sadness overtakes me. Why should Bono need a girlfriend? I don't have a boyfriend, do I? Moreover, what kind of girlfriend would be able to put up with his inhumane working hours, his food-obsessed brain, his impulsive and explosive personality, and, to top it all off, the acute awareness weighing on him morning, noon, and night that each dish he sends out from his kitchen, whether prepared by him personally or by someone under his supervision, is a singular and unparalleled work of art and as such can either make or break his career?

"In New York," he continues, "even a talented, well-traveled chef with experience working for the best chefs in the world may never be able to open his own restaurant. He accepts that this may indeed be the case. He may know all the right techniques: how to cook savory dishes and how to bake sweet treats, how to whip up a salad and do a good roast. He may have mastered the art of seasoning and sauce making, perfected his knowledge of texture, contrast, taste. He may follow the world's contemporary chefs and the latest developments in their cooking styles. He may know how to market himself. But all of that means nothing if he doesn't know how to lead and work alongside others in a cramped, hot space under the pressure of temperature and time. And he certainly needs to know how to inspire other members of the team—"

"So you're saying you know how to do all of those things?"

"How to practice discipline when it comes to oneself and to others, where to find the best ingredients at the cheapest possible cost—"

"Hey! Are you listening to yourself?"

"How to create a bond between one's kitchen and the dining area, how to convey one's personality and passions to every patron, how to cater to the finicky, capricious, and sometimes nonsensical culinary whims of the public."

I pour more wine into his glass and take a deep breath. "You do know that you're completely exhausted, don't you? If you really believed everything you've said, you would just let Arya take over your duties so you could rest. I mean, that *is* his task, isn't it? Execution? Execution doesn't mean he has to introduce something new. Execution means putting into practice what already exists."

I sense something in him relax. Most likely, he's just very tired and needs some time to vent. From what little I know about Arya, he's adaptable, gifted, and possesses a high level of self-discipline. And although his powers of culinary perception are more limited than those of Bono's, he's actually better at working with the rest of Bono's team, which is composed of people like Arya. They're kids who have grown up in small towns like Malang; who graduated from small, private colleges in Jakarta with degrees in hospitality and tourism management; who shoulder the responsibility of helping support their families; and who work within religious restrictions that, like it or not, limit their ability to enjoy all kinds of cuisine to its fullest extent. I really can't blame Arya if he does feel a little jealous toward Bono, whose family isn't wealthy per se, but who has still been fortunate in terms of opportunity. But this isn't the time to defend Arya.

Mercifully, Bono has already calmed down and moved on now to other topics: the condition of my apartment that, though far from shabby, certainly isn't luxurious. My sixteen-year-old cat and her various ailments. My career, which is "running in place." How I don't have to live "like this"—"this isn't the life for you," though God knows what he imagines *is* the life for me.

He tries to sympathize with me about my job and ask incisive questions to show he's interested—like why the farmers whose poultry has died haven't been affected by the avian flu themselves (my answer: "See? Exactly!") and whether autopsies are always carried out on those who have died of avian flu (my answer: "No, never")—and I try to answer them as best I can.

Then I ask whether he's really from East Java, and he says yes, from Madura to be exact: his mother is Madurese; his father is ethnic Chinese, from Surabaya. And I ask again whether he wants to come with me, even as I try to refrain from asking in the same breath about whether there's any religious tension in his family, though it's kind of obvious: his Madurese mother is most likely Muslim and his Chinese father is most likely not. I'm sure he isn't interested in coming along since the last thing he probably needs is to revisit his childhood and all the varieties of *petis*—a sweet black variety of shrimp paste—for which his hometown is famous. What he really needs is sleep: a long, deep slumber that will get his creative juices flowing again. But he doesn't say no.

"So you want to come?"

"Yeah, sure." He sounds a bit uncertain.

"Really, seriously. You're coming?"

"Yes. Seriously."

"Fantastic!"

"I'm just coming along out of curiosity. I was born in Madura and all, that's true, but I don't remember much of it. My family moved to Jakarta when I was quite young. Nowadays, though, my mother tells me that people have such bad impressions about the Madurese."

"What kind of impressions?"

"She says people think the Madurese are coarse, quick-tempered, wild. And sure enough, every time I say, 'Let's go over to Madura,' people say, 'Huh? What for? Watch out, the people there are *fierce*. Say the wrong thing and they'll *cut* you.'"

I laugh.

"Anyway, if my mother's to be believed, the Madurese are tough. In a good way. And iron-willed. A proud people, smart and strong, with a great sense of humor. And the farther east you go, in cities like Pamekasan, the people are more refined. Their food, too."

"So you're serious about coming?"

"I just told you I am," he says with a new edge in his voice. "But promise me one thing."

I ask him what more he could possibly want from me in this world.

"I want to leave Vanilla here while we're gone. Is that okay? And I want you to let Job stay here and cat-sit for us."

Job—I don't know his full name—is Bono's roommate. He always claims he's a distant relative of Bono's, even though Bono has never felt the need to explain Job's presence at his place. What Job does to support himself remains a complete mystery, as does whether he recognizes the irony of this mystery, given his name. He spends almost every day dashing from mall to mall. Sometimes he stops in at Bono's restaurant and hangs out at the bar long into the night, chatting with the mixologists, who, God knows why, often share their cocktail recipes with him.

I don't particularly relish the idea of Job living in my space for the next two weeks, breathing and polluting the air in my apartment. Though I do need someone to take care of Gulali. But in my relationship with Bono, which is quite possibly the strongest relationship I have, I've let myself fall into a role where I surrender to his demands, in the same way that everyone whose lives overlap with his surrenders themselves to him as well. How exactly? Picture, for example, three investors—three restaurant owners, three people accustomed to being in charge—and picture not one of them having the courage to say,

"But we don't want cauliflower and squid. Everyone knows that's Jason Atherton's signature dish. Everyone knows Siria should be more than the Jakarta branch of Pollen Street Social." Or, "A quarter of the dishes on this menu have pork in them. Indonesia's not an Islamic state, but this is going to severely limit our clientele. It's time for a reassessment."

Instead, the concessions Jonas, Tanya, and Michael have made to Bono's whims have their roots in business calculations that rely at times on instinct, not logic. The decision those three young entrepreneurs have made to put their money and faith in a chef as young as Bono, I'm sure, isn't just borne out of naïveté, and their willingness to agree to whatever Bono desires isn't as farfetched as my readiness to order my life in accordance with Bono's worldview. Ironic, yes, but there it is. Bono feels empowered when those whom he loves live for him; I feel powerful when I don't have anyone in my life at all.

"Okay, but Vanilla has to bring her own food," I insist. "Also, tell Job that everything in my fridge is strictly *off limits*. Oh, and most importantly, he is *not allowed* to sleep with Gulali."

4

Farish

My father wasn't always the man I knew (or at least I thought I knew) growing up. That's what my mother would tell me after he passed away. "You were his only daughter," she would say with a sigh. "To you, your father was and always will be the man of your memories."

Still, she acknowledged, in many respects my father had indeed remained constant. Though he wasn't very good at earning money, he wasn't a drunk and he wasn't dishonest. He wasn't coarse either, or violent. He was always pleasant toward his wife, even more than accommodating. He never lost his temper. And he wasn't the acquisitive sort either, except when it came to gambling.

Even before I was born, the nights he spent at the tables taught him how to remove himself from my life. Later, he would claim it was for my own good. A child who couldn't manage the loss of a parent would never be able to stand on her own two feet, he'd say. Only by losing a parent could a child become a true adult. He wanted to teach me to love solitude, to learn how to make do with whatever options life presented. Perhaps he became such a quiet man because he was never there—after all, an absent man has no voice.

One day I'd realize: the gambling dens provided him with many things—sweaty faces and painted lips, flashy clothes and false flattery, fortunes told by amateur astrologers, beer-scented kisses, and meals of chicken porridge taken in the early hours of the morning. But there was a void in his heart that remained unfilled. A void deep and dark, whose echoes kept him awake all night and finally forced my mother to retreat to another room. I never told my friends at school that my parents slept in separate beds.

One day, when I was ten, the echoes turned into long coughing spells—spells that persisted till the day he died, on a mountain of debt, his lungs riddled with holes. I was twenty-four years old.

What can I say about my father, really? He was never there, yet I always miss him. I miss him the way a child whose parents have divorced misses the parent who has gone away because he or she will never live in the same house as that parent again. I miss him in a way I never missed my mother because I knew that my mother would always be there for me. As for my father, I'm not sure whether he even understood what "being there" meant.

To this day, the love of solitude he instilled in me means I'm happy living alone, to the point that I hardly ever call my mother, much less do all the things a good daughter should do: take her on visits, organize lunches and dinners, go shopping together, plan excursions. Sometimes I feel guilty. After all, I'm the only one she has left in this world, and she's never demanded anything of me.

But my mother changed after my father passed away. She worked hard to pay off his debts and succeeded, with a little help from my wealthy grandfather. She began keeping birds as pets. And every time I did visit, she would cook my father's favorite dishes, as though in late affirmation of his actions, a sign that all was forgiven. It was as if she wanted to say, "See? You're not the only one who needs space. The three of us were always individualists at heart. Who knows why God brought us together only to break us apart." (My father and I were never devout Muslims, though my mother, despite the polytheism of her Balinese–Hindu upbringing, believed fervently in God.)

I guess that was her way of saying sorry to my father, so quiet in life and so quiet in death.

Oh, I should say this isn't a dream. But bits of it do pervade my subconscious. This is why I never want a partner who will remove himself from me in the same way my father did. That is, if I ever try to find one at all.

〰️

It's Saturday, but I decide to go into work, though yesterday was so long and tiring I didn't think I'd be able to return ever again. But since I'll be away for a while, I have to tie up loose ends.

Today I'm even quieter than usual, meaning I'm practically mute. Usually I only open my mouth if someone asks me something or if I have a question that needs answering. Because no one is in today, I don't need to open my mouth at all.

I check my e-mail. The OneWorld secretary, Talisa, has sent Farish and me our flight itinerary. It looks grueling. We have to return to Jakarta constantly between destinations, thanks to the lack of direct flights between cities. And this itinerary doesn't even mention all the places we'll have to drive to by car.

Which means three things:

1. Before I start out (that is, from this point on) I have to refrain from eating corn, water spinach, cabbage, and peas—the four vegetables that make me feel bloated and would therefore (a) make me sluggish, (b) make it hard to pick out which clothes to bring, (c) make me look like a water buffalo no matter what I wear, and (d) make me grouchy and unfocused because I look like a fucking water buffalo.

2. I should bring several packs of Pankreoflat and at least two bottles of Norit—the first to relieve any bloating and the second to alleviate any diarrhea (especially since I plan to try the infamous *sate lalat* of Pamekasan).

3. I should pack a head scarf so I won't be arrested by the police in Sampang or Banda Aceh, where Sharia law is in effect. Being arrested would also mean never consulting for OneWorld ever again.

A number of hospitals in Banda Aceh, on the outskirts of Medan, and in Surabaya have suggested specific dates and times for meetings. Talisa will arrange anything further.

I log on to a forum I subscribe to.

Online debate continues to rage over the formulation of the vaccine for the latest strain of avian flu. The people involved are mainly outbreak experts such as myself, researchers, faithful followers of everything to do with Extraordinary Events (or EE, the official government term for what I prefer to call "outbreaks"), and some unusually technologically savvy government officials.

A professor of epidemiology—a creature like me but a million times smarter—has written the following:

> *Look, viruses mutate. That's what they do. Therefore, anticipation is key. Okay, so let's say the new vaccine is ready in two to three months. Then what? How will the vaccine be distributed? Is every bird in the entire archipelago to be vaccinated? If so, how? By people in spacesuits descending into every village in the country, from Sabang to Merauke? It'll cause mass panic. Look at what just happened in North Sumatra.*

Furthermore, will said vaccine provide sufficient protection? What we need, as I keep saying, is to fix the animal health care system, which has been broken for so long.

Afrizal Fuadi, an NGO researcher—I don't know him, but he's always providing commentary on these kinds of forums—writes:

Geez, why are people still talking about this? It's not like the screw-up in handling the EE avian flu crisis popped up yesterday. It's just the same old song.

And did you see the latest interview with the representative for the Avian Flu Action Coordination Committee? How can he speak in such stock phrases? "We remain vigilant about X." "We appeal to Y." "There should be better cooperation between the Ministry of Social Wellness and Fitness, the Ministry of Livestock, and regional authorities along all shared infrastructural channels involving matters that fall into the categories of human health and animal health." "Surveillance of interregional poultry trade must be tightened." Etc., etc.

Sure, we'd be ecstatic if all of that really did happen. But why hasn't the AFACC answered the questions we're all asking in our heads? What have they done so far and why hasn't it worked? And what are they going to do this time round that will work?

Buntaran A. S., a high-ranking official at SoWeFit, offers his response:

Dear wise sirs: First of all, thank you for your input. In fact, the very points you gentlemen raise have already been addressed by recommendations made at a recent ministerial-level coordination meeting. Now I know none of it has been implemented yet (it's still early in the process). But I beg you to be patient. There's no point in making something so difficult to implement even more complicated than it already is.

Rest assured, the Ministry of Home Affairs has already consented to circulate an official statement concerning the avian flu to the regents and mayors throughout the country. We have also engaged a team of avian flu experts to keep us updated on new developments to ensure maintenance of the status quo (i.e., that this strain does not spread to the human population).

However, good sirs, as you yourselves know, there are a number of ever-present obstacles that make implementation difficult. The avian flu outbreak has been officially classified as an epidemic, and thus the funds to deal with it must come out of a budget specifically allocated for non-natural disasters. But no such budget exists. If the current system doesn't change, the federal government's ability to provide assistance to regional authorities—in the form of operational funding and in matters concerning health and the environment, among others— will always encounter impediments.

Ah, so now the question is this: What can be done to make the proper authorities aware of this problem? Heaven knows.

To which someone named Eko Sayidiman replies:

To the Honorable Mr. Buntaran: Will the vaccine be given to farmers free of charge? According to one media source, the losses sustained by the poultry farming sector account for 30 percent of those sustained by the entire poultry farming industry. Which comes to about 5 billion rupiah. Is there any truth in this? What measures will the government take with regard to compensation?

Buntaran A. S. answers:

Dear Eko: The poultry farmers will still receive compensation, not to mention a certain amount of special consideration—for example, assistance in acquiring replacement eggs, extensions on bank loans, etc. Do believe me when I say we are serious about developing a vaccine for this new strain of virus.

Eko Sayidiman:

Mr. Buntaran, keep your empty promises. You're a filthy liar.

I shake my head at how invested everyone is, how excruciatingly serious they all are. Though at the end of the day, it all comes down to money. I think about a recent meeting that turned into a fight after a co-worker of mine—Farish Chaniago—informed us that the "master seed" for the development of the new vaccine had already been established and that it was already undergoing tests at the Animal Biology Resource Center in Surabaya.

"My friend happens to be involved in the project," said Farish. "He told me they're using a virus isolate to develop the vaccine. The isolate came from a blood sample from one of the birds that died in Sukoharjo. For some reason, they've classified it as a vaccine for 'infectious bronchitis.' Go figure. The thing is, even though they'll be able to release the vaccine relatively soon, they won't be able to produce five million vaccine capsules in one month. And that's how many capsules *they say* are needed, which I doubt very much."

When asked how many he thought would be needed, Farish said breezily, "A million at most. And even that figure will depend on how effective it proves. But we'll see. The news is they plan to finish it by the third week of March."

Farish is a vet. He worked at the Ministry of Livestock for five years before he moved on. Though wildlife conservation is his real passion, everyone keeps their mouth shut whenever he speaks up on any animal-related issues. OneWorld always asks him to attend meetings with the Avian Flu Action Coordination Committee. He should have been at the meeting on Thursday. There was no sign of him on Friday either.

But now his voice drifts in from the doorway to my office. Great. Just great.

"Hey! And I thought I'd be the only one in here today."

What's with the smirk on his face?

He keeps talking. "Did you see the e-itinerary Scoop! sent us?"

Scoop! is OneWorld's contracted travel agency.

I nod vaguely, a little annoyed because he seems oblivious that he's done anything wrong. I realize that we'll both be flying out tomorrow. And that means I'll be spending the next few days in his company, seeing his face, listening to him flapping his gums. I don't know how I feel right now. I don't know how I feel about *him*. He's a special breed of human being—the kind who seems to know how to succeed without really trying. He'll show up at a meeting and nod his head without uttering a single meaningful opinion, unless we're speaking about animal health. Or he won't show up at all and contribute absolutely nothing. And always with the same end result: I'm the one who has to work my ass off, while he's the one who gets to regale everyone with stories about our work trips once we're back in Jakarta, as if he did all the work.

Irma says there are lots of people like Farish in Jakarta. They don't need to go to a good university. They don't need to distinguish themselves at their workplace. They don't need to have any special skills. They don't even need to speak fluent English. The important thing is that they go to a prestigious high school—become buddy-buddy with the kid of this big shot or that, who'll grow up to be a big shot himself at this firm or that, winning contract bids for this project or that, and thus be guaranteed a lifetime of wealth and success. A good fucking network is all you need.

People like Farish will always find work, will always have a decent job, and though they won't necessarily rise to the top, they'll never sink too close to the bottom.

In short, I can't be bothered to waste time talking with him. Though I have to admit, he has an okay face. Not as handsome as Leon's, but then again, no one is as handsome as Leon. Unfortunately, he doesn't seem to have any intention of leaving me alone in my office. In fact, he steps inside.

"You're coming on the trip, too?" I say.

"Yep," he says, sniffing around the piles of paper on my desk, like a pig hunting for truffles.

Quickly, to hide my nervousness, I open my web browser and Google "Avian influenza." A long list of avian-flu-related articles from the past ten days appears on the screen. One article description stands out in particular: "Controversial research on making avian flu easier to spread among humans will resume after a yearlong hiatus."

I want to skim it, but not while he's here. Yet another annoying thing about Farish: he's always claiming that he's read about something, or heard about it, or knows about it before you have. He hates to lose. I wonder if he's read this article already.

A new e-mail appears in my inbox.

Sender: Talisa Sumampouw <t.sumampouw@one-world.co.id>
Recipient: Aruna Rai <a.rai@oneworld.co.id>
Date: 24 Nov 2012 10:05:12
Subject: (no subject)

Ugh. Kill me now.

I glance behind, through the doorway where Talisa's desk is located. I see her head poke out from behind her cubicle. I didn't realize she was here as well. I grin.

Sender: Aruna Rai <a.rai@oneworld.co.id>
Recipient: Talisa Sumampouw <t.sumampouw@oneworld.co.id>
Date: 24 Nov 2012 10:07:14
Subject: (no subject)

FC?

I glance at her again. FC grins, but appears to be oblivious that he's the topic of discussion. I grin back. *Yup,* answers Talisa, and at that moment I feel strong, empowered. I watch as Farish pauses in front of the photo of Gulali and tries to suppress a smile, as if having a photo of a cat on one's desk is a sign that the cat's owner has no life. I let him continue snuffling around until he gets bored.

"How come I've never seen a photo of your family, Run?" he asks.

Fuck you, too, I think. "I guess I just don't have any good photos," I say.

He spends a few silent moments perusing my desk. "Good thing we're leaving tomorrow."

"I guess. There won't be any traffic."

"No, I mean it's good because we won't have to spend Saturday night on a work trip. I mean, what if one of us had a hot date?"

Is this some kind of trick? Is he trying to find out if I have a boyfriend? I say nothing. But he still doesn't show any sign of leaving.

"Good thing Leon won't be coming along this time either," he continues. Extending a finger, he bats at the tufts of a cassowary feather I've tucked between the pages of a book. "We can enjoy a little more freedom."

"We" my ass, I think angrily. What the hell is he talking about? Freedom to do what, exactly? But still I say nothing.

"Did you catch the press conference with the head of AFACC the other day?"

I nod, keeping my eyes on the screen.

"People are going crazy on the forum. They're saying AFACC is surrounded by idiot consultants who've been giving them bad advice."

"I'm not one of AFACC's consultants," I snap.

He looks stunned for a moment. It looks like he's beginning to get the message, but not quite enough to get him to leave.

I turn back to my computer and quickly skim the article that caught my attention.

> *The project was discontinued due to heated debate about the virus potentially escaping the lab or being used for bioterrorism. But now, after a one-year moratorium, forty virus experts from all over the world have signed a letter published in the journal* Nature vs. Nurture *declaring that research must resume immediately . . . A Nobel Prize winner from X——University has stated, "The world simply cannot wait another year or two . . ."*
>
> *And yet, not all research groups agree . . . The US government, for one, has yet to set the conditions under which the experiments will be allowed to continue, and this will also affect research projects funded by the US government in other parts of the world . . . A research scientist from Y—— University reminds us that, historically speaking, thousands of people have contracted diseases in world-class laboratories with impeccable safety records. In his opinion, the world will be much safer as long as the moratorium remains in effect . . .*

Suddenly the left side of my head begins to throb. I'm aware I haven't eaten, but I'm not hungry. And, strangely, my brain isn't overwhelmed with ten different options of where to go for lunch, as it usually is.

I feel very small right now. For the umpteen-thousandth time in my life since I decided to become an epidemiologist, I find myself struggling with the same phrases, the same numbers, the same dilemmas. And still, I don't feel any smarter, any more able to effect change.

And even though I have other fears—my overconsumption of beef, for instance (beef is known to cause cancer)—the same questions about avian flu continue to gnaw away at me: Is the virus destined to continue killing only a tiny handful of people in territories uncharted on the world map? Will it, or when will it, undergo a mutation somewhere in this wide world that will enable it to join forces with a human flu virus, thereby creating a new virus that will start infecting people?

Every time a virologist says such mutations take time, that the genetic code of the avian flu virus will need to undergo at least five to nine mutations to produce a potential pandemic, other statistics terrify me anew. On average, pandemics occur every twenty-seven and a half years, and it's been forty-four years since the last one.

A commentator on our latest foodborne disease has noted that the Pandemic of 1918, otherwise known as the Spanish flu, was responsible for a greater number of deaths in a shorter period of time than any other outbreak in history. While AIDS took about twenty-four years to kill twenty-four million people, the Spanish flu killed twenty-four million people in twenty-four weeks. And the darnedest thing is that every virus that has caused a human pandemic shares genes with the avian flu virus. Not only that, but according to a research paper by a historical archaeologist, the Pandemic of 1918 felled many throughout Java and Kalimantan. Which means pandemics aren't just a problem for countries with four seasons—they also happen in the tropics, and they happen *right here*.

And so: When will the avian flu start spreading from human to human?

No clue. As I often say when I get into these discussions with Irma and my other colleagues at OneWorld, what do we know, really, about a risk that we can never really know? How do you measure its probability?

I turn to look at Farish, who's still poking around the few personal possessions I keep in the office. "So tell me," I say. "In your opinion, what is the probability of an avian flu pandemic?"

"I'm not an economist," he says calmly, "but my economist friend always says that probability is derived from the mathematical analysis of past events. And yet we know that events are never exactly the same as what has occurred in the past. Nor are they exactly the same as events that will occur in the future. We also don't know what will change with time, or how things will change, or how quickly they'll change. We can turn to gods, to prayer, to witch doctors, but we will still live in fear—that is, *if* we insist on living in fear."

Something in this speech impresses me. Still. It does nothing to reassure me or make me feel more hopeful. I try not to think about tomorrow's trip—the discoveries we'll make, the conclusions we'll draw, the new hope we'll have. Is that what awaits us?

And then, at that very moment, Farish decides to saunter out, leaving me with my head swimming.

❦

A few minutes later, Talisa pokes her head into my office.

"Hey, Run. Lunch?"

As usual, her expression is cheerful. Though she isn't completely free of obligations—her mother is terribly sick and her father senile—she's the happiest person I know. But wait. There's something different about her hair. It's so black, so straight, so glossy. Has she just come from the salon? Is she going out tonight? Suddenly, I feel like my body is being drained of something. Energy? Hope? But this is not the time to get carried away—and not, of all people, by His Royal Smugness.

But here it is again.

I shake my head. No, I don't want lunch. What I want is my freedom. And what is freedom if not departure—going far, far away, removing myself from other people's concerns? There's only one place for me to turn: Nadezhda.

5

Nadezhda

When I arrive at Siria, I find Nadezhda sitting in her usual spot—on a curved-back leather chair, typing away on her MacBook.

Her brow is furrowed and her lips are moving, as if she's a musician trying to play in her head the melody she's just finished composing. None of which detracts from her stunningness. Both her parents are Indo, or mixed—her father is half Acehnese, half French, and her mother is half French, a quarter Sundanese, and a quarter something else. Not that such a combination guarantees stunningness, but you get what I mean.

On the table in front of her, there's a tumbler of something—wine. After all, it's only lunchtime, and she has certain principles when it comes to matters of drink, based on not only international standards regarding what constitutes good taste but also the practicalities of prudent calorie consumption. This means, as I've been repeatedly taught: wine only with meals; gin and tonics, martinis, sherry, Negronis, white wine/champagne/"bubbly" in any form (depending on social context) as aperitifs; red or white wine with food (again, depending on what type of food, and only the right red, the right white); port and sweet wines with dessert. Thereafter—and Nadezhda's nights can be long indeed, nights that flow into mornings, melt into afternoons, and burst into nights again—she always returns to wine.

Catching sight of me, she hails a waiter and points at her glass. "One of these for Ms. Aruna!"

As usual, there's no point in protesting.

I sit down beside her. It is three o'clock on a Saturday afternoon—the perfect time for an afternoon nap—but the restaurant is still packed to the rafters with beautiful people determined to drink life to the lees, to lavish all their time and money on a taste of the high life. Also present are the members of the freelancing brigade—those like Nadezhda who work to live and who live to work.

But there is only one Nadezhda in this world. Nadezhda, who, at four months old, moved to Paris with her parents. Who, at twelve years old, returned again to Jakarta and who, at seventeen, left for New York to study at Barnard. Who four years later obtained a scholarship to do a master's program at Cambridge in the UK. Who doesn't just speak several languages beautifully, but can also dance and sing in a way that undermines and enfeebles those around her. Who can turn rant into song, silence into sound. Who loves to reach and reaches. There is only one Nadezhda in this world. And as it turns out, she has reached for and claimed the gravest part of me, too.

The look in her eyes tells me she's been here for more than an hour, which means that she's had at least two or three drinks and has probably composed anywhere from half a page to a full page of text.

"What're you writing about?"

Nadezhda has her own column in a respected culinary magazine.

"The term 'foodie,'" she says. "I prefer 'foodist.'"

I raise an eyebrow. "Oh really? And what's the difference?"

"I just like it better, that's all," she replies. "A foodist is, oh, I don't know, on par with an environmentalist, a terrorist, a nudist. It's more political, gives off the impression of a serious 'ism.' And why shouldn't it? For me, food is an ideology, a worldview."

"Hmm."

"Actually, the term has been around since the late nineteenth century, when it referred to advocates of various trendy dietary philosophies. Gael Greene. I told you about her once. The *New York Times* food critic. Well, she was the one who started using the term again and gave us another word for 'gastronaut.'"

I nod, nodding being the thing I do, unsure whether to contribute my two cents or whether I have any cents at all.

"Anyway, I'm experiencing a crisis of faith."

"Regarding?"

"Regarding food."

"How so?"

"I mean, not food in general. But the way food dominates life."

"In what sense?"

"Just look around. At the culinary programs and articles saturating television and print media nowadays. At the number of amateur blogs devoted to food and restaurants. At the online food porn we live with as evidence that their eaters lead interesting lives!"

"Not exactly bad news for you, is it?"

"But just think about it. These days, visual and written rhetoric about food has lost its connection with any concern about nature or nutrition. Food has become this . . . this . . . ersatz spiritualism. The gods this world worships aren't politicians or spiritual leaders anymore, but the kings of the kitchen. Just think of all the TV shows about cooking and food. We watch them in search of enlightenment on all lifestyle matters, and metaphysical ones, too. Gordon Ramsay and Anthony Bourdain are far more famous than the president of the EU or even the winners of the Nobel Prize. I have to agree with whoever said that food is more than a mania these days. It's, like, a psychosis."

"But isn't that more of a problem in the West? I mean, not that I know anything. But does what you're talking about even apply to us? Since when have local chefs in Indonesia been elevated to the status of gods? Who in Jakarta cares if Chef X from Restaurant Y creates the most amazing version of sweet-and-sour soup in the whole archipelago? For your average Indonesian, food is still just a basic need. I mean, just try striking up a conversation here with someone who isn't a foodie—sorry, *foodist*—and mention Ramsay or Bourdain. Or try telling them stories about how you can afford to eat at expensive restaurants like Siria three times a week. They'd probably sock you in the face."

Hmm. This seems to give her pause. But I bet it's coming. I bet if I upped the winds on my own argumentative will, I could get her to let it out, whatever it is she needs to get off her chest. So I wait.

"Run," she says, anticipating me, "I'm really stressed out."

This is new. Nadezhda is never "stressed out," even when she's being brilliant or productive. "Stressed out" is for mere mortals like you and me, whereas *she* finds herself in "a conundrum," or is "wholly unconvinced," or is "fundamentally vexed," or, more recently, is "epistemologically tickled." Probably all the time.

"Didn't you just come back from Paris?" I ask, sensing myself softening. "Paris . . . as in your heaven on earth?"

"Yes, yes," she says impatiently. "But, the thing is—well, I'm scared. You see, I've become aware of the possibility that, maybe, all this time everyone has been thinking that I'm . . . well, frivolous."

And before I can reply, she continues, as if not trusting my ability to realize the word's scope and magnitude. "Frivolous, obsessed with trivial matters, and—this is the worst of it—not just frivolous and obsessive, but *active* in promoting my brand of frivolity and petty obsessiveness! I mean, how do you think people rate me as a writer? Think about it. People hear my name and they go, 'Oh, her! That's Nadezhda—that food and lifestyle writer, that self-styled writer, that *second-rate writer.*'"

"*That's* what you're afraid of?"

She shrugs.

"You're *really* afraid that's what people think?"

"But think about it, though. What kind of serious writer would have food on the brain twenty-four hours a day? Obsess about this restaurant and that restaurant or this and that food trend? Worry about being seen as behind the times or uncool if she doesn't try this or that dish and this or that restaurant, just like the millions of other foodists in the world who consider their tastes, their selves, worthy of more respect than your average person, when in reality, they're just a bunch of idiots?"

"Well, excuse *me*. *I* like my food, but I don't think I'm an idiot."

"Yes, yes. But can't you see that food is a safe passion? It's safer than politics, religion, literature. People *assume* that everyone can spend hours chitchatting about food. It's safe and it's also no big deal. And food by its very nature is, oh, I don't know, subjective. Yes, that's the word I'm looking for. Subjective. The way it tastes varies from palate to palate: it's not like the world really needs experts on it, you know."

"Okay, but there are also a lot of people in the world who don't give a shit about food. Or who only eat at KFC and McDonald's when they go out. Or order chicken all the time, or expect their veal parmigiana to be presented atop a bed of spaghetti. Or who have no taste at all." I'm not sure what I'm trying to do, lighten her mood or rile her up even more.

"But that's also the problem. I'm worried that foodism is a class thing. I may worship Brillat-Savarin, but I'm not entirely convinced when it comes to his oft-quoted pearl of wisdom: 'You are what you eat.' Imagine if I could understand the complexities of Bono's mind just by analyzing what he ate for breakfast. Heaven forbid! When people see the menus of the restaurants I've visited in this goddamn world, all they know is I have money. And that I'm a snob because I refuse to eat curly fries at a fast-food joint, even though I'll eat truffle fries at a high-end restaurant."

"Now that you mention it," I say, "why *won't* you eat curly fries at a fast-food joint?"

Nadezhda gives me a withering look. Everyone knows how much she hates fast food. But, quickly, she returns to the matter at hand, this time in an even more roundabout, philosophical way.

"What if we really *were* moved body and soul by food and by everything that revolved around food? Who could confirm whether we were idiots or only parroting global trends? Just yesterday I was revisiting the works of the materialist philosopher Theodor Adorno."

Unintentionally, I yawn. Here we go again. But she won't let it go.

"It got me thinking. Adorno says it's not the mind that establishes the body but the body that establishes the mind. To him, when someone speaks of fried potatoes transforming civilization, or a perfect cut of meat stirring the soul, it's all hot air. To him, foodism is nothing but an attempt to intellectualize and aestheticize food, even though in the end food is just that: food."

I have to admit that following Nadezhda's train of thought isn't always easy for me. Her brain never stops dissecting, quoting, pondering. She regards anything and everything from every angle, every possible perspective, to the point that what issues forth from her mouth, more often than not, is a combination of question, answer, interpretation, enigma, and something someone else has said.

"If you're going to start quoting Adorno, you're really going to get on my nerves," I say. "What *is* it that you're really afraid of?"

She looks crestfallen.

"Look. Let me tell you this," I say. "First, you don't just 'write about food.' Your articles on travel have been published in magazines of international repute. Second, you have your own opinions about food, and people have a lot to learn from you. The thing is, you don't just report what you've eaten here or there. You always try to delve deeper, connect whatever you're eating with other things. Third, you're thoughtful. You're always willing to seek out new ways of thinking about food for those who may not have time to read about it themselves. So you're doing a good thing. And this whole thing about being too hard on yourself—really, it doesn't become you."

Okay, so that last part was probably unnecessary—and a bit mean. But how else should I convince her? Again, she's quiet. And this unsettles me. As if she wants to believe me but can't.

The drink she ordered for me arrives.

"Riesling," says Nadezhda, forgetting for a brief moment that she's suffering an existential crisis over her profession. "From the Pfalz region. One of the top five Riesling-growing areas in Germany."

That's better. I raise my glass.

"Prost," she says, which I know is German because she's talking about Germany, and because she's always the one to say cheers first.

I echo her brightly and think about lightly swirling the wine in my hand, as would anyone who considers herself a true wine connoisseur, or so I think, to let it breathe, to intensify its bouquet, its aroma. But I don't. This afternoon I don't want to be a connoisseur. I want to enjoy my wine with the charming naïveté of a dilettante, though I do feel a bit guilty about swigging wine in broad daylight just because I don't feel right with the world. I mean, I'm not Nadezhda (and I mean this in the nicest way).

The feeling doesn't last. Soon, my head feels lighter, my tongue looser, the world more fluid.

And it isn't long before Nadezhda begins to talk about Paris.

For the first fifteen minutes, she tells me nothing new. But listening to her makes me happy nonetheless, like the strange and soothing distance across which different worlds may, like opposites, attract: how Paris is the most lyrical city in the world, a veritable paradise for the flaneur (for it is only on foot, free of plans, of supervision, of maps, that one can truly experience a city); how on the surface, the city can reshape itself dozens of times, from moment to moment, but how tiny details—ones that establish the character of a place but that aren't necessarily concrete—render it eternal; how easy it is for someone to be alone there and yet never feel lonely.

I enjoy her descriptions of the morning sun conjuring marble into whiteness, of the shimmering waters of the Seine—"an expanse of dew-covered glass." Or of the sounds of the street, like water trickling, flowing around the intersection where she sits, sipping her first coffee of the morning, and how from her table in front of the Café Les Editeurs, a stone's throw away from the Odeon metro station, she watches the citizens of Paris step out into the morning light—waiters, butchers, shop assistants, writers, antique store owners—and melt into the greater swarm.

Gradually, the gentle swell of Nadezhda's voice in my ear returns me to the here and now. "Bistronomy . . . a portmanteau of 'bistro' and 'gastronomy' . . . it's on the up and up . . . gastronomy—fine dining, but served in a relaxed way, in an informal ambiance, with an affordable price tag . . . I visited six of them . . . it's not just hype . . . it's a renaissance in the truest sense of the word . . ."

6

CHAMPAGNE AND POPCORN

Nadezhda Azhari and I are like champagne and popcorn.

Each of us is eminently capable of standing on our own, and we make a fantastic pair. But metaphysical facts are metaphysical facts: she's champagne; I'm popcorn.

A poet once claimed, astutely, that women often can be summed up using adverbs—that their every action is performed purely for melodramatic effect. Or to be more exact, out of the overflow of ephemeral emotions, they act "gently," "coyly," "with blushes," "with sighs," "like a bird taking flight," "like a leaf on the wind." Men on the other hand never waver or wilt. They don't fade away like footprints in sand. And this is because adjectives are their domain, and there they reign with their "faithful arms" and "manly voices" and "knightly deeds."

But Nadezhda transcends all of that.

She is a thing unto herself.

She is champagne.

And that's Nadezhda in a nutshell. Jakarta's arbiters of beauty— editors of women's magazines, designers, directors, actors, artists, writers, restaurateurs—have even named her one of the ten most glamorous women in the capital.

Glamour, as we all know, is different from beauty. Being glamorous isn't just about wearing the right clothes or knowing how to put on makeup. It's also about rhythm and being smart. Nadezhda knows how to move—her body, her hair, her eyes—in front of a camera or onstage, in lighting ranging from bright to dim, in any city in the world, in front of friends and family, and even in front of complete strangers.

She also knows how to speak—presenting herself with the melodies, modulations, and charms of a prizewinning songbird. And she's been blessed with a brain—gifted not only in speech but in writing as well. Versatile, like champagne, she transcends boundaries with ease.

But as with champagne, every Nadezhda has its moment. When the sun is still shining, she is light, crisp, youthful. In the words of a wine critic whom Nadezhda quotes constantly, when she sits down to lunch, she's rosé: ripe, bursting with flavor, gushing red. As evening approaches, she's a blanc de blancs: white on white—like the flash of the final dancer's petticoat before she vanishes from the stage, akin to the last ray of daylight slicing across the evening sky. And when the men begin to circle around, her features grow all the more striking: ripe, round, floral—in short, she's a Pinot Meunier. A man—sophisticated, worldly—asks her to dance, and she transforms into a swan, as graceful, subtle, and mysterious as the fabled Cuvée Sir Winston Churchill. But when the night deepens and she feels herself getting full, that is when she becomes her true self: Krug Champagne. Victorious, she commands the room, conqueror of all.

In contrast, popcorn is never more than popcorn. No one weighs its heft and pitch in their hands or stores it under special conditions. No one analyzes it, or writes songs about it, or includes it in story titles, except when they're talking about watching a movie. Popcorn, unlike champagne, will never know what it's like to be poured between a woman's legs and sipped before it circulates through someone's bloodstream and shoots out the other end as foamy piss into a pot. Its uses are singular: chewed, swallowed, gone. (Note that nobody touches the stuff when it's old and stale.)

If you ask me, passion isn't an emotion—it's fate.

❦

I must confess that many things about Nadezhda make me jealous. I'll tell you five of them—one for each principle comprising the Pancasila, our official national ideology.

1: her family background, its established history, its distinguished ancestry.

2: a set of parents, still alive and still circulating in what we call "society" (as if the term doesn't apply to the rest of us). And "circulating" is an understatement. People go out of their way to greet them at every function and party they attend. Their names consistently make it into newspapers and magazines. And all of Nadezhda's friends love them. ("Uncle and Auntie Azhari? Who *doesn't* love them? They're like our own parents!")

3: her house, never changing, familiar to all, on a street so famous its real name has long been forgotten. ("What's the name of that street again? Well, you know the one—where Nadezhda's parents live.")

4: her cook, who's been with the family for more than forty years, who brings with her certain signature dishes remembered fondly by everyone who's dined there, plus the garden and the pool we and our friends used to spend so much time in as children.

5: tales of her family's exploits, which almost border on myth, not to mention little scandals that are now talked about casually, with knowing smiles, because people have since forgiven them.

Still, I'm not sure I want to be Nadezhda.

Or rather, I don't know how.

❦

My friendship with Nadezhda just happened—like two magnetic particles lying side by side, we happened to meet and we stuck. Sometimes I feel our friendship has lasted because of the particular nature of our differences. Oh yes, make no mistake, difference comes in types.

As Nadezhda often says: "I could never commit myself completely, body and soul, to any of the men from my milieu." (In the circles Nadezhda's parents move in, the word "milieu" is always being bandied about, as if created exclusively for their use.) "When I date someone from my milieu—let's call him X—he and I are both capable of understanding what our parents want for us, and when something happens, or someone says something, we both react in similar ways. And if I get frustrated by the guy I'm dating who isn't from my milieu—let's call him Y—when he doesn't act the way I think he should, I'm able to think, 'Ah, X would understand. He and I were raised with the same values.'

"But as we know, X would never get that other side of our self—our wild self, our untamed self, or even the self that strays just for the fun of it. He would take us aside, scold us, lecture us. 'What's going on with you?' he'd ask. 'I almost don't recognize you anymore.'

"In short, we could never love X like we love Y because at the end of the day, we want to be loved for the unexpected qualities we harbor inside us, the qualities that make us unique.

"And yet, we could never love Y either—Y who is too different from us, who doesn't get why we still respect Mother, though she always thinks we're being stupid. Or why we still love Father despite his philandering ways. Or why we forgive our parents' friends, despite the fact that they're some of the most corrupt people in business and government."

And I think: *You know something? If you were Y, I wouldn't like you much either.*

And that is how champagne loves—with calculations, with theories, with a different logic for each of the four seasons. But because I'm popcorn, my love lacks drama. And is, perhaps, a bit too naïve.

When I say I don't know how to be Nadezhda, what I'm really saying is I don't know how to live like a character in a novel.

Let me give you an example. One day, when I was staying over at Nadezhda's house, on Jalan Saraswati in the Cipete district of Jakarta, I stumbled upon her diary. Who knows why, but I had no qualms about reading it. I've always known there's a part of Nadezhda that yearns to be read, especially by those whom she knows won't judge her—those whom she "loves."

The diary didn't contain much about food. Or her travels. There were no cities named, or even any dates. But there was a love story about Nadezhda and a man named Chrysander. In this section of the diary, Nadezhda's handwriting was small, neat, in print, as if she'd envisioned it as a book.

Her writing was peppered with phrases like "beyond all compare" and "the bitter sting." And there was nothing moderate about any of it. When they first set eyes on each other, at a conference in some town in Europe (France or Italy, most likely), "I knew we were destined to make love." And then, not the next week, not the next day, but the very next *minute*—as if compelled by some mystical force, they left the old castle through a back door, ducked below a bridge somewhere on the grounds, and there, pressed against the cold, wet stone, without so much as a single word, she let him hike up her skirt. Then, "moaning," she "surrendered" herself, "fully," "completely."

That's how they continue to make love for the next few days—"urgently, as if the world were coming to an end"—on the wet bathroom floor (while the other conference attendees are busy conferencing), in an alcove in the garden (while the other attendees are eating dinner), behind a giant wine barrel at a vineyard (while the other attendees are tasting wine).

Chrysander is portrayed as half animal, with the lust of a wild ox: "He needs me every minute, every second, long bouts of it, again and again. I allow him to ravish me with his manhood." And in an old church, gazing at the angel statues and their weeping faces, it strikes her: "I have found my sexual soul mate. He makes me so wet. He satiates me so."

But by day four of the "madness," Nadezhda's tone begins to change—as does the neatness of her handwriting. "He frightens me. And sometimes, without meaning to, he hurts me. Yet I can't imagine my life after this is over, after he's gone."

A few pages later: "Why is he always blathering on about himself and his work?" And: "Why does he compare everything he eats to his mother's cooking?" But such complaints don't prevent them from going at it in the park in broad daylight. The following day, something ends with a "resounding, earth-shattering moan."

By the sixth day, toward the end of the conference, Nadezhda is sure that she's spotted Chrysander squeezing the breast of a sexy writer from Senegal. "Typical Greek," she fumes. "Who does he think he is? Some sort of god? That he owns the world and everything in it?" That night, as dinner is being served, Nadezhda empties her glass of wine over Chrysander's head just as he's pouring wine into Miss Senegal's glass. Nadezhda runs out of the room. Chrysander follows her. In front of a statue of Aphrodite, they exchange slaps. And all of a sudden, just like that, they're kissing, making love until the sun breaks over the horizon.

At that point, I remember closing the diary and putting it down on the bed. I was trembling. Was this what they called Life? This *torrent*? Flammable, full of surprises, like in fiction? If this was Life, then what had I been doing for three decades? Apparently I hadn't lived, didn't know what "Life" meant. Life had banned me—from sex and from bringing forth little Arunas into the world. I hadn't even been permitted an old geezer to nurse in his final days.

What had happened instead: Life had taken a look at me, sized me up, and said, "Aruna, I hereby bestow upon you a deep and abiding relationship with food, for that is all you are worthy of. Unlike your friend Nadezhda, you lack the power of champagne—a power that would entitle you to the blessing of both food and sex. My apologies, but that's Life. And Life isn't fair."

Had God played a hand in this? And if so, on what basis did he decide who got to have one gift and who got to have two?

But there it was. I was an unworthy woman. Because I wasn't a woman. I was popcorn.

Once I'd calmed down, I opened the diary again. I wanted to finish the tale of the Greek and Champagne. Were they still together? When Champagne went abroad, did they meet up and continue their quest to master 1,001 different sex positions? Why hadn't she brought this guy back to Jakarta so Bono and I could meet him?

Then my eyes came to rest on a different name. It was a different story, a different city, and probably a different year. Even the handwriting had changed—not print, but a slanting cursive, penned in a civilized, Westernized hand.

His name is Aravind. I must give credit to Nadezhda, though, for she truly is an epic kind of gal—from Greece, she swims on over to India, still looking like a million bucks. But the city she's talking about clearly isn't in India at all.

Her language changes, too.

She isn't describing what's happening to her anymore. She's imagining herself as someone else—a "she," not an "I"—a character in a film or a dream.

"She stands on the sidewalk. Tall, slender, with long, glossy locks hanging down her back. She looks up at the window, her lips parted. A fine mist winds among the towers, like a hazy, incense-filled dream, and the city bows its head in sadness . . ."

Then, lo! He appears. The man she's been waiting for, a writer whom she has long admired but has only met once, by coincidence, for a mere three minutes.

He, Aravind, had sent her letters filled with words that made her fall in love, that made her feel justified for being awed by him from the start.

"Sometimes," she writes, "three minutes last a lifetime." They'd agreed to meet here, in this city.

It's their first night together, and he offers to cook dinner for Nadezhda in the kitchen of her "thumb-sized" apartment, "barely big enough for both his body and mine."

He turns out to be pretty skillful in the kitchen, as skillful as he is with his sentences, which are refined, but whoa, don't they "pack a punch"! A plate of tomato and mozzarella salad, drizzled with Spanish olive oil, followed by a simple, classic pasta dish. A bottle of elegant Burgundy, and a few macarons from Ladurée for them to share. Later, they nibble each other's tongues to find out if the taste of white chocolate changes from mouth to mouth. The next moment, they're lying together naked, listening to a Monteverdi aria rising above the peals of laughter and the footsteps of people passing below.

At that point, I longed to return to the language she used to describe Chrysander, to his untamed passion, explosive and laugh-out-loud funny, for there was something about Nadezhda and Aravind's story that verged on cliché.

See for yourself:

He bolted upright as if he'd lost track of time. Glancing at his watch he scrambled to his feet and snatched up his collared shirt and trousers, which lay in a heap on the floor.

"Sorry, darling," said Aravind. "But I have to go back to my hotel. My partner calls my room every night around now to make sure I'm back. She's very suspicious."

And strangely enough, Nadezhda doesn't pour wine over his head or slap him silly like she did with that lecherous Greek. "There are times when we must heed our mother's wise counsel and swallow our pride," she writes bravely. "For not all men are the same."

At that point, I wanted to strangle Nadezhda, especially when I read: "I'm positive we're destined for each other. It's only a matter of time. Someone who respects his wife so much will be sure to respect us."

I read the diary from cover to cover, and for the first time I was unsure of my feelings toward her, and, also, about my jealousy. Should I have been jealous? Or should I have pitied her instead? Pitied her because she was so attractive to men, and so attracted *to* men, yet incapable of building a future with any of them? Because at her age (she was in her thirties, like me) she'd never had a serious boyfriend whom she could introduce to her family and friends. Then again, how did I know she didn't like things just the way they were? Maybe that was exactly what she wanted: freedom. Freedom to have sex without any commitments. Without making future plans. And maybe that was what made her so lucky.

One thing was clear: I didn't feel like I understood Nadezhda any better after reading her diary, much less feel like I had any power over her. She'd concealed this side of herself from me because all her life she'd been expected, forced even, to uphold the values and desires of her family. Minor infractions weren't forbidden as long as they were hidden away, as long as they didn't interfere with the order of things or appearances. And who was I not to respect this way of thinking?

Nadezhda is champagne, and this also means that she's generous. She gives off bubbles—and what are bubbles if not diamonds in water? She's not the type to be easily offended or enraged. I'm sure she wouldn't be mad if she found out I'd read her diary and that I know about her crazy urges and powerful emotions, even if she has to suppress them once she steps foot on Indonesian soil.

So you see, it's impossible for me not to love Nadezhda. In fact, I love her so much, often it makes me weep. For, like Bono, she's such a slave to passion, to the hope of greater heights, and yet she can't give free play to all that she is. Like me, she's lonely as hell.

❦

After talking, eating, and drinking our hearts out at Siria, we go back to my place.

"Really? You want me to come along?"

"Yes, why not?"

Nadezhda stops sniffing around the contents of my fridge (in this respect she's exactly like Bono) and stares at me in bewilderment.

"But you'll be working," she says. "You'll have things to do."

"Yes, but it doesn't mean you can't be in the same city. And it doesn't mean we can't eat together when I have free time."

She walks over to the sitting area. I trail behind her, trying to not let the smell of the leftover Big Mac in the fridge follow me like the stench of some infectious disease. I didn't plan any of this—Nadezhda coming here. But after drinking so much she seemed eager to chat. The more she drinks, the more alert she becomes.

She sits on the sofa and slips off her high heels.

"Bono's coming, too," I say. "But we're taking different flights. I'll get there at eight in the morning; he'll get there at ten."

"You're going to Surabaya first and then on to Madura? Are you spending the night in Surabaya?"

"Yup."

"Bono's going to Madura, too?"

"Yup."

"And Bono and I are allowed to ride in the same car as you and your co-workers?"

"I haven't said anything to my team, but I don't think there'll be a problem."

To be honest, I'm not sure whether I'm allowed to bring my friends along on official business. Sure, Farish and I will be the only ones from Ministry headquarters in Jakarta, but I'm anticipating the Ministry will assign people from its local branches to join us in each city and on several of the field assignments.

When we're in Surabaya, Bono will meet me at restaurants we've read about. In a pinch, he can figure out how to get to Madura by himself, too. The main thing is that we agree to meet at such and such place, around such and such time. This is the good thing about planning a trip with other food-obsessed people. They don't feel like they've lost out if petty little details don't go their way—like transportation, or weather, or distance, or cost. They'll only feel cheated if they don't find the restaurant they're looking for.

"Hmm. It *would* be fun," says Nadezhda, mulling it over. "I've been wanting to visit Palembang and Banda Aceh for ages."

Briefly, absurdly, I see myself and Nadezhda sitting in jail, rounded up by the Wilayatul Hisbah—the Islamic police in Aceh province who enforce Sharia law. Nadezhda, with her swanlike neck, her full, *poori*-like breasts, her hot ass. I can't imagine how I'm supposed to go anywhere with her in Aceh, even if she wears a burka. Not Banda Aceh, the provincial capital, and certainly not the more conservative towns like Meulaboh and Lhokseumawe.

"All right," I tell her. "But that means you have to come to Medan, too. From Palembang, we're going to Medan for two days before heading to Banda Aceh."

She looks agitated. It's like something inside her doesn't want to be left alone, doesn't want to surrender herself to routine. It's the same confusion I saw in Bono on Thursday night. Perhaps she's unwilling to stay behind while Bono goes, or she's unwilling to let me and Bono go together and leave her behind. Or she's thinking, with that somewhat complicated brain of hers, that this is her chance to prove she's not a hedonist who feels comfortable only in the more permissive societies of temperate climes. This is her chance to get to know her own country.

Suddenly: "All right!"

"Huh?"

"My schedule next week is pretty clear," she says brightly. "I'll join you guys. But only when you get to Palembang, okay?"

"Okay," I say.

This is what happens with Champagne and Popcorn. One makes a request and the other grants it.

7

THE FIRST CASE

The sign reads "Dominica." It's an old building from the looks of it, built during the colonial period under the Dutch, and I imagine that from behind those dew-covered windowpanes, I'll be able to see the orange of the trembling horizon in the distance—like something out of Once Upon a Time in the West. *Pure Sergio Leone land.*

As I approach, however, I realize that the building has recently been renovated and now houses a bar.

When I was a little girl, I wrote in my diary almost every day. I also had a fondness for everything French. One of my favorite names was Dominique. And because my name wasn't Dominique, that was what I called myself in my diary. I even changed the name of the boy I had a crush on all through elementary school to Alain. (His real name was Ananda.) Whenever the Dominican Republic was mentioned in the newspaper or a magazine or in the news on TV—and you could count the number of times this happened on one hand—I had to know. And who doesn't love Sundays—dies Dominica, the day even God takes a break?

I enter and see Leon at the bar. He's not alone. I don't need to wait for the woman to lean her face close to his to know that it's Katrin. And when

*her tiny purse falls to the floor, I know she's dislodged it from the bag hook
underneath the counter on purpose.* You've got to be kidding me, *I think.
Katrin is sexy, no doubt about it, but her tactics are stale. Naturally, she
wants Leon to get a good look at her big breasts when she bends down to
pick up her purse.*

Still, my pulse quickens. For a second, I think Leon is going to kiss her.

*But then I hear the bartender. "A Baileys on the rocks for the lady and
an old-fashioned for the gentleman."*

*All of a sudden, the sound of my own laughter echoes through the bar.
From their choice of cocktails, I know it'll never last.*

❦

I love arriving in a new city in the morning. The morning never tells
you how it really feels. It slows everything down. It's kind when it comes
to facts. The morning brings things to light gradually, layer by layer,
so that when the city finally makes its appearance, it's not as a thing
ready-made, but rather a thing not yet final. Something that can still
be shaped. Something full of promise.

At 8:20 a.m., Farish and I are in the middle of the city, amidst
the smog and the sunlight, inside a Toyota Avanza. With us is a young
woman in her midtwenties named Inda, from SoWeFit's local office
here in Surabaya. She's not *pretty* pretty, but she's interesting pretty and
good natured. Her lips have a curious shape to them, irregular, a little
plump, and it's easy to make her smile. Guys seem to like this combination. Most of them are not out to date beauty queens anyway. For a
split second, I'm jealous. But not for long.

It's a good thing she's here, I think. Good for Farish, and good for me.
Farish and I met at the Lion Air check-in counter at the Jakarta airport
this morning, and between now and then we've spoken to each other a
total of three times:

1.

Farish: Morning.

Me: Morning.

2.

Farish: I'm sitting in 8C. You?

Me: 19F.

3.

Farish: Is someone picking us up when we arrive?

Me: Yep.

I leave Farish and Inda to it so they can work their magic on each other.

"Yes, that's right, Farish," says Inda. "The word is that thousands of chickens in Tulungagung are dead as well. Not just ducks." When she says "Farish," she draws it out—"Fariiish." It makes me wince, but I say nothing.

"Hmm, yes. Very strange," says Farish from the front seat, in a heavy, ponderous voice.

As he speaks, the idiot turns his whole body around so he can get a better view of Inda. I look out the window. I can't bear to watch.

He continues. "As far as I know, the clade strains of the virus only affect ducks."

"Yes, it is strange, Fariiish," says Inda with exaggerated sadness. "We've already checked with several chicken farmers over there. They all say the symptoms correspond to those of avian flu. Who knows how many hundreds or thousands of chickens they've already slaughtered since."

"They've incinerated all the carcasses?"

"Yes," says Inda, this time sounding genuinely upset.

I can't help feeling upset as well. I enjoy a good barbecued bird, but I don't like it when scores of chickens are being turned into charcoal just because it's suspected they've come down with a virus. I show some delicacy and try not to ask her about the various restaurants I've been thinking of visiting while I'm here—the ones specializing in fried duck.

"Well, it's a shame," Farish says, grinning stupidly. "But I suppose barbecuing them is all for the best."

Two-bit playboy.

I steal a glance at Inda. She looks all bashful, like a country maiden.

Suddenly I have a headache, a persistent frontal jab, like a shard of glass trying to break through the surface or a giant mite trying to find its way out of the hostile environment that is my head. I can't bear to watch this bad soap opera scene any longer, so I look outside. Then I realize it's been fifteen years since I was last here.

The Surabaya of my memories is dirty, dusty, disorderly. When I last visited, in the late nineties, the air was roasting, to the point of torture. Sometimes, as I took it all in from behind a car window or from the side of the road, it seemed as if the pavement was swelling with heat, steam rising in plumes from the asphalt.

"Here, the heroes of the revolution are not dead"—so wrote the poet Hr. Bandaharo of the city of Stalingrad. But on my previous visit I had trouble seeing Surabaya the same way. Sixty years ago, this city's sons were dying in the streets for country and for freedom. Yet the same streets seemed so unfeeling, so mercantile. It was as if the city was devoid of sacred spaces—spaces to be kept from progress, from the future, so they could continue to honor the past. Sure, there was the Heroes Monument, and the Majapahit Hotel, and the valiant-looking statues scattered throughout the city. But it was all too hot, too chaotic, and I was too weary to pay my respects.

But now something feels different. The roads seem wider, cleaner, less crowded. There are more sidewalks, more trees. Every aspect of the city, including the majestic, newly restored colonial-era buildings, shaky in their old age but charming nevertheless, leaps out at me. The residential areas near the governor's and mayor's houses—beautiful structures, both of them—are lined with mansions and spacious gardens that bespeak an order, a system. The images of sharks and crocodiles found throughout the city—the *sura* and *baya* that make up Surabaya's name—don't feel like contrived mythology this time around. Even the Red Bridge, where Brigadier Mallaby was killed in the Battle of Surabaya, is impressive in its authority.

In the background, I hear the voices of my two companions—one growing more coquettish by the minute and the other more annoying.

We agree that Farish and I should check in at the hotel first and we'll all meet again in the lobby at ten. After that, we'll go straight to the hospital. When Farish says "check in," there's a rascally glint in his eye.

But the only thing on my mind is the name of a certain dish—a local specialty of Banyuwangi, not too far away. *Rujak Soto.*

❦

"Hey, I'm in Surabaya," says Bono over the phone. "Just landed."

"Great. I'm on the road right now," I say, looking at my watch. "We'll be at the hospital in ten minutes. My team and I have to talk to some patients."

"Where are you staying?"

I tell him the name of the hotel.

"Okay," he says. "I'm staying nearby. So where are we going for lunch?"

I lower my voice because I don't want my car-mates to think I'm shallow. (As if the only thing I have on the brain is food. Even if it's true.) "There's a restaurant that serves Banyuwangi cuisine. It's in the city center, not far from your hotel. I'm dying to try their rujak soto. And I've heard they serve other kinds of rujak as well—ones you can't find anywhere else."

"Oh," I hear Bono say on the other end. "Rujak soto?"

As a rule, the word "rujak" doesn't inspire much enthusiasm in men. Bono is no exception. These beautiful medleys of fresh fruit and vegetables doused in spicy palm-sugar-based sauce are associated with women, with pregnancy cravings, with the emotional sweet-and-sour fieriness of Eve's daughters. But there's more to rujak than this. Poor rujak. It's really not fair.

"Soto rujak or rujak soto?"

"Rujak soto."

"Are you sure?"

"That's what they call it. Who am I to argue?"

"Hmph."

Don't tell me Bono's getting all Nadezhda on me.

"There's a reason I'm asking. Soto rujak is more soupy, like soto. Rujak soto is more like salad, like rujak. At least that's how it should be, in theory."

"All right, all right. Why don't you find out for yourself?"

"I will," says Bono, sounding like he means it. "Text me when you're finished at the hospital."

I'm sure the only reason he's willing to give the poor dish a try is because of its sotoness.

"Okay," I say before hanging up.

Farish asks me who I was talking to.

"My boyfriend."

This time he spins around a full 180 degrees. His expression is one of total shock.

"For real?"

"What do you mean, 'for real'?"

"You have a boyfriend? Seriously?"

I ignore this question.

When we get to the hospital, I lag behind as Farish and Inda leap out of the car and scramble toward a redbrick structure that looks depressingly empty and abandoned. I imagine the pair of them running up the stairs and kicking open the door to the epidemiology department like two members of a bomb disposal team, or *CSI*, or fucking Castle and Beckett, racing to save the city from destruction.

The hospital doesn't even look like a hospital. A facility, more like it—squalid, low security, a shelter for petty criminals instead of the infirm, the sick instead of the sickly. It even lacks the harsh fluorescent lighting usually associated with heartless functionality. Instead there are broken bulbs, rain-stained walls, and crummy corridors from which I almost expect a zombie or two to pop out. I take a deep breath and try my best to look at ease.

By the time I join Farish and Inda on the third floor, which in comparison to the rest of the building is better staffed, better lit, and better equipped, they're already talking with a senior nurse. She doesn't look very enthused. From the grim expression on her face, it looks as if she's thinking, *I should have just gone through the trouble of taking the final practicum to become a doctor. Then I wouldn't be stuck having to field questions from these busybodies.*

I overhear them mention "the Mojokerto case." It happened a few years back, in 2007. A resident of Bangsal in East Java had a fever of over 102 degrees Fahrenheit and a leukocyte count of 1,000 cells per microliter—way below average.

"The patient's symptoms back then are almost identical to those of the patient we've just brought in," says the nurse, the expression on her face still sour. "The difference is, back then, there were other patients coming in with similar symptoms. There were a fair number. Now there's only one. But from what I hear, it's the same in other areas: only one case here and one case there. Talk about weird."

"You mean that there both is and isn't an outbreak going on at the same time?" Farish asks pointedly.

The nurse doesn't respond.

"Has a blood sample been sent to R&D at SoWeFit headquarters in Jakarta?"

"Yes, but we'll only get the results back tomorrow."

"Which courier service did you use? Elteha or Caraka?"

Really. What's the point of asking a question like that? But I don't interfere. Let Mr. Hot Stuff feel like a big man.

"So how many people are undergoing treatment in the special wing?" Farish asks the nurse.

"Just the girl."

"And she was brought in from Malang?"

"Yes."

"But isn't there a hospital in Malang? Aren't they also one of the hospitals designated to handle avian flu cases?"

"Yes, but from what I've heard the facilities are inadequate."

"Can we look at the patient? We'd like to ask her a few questions."

"Sure," the nurse says as she hurries toward the door. "But don't take too long."

She looks relieved at being able to send us big-city folks somewhere else—where she won't be responsible for providing us with information that might be wrong, incomplete, or not yet vetted by the hospital admin.

In the wing set aside for avian flu patients, protocol is, surprisingly, followed to a T. This at least allows for some hope. How many times have I visited other hospitals where people are allowed to come and go as they please? Here, the signs that read "No Public Access" are taken seriously. The door is locked from the inside. In order to enter we have to press a button and get permission from the nurse on duty.

Once inside, we're subjected to interrogation. At this stage, the staff is still relatively suspicious of us, as if we're asking to interview the president himself about the outbreak supposedly sweeping across our archipelago. Then, when they're convinced we really have been dispatched from the Ministry and not some bioterrorist organization, they ask us to wash our hands with antiseptic soap and don special gowns before entering the patients' rooms. As Inda puts on her gown, I watch Farish discreetly eying the cleavage that pops out of her blouse.

The coordinator for this wing is also a senior nurse. But she's much friendlier than her colleague. It's as if someone has tuned her face to broadcast two rows of white teeth, top and bottom, morning and night, come rain or shine, hell or high water, twenty-four hours a day, 365 days a year—as if smiling is her only safeguard against disaster. She accompanies us as we visit all the wards. I can tell from her accent that she's from Malang, and she expresses annoyance at the public hospital there, which "time and time again" lacks perception, "time and time again" lacks initiative, and "time and time again" fails to submit requests to the Regional House of Representatives for increased funding to handle emergencies.

"Why are almost all the patients they send to us in such terrible condition?" she asks vehemently before answering her own question. "Because of the inadequate treatment they receive before they're referred to us, despite the fact that the kind of treatment a patient initially receives in such dire situations is critical to ensuring their survival." Before any of us can respond, she continues. "I happen to be friends with the secretary of economy and finance for the regency of Malang. He told me that he didn't see a single proposal for increased funding from the local hospitals during the discussions of the draft for the 2013 regional budget. It's so depressing. And still this happens year after year."

"But even if there were such proposals, would they receive any support?" asks Farish.

"My friend says he's positive they'd receive support—especially since suspected cases of avian flu are on the rise in Malang. The only problem is that these hospitals have no initiative. Zilch."

"Well," I can't help but interject, "as you say, the cases *are* suspected, not confirmed."

The nurse seems momentarily taken aback, but not for long.

"Yes, but it doesn't mean we shouldn't improve our facilities to anticipate the real thing."

"But there's only one suspected case at the moment." Again, I can't help it, though I intend it to sound more like a reminder than a reprimand.

"Are you saying we need to have lots of suspected cases before we do anything about it?"

So she's one of those seasoned senior nurses trained in internalizing an officially imposed institutional myth and voicing it as though it were her own, contradictions be damned. I shoot a quick glance at Castle and Beckett, who are suddenly quiet as mice—*Can you geniuses help me?* But they can't; they won't.

I let it go, even if the institutional thinking is clearly absurd. Are we missing something?

"I bet they have more suspected avian flu patients inside," Farish whispers. "It's just that they've all been injected with an invisible serum so we can't see them. If they have no patients, there's no justifying the wing at all. There's no point to the facilities, there's no point to the corruption, everybody's out of work." And before I have the chance to open my mouth, he says, "And if the right honorable secretary of economy and finance of Malang is apparently aware of the situation, why doesn't the secretary propose a solution to the hospitals' problems himself? Especially if the depressing situation repeats itself year after year? Couldn't he have done so through an informal channel like his good friend standing before us?"

I'm too tired to argue. In this country, asking which member or division of the civil service is most at fault is equivalent to asking which came first, the chicken or the egg. Inappropriate joke, I know, but there you go. That's how low I've been brought.

My headache returns. Soon afterward, we're gathered around the bed of a young girl. She looks weak.

"Her condition is quite serious," whispers the senior nurse. "She was only brought to us five days after she began showing signs of fever. I'm not sure if she's going to make it."

The patient's name is Nuraini. She's fourteen. According to the report I'm reading, she has all the symptoms typically associated with avian flu: high fever, difficulty breathing, stomach pain, diarrhea. She's very thin, as if her body is being gnawed away from the inside out, and she has no energy to resist. Once again I'm ashamed because even at a time like this I find myself thinking of all the things she can no longer enjoy: smell, color, texture, taste, not to mention life itself.

Fifteen minutes later I leave the wing so I can text Bono: *Another 45 minutes, Bon.* When Bono texts back with an okay, I feel a little calmer, despite the fact that my stomach has begun to protest and is making the kind of gurgling sounds you hear in a sci-fi film. Maybe it's better if I stay out here for a while.

A moment later I realize there's an old man sitting beside me. The look of complete and utter devastation on his face compels me to speak.

"Who are you waiting for, sir?"

"My daughter," says the old man, pointing feebly toward the wing.

"Nuraini?"

The man nods. His eyes are tired.

"I don't have any family or friends here. Every night I sleep on this bench." He says "don't" in a thick rural Javanese accent: *n'don't*.

"Sorry, sir," I say, lapsing into the automatic Javanism of apologizing before asking an awkward question. "If I may ask—what is your name?"

"Nurhasan."

"Mr. Nurhasan, sir, may I ask when Nuraini began to feel sick?"

"About twelve days ago. She was burnin' up. Two days later the fever still didn't go down so we brought her to the health clinic near our house. But her condition got worse and worse, and she started hallucinating. Then they took her to Kanjuruhan Hospital. She was there for three days, but then, well, she just got worse. Only then did the doctor there say it'd be better to send her to Surabaya."

"Why wasn't she referred immediately to Surabaya, sir? Or to the main hospital in Malang? Why keep her for three days in Kanjuruhan? The hospital isn't equipped to handle patients suspected of having avian flu. The procedure to follow in these situations should be more than clear."

"Oh, I n'don't understand all that. N'don't understand what went wrong. Maybe they just thought she had wind in the body and that they could handle it themselves."

I try not to wince at the mention of "wind in the body," which is what people say when someone has the chills. It's a common diagnosis, but folk nonsense nonetheless.

"But all the health clinics and hospitals are supposed to know how to detect the symptoms of avian flu immediately. They've all been given directives—"

I stop because I suddenly realize that the last thing this poor old man needs is to be made more miserable. What he needs are hope and encouragement.

"Sir, if I may ask another question: Before your daughter began showing signs of fever, did she have contact with any birds? Geese, chickens, ducks?"

"No. Not directly. But I've thrown away chicken carcasses behind our house before."

"Chickens? No ducks?"

"Yes, chickens. Wait. *And* ducks."

"Is it possible that your daughter came into contact with any chicken droppings? Or duck droppings?"

Suddenly the old man's eyes are wet. "Oh God. If this is my fault, I n'don't think I could live with myself."

And with that, he begins reciting verses from the Qur'an and retreats into himself, into the fate ordained for him and his daughter by God.

An old man, a stranger, is so thin and broken. And I feel so sad for him. So sad that for a few seconds I feel wobbly, unsure whether to stand up or stay in my seat. He hasn't even asked me who I am, where I'm from, why I'm asking him all these questions. Yet I know it's time for me to go, for me to also retreat into myself, to get back to work, if work helps anything, if it helps make things better, for him and for me and for his daughter.

I comb my memory for something Irma once said: "You know what they say about doctors. They're cold, aloof, callous. They have to dull their feelings so they can remain objective and not get too emotionally involved with their patients. And yet they have the power to heal at least one person a day."

Try to imagine what people must say about "outbreak experts" like us. We speak with patients and their families, but we bring no treatment with us, no healing. We come with our notebooks to beds where patients lie prone and feeble, and we bombard them with questions about what happened, how it came to be this way or that, like bumbling police inspectors in pursuit of a criminal mastermind. But we can't catch the culprit or bring the wrongdoer to justice. All we can say is, next time be sure to keep your chickens in good health and don't forget to wash your hands.

Next time. If there is a next time.

Just as I'm about to push the button to re-enter the wing, Farish and Inda emerge. I hear the senior nurse behind them: "Thank you so much for visiting. Don't forget to send us a copy of your report, okay?"

"Damn, I'm starving," Farish mutters.

8

BOTOK PAKIS AND RUJAK SOTO

From behind a plate of *Rujak Cingur*, so pungent it makes me dizzy, I watch Farish stare at Bono sitting beside me—as if this Bono person has just dropped out of the sky and Farish isn't quite sure whether he's human or not. This Bono person, on the other hand, is completely unaware of Farish's presence; he has eyes only for the bowl of rujak soto in front of him.

There isn't a square inch of the table that isn't covered with food. There's the house specialty, which, it turns out, is just your usual rujak cingur—fresh vegetables, fruits, and tofu, plus slices of boiled cow snout topped with a salty-sour dressing. There's also *Rujak Tolet*, a fruit-heavy rujak with a dressing made of palm sugar, sweet soy sauce, and garlic; a dish unfamiliar to me called *Rujak Deham*, fruit slivers and bean sprouts doused in salty dressing; and *Rujak Cempling*, fruits served in a clear coconut-water-based sauce. And there's more: *Nasi Soto Babat* (tripe soup with rice), *Nasi Empal* (sweet-spicy fried beef and rice), and who knows how many different varieties of botok, along with *kerupuk* (prawn crackers, tapioca crackers, fish crackers), deep-fried tofu puffs, crumbed *risoles*, crispy *pastel* puffs, sticky lemper dumplings, and croquettes, all selected by Bono from the glass display case near the cash register, as if he were the rich wife of a high-ranking bureaucrat in a shoe store ordering every model in twelve different colors. Even I, with my secret desire to try everything this humble eatery has to offer, am a bit embarrassed at this theater of excess. After all, my mother taught me to always finish the food on my plate.

But it's impossible not to be drawn in by Bono's energy. It's as if we're stranded on another planet, a space with its own gravitational pull, with its own air pressure, that demands its own language and tone.

Bono is still preoccupied by the rujak soto in front of him.

"Hmm. Interesting. *Very* interesting. Try some, Run. There are soybeans, bean sprouts, cucumbers, water spinach, and—get this—there's fucking tripe broth in the sauce. *Tripe broth!*"

He lets the moment swell and deepen.

Then he goes on. "What do you think are the three or four most important ingredients in this dish? What do you think makes it so sexy?"

Easy. "The tripe broth, because it provides body and aroma; the soybeans because they give it an added crunch; the cucumbers because they enhance the fresh zinginess of it." I pause. "Oh, and the petis, which enhances its oomph." (Even though I hate the stuff.)

Beautiful dish, no doubt about it. Layered, sophisticated almost. And no genius from Banyuwangi to credit for it. I'm almost dewy-eyed at the thought of the countless culinary pioneers who have made our nation's cuisine what it is today, their names and achievements lost to the ages, swallowed up by time. And yet their recipes endure, made a million times over in kitchens throughout the country.

The other kinds of rujak we sample after this one taste flat. They're like novices, unseasoned, lacking life experience. After the religious experience that is the rujak soto, it's hard to enjoy anything as much. But the rujak tolet isn't half bad. Bono doesn't share my opinion.

"Why?" I protest. "It's so deliciously garlicky."

"Ah, but that's the problem," says Bono. "Garlic and sweet soy sauce are already the epitome of a perfect combination. Any Indonesian who likes food knows as much—spit-roasted lamb, lamb satay, the sweet soy-sauce-glazed fried chicken dish they serve in Chinese restaurants. Garlic and sweet soy sauce—that's it. Perfection. But add palm sugar and it goes blech."

And damn it, he does it again, the thing he often does—making me doubt my own palate. Should I order another bowl of rujak soto? As Bono flits from rujak to rujak, I listen to him clucking in dismay.

"Hmm, too thick, too spicy, not salty enough, not sweet enough, too much coconut . . ."

"So, Mr. Bono . . ." It's Inda. She looks confused about how to address him. They've only just met, but "Mister" seems too formal, and besides, they're the same age. "Um, B-B-Bono," she tries again, "try the botok pakis. I think it's delicious. The best kind of pepes. Maybe even the best dish here."

Bono, as if suddenly aware that there are two other people at our table, slowly picks up one of the botok pakis. I see the change in his expression as he unwraps the fiddlehead botok, removing it from its banana leaf covering. The texture and fragrance is promising. He bites and chews. He does this again. And again.

"Hey, you're right," he says to Inda. "What's your name again? Inda? Wow. This really is very good. Very refined."

Hastily, I snatch a *Pepes Jangkang* from under Farish's nose. (He's spent this whole time just staring at us.) I bet it's just as good. More importantly, I'm not willing to let Inda suddenly become the center of attention. She may be sexy, and she may have an okay sense of taste, but tell me, what great contribution has she made to the culinary world thus far? (Then again, what great contribution have *I* made to the culinary world thus far?)

Not wanting to lose momentum, I quickly thrust my crabmeat pepes at Bono before tasting it myself.

"Try this," I say.

But Bono's not impressed. "Hmm. Well, it's okay, I guess. Texture's decent. It's dense, but it's also moist. The soft-shell crab has a nice kick, too. But I don't know. For some reason, it just can't compare to this botok." He pushes my pepes away, as if ordering a *Master Chef* contestant who's failed to make it to the next round to pack her bags and get out. *Good-bye. See you in the next life.*

"Bizarre," says Bono, in the tone of someone watching television for the first time or who's just landed on the moon. "I've traveled all over the US, and I've come across a lot of dishes—West African, Surinamese, Caribbean, even a few versions of crab cake on the East Coast—that were essentially a type of pepes. But none of them were as good, because, truly, only Indonesia has mastered the art of the pepes. Our pepes could go global! We've perfected the technique of making the softest, densest, and tastiest pepes possible, in the same way that Neapolitans have perfected the technique of making pizza chewy, crispy, and airy all at once."

Inda looks extremely pleased because she's succeeded in gaining yet another fan. I see Farish is beginning to get annoyed.

"I agree," says Inda, as if her expression of support, like the UN Security Council power of veto, will change the course of world events. "I also think how strange it is that pepes, despite being both healthy and delicious, isn't appreciated more by us as a people, much less known abroad."

But Bono doesn't seem to be listening. It's as if he's transfixed by the botok pakis in front of him—it's already his third one. And all of a sudden I realize: it's my dream! The details may be different (Inda isn't Bono's mother; Farish isn't Bono's father, though sometimes he's just as annoying; this time, I've entered the picture not as an observer but as a participant; and Bono is no longer cowering and small), but I've seen this same scene in my dream. How crazy is that? I'm not just Aruna the chubby old maid who's obsessed with food. I'm Aruna the chubby old maid who's obsessed with food and can see into the past.

"Sorry, but I'm genuinely confused," Farish says, rediscovering his voice. "Or amazed. Or maybe a little stressed. I'm not exactly sure. But I've never gone out to eat with anyone who's ordered this much food, and my question is, why do you spend money like this? What's the point? Are you really doing research? Don't tell me you always eat like this wherever you go?"

Bono looks up. "Yes, I do. If I'm genuinely interested in the food being served."

"But your restaurant in Jakarta serves mostly international cuisine."

"True," says Bono breezily. "But I still have the right to try whatever I think is interesting."

"Um, okay. But do you think quantity is more important than quality?"

Moron, I hiss in my heart. Feeling clever, I want to point out that it has to do with the theoretical difference between a *gourmand* and a *gourmet*—someone who is interested in food per se (whatever, wherever, as much of it as possible) versus someone who is more interested in how something tastes, in the dining experience as an aesthetic act, and who therefore is more discerning about what he puts into his mouth.

But how can true taste-spotters ascertain which is the tastiest of them all, which food truly ranks several levels above average, if they don't try everything on offer? Farish, I'm positive, is just shooting off his mouth because he can't stand the fact that Inda has managed to work her way into Bono's good graces. I can read his thoughts: *What exactly is so great about this guy? He's not good-looking; he's not in shape. All he can do is cook, and who knows if he's the one making the food at that restaurant of his.*

I wait for the explosion.

It doesn't come.

"It's not about quantity, my man," Bono says calmly. "It's about variety. And variety, in this case, is very important in the search for quality."

Bono knows he's right, of course. And what he's really saying is, "I don't need to take you seriously. I'm not even competing with you. You don't have the right to comment on how I live, on how I do things. But since I'm a civilized man . . ."

Before Farish can respond, Bono turns his gaze on Inda. In the same way he's able to deal with me, he's adept at showing interest in the pastimes and pursuits of others, even if it's usually only after others learn what his own enthusiasms are.

"So, Miss Inda," he says sweetly. "What happens next in this investigation?" He's even remembered her name. What a champ.

Inda, surprised that this up-and-coming chef is still paying attention to her, cheerfully explains the rest of our plans. Next stop, the island of Madura, just next door, on the other side of the Madura Strait. More specifically, the towns of Bangkalan and Pamekasan. The original plan was to stop only briefly in Pamekasan for a bite to eat. But it turns out an avian flu case has popped up there as well. We'll leave after lunch.

Their conversation flows quickly and smoothly.

"What's over there?"

"More of the same: patients with avian flu. One in Bangkalan and one in Pamekasan. Both of them are young and still being treated at the local health clinic where they were admitted."

"Why weren't they transferred to the hospital in Surabaya?"

"That's what we'll try to find out. Apparently the patients' families have issues with it. Maybe they can't afford it. Maybe there are religious reasons. Or maybe the patients themselves don't want to go to the hospital."

"Really? What's the difference between getting treated at a health clinic and getting treated at a hospital?"

"They *are* different. One would be closer to home. The other would be far away, in a big city."

I see Bono look at me, eyes gleaming. I don't oppose him. Of course he's been dying to go to Madura. Been counting the minutes, even. The guy's half Madurese, after all.

9

THE KING OF DUCK

This dream is downright weird.

One morning, several people in uniform come to my house and take me away. I'm a negligent mother, they tell me. One of them spits on the floor in disgust. Then they gag me.

After several hours in a cramped cell, I'm brought to a courtroom. A grim-faced civil servant reads out the charges I'm facing:

1. My children eat too much.

2. My children are unattractive.

3. My children are vectors of disease.

4. My children aren't interested, much less skilled, in anything except eating.

5. I've never disciplined my children. They don't know what it's like to be given the strap, to have their allowance reduced, to have their TV-watching privileges revoked, and this means I've done nothing to build their character.

6. I bribe my children with food so they'll love me.

7. I didn't do anything when the staff at Bagel Peres et Filles caught them stealing a sack of salmon from the kitchen. And worse still, I secretly bribed the management so they wouldn't haul my kids off to the police station.

8. *I also didn't do anything when, one afternoon, I found them cooking the neighbor's pet turtle. ("Come on, Ma, I've been wanting to try turtle soup for ages!" my eldest said, a pitiful expression on his face.)*

9. *I'm afraid of my own children.*

10. *I'm a coward who engages in shameless bribery, and the children I've brought into the world are no good.*

"Based on the aforementioned charges, this court has decided that you, Ms. Aruna Padmarani Rai, have no right to any defense at all. You are hereby sentenced to five years' imprisonment, effective immediately."

Because I'm a coward and worried they'll accuse me of attempted bribery, I offer no resistance.

That night my children pay me a visit. The next day at sunrise, I'm scheduled to be transferred to another prison, who knows where. I probably won't see them again for a long time. I try not to look sad.

They've brought me a box with a cake inside. They don't seem upset at all. When I open the box, I find a small chameleon. It looks dazed. Its eyes are bulging out of its sockets. Suddenly, I recall something someone once said to me—animals have souls. It was a person I didn't particularly like.

"Here you are, Ma," my second eldest says happily. "It'll taste great deep-fried with a little butter sauce, don't you think?"

✴

I fall asleep in the passenger seat for who knows how long. The Toyota Avanza zooms across the Suramadu Bridge. We've covered 3.3 miles in the blink of an eye, and just like that, we're in Madura. Madura, technically part of Java, and yet not part of Java at all.

As usual, whenever I arrive someplace unfamiliar, my eyes and mind open wide, searching for anything that bears traces of history. But moments pass, and all I see is a long stretch of empty buildings, gloomy, weather-beaten, and a little scary, along with fields covered in nothing but wild growth. Everything is so still, like a photograph.

During the ride, Inda has been telling Bono about Nuraini and the direness of her condition while also stressing the strangeness of the situation we're facing. Different cases, different cities, all happening at the same time. Because we're in his territory now, Farish can't bear to keep quiet. I'm dimly aware of his voice as it fills the car: "Animal health . . . veterinarians are the first line of defense . . . to poultry, viruses . . ."

"Smooth bastard," whispers Bono with a snicker.

I try to remember what I know about Madura. Total population: around 3.7 million. One of the poorest parts of East Java. Composed of four regencies: Bangkalan, Sampang, Pamekasan, and Sumenep. The agricultural sector is weak due to the infertility of the soil, but from the mid-to-late 1800s, it was the largest producer of salt in the Dutch Empire.

A friend of mine whose family left Madura for Jakarta many years ago says she knows a lot of other people who'd left to seek their fortune elsewhere.

The reason I remember is that she's a happy girl. Loves to laugh, makes other people happy, is open-minded. She never criticizes anyone and never gets angry when people criticize her. And I think about how this is no easy feat, for she lives in Jakarta, and Jakarta is in Java, and Javanese people often look down on Madura—poor, filthy, religiously conservative, and incapable of progress because it doesn't like progress. But right now, from where I'm sitting in this Toyota Avanza, approaching Bangkalan City—Bangkalan's capital—there really isn't very much to prove them wrong.

I focus my attention again on the file in my lap. The official report from the Ministry's headquarters is a bit disorganized, as if they themselves were still trying to figure out what happened based on conflicting reports.

Rizki, A. L.: Male, seventeen years old, the son of a Muslim cleric (so reads the report), exhibited classic symptoms associated with avian flu and was eventually permitted by his family to receive treatment at the nearest health clinic. He's been there for four days now, and his condition is getting worse, but his family still won't give their permission to transfer him to the public hospital in Surabaya.

Inda is the most familiar with the case because two days ago she was part of a team from the local Ministry office who tried to explain to the boy's father that if his son wasn't given proper treatment right away, he could die. But the *kyai* remained unmoved. "Life and death are in the hands of God," he said doggedly.

"We've given up hope," says Inda. "How do you convince a kyai? We've already promised that the son won't be 'defiled,' if that's what he's worried about. We promised that he would only be handled by male nurses, that he would be under twenty-four-hour surveillance, that someone would guide him in his prayers, the whole works. But this kyai—he's so stubborn."

"So we're headed to the health clinic?" I ask.

"That's the plan," says Inda. "It'll be best if we do a thorough investigation of Bangkalan before moving on to Pamekasan. From Pamekasan, we'll return to Surabaya."

"Shouldn't we examine the patient's home first? Before the sun sets? My sense is we won't get any useful information from the health clinic about probable cause."

I watch Inda think this over. Her brow is furrowed, but she still looks as lovely as ever—damn her. Bono and Farish are debating the benefits of eating meat and the importance of not eating meat. (Bono is a first-class butcher. Farish, on the other hand, is trying to adopt a stance as a warrior-defender for all creatures with souls.)

"You don't eat chicken and duck?" Bono asks.

"Well, sometimes," says Farish, a little sheepishly.

"Do you think chickens and ducks have souls?"

"Sometimes they do; sometimes they don't."

"Which one is it? They do or they don't?"

"I mean, it depends on the context."

"Okay. So why don't we make a quick stop at that famous restaurant—the one that specializes in duck. I forget what it's called. That way we won't have to try to squeeze it in this evening. Let's see how long you can stand sitting with us without eating anything yourself."

"Okay," says Farish, despite the overcast expression on his face. *If you all die of the avian flu, good riddance,* his eyes seem to say.

"Okay," Inda says to me. "I think it does make more sense to go to his house instead. That way we can also examine the surrounding area." She gives the address to the driver.

"But we're stopping at that duck place first, right?" Bono chimes in, his voice ringing urgently from the back of the car. "It shouldn't be too far from here—fifteen minutes, max."

✴

Is there anything more pleasurable than a perfect leg of duck confit? For, at the end of the day, the legendary *Nasi Bebek Sinjay*, or Sinjay-style fried duck served with rice, whose fame exerts a magnetic pull over those who visit Madura is a specimen of that exact thing, that near impossibility: the perfect duck confit.

In other words: a duck that has been smeared with salt, garlic, and aromatic herbs and stored in the fridge for three days, then rinsed and dried before being put into the oven on low heat, no more than 275 degrees Fahrenheit, for four to ten hours. A duck that, after being cooked in its own fat, is removed from the oven to cool before it's fried and then gobbled up piping hot. A duck, rich, oozing—a heavenly thing.

For half an hour the only words to be heard at our table are: "Oh my God," "No way!" "It's sooo good." "I think I'm gonna die." There's no looking around, no soaking up our surrounds.

Farish has given in. He and Inda have ordered duck rice, the kind you find listed on menus as a cheap lunch special: a plate of rice along with a piece of fried duck, sprinkled with a mixture of dry-fried garlic, shallots, candlenuts, and coriander and garnished with a slice of cucumber and a few leaves of Thai basil. And of course, there's some spicy green-mango sambal on the side. Bono and I have each ordered two portions of duck, no rice. When it comes down to it, we're the same kind of person. Although we're crazy about rice in every form, in every language—bibimbap, coconut rice, *Nasi Begana*, risotto, paella, Japanese garlic-fried rice, and good old Indonesian lamb-fried rice—we couldn't bear to tuck into something that demands this much respect, this fried duck, for instance, if it came on a mountain of steamed rice. The composition would be all off. Rice, which by right should provide balance, would only ruin one's appetite, not to mention a work of art.

Luckily Bono and I have ordered those two extra portions of duck, which comprises three pieces each. That way, unlike Inda and Farish, we won't have to go back if we want more and start the whole process from the beginning. This means lining up at the cash register, which feels more like a ticket booth at a soccer stadium; jostling with other fried-duck aficionados at the serving stations that consist of long tables laden with rice, sweet soy sauce, and sambal; grabbing one another's orders—first come, first serve!—and gawking at the sea of Sosro Tea bottle caps flooding the filthy tables and floors.

To add to all this, the restaurant doesn't feel like a restaurant at all. It feels more like a cafeteria—the kind you might find in the middle of some parking lot, with blazing red walls and a makeshift zinc roof, sprawling, shoddy, crammed with long tables, with ads posted in every corner and signs written in big red, yellow, and green letters.

When we further scrutinize the serving stations, we become truly aware how absent hygiene is from the place. There are the bowls of mango sambal on the tables, whose contents have spilled everywhere and been left for hours for flies to swarm around. The Thai basil leaves and cucumber slices have been left out in uncovered plastic boxes until the servers pick them up with their hands and plop them onto our plates. There are abandoned duck remains in shallow woven rattan baskets, which have become arenas for fly-to-fly combat. There's the floor, littered with drink cartons, plastic wrappers, bottle caps, and who knows what else.

But nobody cares. Wherever you look it's as if the world has stopped spinning and all that exists is the relationship between man and duck.

"Damn," says Bono. "I've made the rounds of all the bistros in France, and even then there was no guarantee I'd find a genuinely decent duck confit. And it's a fucking French staple! Next thing I know, I go to Bangkalan, in Madura, in the Republic of Indonesia, and what do I find? A confit-like dish with a texture that would floor any French chef."

"I suppose the only difference is that this version uses cooking oil," I say, trying to sound just as worldly. "That's what a French chef would say in his defense."

"And the ducks they use here. Sickly. No good." Farish's tone is bitter, because he's lost the bet.

"And, probably, the fried spices they sprinkle on top," Inda quickly adds. "Like it or not, it's this feature that makes the dish Indonesian— it's how fried chicken and duck are usually served in Java."

This Inda woman really isn't bad at all. Turns out her knowledge extends beyond infectious diseases. I'm even growing to like her.

"I want there to be two types of duck confit in my restaurant," says Bono. "The first, already on the menu, is in the French style, served with *pommes de terre àla sarladaise*—potatoes roasted in duck fat. The second would be cooked in the Madurese style, like this one. The only thing I'd change is the sambal, and the rice would come as a side dish."

"Seriously?" I ask. "You don't like the sambal?"

Bono doesn't look entirely convinced about how he feels. "Honestly, if you ask me, it's a bit too sour. Too strong. And its sourness is a spicy kind of sour, but so what. Not everything spicy is tasty. I mean, the whole sambal lacks complexity."

"They probably did it on purpose," I say, "to avoid having it be too sweet, too stereotypically Javanese. To make it more distinctive. Or maybe they want the contrast to be sharper—to have a sauce with enough character to penetrate the meat's succulent core. A sweeter sambal would only be compounded by the sweet soy sauce, and the texture and flavor of the duck would be lost."

"As far as I know," says Inda, "even in Surabaya the sambal that comes with fried duck is usually of the mango variety. If there's time before your flight to Palembang, you should stop at . . . you know, that place. I forget the name. Their duck doesn't compare to this one if you ask me, and the same goes for their version. Nothing special, I mean. The point is, you can't escape the damn thing."

"Either way," says Bono pointedly, "I'll have it in my restaurant, too. Just you wait. But it'll be a much better version, I can promise you that."

"Thai style?" asks Inda.

"Bono style," says Bono, without the slightest hint of arrogance in his voice.

As we head back to the Avanza, watching the crowds of people still thronging to the restaurant, Farish suddenly pipes up.

"Unbelievable. Look at these people. No one seems to be affected by the avian flu scare. They'll act like there's no tomorrow, all for the sake of eating duck. Bizarre."

10

The Troublemaker and the Legendary *Warung*

Two banners, both green—the color associated with Islam—greet us on the road into Village T.

One is aimed at sinners: "Offenders of Sharia law will be severely punished."

The other is aimed at the police: "Untrustworthy police officers and those pretending to be police are not welcome in this village."

I think about putting on a head scarf, but I see several young women on the road who aren't wearing them, so I decide not to. Then I wonder what's going on with the police.

"Oh, it's nothing," says Inda. "It's the *jamu*-makers' way of protesting. There've been a lot of bogus sweeps recently. The police claim the raids are targeted at those who use illegal chemicals in their jamu, even though most of the jamu-makers here have returned to making their medicines from herbs. They're probably the ones who are mad as hell. Clearly they refused to bribe the police."

"But, miss." Our driver interrupts us with a heavy Javanese accent. "The jamu they make here really n'doesn't hold a candle to those from some of the other regencies in East Java. Take Banyuwangi, or Ponorogo. The jamu here n'don't cure nothin'."

Inda is silent. "He's right," she whispers. "The jamu here is crap, really. More often than not, they're just homemade concoctions to make you stronger or help you lose weight. Of course it 'don't cure nothin'.'"

Then she adds, still whispering, "You have to be careful when you hire a driver in Surabaya. Often, they have friends or family in Madura who make jamu, and before you know it, you're being driven there for a visit. There won't be anything you can do about it, and in the end they'll force you to buy jamu. And, um, other things, too. Like medicines to decrease vaginal discharge or odor, Madurese miracle wands—"

"Miracle wands?"

"Um, I'll explain later," says Inda, suppressing a smile. "As it is, you can't tell whether the jamu you buy is purely herbal jamu, which usually isn't very effective at all, or jamu that contains chemicals as its main ingredients. Chemical-containing jamu is obviously dangerous because it can kill."

"Yes, you really should be careful," Farish suddenly chimes in. "It's dangerous business dealing with chemical substances. Making counterfeit medicine is on the rise now, and very lucrative. Word is the ringleaders have connections to several high-ranking officers on the federal police force. How could they not be above the law if they're paying thank-you money every month?"

Suddenly, Nadezhda comes to mind. "I only buy expensive medicine," she always tells me, in that imperious way of hers. "Imported medicine. I don't do it to be irritating, darling. But one has to have standards. The odds that they're fake are much slimmer."

Costly Nadezhda. Cautious Nadezhda. Irritating, yes, but so hopelessly irresistible.

The house is quiet. The only person at home is the patient's mother, Hajjah Delima—"Hajjah" because she's made the pilgrimage to Mecca.

She's about to go to the clinic to see her son. Her husband, the obstinate kyai, is nowhere to be seen.

"The kyai is busy," says his wife. Her face and her voice are weary. The plants and trees that surround the house look weary, too.

Hajjah Delima isn't more suspicious of us, because we're with Inda, who's visited before. But it's obvious that Bono is making her a little uncomfortable. How could he not, dressed all in black, with his spiky hair, his quirky glasses, his bee-stung lips? I think about telling Bono to wait in the car, especially since he really doesn't have any business being here. When I suggest this to him, he says, "Okay, I'll just walk around for a bit."

"Rizki's my only boy," says the woman, who is now starting to cry. "Always getting into mischief, that kid. Cuts class all the time and doesn't come home for days. One thing's for sure, if he came into contact with any infected chickens or ducks, it definitely wasn't here. N'aren't any farm animals 'round here, sister. Hardly any chickens or ducks neither. Take a look yourself if you n'don't believe me. Half a dozen chickens belonging to the neighbors at most. But that kid of mine! Mercy me, sister, he's a handful! Just turned seventeen, but when he fights with his father, the whole village can hear it. It's just plain embarrassing! The other day he even joined in n'beatin' on some Shiite folks living in Sampang, though the kyai already told him there ain't no use n'poundin' on people who've strayed in their faith like that. After all, God Almighty'll judge them, too. Me and the kyai just think it's hopeless sometimes. Who knows what'll become of that kid."

"Ma'am," Inda asks carefully, "would you mind telling us again how and when Rizki began feeling ill? Mr. Farish and Ms. Aruna here are from SoWeFit's central headquarters. They just want all the information to be complete. And perhaps we could examine the area around the house? With your permission, that is."

But it's as if she hasn't heard us at all. "The kyai's always saying, 'Don't forget, all people have minds. We can think for ourselves. Don't just follow what other people say, even religious scholars.' And he's a religious scholar himself! But Rizki keeps saying minds are weak, they need direction. 'The mind is the devil itself'—that's what he said to my husband. Ain't that disrespectful? In the end, he went and beat up those Shiite folks, and one of the people who died was my little sister's husband." Really crying now, she points to the photo on a table: a young man in his late teens with stony eyes and a mouth set in a hard line. "Now God is punishing the kid. And n'don't we have to accept God's judgment? The kyai n'doesn't even want to visit the clinic. In his heart, he's already let Rizki go."

Who knows what moves me to speak up—after all, what do I know about religion? "Ma'am," I say carefully, "you said just now we all have to think for ourselves. That means we have to act for ourselves, too. I believe in miracles, but I don't believe that such miracles are determined entirely by God alone. I believe that miracles are inseparable from human action. Isn't that so? It means we should try our hardest before we surrender everything to God."

The woman looks at me, almost in disbelief, then suddenly she grabs my arm. "But isn't it too late already? Isn't it too late to move him to Surabaya?"

Everything happens quickly after that. Inda makes a few calls, Farish, too, and all of a sudden, I hear that an ambulance will transfer Rizki to the hospital in Surabaya. Inda has already entrusted one of her colleagues at the SoWeFit office there with the responsibility of monitoring him. That same colleague will also ride with Rizki in the ambulance and deal with various odds and ends on the hospital side so that Inda can still come with us to Pamekasan.

Hajjah Delima squeezes my hand.

Afterward, Farish, Inda, and I circle the area surrounding the house—clusters of bamboo and trees that look like they've never even seen water. Hajjah Delima wasn't lying—not a single chicken or duck around. We ask all five neighbors, and they say the area's never had much poultry. When Rizki came down with avian flu, it was obvious he caught it somewhere else.

Farish, Mr. Animal Expert, seems offended by the absence of any field evidence. "I really hate my job," I hear him grumble.

In the end we give up and go back to the car. I ask Inda to pass on this information to her colleagues so all the records will be complete.

By the time we reach Bangkalan City's downtown, I suddenly feel something. Don't tell me I'm hungry. It's pretty clear the driver is.

"If you want to know what real Bangkalan food is like, you should try the warung near the main mosque." As he speaks, he points to a small eatery painted bright green, with swinging doors, like in a Western. It's located just a few doors away from the Bangkalan Grand Mosque, right next to an ancient-looking bookstore. "Everyone in Bangkalan's been eating there since my granddad's time."

It's clear he's requesting that we stop there.

I'm intrigued, and I can tell Bono is, too. And this time, my fellow teammates don't need to be asked if they agree.

The five of us go in. Five—this time we're with our driver, his eyes shining. The warung is tinier than tiny and impossibly packed. Most of the patrons are locals. Most of them know each other—religious students from the mosque next door, civil servants, truck drivers, parking attendants. When confronted with our group, especially Inda and me, who aren't wearing head scarves, their attempts to act indifferent are obvious.

The space, which consists of two long tables facing a wall, is dominated by browns and greens—a brown-tiled wall and a wood-veneer table, along with a fluorescent-green plastic cupboard stocked with bottles of soda. The patrons are old and young, rich and poor, male and female. They sit in rows, side by side, each one intent on his or her dish. There's rice with lamb curry; rice with *rawon*—a sweet beef stew; rice with tripe soup; and *Nasi Petis*—a combination dish with chunks of beef and a hard-boiled egg, doused in that odious petis sauce. As they eat they take turns reaching for the free sweet soy sauce and sambal that have been placed on the tables.

I'm momentarily startled by the menu on the large board above the counter: seven dishes, all of them involving rice and something else. Worried that I'll cause offense, I ask Inda, "Would it be rude if I ordered something and told them to leave out the rice? I'd still pay full price."

For the first time, Inda looks at me with a barely concealed smirk. *You city folks. You think everything has a price.* "Just order a complete set. I'll eat your rice."

Probably because I look so indecisive, the man behind the counter snaps, "Come on! Move it!"

Hastily, I approach the counter, but once I'm there, my mind goes blank. I still don't know what to order. I know that this isn't the kind of place where Bono and I can order a variety of dishes just so we can taste a little of each. And as it turns out, I'm not that hungry. It's my eyes that are hungry, and they've sent a signal to my brain to convince me that I feel the same way. But my stomach is telling me something else entirely: that it's still kind of bloated from the mango sambal and rivers of oil from lunch. That it feels like it's going to explode.

"Go sit over there!" snarls the man behind the counter, a disgusted expression on his face as he points to an empty chair. He gives me a menu to look at.

I finally make my decision and whisper to Inda, "One nasi petis."

"Pay me back later," she says, waving my money away. She returns to the cashier with confidence, and I see the surly man write our orders on the counter with a piece of chalk.

As we wait for our food, Bono and Farish grin sympathetically in my direction. "Good job," Farish says, his voice tinged with good-humored sarcasm. "And now we won't be eating dinner in Pamekasan, even though everyone says the food is better there, more refined . . ."

"Nah," sneers our driver, the Bangkalan patriot. "All Pamekasan has is sate lalat. That stuff's no good. Oh, and *Kikil Kokot.*"

My instincts were right. When the nasi petis is set in front of me, the very sight almost knocks me out. "I think I'm going to be sick," I say weakly. The mound of rice dominates the plate, but there's too little of everything else. There's a single slice of boiled egg drenched in some sort of meat curry, a single piece of tough dry-fried *empal* beef, and a single pinch of shrimp-paste sambal on the side. I don't even like petis to begin with! But yet again, I feel guilty as I watch how the people around me are eating with such gusto. To them, this isn't just a restaurant. It's a part of their childhood and their history, and it represents happiness for a countless many.

In the end, my good-natured teammates help me finish my food. I'm especially astounded by Farish, who, after devouring his rice and lamb curry, is still willing to eat half my rice.

"You know," he says as he gently inches closer to me, "this is the first time I've met a food lover who's scared of rice."

But it's okay. He bothers me less and less somehow. Besides, he's right. And I like that he's getting along with Bono, despite the odds.

Once we're done eating, out of lingering guilt, I put twelve thousand rupiah into the charity donation box—the price of a plate of nasi petis—as if this action will absolve me of the falsity of my gesture. Then I buy two clusters of *rambutans* from the old woman slumped in front of the bookstore next door. This perks her up.

It's already afternoon, but it doesn't feel like it. We drive off to Pamekasan by way of Sampang.

11

SAMPANG AND PAMEKASAN

I still can't believe I'm here, in Sampang. For the past few months, the air has been abuzz with the name. The news is constantly reporting what's been happening in the regency. I still recall, some three months ago, that at least two lives were lost, dozens wounded, dozens of houses burned down, and the regency's Shiite Muslims were driven out of their hometowns. The country's intellectual elite hastened to note that the incident was linked to preceding incidents of conflict. They offered a wealth of historical evidence. But as usual, the federal government, the House of Representatives, and the country's top religious authority—the Indonesian Ulema Council—all failed, perhaps deliberately, to take heed.

I search for traces of the violence among the stretches of field and brush, the stores lining the streets, and the markets closed for business, but without success. The landscape looks lifeless, like it's been turned into stone. None of it seems real, and I feel like I've come in late, right in the middle of the movie. Wherever I look, the signs of filth are so apparent and the city center so gray. Surely what happened here a few months ago can't be reduced to a story of tragic love, which is what government officials and religious experts keep saying, and what the general public keeps saying as well, to the point that it has become fact. What could transform love into tragedy? Every tale of violence has its roots in something deeper than what's visible on the surface.

As though trained to read the minds of the passengers he drives through Sampang—visitors not from Madura—our driver speaks up. "You know about it, don't you? What happened here with the Shiites and the Sunnis?"

"Yes, horrifying," says Farish. "And incredibly inhumane. Imagine how the Shiites must feel being forced to flee en masse, not even knowing where they'll go. What are they, for God's sake? Livestock?"

"I know," says our driver. "And to think that love did this. You know what happened, right? As always, it started with a conflict between two brothers. They were both Shiites, both totally stupid, both totally in love with the same girl. The younger brother was put in charge of the local branch of the national Shiite organization. You know the one, IJABI. The older brother was appointed to the branch's advisory committee. The older brother, unwilling to be in the same organization as the younger, converted to Sunnism. But he still wanted to bring ruin to his younger brother, out of spite. In the end, sometime in December, a mob set the brother's seminary on fire. After being driven out of his village, the younger brother was charged with blasphemy and sentenced to two years in prison. People who n'didn't understand what was going on, well, they got mixed up in the whole affair."

"Yes," I say, "but doesn't that just mean the older brother used existing religious tensions to give vent to familial ones?"

"Ah, but of course," says Bono. "Once again, it's the classic problem of the chicken and the egg—which came first?"

"If hatred and mutual suspicion already exist, anything can be turned into a reason for conflict," I say obstinately.

"But if my little brother dared to like the same woman I did, and if everyone knew about it, I'd want to beat the shit out of him, too, miss!" the driver exclaims, equally obstinate. "It's a matter of dignity. What's one supposed to do?"

No one says anything. It occurs to me that this is another useful thing about food: unlike religion, it brings people together. But then again, bad food may have more in common with displeasing interpretations of religious doctrine.

As if they can read my mind, none of them suggests stopping in Sampang for a snack. They're all busy, or pretending to be busy, doing their own thing.

Inda is talking on her phone with the colleague who is taking over her duties in Bangkalan. "Try to find out from Rizki where he's been. Before it's too late." She speaks in an authoritative tone. "His parents won't know, only him. Then we'll check those areas for outbreaks."

Bono is busy on his iPad. He's probably watching *Top Chef*. He's a huge fan of Padma Lakshmi, though in his eyes no beauty could surpass Nigella Lawson. Farish is also absorbed in his phone. He's probably committing the latest news to memory so he can yet again sound smarter than the rest of us.

And, as usual, I'm alone with my thoughts.

⁂

The regency of Pamekasan. The landscape suddenly changes. Not radically, but still, the difference is tangible.

We pass an expanse of salt pans, a tobacco plantation, a health clinic in front of a dock, and a military building curiously named "Gunfire Artillery No. 8." Seminaries flash by, along with elementary and middle schools with religious names like "Al-Islami," mosques with pale-green cupolas, and people equipped with banners and megaphones, soliciting donations by the side of the road for a mosque. We enter a part of the city that isn't just neat, clean, and well maintained but also so impossibly pretty it looks like something straight out of a travel brochure.

We pass the Ministry of Religious Affairs, the attorney general's office, the Bureau of Logistics, several large mosques, the University of Madura, and the offices for district-level executive boards of the major parties. They all look majestic and important, each one vouched for by a beautiful lawn. Almost every bridge, streetlamp, and gate is painted the color of candy: fluorescent-green, purple, orange, pink. Banners in support of Sharia law scream next to banners that read: "My city is clean and green." Ads for sausage suppliers and Melt in Your Mouth meatballs are also present to add a comic touch.

Our driver explains, cattily, that the regent elections are being held today, so the city has, of course, been beautified. No one can make a city beautiful in the blink of an eye, I want to say. People aren't creatures with supernatural powers. But I decide to let it go.

As with the other places, Pamekasan's track record of avian flu infection consists entirely of one patient, in this case a thirty-five-year-old woman who lives with her parents. Her name is Siti Huriah. After having a high fever for several days, she was taken to the nearest health clinic, and for some reason she still hasn't been transferred to Surabaya. From the looks of things, inadequate facilities aren't our only problem; we also have trouble on the ground with interdepartmental coordination. The local authorities representing the Ministry don't have any teeth, especially when it comes to tackling deeply rooted systems and values, like those in Madura.

"She's thirty-five? And still living with her parents?" I ask.

"Yes, why not?" says Inda. "It's obviously a lot cheaper."

"Think how it must feel—living with your husband and children while staying in your parents' house." I shudder. I can't imagine living like that: not being able to eat what you want all the time, not to mention being ordered around and criticized constantly.

"What's her line of work?" says Farish.

"The records don't mention it," I say. "But according to the nurse on the morning shift—Inda's colleague spoke with her and included her report in this file—the woman wasn't having that much difficulty breathing. Her fever wasn't that high either, only between 101.3 and 102 degrees Fahrenheit. And yesterday it was back down to 101. So basically, her temperature's decreasing. That's what the nurse's observations say. However, a report by another nurse, the one working the afternoon shift, always reports it as over 102 degrees. Close to 104, even."

"Huh. That's strange. Have the blood tests come back?"

"Yes. And they're negative. Anyway, based on the two clinical reports, the doctor has asked for another test. So now we're waiting for the second lab test results."

"She's probably not married yet," says Farish. "That's why she's living with her parents."

"Or maybe she was widowed," Bono chimes in. He's clearly enjoying playing the stowaway on this mission. "You know what? She's the same age as you, Run."

"But I don't live with my parents," I snap. "So actually, I'm free to bring home different men every night if I feel like it."

Good grief. I can't believe I took the bait.

✺

Siti Huriah isn't the old maid of Farish's imagination. Her face is in fact quite beautiful, like that of an actress playing the part of a country girl. Her teeth look as if she's just had them whitened at a dental clinic. Her skin is radiant and smooth, and this makes her look ten years younger. She doesn't look sick. Even though the nurse's report says her blood pressure this afternoon is fairly low, 90/60, and her temperature is almost 102 degrees, she looks curiously healthy. Anxious, but healthy.

Even Farish can't help noting, "Maybe Madurese jamu does cure somethin' after all."

A little before this, upon arriving at the health clinic, we found that Inda's colleague from the Ministry's Surabaya office was already here. I must say I'm very impressed by their efficiency.

"Where's the nurse you spoke with?" I ask her now. "The one whose report I have in this file?"

"As it happens, she was on the morning shift," she says. "She just went home."

"How many nurses are here now?"

"Two. They'll be here till tomorrow morning."

"The morning shift nurse—can we contact her?"

"Yes," she replies. "Here, I have her number."

Then I speak with the two nurses on the afternoon shift. Twice I ask them why the doctor ordered a second test, even though the results came back negative. They say the doctor thinks the results should be positive.

"Why?" I ask.

"The clinical data doesn't support it. The blood tests must be wrong."

When I examine the reports for her temperature, taken every four hours, sure enough it mostly hovers above 102 degrees Fahrenheit. The instances where it's noted as being above 102 occur only when the nurse on the morning shift has gone home.

Inda is talking with a head nurse and her colleague from the Ministry's local office. She doesn't seem particularly concerned about our patient's condition. Or maybe I'm just jealous—too quick to dismiss a pretty face.

"There's something strange about this, don't you think?" I ask Farish.

"Yes. Very strange."

"So, what do you think—"

"She looks like Ida Iasha," says Farish. "You know, the actress."

"Ida Ia . . . ," I sputter in frustration, but trail off as Inda approaches us. Her brow is furrowed. From the expression on her face, she wants to go somewhere else to talk. Once we've moved away from the patient, she clutches both of our arms.

"Guess what? Curiouser and curiouser." She gives our arms a good shake. "Why do you think this patient hasn't been transferred to Surabaya?"

We stare blankly at her. Why, indeed? Has her family forbidden it? Has her religious teacher forbidden it? Is she scared of leaving home?

"It's because the local SoWeFit office—my colleague over there—isn't sure whether she really has the avian flu."

Now this is news.

"But the test results."

"That's what's still under debate. The two afternoon shift nurses insist she has a high fever and that it tends to be even higher at night. The doctor on night duty thinks the same thing. They're all positive there must be some technical error at the lab. Perhaps her blood test results were mixed up with someone else's. That's why the head of the health clinic, with permission from my boss at the Ministry's Surabaya office, is running another blood test. We'll find out the results tomorrow.

"But here's the interesting part. My colleague was holding the patient's hand just now. She wanted to check whether her temperature really is that high. Turns out it's nothing unusual—like someone who has a regular flu and maybe a minor throat infection that causes fever."

"Hmm."

"And apparently the one who's been pushing for a transfer to Surabaya is the patient herself."

"Well, it's obvious, isn't it?" says Farish breezily.

Inda and I both look at him. What does he mean?

"Can't you see it?" he says. "I'm certainly not surprised. She's thirty-five, she looks like Ida Iasha, and she still lives with her parents. She obviously wants to get the hell out of here. When I was in Australia doing two months of residency, I became pretty good friends with a vet who worked in the countryside. He was thirty-five and psychotic, with a support system made up of nine psychologists, none of whom succeeded in helping him; three psychoanalysts of the Reich school of thought; three masseuses; five yogis; two Pilates instructors; two life coaches who conducted sessions with him over Skype; and a shaman from Germany. Why am I telling you about him? Because he lived with his parents, too.

"So, let's go over this again. Our thirty-five-year-old female patient lives in Pamekasan. Wherever she goes, she's surrounded on all sides by Sharia law and dubious jamu concoctions that probably have disastrous effects on the brain. I can almost guarantee that she's wanted to run away from home time and time again but has no idea how. The older she gets, the harder it gets. Her wits grow duller. Her nerve shrinks. I bet she's pretending to be sick so she can get to Surabaya. Without this excuse, she has no reason to leave Pamekasan unaccompanied."

It's quite clear. Farish is the official Scientific Authority on Old Maids.

Inda looks impressed, too. "Ida Iasha?" she exclaims. "The actress from the eighties? Who remembers Ida Iasha?" She lets loose a ripple of laughter as she goes back inside to speak with her colleague. A moment later, I see her walking to the clinic head's office.

Farish and I decide to return to the patient's room. There on the bed lies Siti Huriah, like a child pretending to be sick so she can skip school. I can see it in her eyes: she knows that we know.

When I ask her if she has any kids, her eyes instantly fill with tears. She says she used to be married, but her husband made eyes at other women and left her when she was one month pregnant. She had a miscarriage and fell into deep depression. Later, she returned to her parents' house because, what to do? That's what people did. "That was fifteen years ago," she says, her chest heaving. She then confesses that the two nurses on the afternoon shift, the ones who are adamant about her having a high fever, are related to her. They promised to help fake her records to make it look like a case of avian flu. Even better, they said, avian flu patients didn't have to pay for any medical treatment.

Inda's colleague is right; it's just a normal flu. Farish is right, too; Siti Huriah wants to get out of Pamekasan. She wants to breathe freedom.

12

"Fly" Satay and "I Love My Son" Duck

It turns out that the renowned sate lalat, or "fly satay," of Madura is not entirely metaphorical in name: the pieces of skewered meat really are the size of flies. Or, to use a popular expression, "as small as a snotball." They're served in the same way as regular chicken satay—ten skewers smothered in peanut sauce mixed with sweet soy sauce. But, well, that's the thing: they're small as snotballs, and they make my blood boil.

"What were you expecting, exactly?" asks Bono, laughing. "Real flies? Or 'chicken' meat made out of flies, like vegan 'meat'?"

Who knows how many photos he's taken with his iPad. I can imagine the tweets now: *Yo, behold!* Lord of the Flies *in the flesh*. Or: *Fly Satay Air*. Or: *Snot Satay*.

"Flies posing as chicken?" says Farish, joining in as if he isn't secretly disappointed as well. "Aren't the viruses they spread enough?"

"It's because chickens spread even more diseases," says Inda. "So it's healthier to eat flies." As Inda laughs at her own joke, she fiddles with the red cloth sloping over our heads, as if touching it will transform the roadside tent warung into a fancy restaurant.

"I'm serious," I say moodily. "This is god-awful. Worst food I've ever seen. What's there to *taste*? There's nothing!"

"How about trying some authentic *Soto Madura*?" asks Bono. "Good thing we're in Pamekasan, come to think of it. You can always get two kinds—one made with chicken meat and the other with beef."

This meal wasn't planned. At this point, we've been stuffing our faces so much we can't possibly be that hungry. But since we're already in Pamekasan, it's ridiculous not to steal the opportunity to sample the local wares.

I look at Bono. He mentions the name of a restaurant.

"That's not far," says our driver, from the bamboo platform where he's sitting and hanging out. I see that he's not eating, though. And I'm sure it isn't out of fussy taste buds. It seems he recommended the warung near the mosque partly out of childhood nostalgia. "They say the food is good," the driver continues, "but it's expensive. And today they'll be closed because of the election."

"Gah," says Bono. "So what is there to eat apart from these stupid flies?"

"Have you ever tried kikil kokot? Cow-hoof soup, Madurese style. It's a favorite dish among us Madurese. But we'll have to go to my little brother's house."

I must say, our driver is a strange but interesting guy. According to his worldview, Madura serves as the benchmark by which to measure all matters. Large matters are sized up in relation to Madura at large. Small matters are sized up in relation to Bangkalan.

"Enough," says Bono, snatching my plate away. "You shouldn't finish them all if you don't actually like them."

Less than fifteen minutes later, the car is pulling over to the side of a small road in front of a warung operating out of someone's house. But the place is quiet—more house than warung.

"This is my little brother's house," says our driver, eyes shining once again. "His wife, my sister-in-law, is a whiz at making both *Kaldu Kokot* and *Lontong Kikil*."

Bono and I glance sideways at each other like two detectives who've just entered the scene of a grisly murder. We're both thinking about the two dishes just offered to us: mung-bean and cow-hoof broth and rice cakes drenched in cow-hoof soup. I'm on the verge of yelling, "Nah! Never mind! Let's just go back to Surabaya!" Especially since we never said yes to coming here. But I don't want to hurt the driver's feelings. Besides, I'm actually curious to try beef bone marrow in a mung-bean broth.

The driver's sister-in-law doesn't talk much. Her expression is a little sour. It's almost as if she's a bit scared, or suspicious, because she's suddenly been inundated with so many guests—all of whom look so out of place.

Fifteen minutes pass, and we begin supping on our respective bowls of kikil kokot. I go numb. The dish has been served practically cold, and the marrow, which is meant to be scraped from the inside of the bone or sucked up through a straw, looks like a chunk of splattered brain. When I take a mouthful, it tastes like filthy grease congealing in and around my mouth. Lips, tongue, palate—it's as if all of them are suspended in fat.

I give up. Before long a troop of flies swarms what remains in my bowl. Let them have my kikil kokot. I don't like losing, but my mother taught me to let those who are smaller win.

I don't dare ask the others what's going on inside their heads.

On the drive back to Surabaya, almost nobody speaks. Farish is sprawling unconscious in the front seat, mouth half open. Inda is busy on her phone, probably listening to colleagues make their reports. I'm WhatsApping with Nadezhda. As usual, she's complaining.

You know, being a restaurant critic isn't easy.

No one said it was.

Just look at the restaurant columns in all the famous newspapers. They're all short. And even though they have to deal with a restaurant's history, ownership, and concept, its ambiance, service, and menu, in the end what sets one column apart from the others is the quality of the analysis of the food. So tell me, how is one supposed to review a degustation menu comprising nine to fifteen different courses, each one a work of art? And what if the restaurant also has a rich history? Or if it's rich in, I don't know, production detail?

Yep. Sounds tough.

It is. I should become an art critic instead. Or write about architecture.

I turn my thoughts to fly satay, to fly hooves, and to flies in general.

Hey, I'm dying to get my hands on some Pecel Semanggi. *The dish is virtually extinct because of all the road construction. Just try searching for* semanggi *clover around here. You won't find it.*

But semanggi tastes like shit. It's just a weed that grows by the side of the road.

Yes, but I'm curious.

You're not curious because it's supposed to taste good. You're curious because it's rare.

I don't respond. The minute Nadezhda gets argumentative, I shut down. Anyway, my head is suddenly flooded with images of fresh oysters, prawns in spicy sauce, fried squid in butter sauce, stir-fried *genjer* leaves, bean-sprout-and-salted-fish stir-fry, *belado*-style eggplant swimming in chili and oil, crab and corn egg-drop soup, clams in salted bean sauce, and mango sambal—all to be found at my favorite Chinese seafood restaurant in Surabaya.

"Bon," I say.

"Yeah?"

"You still hungry?"

"Of course."

"Wanna go out for seafood a little later tonight?"

Bono turns to me and grins. "Of course."

In the morning, while I'm checking out, Bono appears behind me. He was staying at a nearby hotel, and it looks like he's checked out, too. His belongings are parked near the sofa in the lobby. He's fresh-faced, and his rose-apple lips are even rosier than usual. He bears no trace of last night's wild seafood rumpus, when the two of us ordered enough food for ten people.

"We still have time for breakfast, right?" His tone is that of a child who's found buried treasure in his backyard.

I nod. There's still time. Enough for Farish, him, and me to hit two or three places, even. The plane doesn't take off until four.

"I found a place that serves pecel semanggi," he tells me. "It serves all kinds of East Javanese specialties. If we hurry, it looks like we'll have time to try other places, too. Where else do you want to go?"

I rattle off the foods on my list: the locally famous *Sate Klopo*, aka satay mixed with grated coconut and special seasoning; the soto madura at the place next door to the place known for its sate klopo; and the famous fried-duck restaurant here in Surabaya that attempts to compete with the king of duck in Bangkalan (but apparently, to no avail).

It turns out Nadezhda is right—*of course* she's right. Pecel semanggi is nothing great. It's survival food—the kind of food that springs up and becomes popular because its ingredients are cheap and can be found anywhere. But I'm happy because I've finally tried it for myself.

I'm even enjoying sitting with Farish on the corner of Jalan Wolter Monginsidi, at an establishment that an industrious woman and her family have kept going for forty years by the sweat of their brow. I take it all in: the large number of customers; the thick smoke from the grill by the veranda; the hundreds of satay skewers waiting to be grilled, which have been placed on top of broad banana leaves beside trays of tempting peanut sauce and big buckets filled with charcoal; the newspaper clippings displayed on the walls, all of them praising the delicious satay.

Quietly, I also observe a change in Farish's body language and demeanor. He seems more sincere, more open. It pleases me to see him eating with such gusto and having a laugh with Bono, as if he belongs with Bono and me. It also pleases me that Inda's departure doesn't seem to have affected his mood. Quite the reverse, in fact: he almost seems glad.

Though I'm stuffed and can hardly walk, I'm glad, too. And from the looks of things, so is Bono. So we offer no resistance when our driver brings us to the house of another little brother, who has mastered the art of fried duck.

"How many little brothers do you have, Dar?" asks Farish. "Pretty amazing, if you ask me. That all of them can cook, I mean."

With a sheepish grin, the driver says, "He runs a tent warung in the evenings. When we spoke on the phone just now, he said he wanted to cook a meal for us. Good thing we have time."

I look down at my watch. It's true.

"Actually," continues our driver as he lights a cigarette, "his duck is just as good as that overrated duck in Bangkalan everybody raves about. But we live in Surabaya, and we're Madurese, so that's that. They'll never acknowledge he's the true king of duck."

In contrast to the other younger brother with the mean wife, this brother is super-friendly. He's in his midthirties. He eagerly invites us to sit on the veranda, which from five o'clock onward transforms into a space open to the public. "Sorry," he says. "My house is small and cramped. It's more comfortable here."

A few moments later, atop slightly wobbly wooden chairs, at a slightly dusty table, amidst car smog and carbon monoxide, we're gorging on some pretty decent crisp-skinned fried duck. But all of that seems to pale in significance with the good faith and hard work implicit in the words "I Love My Son" painted on the front of the house.

"My little brother is recently divorced," our driver whispers. "After it happened, he n'didn't have anyone to help him in the kitchen. N'didn't have anyone who knew how to cook duck like he did, except for his ex-wife, who got remarried right away. The warung almost folded. He was so stressed. He tried to commit suicide. But I always reminded him that Dirin, his son, n'didn't have anyone else to rely on. Just him—his father. After a while my little brother began to get back on his feet. Now he has two assistants. And his business has grown. Folks like eating here."

And so the economy may go to pot and the market may crash, the gap between rich and poor may widen, and politicians may continue to be corrupt and inept. Yet people are still starting new businesses, still cooking, still giving each other food.

I'm touched.

13

The Princess Has Landed

This is not a dream. This actually happened.

I'm five years old. One day I come home from school and start bawling my eyes out when I realize my mother has secretly thrown away my beloved pacifier. That's not all—my mother's a coward, for she's callously laid the blame on our Javanese housekeeper, saying Mbok Sawal threw it away by accident. Mbok Sawal is just as cowardly, for she just accepts the blame, even though it's obvious she was acting on orders from my mother, who secretly thinks I'm too old to be sucking on a binky.

For three long months, without my mother's knowledge, Mbok Sawal has been trying to regain my affection. She offers me pacifier after pacifier, pink ones, cute ones, costly ones, but I refuse them all. In response, I begin sucking on lollipops every day.

One day she gives in and asks, "Miss Aruna, why are you giving me the cold shoulder?"

I don't reply.

Ten years later, when I'm out of town, Mbok Sawal has a heart attack and dies. I bawl my eyes out because I never had the chance to explain why I so mulishly refused her offerings. Many times I wanted to tell her, "I don't want another pacifier. It's the taste of my old one that I was utterly addicted to." But I thought, *She knows. It's impossible for her not to.* So I never said anything.

One day, when my mother is going through Mbok Sawal's possessions, she discovers a plastic bag with "Aruna" written on it. Inside are fourteen brand-new pacifiers and a bunch of Chuppa Chup lollipops.

Above and around me: Feet brought to a halt and so many different kinds of shoes. Voices. Then bodies crouching over me, startled, worried. *Are you okay?*

I'm sprawled on the floor, not comprehending what just happened. A pause.

Shoes. The sound of shoes. And not just any shoes.

Then that face: a woman's face. Not just any woman. "My goodness, Run, what's wrong? Are you okay? Why did you keel over like that?"

Purse. Phone. Another phone. Wallet.

"Yes, yes," the woman's voice says. "They're all here. I've got them."

Yet another voice: a man's voice. And, like the woman's, not just any man's. "Nadz, she keeled over 'cause she saw you. Only you could make a robust woman like Aruna fall flat on her face in the middle of the Palembang airport."

It's all coming back to me now. Bono, Farish, and I had just arrived at the airport in Palembang, Sumatra. The two guys went down to the baggage claim area, while I went to the ladies' room. Then, as I was coming down the escalator, I saw Nadezhda's stately figure near the entrance. Out of nowhere. Like a ghost.

I knew she was going to join us in Palembang, but I'd never imagined what it would be like for Bono and me to meet her—Nadezhda, so utterly private, who has another life that I don't know about and that she doesn't want me to enter—in a place so removed from what I'd imagined about that foreign life she leads. My steps faltered. Then I fell. Of course, I fell.

Another surprise: Nadezhda wants to share my hotel room.

"It's okay, right?" she asks. "Rather than me having to search for another hotel."

"I don't have a problem with it." I choose my words carefully. "But this is a work trip. I'm worried Farish will tell other people at work. I don't trust him."

"Oh, I'm sure he won't tell," says Nadezhda with her usual coolness. "Relax."

How am I supposed to relax? There's been a change in temperature since she made her spectacular appearance at the airport. Farish seems dumbstruck, as does the man from the Ministry's Palembang office who picks us up at the airport—a guy in his thirties, baby-faced, most likely still a virgin.

"Okay," I say weakly. "You can stay with me. But you have to promise: don't bug me while I'm working."

Nine at night. The road feels open and empty. From the car, Palembang looks like a stretch of commercial space, as long as Mangga Besar or Pluit in Jakarta but far more neat and orderly. I see rows of stores selling electronics, textiles, furniture, and housewares. Department stores, hair salons, and auto mechanics. Law offices and eateries, billboards and campaign posters for the gubernatorial and vice gubernatorial elections, all seemingly without end. Strange how there's no traffic or bustle or swarms of people by the side of the road. No litter or anything filthy or miserable. The government buildings stand tall and removed from the street—structures that seem to harbor no history, to have no knowledge of dust or rust or anything unplanned. The city seems to exist outside of time.

It's difficult for me to imagine the Palembang that once upon a time established dynasties, gave birth to kings, set up monuments, spread its faith far and wide, and disclosed its history onto stones and dried palm leaves of ancient *lontar*. How for almost six centuries it served as the center of civilization for the Srivijaya kingdom before bowing at last, in the thirteenth century, to the power of the Majapahit Empire, and afterward, to other powers whose influences still persist into the present—Chinese traders, Islamic sultanates, colonial powers from the Netherlands and Japan.

I'm reminded of a book I've just recently reread that contains several quotations from the travel records of a seventh-century Buddhist monk from China named I-tsing. He spent twenty-four years sojourning through China and India, collecting and translating sacred Buddhist texts.

In the course of his travels, he stopped—as all Buddhist monks from China did at the time—in Palembang to observe its temples and learn Sanskrit. From India, he even returned to Palembang and stayed there for four years, copying and translating into Chinese the texts that he had collected. From his brush flowed one of the first written descriptions of Palembang:

> *In the fortified city of Fo-che, there are more than one thousand Buddhist monks whose spirit is only turned to study and good actions. They study all possible subjects, like in India. Rules and ceremonials are identical. If a Chinese monk wants to travel to India to listen and read Buddhist laws, he must stay in Fo-che during one or two years to learn how to behave properly. He could then pursue his travel to India.*

The importance of Palembang as a spiritual center for Buddhism in Southeast Asia began to wane after the Chola invasion in 1025. During the invasion, dozens of temples, libraries, and treasuries were looted, and Buddhism in the region eventually collapsed.

Almost a thousand years have passed since then. The driver tells us that in five more minutes we'll be at the hotel. It's in the vicinity of a housing development where little girls, not unlike Nadezhda and me, live. With their fathers, who are lawyers, company directors, factory managers, or owners of stores and small businesses. And with their mothers, who help in the store or with the business and who are also skilled in making *Pempek* and *Tekwan*, the fishcakes Palembang is so famous for. Their childhood memories consist of piano lessons and birthday parties, MTV and *American Idol*, *Top Chef*, and pirated DVDs, not to mention weekends with their families at hotels, afternoons in swimming pools, and the smell of my father's brand-new car. There'll be memories of the latest model of smartphone and tablet and family functions overflowing with food.

"So, about this hotel . . ." Out of the corner of my consciousness, I hear Nadezhda's voice. "Are you sure it has Wi-Fi?"

❦

One o'clock in the morning.

"Thirsty?" asks Nadezhda.

"Huh? Um, no."

"Really?" She sounds disappointed. She doesn't care in the least that I'm already half in dreamland. "Sure you don't want to join me in a glass of wine?"

❦

The first morning in Palembang isn't as trying as I feared. Nadezhda doesn't show up at breakfast. Good. So what if stupid Farish and the baby-faced Palembang kid are all gloomy. But it won't last. How long can they fret about something that isn't there?

There's no trace of Bono either. Again, good. He and Nadezhda are probably eating together without telling us.

I'm enjoying my solitude at the breakfast table, where, as is probably the case at all breakfast tables in Palembang, pempek is available. Is always available. As readily on hand as, say, sweet soy sauce, or sambal, or prawn crackers. But I restrain myself. I want to eat only fresh pempek. I want it hot, straight from the fryer. And, what's more, my first pempek-eating experience in Palembang has to take place at a pempek restaurant of local repute. I've even made a list.

There *is* a pempek restaurant that's popular among the celebrity set. Even S. B. Y., our illustrious ex-president, has been there. But that's precisely why I don't want to go. Too mainstream.

Farish and the baby face—his name is Ewan—are at the breakfast table. They're busily munching on pempek and poring over a bunch of documents. Farish keeps smacking his lips in approval.

"The pempek is really good, Run. You should try some."

"Nah," I say, picking up a menu. "Just coffee for me."

"Know why this particular kind of pempek is called *Pempek Adaan*?"

"Enlighten me."

"It's the adaan from the Islamic injunction to pray—'*adaan lillahi taala*'—because Allah is supreme."

"So?"

A look of disdain crosses his face. But it isn't because I'm being snarky. Rather he seems to sincerely believe that the past three days have transformed him into an expert on culinary matters.

"What I'm trying to say is it's ready on time. In a pinch, I mean. It doesn't need to be boiled before being fried. So you won't be late for prayers."

"I'm not too fond of pempek adaan." *Not fond of praying either,* I think to myself.

"Why? Because of your sinful ways?"

"Ha ha." Wise guy. "No. It's because pempek adaan doesn't have fish in it. It's only made of flour, eggs, and salt. Where's the art in that?"

"Flour, eggs, salt, and prayer, ma'am," says Ewan, suddenly chiming in. "Though, you know, people also call it *Pempek Dos*. Not *doa*—prayer—or *dosa*—sin—but *dos*."

"Because?"

"Because they often explode when you fry them. And that's exactly the sound they make: *dossss!*"

I can feel my appetite plummet. Dos, dosa, doa—they're just not part of the plan.

But we have a bigger problem at hand. Nadezhda. Crazy, wild, unruly Nadezhda. Nadezhda, who's landed in this city, acting like a royal princess. Who can tell what her plan is?

14

A Perfect Cluster of Pempek

In my dream, I watch my mother open a cupboard and take out birds, one at a time. Then she lays them down on the kitchen counter and calmly, with glassy eyes, starts beheading them, one by one.

This time the patient is an old man. Seventy-two years old, in bad health. His file shows that he's been hospitalized three times in the span of five years.

He's old. Of course his health is bad, Priya types over WhatsApp. She's one of my colleagues at OneWorld. She's never once been given a field assignment. It's probably because she always plays the weakling, complaining she's feeling unwell at the drop of a hat or that she's sick with this or with that. Like she's old or something.

Hey, Run. You do know why they've asked you and Farish to investigate, don't you?

I'm about to type *Why?* but stop when I see the text at the top of my smartphone screen: *Priya is typing . . .*

To make it look like DOCIR is working hard.

Before I can respond, those words again: *Typing* . . .

So if the corruption allegations get even worse, they can point to you guys and say, "Look how serious we are about managing the avian flu situation. Here's proof."

Hastily, I type back.

Is it really getting worse?

Haven't you been reading the news?

I stop: *Typing* . . .

The people who've been implicated at DOCIR still haven't been taken into police custody. You don't think that's suspicious?

But hasn't one of them already been labeled a suspect?

Yes, but it won't be long before the others are, too. There's a lot of evidence about who's involved. The Parliamentary Public Accounts Committee isn't just going to keep quiet about it. And that goes double for Indonesia Corruption Watch. Once the CEC takes charge, DOCIR is done for.

Ever since the National Audit Board found things amiss with two of DOCIR's projects—a "system connecting" project and a research project on chicken breeding—the police, attorney general, and the Corruption Eradication Commission (CEC) have agreed that the right to handle the case will fall to whoever obtains approval to conduct an official inquiry. Obviously, the police beat the CEC in this particular matter and have obtained approval first just to prevent the case from falling into the hands of their rivals at the CEC. Once approved, the inquiry, processed so quickly at the initial stages, will suddenly stall.

I recall Irma and the worried look in her eyes. Was she secretly involved in all of it? Why did she look so scared? Was she scared of being seen as a failure when it came to protecting so many people's interests? Or scared of being found out that she was colluding with . . . whatever his name is—that asshole entrepreneur whom everybody suspects but just doesn't talk about, along with that stinking corporation, Proto Medis? Or maybe she's just terrified that the avian flu epidemic will obliterate humankind.

So you're saying that this is all just pro forma? That the findings don't matter and all that counts is that DOCIR is conducting an investigation? To show how seriously they're taking each case of avian flu?

Yep.

So DOCIR is just using us for its own political ends?

Totally.

What if the findings of our investigation do verify that we need a vaccine for human beings? Wouldn't that be in SoWeFit's interests?

Yes. But what conclusion have you reached based on your field research so far?

I reflect on this.

At long last, I reply. *It's still too early to tell, Pri.*

All right. We'll see what you find out.

I reflect further. Something tightens in my chest.

Fifteen minutes later, I type: *The corruption scandal has nothing to do with the scientific validity of this investigation, Pri.*

However, I realize that my faith in anything apart from food is diminishing quickly.

He's been placed in an isolation room, but Mr. Zachri Musa doesn't look like he's suffering too much. And although his temperature has shot past 102 degrees Fahrenheit, he looks like he's only experiencing mild fatigue and chills. He does look very old, older than his seventy-two years, but he still seems strong. When I ask him whether he's dizzy or has trouble breathing, he nods and massages his temples.

"Do you have a cough?" I ask.

He nods and immediately starts coughing.

Of particular interest is the fact that every time I ask him something related to his illness, he talks instead about other things. He prattles about two Palembang delicacies, something called Eight-Hour Cake and another called *Maksuba* cake. He describes the organic vegetable farm his family owns, and the local legends surrounding dishes that were once eaten by the rulers of the Malacca Sultanate but are now almost extinct.

Farish, who can't be bothered with human contact, unless said human is an attractive female, immediately shifts course. "I might as well head to the patient's house with Ewan now," he tells me. "Ewan says the place isn't far. You just keep chatting with Mr. Zachri."

"Okay," I say. "We can meet up for dinner later."

"Where?"

I give him the name of a restaurant.

"Okay," he says. "Just text me the address. Hopefully it won't take too long. So, about your friend, the really pretty one—"

"Yes, yes," I say quickly. "I'll ask her to join us."

Suddenly I'm assailed by worry, but not at the prospect of Nadezhda joining us and all the consequences thereof. I feel that there's something I don't know, something that has disappeared from view, much like the terms of reference document in the scandal Priya was talking about—the unofficial one that Proto Medis drew up to ensure B. S. Incorporated would win the tender for the human vaccine project and that vanished from the radar of the National Audit Board when they audited said company.

Priya's words haunt me: *Once the CEC takes charge, DOCIR is done for.*

Frankly, I don't care if DOCIR is done for. Or if OneWorld loses a client as a result. Corruption is the country's worst affliction, and yet we turn a blind eye to it every day. Enough already. The corrupt must be brought to justice. Serve life sentences if that's what's called for. But Irma . . . Irma is different. I *like* Irma. I don't want her to be publicly humiliated, much less stripped of her position.

Suddenly, Mr. Zachri grabs my hand. His hair, the color of sour milk, gleams in the lamplight. He asks me whether I'm going to try the pempek at the restaurant I mentioned.

I nod.

"It's good," he says, giving me a thumbs-up. "It's from Plaju. The real deal. They use special vinegar. It always has chili seeds in it. And don't forget to order their *Es Kacang Merah*."

"Es kacang merah?" Red-bean shaved ice?

"It's the ultimate local treat," he says with a grin. His teeth still look great. "You boil the red adzuki beans, then mix them with coconut milk, sugar water, red *cocopandan* syrup, and milk. Then you add melted chocolate for good measure. My kids say it's like eating diamonds . . . made of chocolate! It's fantastic . . . it's beyond compare."

A bowl of red-bean shaved ice—the image at once takes shape in my mind, like cake batter in a cake pan.

"But you know what?" he says. "I know another place that serves even better pempek. Where are you from, miss?"

The old man's hand still hangs from my arm. I make no attempt to brush it away. He smells like a combination of nutmeg and bananas.

"Jakarta, sir."

"Don't they have good pempek in Jakarta?"

I smile. "No, sir. They don't have good pempek in Jakarta."

"Would you believe," he says, "that's why I can't live in any other city. The pempek isn't as good as in Palembang. I've been offered jobs in Jakarta, Bandung—Bali, too. But I turned them all down. And why? The pempek in those places is lousy."

"But you can get things delivered from other cities these days."

"Hmph! Why bother with deliveries when you can eat it right at the source? Especially since my wife's already passed, and my kids have already grown up and have their own families. At my age, miss, I don't want to live too far away from the things I love. What's left of them, I mean."

Did my father have a lot of regrets at the end of his life? Did he know death would come for him at the age of fifty, when most men are still in their prime? Besides his birds, which didn't demand anything of him, did he also wish to be near the things he loved?

"Know why pempek is called 'pempek'?"

"Is it true it comes from the word *apek*?" I ask. "Apek" is the affectionate term of respect for an old Chinese man.

He seems to be impressed. He gives my hand a squeeze. "There are actually many versions of the story, miss. But a lot of them are hazy when it comes to details. The most famous one is a folktale from the mid-seventeenth century."

"Oh? How does it go?"

He proceeds to tell me about a sixty-five-year-old Chinese man—an apek—who lived on the banks of the Musi River. The year was 1617, more or less. As the story goes, the apek was furious to see abundant catches of fish not being put to optimal use. So he began experimenting in the kitchen. He ground the fish into a fine paste and mixed it with tapioca flour. He then told his friends to ride around the city with him on bicycles selling this new food. "Pek, apek!" they would cry, their voices filling the streets. "Pek, apek!" And there you have it: "Pe-m-pek."

However, according to Mr. Zachri, this story has several problems. First of all, bicycles were only found in Portugal and Germany in the eighteenth century, and Sultan Mahmud Badaruddin the Second was only born in 1767. Second, and most importantly, tapioca comes from the cassava plant, which only began to be cultivated for commercial use as a staple food in 1810.

I'm just about to respond when the room door swings open. A nurse wearing a surgical mask and gown pokes her head in.

"Mr. Zachri," she says in a low voice, "don't spend too much time talking."

Mr. Zachri gives her a thumbs-up. "Yes, nurse!"

The sweet old man doesn't act at all his age, much less like someone who is gravely ill.

The nurse dims the lights. Plunged in darkness, everything in the room, including Mr. Zachri and the equipment he's hooked up to, seems to shimmer.

The door closes again.

"You must have heard the story about the palace competition."

I shake my head.

"It goes like this. Once there was a king who grieved because his top chef had passed away. So he held a cooking competition. Whoever could invent the best dish using fish as the main ingredient and the right combination of spiciness, sourness, and freshness would be appointed to the position of palace chef."

The end of the story is, of course, predictable, but I wait for it nonetheless.

"Finally, only four contestants were left. Someone who produced a Japanese-style dish, another a Padang-style dish, another a Javanese-style dish, and another a Cuko-style dish. Cuko—it refers to the name of the cook whose dish, pempek, was declared the winner. And so that was how Cuko became the new palace chef."

I burst into laughter.

Mr. Zachri still hasn't let go of my hand.

"Miss," he says. There is a change in his expression and tone of voice.

"Yes, Mr. Zachri?"

"Is it true? Am I going to die?"

My throat seizes up.

Again I see the image of my father, who died seven minutes before I arrived in the ICU. I see also the faces of his friends, the few he had. On the night of the *tahlilan*, as verses of holy scripture were being recited, they tried to lighten my heart, outdoing each other with tales of my father. His voice was like a nightingale's—sweeter than Sinatra's! He was loyal, willing to suffer for the sake of his friends! He was an artist *and* a philanthropist—once, all his paintings were bought up by a rich art broker, and he donated the proceeds to help start an artists' workshop! And then there are the faces of my aunts and uncles, reciting stanzas of the "Surah Yasin" as they share memories of my father that are less than glowing. That incurable swindler! That inveterate gambler! That asshole who couldn't care less about his own wife and child!

And, most of all, I see my mother: her face drawn and wrinkled like an apple that's been left too long in the sun. Her body, shrunken and hunched, weighed down by the pressure of things absent from her life: dancing, laughter, vacations.

I swallow.

"Sir, do you know how you got this ill?"

"Honestly?" he asks.

I feel the old man's hand squeeze my wrist. I nod.

Suddenly I feel the urge to massage his hand with the lotion I always keep in my purse. As if by doing so I can restore his youth, give him the skin of a teenager. But it would be too much. He's not my father, after all.

"Miss, my late wife has come to see me every day for the past two weeks. It's like she wants me to join her. It's thanks to her that I lived eating the best pempek in the world. And the most delicious *Sambal Lingkung*. Have you had it? It's fish meat pounded fine, stir-fried powder-dry, delectably seasoned with galangal, cumin, and coriander. That wife of mine . . . bless her soul. She was a master cook. All our friends said so. Only now, since my wife isn't here anymore, do I sometimes feel the urge to go to a restaurant so I can eat pempek. And that happens only once in a while. Every time she visits, my late wife asks, 'What's the point of living alone, my love? There's no one in the world who can cook for you like I could.' She then reminds me of our maid, Atun, who used to help her in the kitchen. 'That Atun!' she says. 'What a useless maid—making *Mie Celor* like that, with lukewarm water! "Celor" is Palembang for "blanch"! The woman might as well not celor it at all! But in heaven, my love, anything we want to eat appears before us, ready and waiting! And we can eat as much as possible and never get full. Furthermore, you'll become a burden to your children if you stick around too long.'"

"Sir, please don't think like that," I say, because what else can I say? "Sir, could you please tell me one thing? Do you know how you caught the avian flu?"

Suddenly, Mr. Zachri winces.

"Miss," he says. "I don't think you understand. I really do wish I were dead."

Half an hour later, I find Farish and Ewan smoking on the veranda of Mr. Zachri's house. The people from the local SoWeFit office have just finished combing the area and look like they're beginning to pack up.

Since when does Farish smoke? My heart is still in too much tumult to really care. The head nurse I spoke to before leaving the hospital wasn't very forthcoming. In fact, she seemed callous. "Mr. Zachri probably won't last very long," she said, as if she were talking about the latest Nokia phone model. "The way he lives—it's like he's just waiting for the sun to set at the end of the day."

When I examined his file, the pathology test results didn't look promising. I couldn't bear it, and I departed from the hospital with the grief and fury of a child who's just lost a parent.

In the car, for some reason, I thought about withdrawing from my work with DOCIR, about not consulting for OneWorld anymore—and what I'd do next. Maybe I would flee once this investigation was over, to Lima, to Luanda, to Lesotho—to any city as long as it's one that would never cross anyone's mind, not even Nadezhda's. Then someday, five years later, I would return to Jakarta and start my life over again.

What's wrong with me? And now here's Farish, looking at me with some concern.

"Hey. Have you been crying?"

I pretend not to hear.

"What do you think caused it?" I ask, trying to compose myself. "Mr. Zachri's illness, I mean."

"It turns out the next-door neighbor sells quails," says Farish in an even voice. "And Mr. Zachri's maid often buys quail eggs from them."

"Just like the case in Riau," I say. I still remember the details: a two-year-old in Siak, Pekanbaru, who died after ten days in the hospital. The parents ran a quail egg business from home.

A young woman with curly hair emerges from the house with three plastic containers of Aqua water and a plate of peanuts. Her face hangs in folds, like a piece of cloth someone is in the process of ironing.

She must be Atun, I think. Useless Atun, who can't cook.

On my plate roosts a perfect cluster of pempek. Beside it are two handfuls of cucumber slivers and a pinch of shrimp floss.

It's perfection.

Perfection before it's drenched in vinegar and perfection after it's drenched in vinegar.

Perfection in the visual sense: its color and texture, its elasticity and size, its shape—like a jumbo-sized chicken croquette with a puffy center.

Perfection in the metaphysical sense: when the brownness of the vinegar seeps into the crevices, the pempek changes color, from pale candlenut to rich caramel. And the look of the canvas changes, too, from ivory to sugar.

"Hot damn," says Bono.

"Wow," says Farish.

"Best pempek in the world," says Nadezhda.

"Fucking amazing," says baby-face Ewan.

I'm soaring. It feels like my head is being pulled upward, rising, almost detaching, tingling with a pleasurable sensation both salty and spicy, warm and sweet, spreading now through my tongue and neck and chest and stomach. Two forces, then, simultaneously at work—one transporting me to heaven, one grounding me on earth.

15

CEK MIA'S *GULO PUAN*

Due to the simplistic nature of Garuda Airlines' domestic routes, we can't fly directly to Medan from Palembang. We first have to fly back to Jakarta and change planes before flying to Medan. And flying back to Jakarta tonight doesn't work out timing-wise because Farish and I still have to report to the Ministry's Palembang office for data consolidation and the necessary niceties. Only tomorrow in the late morning will we fly to Jakarta, then wait for the afternoon flight to Medan. Yet, I secretly rejoice. We have more time, and more time means more food.

We're done eating several rounds of pempek, and in the end we decide to visit the Grand Mosque for a while. I'm just about to put my bag in the trunk of the car when I see that it's brimming with treats that Palembang is famous for. Bono and Nadezhda must have cleaned out an entire store. In addition to fish crackers, cookies, and *dodol* candies, there are also several packets of civet cat coffee, each one worth 235,000 rupiah.

"Nadz," I say, "how are you going to bring all this with you if you're continuing on to Medan with us?"

"Relax," she says lightly. "Bono and I will divvy them up later."

"Yes, but you're sure to buy more in Medan, and in the end you'll ask me to put some in my suitcase, too. Then I won't be able to buy as much."

"Why are you being so selfish?" Nadezhda asks in a high-pitched voice, though she keeps her tone light.

All of a sudden, Farish, his face bright red—a combination of over-eating and awkwardness—interrupts. "You can put some in my suitcase. I have plenty of room."

"Oh my, aren't you the gentleman," Nadezhda says sweetly.

The sight of all this flirting maddens me. "Why are you being such a softie all of a sudden?" I ask, poking Farish in the stomach.

"I shouldn't have eaten breakfast just now," Farish says weakly. "Before we went to the store, I ate two helpings of pempek dos, with toast. And chicken porridge, too. You were totally right, Run. I should've just had coffee."

"You know," says Nadezhda plunking her butt down in one of the passenger seats. "Breakfast really is the most important meal of the day."

We're in for a lecture. I can sense it.

"But it also can be dangerous for one's health," she says.

"Meaning?"

The car begins to move. I'm not sure if this is the time to formally introduce Nadezhda to Farish and Ewan—watch out, this woman doesn't just prey on animals, vegetables, and tubers. She also feeds on eloquence and romance (when the two are intertwined).

"At base," she says breezily, "we are all creatures in search of variety. But breakfast is the one moment in everyday life when we need to revert to routine. For this is when we feel safe, carefree."

"Your point being?" I interrupt. I immediately think of my panic-filled mornings: waking up late, clothes unironed, no time for breakfast, rancid coffee, work piling up in the office.

"Just imagine," continues Nadezhda in that distinctive manner of hers, part philosopher, part poet, part goddess from seventh heaven, all ethereal, "what the day is like before it's fully light outside, when the city has just woken up. There's a calmness, a looseness one can feel in the air before everything tenses, sharpens, makes demands. Ten minutes, thirty minutes, however much time it may be, that time is truly ours. We enjoy those moments. We enjoy our rituals, whether they be chicken porridge, a slice of bread with jam or honey, or simply fruit, yogurt, and coffee. We read the news online, watch it on TV, read the paper. In essence, when we wake up in the morning, we determine our caloric consumption for that day."

I watch Farish and Ewan gawking at the goddess.

"And yet," she continues, "it is at that very moment, when there is something that makes us happier than usual, a new lover who has stayed over, for example, or the incredible sex of the night before, or a public holiday—one extra day to have more sex—that we often feel tempted to eat more than usual."

"Really?" says Ewan, his face bright red. "How come I never feel relaxed or happy in the morning? I'm the eldest of six brothers and sisters. My mother and I work hard to make ends meet since we don't have Father anymore. It's been that way since I was little."

"Same here," says Farish. "I've lived on the same small street for years, and the noise is really something else. There are always buildings being constructed, neighbors fighting, warung owners fighting, and babies crying all morning. Not to mention the sound of birds chirping and the occasional gusts of wind."

"Oh, also, when I have a new girlfriend, I usually lose my appetite," adds Ewan, his face becoming redder still.

"And come to think of it," says Farish, "I've never brought a girl home for . . ." At this point he stops, as if grasping for the least vulgar word he can find. Suddenly I feel a strange tingle on the back of my neck.

"My point is," says Nadezhda, who is rarely shaken by the arguments of others, "it is when we feel relaxed and comfortable that we feel tempted to eat more than usual. Especially foods rich in carbohydrates. A croissant slathered with butter, a sliver of cake from a friend, a plate of fried rice, the leftover rendang stew from the night before."

"After a big breakfast, wouldn't you reduce the amount you eat at lunch and dinner?" asks Farish in a faux academic tone, trying to overcome his embarrassment.

"Mmm, not always. Someone who breakfasts like a king will usually continue to keep eating like a king. Lunch and dinner too will be eaten as if he were a king. In essence," says Nadezhda, her voice growing firmer still, "the benchmark we set for ourselves will change and, all of a sudden, in the ensuing hours our stomachs and heads will demand the same. The more we grant ourselves concessions, the more our stomachs will demand. And *that* is why breakfast can be so dangerous."

"Well," says Farish, "I always eat like a beggar. Breakfast, lunch, dinner—it's all the same. I mean, except for now . . ."

"Hah!" I say with a grin. "Look who ate chicken porridge and two helpings of pempek dos this morning, followed less than four hours later by still more pempek, two slices of *Bugis* cake, and two glasses of orange juice sweetened with sugar."

I see Bono tilt his head in my direction. Up to this point, he's been quiet, doing things on his iPad.

"Run," he says tonelessly, "there's no point in avoiding breakfast like you do, then polishing off five *kapal selam*-style pempek stuffed with boiled eggs and three fat batons of *lenjer*-style pempek in a single sitting for lunch. That's not optimizing your fish-protein consumption. That's just loading up on bad fat from that garbage they use as cooking oil."

❦

I do want to see the Grand Mosque, but there's actually another reason why I want to go—the *Gulo Puan* vendors. I'm not sure if they'll be there today since it isn't Friday, but what's the harm in trying?

Walking along the footpath from the parking lot to the mosque, I realize that there's something different about this place. For a while I concentrate on taking in my surroundings: the row of leafy trees that soften the sun's rays; the pointed tips of the minarets, two hundred and sixty years old; and in the spaces between them, refreshing bursts of palm trees, green and lush, adding an extra texture to the canvas. The grounds of the mosque, those beautiful new tiles, cool to the touch and strangely moving. Malayness and Chineseness clinging to each and every architectural detail. The orderliness of things.

Nadezhda and Bono seem to be relishing every moment, their fingers working their respective electronic devices, their lips moving nonstop. The two of them have a flair for photography. They never click just any old way, like the people who take photos with the sole purpose of putting them up on Facebook or Instagram. And whenever they upload photos to social media from their trips, they never fail to add an explanation:

Clock towers remind us of older times, when the West dominated public spaces and real life was shut away behind boarded-up windows and doors. (Nadezhda)

My fellow foodies, there's more to the northern Jakarta area of Pluit than perennial flooding and all manner of things forbidden. In the open-air food court at Pluit Sakti Raya, you'll find a Medan-style shaved ice and a giant freshwater prawn soto that will prove you don't need to be a sinner to enjoy life. Carpe diem! (Bono)

I suddenly feel a rush of tenderness toward them. Their passion for the seedy and sublime still surprises me to this day.

I hear the opening lines of a sermon being broadcast over the mosque loudspeakers. The sound fills the air. But I'm not bothered in the least, perhaps because the volume is low, unobtrusive, questing. From different angles I again examine up close the architectural lines of the mosque, the roof corners that jut skyward and the greenness of their tips, the calligraphy adorning the windows, the play of the mosaics across the floor, the solemn, almost stately entranceway—part temple, part mosque.

The sermon continues, like background music. It neither startles nor rankles. I walk toward the majestic reflecting pool and its sparkling fountain. The sound of spraying water sharpens my senses for some reason, and gradually, just like that, the words reach my ears. I don't resist. The longer I listen, the more I realize that what is different about the mosque is that the person delivering the sermon is speaking not about sin, restrictions, or even laws. He is speaking about beauty, peace, the magical. His voice is a steady but inquisitive vibrato, almost full of wonder at its own quiet searching.

I linger by the side of the pool for a long time and lose myself in thought.

I hear Nadezhda's footsteps and look up. Her eyes are fixed on an old woman who holds her hands under a faucet that dispenses holy water. Above it is a sign: "This faucet dispenses certified holy water for ablutions."

The water she awaits fails to flow.

"Ach!" we hear the old woman exclaim.

"Maybe they reserve the holy water for Friday prayers," I hear Nadezhda say to her, trying to make light of it.

The old woman doesn't seem to hear. Yet she won't waste a minute more of her time. Nadezhda and I watch her get up and walk away from the fountain, as if to avoid being crushed by disappointment.

"Don't tell me you're right," I say.

She sits beside me, on the edge of the reflecting pool. She looks serious.

"It'd be so depressing if I were," she says. "Would they really lie about something so sacred? If so, it's doubly sinful—using religion to make empty promises."

A moment later, I notice Bono waving at us from afar. Even at this distance he looks excited. He appears to be holding something in one of his hands—a bowl, from the looks of it—and occasionally he ladles its contents into his mouth. Nadezhda and I approach.

And then I realize my darling friend has found the gulo puan I'm so curious about.

There are so many unpleasant facts in life, and this is just one of them: gulo puan is on the verge of extinction. But here, on the grounds of the Grand Mosque, this snack, renowned for being the food of sovereigns in the days of the Malacca Sultanate, can be found—and usually only on Fridays. If one comes across it on any other day, it will be nothing short of coincidence, like today.

Cek Mia is a mother of four. She had no intention of coming to the Grand Mosque this morning. Like all the other gulo puan vendors, she always tries to get here half an hour before the men finish their Friday prayers. After her children leave for school, on days that aren't Friday, she usually spends the morning shopping for groceries and ingredients for her wares. Sometimes on the way home she stops somewhere to satisfy her hankering for a sweet es kacang or some pempek. But for the past few days, she's been ecstatic.

Her big brother's good friend, a businessman from Bandung, has recently come to visit. He has a potbelly and a booming voice, and seems to have fallen in love. He can't stop talking about how sexy Cek Mia is—look at those curves, look at that skin—even though she's married with four children. Not only that, he feasts on her gulo puan as if it's the only food in the world, and has promised to fund her business. He's even offered to help bring gulo puan to Bandung and Jakarta. "The Javanese love sweet things, dear sister," he said this morning. *"However,"*—here he winked—"to achieve success, you have to be willing to take risks!"

When Cek Mia asked what he meant by "risks," Mr. Potbelly leaned his face in close and whispered, "I do want to invest. But before one invests, one wants to have an idea of how the market will react." And because Cek Mia just stood there staring at him, Mr. Potbelly continued: "Come, now. Are you brave enough to hawk your wares at the Grand Mosque today? How about we conduct a little experiment. Let's see how many people buy it. And how long you last before the authorities give you a talking-to."

At first Cek Mia was hesitant. Why take the risk of being shooed away or arrested, of embarrassing her family and herself? There had been a hiatus for almost a decade since she resumed selling gulo puan at the beginning of the year, long before they spruced up the Grand Mosque to make it what it is today. She still has several loyal customers, even if their numbers are few. And although she gets wistful whenever she remembers her prime—when a day's work would mean selling thirty-three pounds of gulo puan, whereas now she's lucky if she sells fifteen portions—she is still a woman of faith. She believes that gulo puan isn't meant to bring happiness to everyone in this world. Rather, by bringing happiness to just a select handful of people, she is doing something important and useful.

But this morning, something caused her to change her mind. As she was clearing the plates from breakfast, suddenly her husband piped up. "Listen. Have you thought of retiring from selling gulo puan?"

Cek Mia looked at her husband incredulously.

"Come on. Take a look in the mirror. Your income's not exactly ballooning, but you are."

So hurt was Cek Mia that she almost asked for a divorce on the spot. *How dare he criticize me,* she thought. *After I've borne him four children and tended to all his needs like a . . . like a . . . goddamned servant.* But then she recalled that offer: the offer of a man who knows how to appreciate a woman. And she thought, *Want to see what success looks like? I'll show you. I'll become the lady mistress of a gulo puan empire. And once I'm rich and famous, I'll divorce your sorry ass!*

❦

Bono is telling us about his plans to open a second Siria—a Siria II—in an upscale neighborhood in Jakarta. Pondok Indah, perhaps. This isn't an interesting topic of conversation for Farish and Ewan; they're busy chatting with each other as they enjoy bowls of tekwan fishcake soup. Tekwan, the close relative of the pempek.

Nadezhda doesn't look convinced about Bono's plans.

She doesn't look too convinced about this restaurant either, which serves cuisine from the Dempo region of Sumatra, and whose house specialty, the locals say, is pempek made from the flesh of the *Belida* fish. It's surrounded by convenience stores and shops selling auto parts and baking equipment.

"But here, the belida is prized more highly than mackerel." I say this in the restaurant's defense, though I still prefer by far the marvel that is the pempek we ate at that other place. "Originally, all pempek was made using belida. Only recently did people start using snakehead fish instead because it costs less and is easier to find. And after that came mackerel."

"Yes," Nadezhda says, "but pempek's taste isn't wholly dependent on the type of fish. For some reason, these taste too rubbery, too starchy. It's like the difference between the dim sum in Hong Kong and the dim sum in Shanghai."

She's right. I stare at my Pempek Kapal Selam. It's so beautiful in its shapelessness, you can almost taste it. It makes you weep. But when I start to explain this, Bono immediately cuts me off.

"Nadz is right," he says, even though I'm not suggesting she isn't. "The fish is clearly superior, though I also liked the pempek at the other place. They were crispier on the outside."

He dips his spoon into Farish's bowl, scoops up several slices of tekwan, and savors them. "Wow," he says at long last. "Now *this* is good."

In a flash, my spoon and Nadezhda's enter the fray. It *is* a very good, stunning broth: clean tasting, sober—with just the right amount of bamboo shoots and cucumber garnish. And the tekwan are soft and supple.

To his credit, the dish's rightful owner doesn't seem perturbed in the least. He simply leans back in his chair and smiles, having grown accustomed to our antics, like that of children.

"I'll buy you another bowl," Nadezhda says sweetly as she calls a waiter over. "Let's give their *celimpungan* and *mentu* a try as well. I've heard they're good. I want to try the one with papaya filling."

Farish's grin widens. The Nadezhda factor is at full throttle.

I hear my stomach gurgling in protest.

"Come on. The Pondok Indah set will still brave hours of traffic to go to Siria I. After all, this is what they've been doing for months." Nadezhda prattles away, returning to the initial topic of conversation.

I gaze at her full lips and her even white teeth. How is it possible for her teeth to still be so white after being relentlessly assaulted by red wine, coffee, and now vinegar?

"Because that's the consumptive behavior of South Jakarta's upper class. Where they're seen hanging out is very important for their image."

"Wouldn't a Siria branch closer to them be doubly to their advantage, then?"

"Not necessarily," counters Nadezhda. "My point is their response to Siria II depends a lot on the type of people who come and hang out there. If it's only fellow members of Pondok Indah's elite, then what's the point? They want to see the beautiful people from the other parts of town—the celebs, the actors, the models, the super-rich."

Bono scratches his head as he studies the menu. It looks like he wants to order some tekwan for himself.

"If that's the case, I'll give them something they can't get at Siria I," he says. "Crazy, innovative dishes that I'll only serve in the new restaurant. Can you see it? Something like the ABC Kitchen menu, but you won't have to travel to New York!"

My dear heart, my Bono: he really is a true chef. In the face of a sociological problem, he proposes a purely culinary solution.

After ordering his own bowl of tekwan, he returns to staring at his iPad, following with his eyes every one of Nigella Lawson's curves, pondering every weighty phrase that falls from the lips of the great and gorgeous creature as she pours batter into the cake pan she presses to her breast like a baby.

In the meantime, I nibble on my small, sweet, pancake-like *Apem Banyu*. The texture resembles the more ubiquitous *Kue Cucur*, but this quiet beauty is soaked in a sauce heavy with coconut cream, palm sugar, cloves, nutmeg, and cinnamon. It's only served at Islamic funerals in rural areas, explains the owner of the eatery, during the nightlong recitation of prayers. *Ah, but all of us have to return to our eternal home at some point,* I think lightly. The important thing is that all of it be delicious—or, in the lingo of these parts, *lemak nian*.

16

HE'S NO LONGER WITH US

In another dream, I see myself in a hospital, approaching the nurse's station in the middle of the night. I'm an enormous baby, swaddled in a special isolation room gown, whimpering for milk.

When a nurse replies "We're out of milk," I scream like a baby possessed. "Me want miwk! Me want miwk!"

❦

My team of three and I haven't even emerged from the car when a middle-aged woman runs toward us.

"Oh God. He's dead, ma'am. Dead." As she speaks, she shakes her head. From her uniform and figure, she appears to be an employee at the Ministry's local office who doesn't care much for food.

My heart is pounding. Who's dead? My mother? Irma? The two other people I love, Bono and Nadezhda, are with me now. It can't be . . . it can't be Leon. My pulse quickens, like in that wretched dream with Leon and Katrin in it. I hastily brush the thought aside. What I experienced with Leon wasn't love; it was stupidity.

"The patient, ma'am," the woman stammers when I grab her hand. "The avian flu patient you just visited."

Now my heart seizes.

"Mr. Zachri?"

"Yes, ma'am. Mr. Zachri. Just now. Less than ten minutes ago."

"Wha . . . wha . . ." My knees go weak. I have to sit down, and Farish gets me a stool—strangely attentive of him. There I am, sitting down on the veranda of the Ministry's local branch office as if my own world is falling apart.

"How could this happen? I only just . . . I mean, he was fine when I left him."

"According to the hospital, there was some unexpected hemorrhaging in Mr. Zachri's lungs."

"There was . . . there was no direct connection with the avian flu, was there?" I ask a bit stupidly, my head spinning.

A hand lands on my knee. I'm trembling all over.

"Run," says Farish, the hand's master, "you know it's not your fault, right?"

For some reason, I let his hand remain.

This seaside restaurant, though much vaunted, doesn't seem that impressive tonight. In Jakarta, this restaurant wouldn't last long; people wouldn't think it was the real thing. What kind of successful restaurant operates in complete darkness? With some sadness, I consider this difference in standards. Even though the people of Palembang get all starry-eyed when they talk about this place, the facts of life outside the capital still apply: electric lighting belongs only to governors, mayors, the police—those who have the power to do dark deals for their own gain.

After we pass the enormous fish tanks at the front of the restaurant, we decide to sit in the open-air area, which resembles a wharf and where we can freely admire the lights of the Ampera Bridge, their curvature like the broad grin of Zwarte Piet.

In the light of the moon, Nadezhda looks like a mythical creature from a faraway land, as if she is still unwilling to refuse outright the awe of mortals like Farish and Ewan, who in turn know they might as well be the owl in that old saying, pining hopelessly after the moon.

Once again I feel that jealousy—a jealousy that is, really, more a kind of disappointment with myself. A disappointment that I'm so straight, so monotone, not in the least plural like this enchanting sylph who happens to be my very close friend.

It's a matter of some astonishment—Nadezhda's confidence that she'll always be the center of attention. She was raised in a high-profile family, both wealthy and educated. As such, she's used to meeting, befriending, and conversing with people from diverse circles, and she knows how to bring them under her spell. It's like the rules don't apply to her; she's above them, and yet because of this she's open to all kinds of eccentricity and madness. She's not someone who's fated to embrace the full import of her origins or to find what other people call "home." And she doesn't feel the need to explain why she is the way she is.

Bono isn't much different. When he looks at something, he takes in the world. He works hard, learns to play many parts. He absorbs, infiltrates, embodies his surroundings. When he laughs the sun is brighter, the moon fuller.

Look at them now, discussing recipes for *Pindang Patin* and the hemorrhaging of internal organs as if the problems of this world and the afterlife must be confronted, debated, and settled to keep the human race going. Meanwhile, I still can't find the words to express this strange grief of mine. Where are they? How do I call them to me? Or do they come only to those who put themselves in their hands?

"He was already more than sixty-five years old, wasn't he?" asks Nadezhda.

I don't respond.

"How could an aneurysm go undetected by the doctors?"

In truth, I've begun to suspect that the doctors handling Mr. Zachri's case were preconditioned to regard his pneumonic symptoms in the larger context of avian flu, to the point of dismissing the other chronic ailments he suffered that could have caused similar symptoms. It's very likely that he had suffered for a long time from a rare form of bronchiolitis, or a lung condition even more difficult to detect, that quickly spread to the blood vessels and gave rise to pneumonic symptoms. But I say nothing.

"Tamarind!" It's Bono, his voice floating up. "I'm positive there's tamarind in this."

Suddenly, just like that, hemorrhaging as a topic of discussion is forgotten. Nadezhda and Bono begin comparing the pindang patin they're currently savoring like there's no tomorrow. It's tasty as hell, as are the other versions of *pindang* soup around the archipelago: the *Pangeh Masi* of the Minang, the Javanese-style *Pindang Serani*, the *Gangan* or *Lempah* from Bangka Belitung.

"*Definitely* tamarind. Just a hint, dissolved in water. No wonder it's so subtle. I even detect notes of something roasted, but it's not smoked fish. Turmeric, maybe? Shrimp paste?"

Ewan, who's been listening to us this whole time, holding his breath, suddenly chimes in. You can find many kinds of pindang in Palembang, he tells us. There's *Pindang Meranjat, Pindang Pegangan, Pindang Musi Rawas, Pindang Palembang*. The most common version in South Sumatra, in the regency of Ogan Komering Ilir, uses coarsely ground red chili pepper. When you stir the pindang, bits of chili pepper spread through the broth. "Like someone's brains spraying out after they've been shot," he says earnestly.

Nadezhda gazes for a moment at the innocent face of the Palembang boy. She seems impressed—beneath the water's placid surface, there are ripples after all.

Pindang meranjat and pindang pegangan, Ewan continues—probably more confident now that he has Nadezhda's attention—use a lot of shrimp paste, and sometimes smoked fish.

"But this pindang has shrimp paste, too!" Nadezhda exclaims with energy. "I'm sure of it. Not a lot, but enough to enrich the flavor. The combination of the sour, sweet, and spicy is just right as well. Cherry tomatoes, green tomatoes, *bilimbi*, bay leaves, pineapple slivers . . . my God. *So* stylish. Not to mention the lemon basil!"

"And they all make complete sense—they balance out the oiliness of the *patin* fish, which might make this dish too rich," says Bono.

"Even the broth is spot on," says Nadezhda. "Thick, but not too thick. *Full-bodied*," she adds in English before looking my way. "Aruna, what's the right word in Indonesian?"

But I pay her no notice. I still can't erase Mr. Zachri's face from my memory, especially the look on his face when he said he wanted to stay in Palembang for the pempek. I also can't shake off the image of the Grand Mosque and the stillness I felt down to the tips of my toes. Why did that moment feel so arresting, so stirring?

Then I remember someone once told me that silence is God's friend. From the monks and nuns of certain orders who carry out their days mutely, to the Hindu concept, in Sanskrit, of *sunyata*, it is clear that stillness can become a kind of acknowledgment on the part of humankind that God is truly that which is inexpressible.

Before I realize it, I'm crying. And there's that hand again, this time on my shoulder.

"Do you want me to take you to Mr. Zachri's house?" asks Farish. His gaze is gentle, almost like a lover's. "I'm not sure if we'll have time tomorrow."

I nod.

Again, I let the hand remain.

During the ride to Mr. Zachri's house, it feels like something is going to burst out of my chest. I go into hysterics.

"Impossible, Run." Farish tries to calm me down. "It's impossible to push for a histopathological investigation if a patient's already dead. Even when a patient is still alive, who has the right to ask for such a procedure if they're not the doctor? And even if the doctor had the same idea, what hospital would be able to do it? And who would pay for it?"

"What about an open lung biopsy?" I ask stubbornly.

"You can't be serious. That's a mighty expensive procedure. It would involve video-assisted thoracoscopy and everything! Look around you! We don't have the technology, much less the technicians. And as we all know, Mr. Zachri probably never had a real doctor and probably was never given proper medicine. If he really did suffer from bronchiolitis, it's very likely he was never diagnosed as such and consequently was never given corticosteroids or prednisolone."

My tears start flowing again.

Thanks to the hard work of the local Ministry staff, Mr. Zachri's family has been convinced not to bury the old man's body until the next morning, with the excuse that an additional examination has to be performed before the final report is sent to Ministry headquarters in Jakarta. But what they don't know is how many additional examinations have already been performed on his corpse.

However, the local Ministry staff had clearly failed to convince Mr. Zachri's family to let his body stay in the hospital overnight. At half past seven, earlier that evening, while my friends and I were analyzing the composition of flavors in a bowl of sour, sweet, and spicy pindang patin, the body of Mr. Zachri was returned to his house to be prayed over by people who probably never so much as glanced at him when he was still alive.

"Maybe the hospital just wants to wash their hands of the matter," I say, tears still streaming. "Now they can close the books on it. All they have to do is tell Ministry headquarters, 'Suspected avian flu patient died of complications related to pneumonia.' No one will ask why or what triggered the death. And now Mr. Zachri's body has been returned to his family. There won't be an autopsy. He'll be buried tomorrow. Case closed."

"Just let it go, please."

"Look," I say as I swallow, "sorry . . . but do you mind if we go to the hospital for a little while? I want to examine the pathology records again. I probably wasn't concentrating earlier today when I read them the first time."

When we get to the hospital, the nurse who greets us says curtly, "The pathology records have already been sent to Ministry headquarters. We forgot to make a copy. Sorry. You can check them when you get to Jakarta."

It's only when we're back in the car on the way to Mr. Zachri's house that I remember—she was the nurse who kept reminding Mr. Zachri not to talk to me for too long when I was visiting him.

My knowledge is limited where death is concerned. Only two people I know well have died: my favorite elementary school teacher and my father. And even those didn't seem real.

When my teacher died, I hadn't seen her for years, and all I remember of the funeral was the canopy tent that suddenly collapsed, the people baked under the sun's fierce heat, and the *ustad* who hacked continuously as he prayed for my teacher's soul: "May her good deeds always be remembered (cough, cough) and may the family she leaves behind be strong and pure of heart (cough, cough). Amen."

Whenever I recall that afternoon in the cemetery at Tanah Kusir, something stirs within me, near the nape of my neck. It was a day when my teacher sat me down in the classroom and, gazing deep into my eyes, said, "You're the kind of student who'll never be satisfied with what you know." To this day, I don't know what she meant. I don't feel like I know much of anything. But "who'll never be satisfied" implied some kind of strong desire, a struggle even, to fix or change my fate in life. And for some reason those words always gave me strength. So I found it sad that someone who had made my life richer with what she'd said had to leave this world accompanied by words so hoarse, so broken, so banal.

With my father it was a different matter entirely. Maybe it was because I reached the hospital too late or because my mother was trying hard to avoid seeing him. I wasn't even allowed to look at his body in the mortuary, before he was taken to our home to have his face scoured and his body and hair freshly washed and wrapped in Muslim linen.

My memory of that day is groaningly unreliable because death, like birth, circumcision, marriage, and all other important events in a person's life, is a public affair, and as a result is packed with the problems of other people: Is there enough rice for everyone? Have we paid the ustad his fee? Have you called the funeral transportation company? Has the tent been set up? Have the flower arrangements from Company X arrived yet?

After my father was bathed and made up and laid out on a mat in the middle of the house, all I saw was a face, rotund and yellowish. A sad piece of flesh. I found myself thinking, *Isn't now the time to cry? But wait. Isn't now also the time to "be strong"—to dress neatly, to receive guests with a brave smile, to invite people to sit down, to fetch them drinks?*

How many stories were milling around that day among the guests being served sweet tidbits and fruit and small packets of *nasi rames*—rice with assorted side dishes? Stories about my father's swollen face, about the mixture of mucus and blood that rose from his broken lungs and poured from his nose in such a horrible gush that the mask that had been put there to protect his nose couldn't contain it all. But of course life was no longer the same. After my mother had stolen away to her room to cry and my father was no longer able to protect us, those who had come to pay their respects didn't even try to lower their voices as I passed. As if death, from now on, was a part of life best learned through other people.

Later in the day, after afternoon prayers, I watched six men, some whom I didn't know, shoulder the coffin and carry it to the open grave. A hollowness took hold of me, and I felt nothing. What I felt—if it was a feeling at all—was a profound dullness. And I felt the same when, in a flattened corner of my consciousness, I heard the voices of children chasing each other among the graves of strangers, their happy shrieks rising like balloons above the public grief of their parents.

For days I lived in that dullness as a constant stream of people came to visit the house and uttered the same words again and again: "My condolences." "Be brave, child." "Take care of your mother." "Let your father go." "Only God knows what is best for us." It was only after a month or so, when I saw a pair of songbirds—sooty-headed bulbuls—on the veranda of a friend's house that I felt moisture warming my cheeks.

But tonight, as I'm sitting cross-legged on a mat in a dank house that smells of death, about a hair's breadth away from the body of an old man who wasn't my father, wasn't an acquaintance, wasn't anybody, just someone who less than twelve hours ago was squeezing my hand and entrusting his most intimate memories to me, I feel a tightness in my chest. And lo, tears falling.

I'll never know if my sadness has shown itself to such an extent because I feel more involved in his death or if it's because I only knew Mr. Zachri in part—the side of him that moved me—unlike my father, whose entire life had been a long stretch of despair.

I'm also not sure if the tears that now flow so easily from me are because I'm older than when my father was ripped away from me. Because in being older, I see now that the struggle of those who stand face-to-face with death is really a struggle against malaise—the pain of loss.

Whenever a person says he or she wants to win their fight against cancer or some other terminal illness, it is that pain they are fighting against; the pain tells them they will lose. It's the same with the person who stands at death's door, talking about the beautiful things in their life, whether they be the birds that make them smile in the morning or the pempek that keeps them rooted to the city of their birth.

That night, when I return to my room, Nadezhda hugs me. There's a book, she says, about a woman mourning her husband and child who passed away within a short time of each other. In one chapter toward the end, the author writes: *Grief turns out to be a place none of us know until we reach it.*

I still can't imagine such a place.

<hr>

That fiendish es kacang: I never thought it would taste exactly how Mr. Zachri described it, just hours before his final breath.

Chocolate diamonds. Holy fuck.

<hr>

It isn't too hard to imagine one Zachri Musa sitting in a corner of this restaurant from week to week, sometimes day to day, year after year, enjoying a plate of pempek and a bowl of es kacang. To him they must taste of what folks mean by "heaven on earth."

<hr>

The next morning, I hear that the mean nurse has been found out. She received a bribe from Mr. Zachri Musa—a whopping 500,000 rupiah—for falsifying his diagnosis to make it look like avian flu.

"Mr. Zachri asked me to do it," the nurse said in her defense. "It was so he wouldn't have to pay for his treatment. He was tired of living anyway."

17

HEAVENLY CURRY

Angel: All right, let's see here. Your name is Aruna, and you're thirty-five.

Me: Correct.

Angel: My name is Nigella.

Me: All right.

Angel: You may address me as Goddess.

Me: All right.

Angel: "All right, O Goddess."

Me: All right, O Goddess.

Angel: You know I'm not God, right?

Me: Yes.

Angel: Yes, what?

Me: Yes, O Goddess. I know you're not God . . . O Goddess.

Angel: So you know the final decision is out of my hands.

Me: Yes, I do, O Goddess.

Angel: Whether someone should go to heaven or hell is no easy matter. The criteria are very fluid.

Me: (Silence)

Angel: And only God has the authority to guarantee anything.

Me: Yes, O Goddess.

Angel: But this time, God is genuinely baffled. So I've been given the task of interviewing you. Usually, God doesn't need my help. Unlike mortals, he doesn't need judges, mediators, investigation committees, or selection panels. But yours is an interesting case. First of all, I'd like to ask: Do you know what your crimes are?

Me: Yes and no, O Goddess.

Angel: What do you think they are, in your opinion?

Me: I know I wasn't at my father's side when he breathed his last. I rarely look in on my widowed mother. I enjoy being mean to my friends and co-workers because when it comes down to it, I don't like people. Sometimes I'm even mean to other people's cats because I love my cat best. I can cook, but I can't bake cakes. Every time I take a flight or stay in a hotel, I swipe the forks and spoons. I've also been to a restaurant and kept quiet when they gave me the wrong check because they charged me a lot less. My job is to research birds, but I don't like birds. I once slipped a Dulcolax into a friend's drink in middle school because I didn't want her to win the singing competition. I'm often jealous of my own best friends because one of them is an expert chef and the other is an expert writer, thinker, and speaker. Both of them are also expert eaters, whereas I'm just an expert eater, period.

Angel: You don't remember what you did when you visited Bangka last year?

Me: I . . . I went there to look around a village, O Goddess.

Angel: And what was your intention in looking around that village?

Me: To search for kulat *mushrooms.*

Angel: And what are they—kulat mushrooms?

Me: The kulat mushroom is one of the most delicious mushrooms in the world, O Goddess. And also one of the rarest. And most expensive. It is found only on the island of Bangka and grows only at the base of the pelawan tree. It's so unique that many erroneously equate it with a truffle, even though true truffles only grow underground. But the kulat—let's just call it a rare mushroom. Two pounds can command prices of up to 1.15 million rupiah.

Angel: And how are they prepared?

Me: Simple. Put them in a Bangkanese lempah stew seasoned with bumbu putih *or* bumbu merah—*white mixed spice or red mixed spice—and some coconut cream, perhaps. Oh, and the chicken bones you use to make the stock should be free-range. That's a must.*

Angel: Then you must know how important the kulat mushroom is to the people of Bangka.

Me: And I'm always saying, instead of chopping down trees, razing forests, and opening gold and nickel mines, it would be better to plant as many pelawan trees as possible. It would guarantee the prosperity of Bangka's people for decades—no, centuries. Not only that, to preserve the kulat mushroom is to preserve their traditions. The process of cleaning the mushrooms must be done manually and sometimes takes hours. You have to open each one, and the debris has to be scraped out very carefully. . .

Angel: If you know all this, then why did you steal twelve sacks of kulat mushrooms from the village storehouses and bring them to Jakarta? How could you do such a thing?

Me: (Silence)

Angel: Did you hear what I asked you?

Me: Yes, O Goddess.

Angel: So, why did you steal twelve sacks—

Me: I—I don't know, O Goddess. The opportunity suddenly presented itself . . . and I . . . I couldn't refuse.

Angel: But stealing is stealing, and stealing food supplies is a transgression of the highest degree. Surely you know that from the Foundational Food Ethics classes you took in elementary and middle school. They're a mandatory component of the national curriculum.

Me: I do know, O Goddess. I have sinned.

Angel: And your sins are multiplied because you stole from people who are utterly dependent on the food supplies you stole.

Me: I know, O Goddess.

Angel: Is there anything you have to say that might explain your egregious act?

Me: But those mushrooms . . . they're so delicious, O Goddess. I can't stop eating them.

Angel: (Silence)

Me: I'm addicted, O Goddess. I don't know how to explain it.

Angel: And I probably wouldn't understand if you did. I don't know what it means to eat good food. I wouldn't know whether it was "good." I don't know what it means to eat, much less to be addicted to anything.

Me: I stole those kulat mushrooms because I couldn't bear to part with their flavor. It's beyond compare, O Goddess.

Angel: Do you repent it, then—obeying your fleshly desires to the point of not caring whether other people would suffer?

Me: I . . . I . . .

Angel: It is with a heavy heart that I must submit my recommendation to God. I feel like there is no other way. You must go to hell.

Me: I repent of causing other people to suffer, O Goddess.

Angel: Well, surrender all your worldly possessions. Your time has come.

Me: It was a pleasure to meet you, O Goddess, O Goddess Nigella. Before I sinned and had to go to hell, I must tell you I always watched your cooking show on TV. My friend positively worships you—he's . . . he's the expert chef.

Angel: Believe me. When you're in hell, you'll understand how much better it is to be consumed by fire for eternity than to be an angel. Alive, yet unable to feel.

There are always cities that inhabit our imaginations long before we visit them. Medan is one of them—every time I hear "Medan," I immediately think: Commerce.

The word "Medan" is practically synonymous with money and trade, buying and selling, bargaining and haggling, duplicity and deception, cunning fraud, consumerism, market power, chaos, violence, traffic, pollution, the law of the jungle. It's a virtual embodiment of every unsavory thing we know about politics and capitalism: dirty politics, pork-barrel politics, the politics of survival, hired thugs. Nothing is pretty and nothing comes free in Medan. Everything is brutal and ugly.

But these days the impression that has attached itself to the city is that of a food paradise. And if someone from Medan recommends eating at this place or that, I take their word for it. Who knows why, but their palates seem to be accustomed to various options in abundance, all more or less above average. As a result they have to be much more selective when deciding which is the choicest.

Bono, who has many Medanese friends, has made a list, as usual. Sitting between me and Nadezhda on the plane ride over, and during the entire taxi ride to the hotel, he's been talking nonstop about that list, that catalogue of Medan's culinary delights. *Kari Bihun*, "Chicken" *Bakmi, Nasi Campur*, "Crack of Dawn" *Kwetiau*, "Crack of Dawn" *Bihun Bebek, Sangsang*, all the crazy assorted noodles they sell on Jalan Selat Panjang.

"Why don't we go to Jalan Selat Panjang and get something to eat?"

Never mind that it's 11:00 p.m. and I'm completely pooped.

"You two go ahead," I say to Bono and Nadezhda as I drag my suitcase to the elevator, room key in hand. "I'm going to crash."

But as it turns out, I don't. Too accustomed to having Nadezhda around, she who so commands a room, I feel lonely and sad. For some reason, the space feels too large.

I feel like a drink.

❦

There are only two guests at the hotel bar: men. One a foreigner. One a local.

I don't care that I'm a woman or that I'm by myself. Medan doesn't give a damn. It's seen too much.

I order a Campari Orange, my longtime favorite aperitif. Sweet, elegant, safe.

I spend a long time staring at the giant television screens on either side of the bar. Nadezhda would refuse to drink in a place like this. Or if she didn't refuse, she'd grumble, "Why are people so dumb? Why drag yourself to a restaurant to do something you can do in your own home?"

And if we reminded her, saying, "But this is a bar, baby, not a restaurant, and people often go to a bar for the express purpose of, say, watching a soccer match with other people—or badminton, or tennis, or whatever—and drinking at the same time," she would call into question the entire premise behind people's obsessions with sports and quote some obscure Italian or German intellectual about the absurdity of group sports and what makes them so ridiculously addictive.

Basically, she'd opine, the obsession with such physical competition produces nothing but mindless chitchat about sports. In other words, something shallow, superficial, almost akin to a parody of a political discussion: what strategy Team A or Athlete B should have put into play and what they did wrong, what happened versus what should have happened. But, more than that, this shallow and superficial thing would make its discussants feel powerful, incisive, verbally aggressive, as if they were the ones in competition. In short, they themselves would be part of this larger competitive spirit, which requires an outlet for its release.

But I know that all this isn't the main reason for Nadezhda's hatred of restaurants that have television screens. I'm certain the main issue actually has to do with aesthetics. In this matter, she can be positively fascist. It's like she can't tolerate in the least anything she considers gaudy, or ugly, or mass-produced, or kitsch. And yet at the same time, she never treats other people badly, nor does she humiliate them. How can two such opposing attitudes coexist within one person?

Farish approaches my table with his glass of beer and sits beside me, and for some reason I'm not that surprised. Everything about him tonight makes him look handsome. His cool blue-collared shirt. His curly hair, which he wears a little long. The color of his skin in the dim light. His air of spontaneity.

I wake up around six with a startle. Nadezhda's already up. Less than two and a half hours ago, when I came back to the room, she'd already fallen asleep—sprawled on the bed on top of the covers. She's still wearing the same clothes. She's still wearing the same makeup. Clearly, after wandering off in search of food, she and Bono went out drinking, too.

"So, where'd you go last night?"

"Nowhere. I was just downstairs."

"Seriously?"

"I swear!"

"By 'downstairs,' you mean . . ."

"The bar. Where else?"

"Why didn't you ask me to come along? Were you alone?"

"Nah," I say hesitantly. "I was . . . well, I was with Farish."

She keeps her thoughts to herself, but her eyes are wide. And then it comes out: "Farish!"

I feel a pinch of annoyance. Am I supposed to feel guilty? Even though my accuser has made a profession of hooking up here, there, and everywhere on different continents without ever feeling the need to explain herself.

At that moment I really dislike Nadezhda, with her beautiful, accusatory eyes and her slightly aquiline nose—Nadezhda who looks lovely even at this ungodly hour, though her hair is a mess and her makeup is smudged. *I'm not your rival. I—the one who's always giving, practicing self-control, letting things go. In no way, at no time have I ever been your rival.*

"Yes," I say irritably. "Farish. Who are you, the moral police?"

Something tenses in Nadezhda's expression. Her eyes are cold. Five minutes later, or thereabouts, I find myself absurdly trying to apologize.

"It's okay," she says, lying back down. "All forgotten."

It's hard to tell who's won—me, with my oversensitivity, or her, with her refusal to deal with the fallout from a situation she's created and by making the wronged feel bad.

Only two hours later, once we're all crammed in the car OneWorld has hired for our use, do I realize that Nadezhda wasn't trying to accuse me of having sex. She was just a little vexed, and for good reason: What happened? How could Farish Chaniago and Aruna Rai sit together in the same place for an extended period of time, alone, and not tear each other apart?

You tell me.

The annoying truth is that seeing Farish again has unhinged me. Since I met him in the lobby, my tongue has gone dry, as if we did something indecent the night before. Even though we didn't sleep together, there were moments during our conversation at the bar when I was dying to see the body beneath the blue-collared shirt.

Bono seems ignorant of it all. Typical chef. Typical man, for that matter! Just look at him: he's still reading off restaurant names from that sacred list of his, as if uttering them one by one will make him feel like he's been to them already. Still, I'm secretly relieved. It means Nadezhda hasn't mentioned the matter of my returning to the room so late.

And how about the princess herself? Is there any way of knowing? Look at that flawless face, the tip of its nose pressed lightly against the car window, as if she doesn't care about how the smog and scorching sun will distort her profile. (Because they won't.) Is there any way of knowing what's going on inside her ridiculously fine-formed head?

✦

There are those who get and those who give. There are those who eat in the morning and those who think about the morning.

Of the four of us, Nadezhda is the only one who always thinks up a reason for not eating breakfast. We heard her theory on the subject in Palembang the other day. Thus, no one forces her to join us in ordering something at the crowded restaurant we go to. Especially since they only serve one dish: Medanese soto—*Soto Medan*.

Here, old, young, poor, rich, Malay, Chinese, Bataknese, Javanese, Indian, pure Minangkabau (Farish), Balinese-Minangkabau (me), Chinese-Surabayan-Madurese (Bono), and French-Sundanese-Acehnese (Nadezhda) are united. People come on motorbikes and motorized *becaks*, by car and on foot, alone and in packs.

To the right of the entrance, a tall man behind a glass partition chops up meat and gizzards and puts them into large bowls. Behind him a woman with a cheerful face and a head scarf stirs the soto broth before ladling it into serving bowls. Meanwhile, a potbellied man scoops rice from a large tray onto orange melamine plates.

To the left of the entrance, a skinny man stands facing a table and wall made filthy by flecks of sweet soy sauce. He can't be more than fifty but moves like someone twice his age. Two enormous drums of *sambal kecap*, almost filled to overflowing, stand side by side along the wall. Next to them are rows of boxes and plates filled with *Perkedel Kentang*, a type of potato fritter, to be served to each guest.

The man stands there, humped, silent, looking dejected. But such is the fate of a soy-sauce station manager: his duty from dawn to dusk consists entirely of making sambal kecap and plonking it into small bowls arranged in rows across a table.

I feel bad for thinking this and therefore don't say anything, but if you ask me the broth's texture is neither here nor there, as if unsure whether it should be robust and full-bodied or colorless and light. The flavor of the spices, not to mention the aroma from the meat, fails to linger on the tongue, and the impression of overall dirtiness formed from the outset affects its taste.

Even Bono is quiet. Usually he's the one who feels compelled to defend restaurants that are liked by so many, even if their food is nothing special or tends toward the bad. His expression is that of a man wrestling with disappointment but too proud to show it.

After we finish eating, we return to our car parked by the side of the road. I give Farish's arm a deliberate poke. I don't want my awkwardness to continue. The longer I let it go on, the harder it will be for me to return to how things were.

"Hey," I say.

"Hey," he replies.

Is that a blush I see spreading across his cheeks?

But that's as far as my courage goes. I see Nadezhda glance briefly in our direction. Or maybe it's just my imagination.

In our respective confused states, Farish and I are almost oblivious to the fact that our two stowaways have conspired with the driver. He takes us to a fruit market. Nearby, on a street corner, is an eatery—one that has attained legendary status.

Secretly, I'm relieved that I don't have to make decisions—not about what to do with the bizarre avian flu cases and not about what kind of food is needed to erase the bitter taste of our first meal in this supposedly culinary city.

It's only ten o'clock, and almost all the tables in the place, no wider than the small porch at the entrance, are filled with customers. The husband and wife who own the restaurant are busy at their respective stations, and occasionally patrons throng them, wanting to settle their checks or watch them cook.

We decide to sit in a dining area sheltered by a white tent near a large tree. A low stone wall surrounds the tree trunk. A peddler selling Medanese oranges has placed his wares on the wall as he takes a break by the side of the road. For a moment I'm transfixed by the shape and color of the oranges, which, in such abundance, look so beautiful against the stone and the green of the leaves—not to mention the green of the plastic chairs we're sitting on.

"Kari bihun or wonton noodles?" It's Farish. His voice is back.

"Bro, come on," exclaims Bono. "Both, of course!" I've never seen him this ravenous, not even when we were in East Java. "A lot of Medanese friends tell me the wonton noodles are delicious. Even better than the famous noodles from that other roadside restaurant!"

"Better than the kari bihun?" asks Farish.

Bono waves his hand to attract a waiter's attention. "*Cik, cik*, over here!"

And the next thing we know he's ordered for all of us: four bowls of chicken kari bihun, which is rice vermicelli in curry sauce, and four bowls of wonton noodles.

What happens to us fifteen minutes later is a miracle.

And it is at that moment, as I'm letting the gloriously soft strands of rice vermicelli wrap themselves around my tongue—strands which have absorbed the curry's fragrance without letting the sauce overpower them—that I see Nadezhda's eyes fill with tears.

"What's wrong?"

I give her time to compose what she has to say. On an instinctive level I know what she's going through. I'm no writer, but I can understand how the most profound moments for someone who wrestles every day with words and with the nuts and bolts of taste would happen precisely when he or she encounters something whose beauty surpasses description.

"I've always loved quoting Brillat-Savarin—ever since I started writing about food," she says, at long last. "You know that. But, to be honest, it was only two years ago when I sat down and really read that magnificent book of his, *The Physiology of Taste*, that I began to internalize what I'd been parroting. I devoured every subject, every chapter, every section of every chapter, page by page. And only now do I truly understand that when he says 'the number of tastes is infinite,' he's really telling us how lucky we human beings are."

"So what are you saying?" asks Bono, already moving on to his bowl of wonton noodles. "That, from his perspective, the world has many tastes we don't yet know about? As if it's still holding out on its greatest treasures?"

"Ye-e-e-s . . . ," says Nadezhda. "But what I mean to say is this: which one of us could guess that a taste like this even existed? Take the vermicelli in this curry for instance. It's a taste we should be familiar with, that shouldn't be this astonishing. Nevertheless, we still have the capacity to be surprised. We're like, oh my God, where has this taste been all my life? Where have *I* been all my life? My point is, who hasn't eaten rice vermicelli, and who hasn't tried curry? But both in this particular combination? These *bihun* noodles . . . they just . . . they just . . . melt in your mouth. This *kari* sauce, too. I know nothing sounds stupider, coming from my mouth especially, but how else can you say it?"

At this point I half hope that the wonton noodles in front of us won't be as good as our kari bihun. How could they possibly be? If all the pleasures of this world were to be found in one kitchen, where would be the justice in that?

Turns out I've been let down. Let down by life, which insists, in this instance at least, on defying the laws of nature. Disappointed because at this hour, on this day, the god of ambrosia wants to slip into these pale-blue melamine bowls on the table as well, into the soupy wonton noodles that resemble a study in accents—the crisp brown skin of the meat, the green of the scallions, the fire of the sliced chili peppers, the pink of the pickled shallots.

Unfortunately, miracles often produce hubris in both those who enjoy them (Bono) and those who are made happy by them (Farish). I say this because after Nadezhda and I pay the cashier, we return to the car to discover those two have disappeared. For several minutes, Nadezhda and I stand there by the car, confused.

"Feli always warned me," Nadezhda fumes. "Medan is the rottenest place on earth!" I don't know who Feli is, nor do I care, but before I ask, Nadezhda quotes her: "'Drivers in Medan are a mess. Their brains don't function. Either that, or they're crooks. They promise to pick you up, and they arrive late. Or they don't show up at all. They promise they'll wait here, and they wait there. They promise you one price and demand another.'"

I'm always irritated by such generalizations. Nadezhda herself likes to say that she hates "essentialism." But I let her continue grumbling like an old woman.

Then I see them: two eateries across the road, side by side. One serves rice porridge, and the other is resplendent, with illustrated bowls of chicken noodles on a banner beneath its signboard. I remember that the restaurant is on Bono's list.

I grab Nadezhda's arm. "Come on," I say, "I know where those two rascals are."

And sure enough, the moment we enter, I see them slurping on their chicken noodles. There are no other customers in the clean, air-conditioned restaurant. They grin sheepishly when seeing us, like two kids who've been caught playing hooky to pig out all day.

I make a point of not saying anything. I just sit down next to Bono and watch him eat.

"This place can't be as good as the restaurant across the street," I say finally. "I'm right, aren't I?"

"Ha!" Bono says, giving me a hug by way of apology. "Eating things that aren't really good is also part of doing research. Only in this way can we continually sharpen our palates."

"Yes, but there's no way you came here hoping that the quality of the food would be lower than that incredible restaurant where we just ate."

"Of course. What do you take me for?" he says, still grinning stupidly. "I mean, how could I be wrong? *Me!* I'm never wrong. Frankly, when I first saw those wonton noodles at that restaurant, I was dog-gone certain they couldn't be all that good, no matter how delicious the broth. You could have told as much from the giant photos out front! The noodles were the curly yellow kind. And so thick! You know me. I always believe that the thinner the noodle, the more easily it absorbs broth and seasoning. So, when we got here and I saw that the curly noodles they use are thinner, I got carried away. But I suppose this kind of thing could be misleading."

"You've never liked curly noodles," says Nadezhda. "I knew it. You were biased from the start."

"Yes, but I have my reasons. People always tend to focus too much on the kind of noodles, rather than assessing how the dish tastes as a whole. But curly noodles, for instance, can also be very good. I mean, look at the majority of noodles in Jakarta's Chinatown. They're awesome."

It's my turn to smile. If ever there were a reason for Bono's downfall, it would be this. After all, he's Bono. From the way a dish looks, he can imagine how it will taste, from when the food is still in his mouth to when the food has reached the back of his mouth and the food's aroma and taste have begun to envelope his nose and taste buds in their entirety. Sometimes he can even anticipate how he will feel after the fact, when he's ruminating about said food. To him, admitting he's wrong is as bad as confessing he's impotent.

But I'm completely unprepared for the toothy smile Farish suddenly throws my way.

"I think this tastes good, too," he says. "The only reason I can't finish it is because I'm full."

And my heart goes all soft and gooey, just like that.

18

Conspiracy

Shortly afterward we find our driver. Turns out, he dozed off after eating lunch at a nearby warung. We immediately agree that we should drive around for a bit, to take advantage of the fact that we have a car. The hospital we're headed to is some distance away from the city center, and I worry that if we hurry over we won't have time to get a full impression of Medan.

After summoning my courage, I poke Farish's arm again. He looks at me.

"Hey, where's that file?"

I'm all coy. I mean, of course I am. We were able to spend almost three and a half hours talking to each other last night without once touching on the subject of work, and now . . . and now, work calls. And here we are.

He rummages around in his bag for a few minutes, as if only now reminded of its existence. Then he produces a transparent folder full of documents.

"How serious is this case?" I ask.

His eyes pierce mine in that way again—they don't belong to the Farish I know, but to someone who, heaven forbid, *cares*—and for a moment I feel wobbly. The memory of being on the veranda of Mr. Zachri's house returns once more, rolling over me like a wave.

"From the most recent report I received via e-mail early this morning, it seems like it's under control." As he speaks he points to the report, trying to sound all businesslike. "But it might be good to interview the patient and hospital staff anyway and take a look at the place where the patient lives."

His tone gives the impression of something going slack—like a pact he's made that he no longer has faith in. How often do I see a similar fatigue in my colleagues' faces at the Ministry, at DOCIR, at OneWorld. How difficult it is to live life and continue to have faith.

I quickly read over the report. The suspected avian flu victim—initials: J. T.; age: thirty-five; a resident of Seribu Dolok; subdistrict: Silimakuta; regency: Simalungun—was rushed to the large referral hospital in Medan four days ago. At one point his temperature reached a high of almost 104 degrees Fahrenheit, with a blood pressure reading of 110/80.

The head of Avian Flu Eradication and Control at the hospital (Prof. Dr. H. L. S.) said the patient's condition stabilized after he underwent treatment in an isolation room. Beforehand, not too far from the victim's house, a dead chicken was found. When workers from Simalungun's Department of Cultivation conducted an examination, they found the chicken was indeed infected with avian flu.

"Finally," I say. "Some good news."

"I hear the hospital we're headed to isn't bad at all," says Farish, though his voice is still tired. "It's a general hospital. But the facilities are okay, procedure is strict, and the doctors are professional."

"It also has efficient channels of communication with other hospitals," I say. "Meaning whenever patients are sick, they immediately take them to the referral hospital rather than letting them stay overnight in a crummy one. It's great."

"But there's still one problem."

"And that is?"

"The details of this case are exactly the same as those of another case six years back. The location is the same. The symptoms are the same. Only the initials of the patient's name are different. The patients' ages are the same, too."

The hairs on the back of my neck suddenly stand on end.

"Which means," Farish says, lowering his voice, "there are four possibilities. One: the cause of the virus is the same, which means the local Department of Cultivation didn't do their job properly or thoroughly enough. Two: someone is falsifying the reports. Three: someone accidentally gave us the wrong report. Four: by extraordinary coincidence, the two cases are practically the same."

It seems the car ride will never end. Meanwhile, I receive news from Talisa back at the office in Jakarta. This time nobody from the local office of the Ministry will be accompanying us.

"They're short-staffed," says Talisa, her voice sounding funny. Maybe it's because she unsuspectingly picked up when I dialed her extension at the desk she keeps at the Ministry, and now it's too late to avoid my call. "After all, now that the patient is showing signs of recovery, this isn't technically an avian flu case anymore."

"What? Since when?"

"Since when what?"

"Since when is a positive case of avian flu not considered an avian flu case? Even if it's being dealt with, what does it matter?"

Talisa's voice sounds increasingly nervous.

Suddenly I hear her whisper, "I can't talk long . . ."

I stiffen.

"I don't know what's going on," Talisa continues, still whispering, "but it looks like you guys are going to be asked to return soon."

"What?"

"I don't know for sure, but word is they're going to send another team in a little bit."

"Says who?"

"That's just what I've heard."

"What does Irma say? I haven't heard from her at all."

Talisa sounds as if she's swallowing, a very strange noise indeed.

"Really?" she says. "Irma hasn't told you anything?"

"Lis," I say, beginning to panic. "We've been friends for a long time. What is going on?"

"A lot has been happening in the office these past three days," whispers Talisa. "Confidential meetings with outside parties, people from Proto Medis and a bunch of people who look like they're from B. S. Incorporated, and reporters who've sneaked in that we're ignoring. They say all they want is an interview. Some of them just sit here from morning to night. There are people here from the CEC, too. And the National Audit Board. It's madness."

"How about Irma? How's she responding to all this?"

But Talisa doesn't seem to hear my question. Or she pretends not to.

"You know about the document, right?" she whispers.

"What document?" I ask, my pulse quickening. "You mean the secret terms of reference document? The unofficial one that everyone is talking about?"

Once, when Priya, a bunch of other friends from R&D, and I were eating lunch in the DOCIR cafeteria, some DOCIR employees came and joined us. I didn't know all of them. There was someone from the Bureau of Law and Organization, the Bureau of Logistics, and the inspector general's office. They seemed to be mad about something and whispered to each other about a confidential document 139 pages long that had been compiled around mid-2008. Its contents: "a funding proposal for equipment to construct facilities in support of the supply committee for the human vaccine project." Which is as bogus as bogus gets, but has a ring of plausibility. It was rumored that all the pages were initialed by a high-ranking executive at Proto Medis.

Now, several months later, I'm hearing that DOCIR hid the documents when the Finance Audit Board paid a visit.

"And that's the problem," Talisa confirms. "Now, last I heard, the documents have fallen into the hands of a bunch of reporters."

"For real?" I say. "From what newspaper? What magazine?"

"Dunno," says Talisa. "One thing's for sure. Irma's in a bind. As DOCIR's unofficial PR person, she's responsible for all communication with the media."

I feel faint. The question is on the tip of my tongue: Will Irma be made the scapegoat? But I'm afraid to voice it for fear it'll become reality.

"I'll try to contact her," I say at last.

Dead silence. I can almost hear Talisa holding her breath.

"Listen," she says after a few moments, "maybe it's best to let Irma contact you."

What the fuck is she hiding from me?

Through the car window, Medan goes by as if in a dream. The bad and the good intertwine, then separate, then are joined once more: the castles of the nouveau riche, garish beyond all measure; the campaign ads for the upcoming gubernatorial elections, rabble-rousing and yet the subject of censure and derision by the rabble themselves; the signs marking district branches of the thuggish Pancasila Youth, whose orange-and-black-striped uniforms seem to be popping up everywhere; the serene boulevards bequeathed to us by Europe, which continues to leave its mark on its former colonial possessions.

At last, Irma contacts me, but not through WhatsApp or BlackBerry Messenger. I'm guessing she doesn't want to feel pressured to respond immediately, since both apps show whether the recipient has read a message or not. I'm also guessing she doesn't want me monitoring her, since both apps also show whether a person is typing.

Hi Aruna. Are you in Medan yet? That's her text message. Not Run, or Runi. But Aruna.

Hi! Medan's amazing! Esp. the areas w lots of Dutch colonial bldgs!

For some reason I refrain from talking about food, though it's a dynamic we have that's long been in place. I don't want her to think I'm having fun on company time.

Yes. There's city hall, the water tower, the Titi Gantung Bridge . . .

That's another thing about Irma: unlike your usual government functionary, she's a history buff. Every time we go to Chinatown in Jakarta in search of food, she always takes me walking through the streets around Fatahillah Square. She's even taken me to the Wayang Museum, the Museum of Fine Arts and Ceramics, the Fatahillah Museum, the Kedai Seni Djakarte—an art café whose art and caféness are of equally minimal quality—and breathtaking old buildings that are now, sadly, dilapidated, half debris, some with their roofs blown off.

Then another text message from her appears, like an afterthought or a guilty missive: *The buildings near Jalan Kumango. Very lovely indeed.*

A moment passes. Five minutes. Ten. Fifteen.

I'm not sure whether I should wait for her to touch on the problems at DOCIR first. I've just begun to type something when suddenly I receive a message: *I've read your last report about the patient in Palembang . . .*

My heart races. Do the dots indicate that she hasn't finished typing and that she's going to continue, or do they indicate the typer's wariness about the recipient? Once again, I wait.

Six minutes later, I receive another message: *I've just met with the head of DOCIR. I'm so sorry, Run, but they've requested that your team discontinue the investigation for now.*

❧

What's been going on in Jakarta while we've been away? Isn't DOCIR counting on the results of our team's investigation? What caused Irma to hastily switch off her phone when I tried to call after she didn't reply to my response to her last text? Why didn't she want to be honest with me about us being pulled off the investigation? Was there a direct connection between this decision and the report I sent about Zachri Musa?

When I raise these questions, as if to myself, it's Farish who responds. "Maybe there really is a connection."

"What do you mean?"

"Stay calm," he says. "Try to remember the gist of your report."

My mind is in chaos, but I know exactly what it was: the patient died because none of the medical personnel he encountered over the course of his life had enough knowledge about different illnesses, much less how to treat them. Not only that—they didn't have enough sense or responsibility to arrange any further investigations into the patient's condition. They didn't consult fellow doctors or specialists. And they definitely didn't read up on research or recent findings in the world of medicine. So when the patient exhibited symptoms similar to those of a virus receiving so much attention, they simplified the situation and brought their diagnosis in line.

My crime was that I didn't say what the people who sent me into the field needed me to say. I didn't say, "Yes, it may be possible that the case in Palembang indicates an outbreak, and we should be on our guard." And I didn't say it for any of the previous cases either.

There's a tightness in my chest. I recall a friend who married young—whose first child was born with a cleft palate. The baby cried

190

continuously, loudly, as if she had colic. But her pediatrician wasn't in the least concerned. "Just keep breastfeeding as normal. This really isn't that unusual." That's what the pediatrician told my friend.

A week passed, and though my friend had been diligent in breast-feeding, her child suddenly began losing weight, to the point that they had to return to the hospital and put her in an incubator.

Everyone in my friend's life was powerless to help. Her husband was working out of town at the time, and her mother and mother-in-law had both come down with a bad flu and were worried about infecting their already frail granddaughter. Everyone blamed my friend. Her family believed she wasn't nursing the child properly. So did the pediatrician. They thought she was too young to be a mother, that she didn't know the meaning of responsibility.

One day, she called me to ask which doctor she should see. Because she'd had a cesarean, she still needed a few more days to completely recover. She was so weak, she couldn't do research and was made helpless by all the stress. "My child weighs only four pounds," she said, sobbing. "The doctors say she probably won't make it. Please, Run. Help me. Maybe you can ask around at other hospitals. Ask if they have a unit dedicated to treating cleft lips and palates."

Back then the Internet didn't dominate life. People weren't used to the luxury, or necessity, of looking up information on Google before even making an appointment to see a doctor. It was an era when the various specialty units in a hospital weren't interconnected, and a pediatrician had no way to communicate directly with an orthodontist or ENT if a patient had a cleft palate—an era when even a pediatrician didn't understand that the field of oral surgery had already developed new tools and technology easily able to overcome the difficulty of feeding an infant with a hole in the roof of her mouth. There was no need to unwittingly kill a child.

As it turned out, the right tool did exist—a German-made bottle with a nipple designed especially for such babies. The bottle was available at a clinic in Jakarta specializing in cleft lips and palates, at a private hospital, in a unit founded in conjunction with a Japanese university.

I'd heard about the clinic when I ran into my gynecologist at a seminar on public health services. When I told her about my friend's troubling situation, my gynecologist immediately got in touch with her colleague, an orthodontist, who had just been involved in the clinic's establishment.

"Why hasn't news of this clinic been disseminated among pediatricians?" I asked.

"I wish," said my gynecologist. "But that's the way it is in this country. There's so much to be depressed about."

The moment my friend arrived at the clinic with her baby, they immediately began feeding the infant from the special yellow-colored bottle. The tiny creature kept sucking nonstop, as if she had never drunk anything in her entire life. And, as it happened, for the first ten days of her existence, the baby hadn't drunk a single drop from her mother's breasts, which had deflated quickly. Like busted tires. For ten days she had been suckling on air.

Every time I think of my brave friend and her baby, I'm plunged into a deep sorrow. I think of how fragile human life is when people still have to rely so much on good fortune and not on a system that they can trust. Where all that brings goodness and improvement—science, doctors, hospitals, teachers, schools—isn't always accessible. Imagine my joy then, that I, a mere layperson, was able to save someone in that tangled mass of widespread ignorance and obliviousness.

But this time there is nothing laypersonish, much less coincidental, about either my position or my situation.

I'm someone who possesses competency in my field, someone who should have an interest in bringing about improvement. I'm a part of the system, not one of the many people whose brains aren't used to thinking in clinical terms. I don't cite stress and that folk nonsense about "wind in the body" as the root of all maladies. I'm a part of a system far worse than the one that nearly killed an innocent baby thirteen years ago. It's far worse—not because it can't be accessed, but because it's so grand and impressive in appearance, and in reality, so false.

19

SHRINES, KITSCH, AND TREACHERY

The shrine was truly miraculous. I've experienced things that look both authentic and fake before, kitsch in all its forms: houses in Pondok Indah with statues of Roman soldiers and Apache chiefs flanking each other on their front lawns; apartment buildings near the Grand Sahid Jaya Hotel with absurd ancient Greek columns; Venetian canals, replete with a gondola fleet, in the middle of a shopping mall in Kelapa Gading; gaudy building facades trying to outshine each other, shouting, "Look at me! I'm even more gorgeous than the real thing!" But never in my life have I encountered anything like the Graha Maria Annai Velangkanni.

How was it again that Farish and I ended up there? I have a dim recollection of the driver insisting we make a pilgrimage to the place he called the eighth wonder of the world. And suddenly, here I am, in the backyard of a Hindu-Tamil-style Catholic shrine visibly eager to impress, alone with Farish, a mere stone's throw away from a statue of Jesus.

This Jesus looks very much like the Jesus in the Catholic comic book series that made the rounds back when I was in elementary school. Caucasian, with wavy golden hair, Jesus sits peacefully in a park surrounded by five children who represent different ethnicities and races.

There's a black child, an Asian child, a Caucasian child, an Indian child, and, I think, a Hispanic child. I can't be sure because the child who I'm guessing is Hispanic has its arms around Jesus's neck and its back facing us. And I say "it" because for the life of me, I can't tell whether the child is a boy or a girl.

Not too far away there's a water faucet and a blue-painted wooden cross. Above the faucet is a handwritten notice:

ATTENTION
To PREVENT WASTAGE OF HOLY WATER,
DO NOT WASH YOUR FACE/HANDS/FEET
DIRECTLY UNDERNEATH THE FAUCET.
FILL YOUR BOTTLE AND USE THE WATER FROM THERE.

THANK YOU FOR YOUR ATTENTION AND COOPERATION.

Nobody is paying the slightest notice. Visitors are still washing their faces, hands, and feet directly underneath the tap rather than using the empty juice bottles they've brought—unique juices Medan is famous for, squeezed from the *kietna* and *martabe*, the *terong Belanda* and *kesturi*. They fill these bottles—and not just one or two of them, but several—only after they're done washing . . . you guessed it. Directly underneath the tap.

The story goes that this enormous shrine, reminiscent in shape of a cheerful-looking Indian temple, was built in 2001 under the initiative of an Indonesian pastor. He is said to have been inspired by a vision of the Virgin Mary that occurred during the sixteenth century in a faraway coastal village in Southern India. The signs throughout the religious complex, in turn situated within a housing complex, attempt to convince us that this is a perfect replica of the original grotto.

I'm skeptical. How could a grotto in a poor village on the Bay of Bengal be transformed into a three-billion-and-seven-tiered structure with two stupas on the fourth floor, one stupa atop a tower, and two winding paths on either side of it like the ones surrounding the rollercoaster at Fantasy World?

What have I actually been reporting to DOCIR? I think about the cases so far. Only two of the five reported incidents have been genuine avian flu. Not much to suggest an epidemic at all.

"Can't they wait until we finish surveying all the sites?"

To my surprise, Farish smiles. He doesn't seem upset at all. In his gaze there's even something bordering on relief.

"Maybe it's better this way," he says. "What's the point of us working so hard if they have such a clear political agenda?"

They. He doesn't think this is my fault at all.

"What political agenda?" I ask.

"Come on," he says. "We both know what's really going on, don't we? SoWeFit *needs* empirical evidence that there's an avian flu outbreak going on. Think about it. B. S. Incorporated and the higher-ups at Proto Medis could blow the whistle anytime on which Ministry officials they bribed, especially given the fact that the media is calling attention to the most serious offense in the whole affair—the Ministry's conspicuous absence when it came to submitting a budget to the House of Representatives.

"The consequences are no laughing matter. It's a violation of the law. Furthermore, Government Regulation 21/2004, regarding the Preparation of Work Plans and Budgets by Government Ministries and Agencies, states that all work plans must be drawn up even before the budget is okayed. And that's why they have to keep going with the human vaccine factory. SoWeFit will have, *must* have, empirical evidence that the fate of mankind rests in the hands of birdkind in order to justify their position to the House of Representatives later. As long as we're not providing that kind of evidence, DOCIR has no use for us."

"But who knows what we'll find in Aceh? Or Pontianak?"

"No way, my dear," says Farish. "No matter what we find, our analysis of the situation is definitely tending toward the negative already—that is, the danger of an outbreak is nowhere near any cause for alarm."

In front of us a pair of teenagers are making out behind the statue of Jesus. Then they take turns washing their faces below the faucet dispensing holy water. The holy water is looking increasingly murky.

"Anyway," Farish continues, "who says the cases we've been sent to investigate haven't been made up? This case in Medan, for example. It's obviously a bogus case. I bet DOCIR is asking us to stop now because they don't want to take any more risks. They've probably just realized that you're a true idealist, that you can't be paid off. Or, if you're not idealistic, that you're naïve."

When Farish says "DOCIR," he clearly means "Irma." But, as I keep saying, I like Irma. I feel like I know her outside the constraints imposed on her by her job. My relationship with her is more than just professional. And for this reason, Irma's treachery, so subtle, so spectacular, leaves me speechless.

Could she really have misread me so? Could she really have sent me here, hoping I would understand the results she wanted, even if she was too elegant to spell them out for me? Who are my friends? Who are my allies? I don't know anymore. Nor do I know why, all of a sudden, without any warning, I've been lumped into the same category as a guy I used to find so annoying.

"How about you?" I ask in a slightly defensive tone. "We're the same, aren't we? Equally idealistic? Naïve, even? After all, we've been given the same assignment."

"The difference between you and me," says Farish, "is that I know about all the shady things that have been going on. I've known for a long time. But I don't care." He follows this up with a laugh. "I'm kidding," he says. "I *do* care."

It is a strange, lucid moment. Maybe now we can be friends.

He's being sweet, but I feel genuinely bitter about all this. And scared. The thought of us having to return to Jakarta like soldiers defeated in battle is giving me stomach cramps. No, wait. This is worse. There is something heroic and poetic about war—and a lot of it has to do with how victory and defeat are determined by fate. But this—this is about something else entirely. This is about letting those in the wrong freely determine who will suffer defeat.

"Hey," says Farish, his tone more serious. "Sorry. I shouldn't make light of this. To be honest, I've been wanting to remove myself from DOCIR for a long while now. I've talked to Darius about it several times—asked him to cut me loose from all DOCIR-related projects and put me back in wildlife conservation. But it's like he just doesn't get it. Apart from leaving OneWorld, what choice do I have?"

"What are Darius's reasons?" I ask. Darius Sinaga is the director at OneWorld who handles wildlife conservation and forestry. My interactions with him are few and far between.

Farish grins. He has nice teeth. A bit big, but nice. It's the first time I've really noticed.

"He keeps saying he needs people he can trust—there are too many politics involved when it comes to avian flu matters."

This trust, I'm convinced, is more out of friendship than anything else. Farish and Darius have been pals for ages; they've been in the NGO world together since they graduated from college. Where there's Darius, there's Farish. So whatever Farish decides to do after this, his position at OneWorld is safe. If he insists on having nothing to do with DOCIR, it's fine; he'll still have his job at OneWorld.

Me, on the other hand? Me, the "outbreak expert" who relies on outbreaks to stay employed?

Is this what Irma meant when she spoke about the Farishes of the world? The people in the business world—in the "professional" world—who'll always stick around because they're part of a firmly established network of friends? In the meantime, the Arunas of the world drift around like loose, directionless kites, having never known the meaning of home—unless the term applies to a house of free spirits.

"Remember, kid," my father said a few weeks before he died. "You get as much as you give."

"But?" I ask. Farish's comment still hangs in the air.

"But?" he repeats. "There is no 'but.' I really don't like being involved in this project. DOCIR clearly has an interest in ensuring the continuation of the vaccine project, and that goes against my conscience. Them stopping this investigation is more a blessing than anything else. Like God's giving me a way out."

Now he's bringing God into it—probably because we're in front of a shrine dedicated to the miraculous.

In the background, I hear Nadezhda yakking. It's getting closer. Is she chattering away or pontificating? (With her it's difficult to tell where one begins and the other ends.) Bono doesn't seem to mind—as usual he's indulging her with a similar degree of enthusiasm.

"But this is different from kitsch. Kitsch is about showing the reproduction is more authentic, more awe-inspiring, more worthy of admiration than the original. In so assuming, it exaggerates the original until we find ourselves convinced of the greatness of the past. But this shrine is different. This is pure tastelessness, pure common ignorance."

"I see things a little differently," I say suddenly. For the first time since that liquid night, I gaze deep into Farish's eyes. "I don't object to a factory that will produce human vaccines."

Farish seems startled.

I keep talking. "What I object to is the process. What I object to is collusion between private parties, whoever they are—Proto Medis, parliamentarians, or ministerial bureaucrats. But I don't disagree with the science behind it. Or its urgency."

"You've said it yourself. There's no urgency yet."

"Yes, but I am a scientist," I say. "If you ask me, it's always better to take preventive measures rather than reactive ones. If we really do have the infrastructure and technology, and the funds as well, then why shouldn't we prepare well in advance? Think of it as an investment for the future."

Seems like it's his turn to be dumbfounded. I move in for the kill.

"You can't tame a virus, Farish," I say. "They're small, they're patient, and quietly, they multiply. Nobody keeps track of how old they are—but they never forget. One day they'll come for us. They'll attack. And we're powerless. We won't be able to offer any defense."

❦

"We're going back to Jakarta tomorrow?"

"Oh man! So what are we supposed to do with this list?"

The car drives around aimlessly. The city is like a montage: fish markets, the Sinar Aquarium, a row of Indian restaurants next to Sun Plaza, the famous restaurant Simpang Tiga (also known as "happiness"). There's the textile district, where you can find fashionable Muslim-wear, traditional Sumatran garb, holy water, and dates from Mecca; stores selling machines and appliances; the automobile and electronics repair stores all along Jalan Pandu, followed by the Indian quarter, known as the Kampung Madras district. Soon we are cruising along streets lined with florists who specialize in funeral wreaths, the kind where the flowers are toothpicked into elaborate patterns on enormous boards. We turn into an area where the street signs for the narrow roads in downtown Medan all start with *lorong* or "alley" and remind me of the roads in Singapore's Geylang district. We see pleasant tree-lined boulevards bearing the names of Javanese cities or national heroes, and colonial Dutch buildings softened but by no means enfeebled by cobwebs and dust.

I never thought Bono and Nadezhda would be this upset about the prospect of leaving.

"But, Run," says Bono, "there are so many restaurants we still have to try . . . if we want to go to that famous bihun bebek place we have to go early in the day. The same goes for the Medan-style *Kwetiau Goreng* place, too. And then there's that barbecued pork restaurant we just *have* to visit—they're usually completely sold out by noon. Not to mention the restaurants all along Jalan Selat Panjang. We didn't get a chance to sample anything last night except for that incredible nasi campur. I can't leave Medan without trying all the different kinds of bakmi."

"Excuse me," Nadezhda says irritably. "I was hoping to go to Lake Toba while you two were busy at the hospital. I'd hoped to experience more than just restaurants . . . I wanted to check out all the nooks and crannies, to see how the locals themselves cook, the spices they use, their views on the staple foods of their surroundings."

"I wanted to do all that, too, Nadz," I say, my sadness genuine. "But my work is the only reason we're here, after all."

Nadezhda doesn't seem to hear me. "A friend was telling me about *Naniura*—Lake Toba's version of ceviche. It sounds like an interesting dish—more than just a traditional food unwittingly perceived as 'modern' on the other side of the world. It also has an important social function. In fact, it plays an important part in traditional ceremonies, like Maksuba cakes do in Palembang—"

Farish interrupts. "Actually, there's nothing forcing us to go back." His tone is light, casual. And I like that he's looking at me, not at Nadezhda. "Let's just stay in Medan another day. Go to Lake Toba. Or to Pematangsiantar for some fried paddy squab. And when we're done, let's just keep going anyway and wander around Banda Aceh,

Pontianak, Singkawang, and Mataram. We have an eating agenda, don't we? And we can't let your friends down after they've come all this way."

The possibility never even crossed my mind. But it's true that there's nothing in my contract with SoWeFit that says I have to put an end to anything as long as I don't claim any expenses once the project has been discontinued—especially in this case, since SoWeFit was the party who hired me and drew up the terms of my employment. As a consultant who gets paid by the day, one might say that I'm the one who's losing out.

I don't know the details of Farish's terms of employment. He probably has a lot of days left on his current contract with OneWorld, and as such is still getting his pay for this project from OneWorld, not SoWeFit. But because the project is being cut short, it might work out if he takes a few days of impromptu leave before returning to Jakarta. Anyway, his job is safe, as evidenced by him being so calm, and desirous, even, to speedily extricate himself from the project.

The prospect of continuing our eating mission without being burdened by work makes me feel relieved. There's just one thing. I should hurry up and e-mail Talisa—ask her to forward a letter from me officially stating that I'll compensate DOCIR for the full cost of all the flights they've already paid for from this point on. And I should send an e-mail to Diva, my supervisor at OneWorld, saying that I want to take a short leave of absence.

Suddenly I realize there's a good chance I'll never work at DOCIR again—never have lunch with Irma, just the two of us, while we discuss the conflict between public professional roles and private life, or where to find the most delicious *Bakso Lohwa* in the Tangerang district or the most mouthwatering *Sambal Kecombrang* in Jakarta, or even being willing to make sacrifices for our work, despite how polluted it's been by greedy hands.

I ask Farish why he's still proposing that we visit the hospital.

"Idle curiosity can be useful," he says.

And what was it that made me say yes? When we arrive at the hospital, we don't even try to meet with the people we should have met, those whose names are listed on the itinerary that Talisa put together a week ago. We're not here to look for anything or see anyone. Maybe we've come for the sole purpose of honoring what we said we would do. We don't want to betray ourselves.

Funny that Nadezhda and Bono are dead set on coming with us. They seem to take our misfortune as a blow to them as well. Or else they feel responsible, too. Maybe. Or maybe they have nothing better to do.

On the way to the hospital, which is some distance from the city center, we pass that famous Medanese institution, Kedai Durian Ucok. The driver immediately slows our car down and asks if we want to stop by. Durians are cheap right now because they're in season, he says. It might be as low as 15,000 to 20,000 rupiah per fruit.

From where I sit in the car, all I can see are piles of durians. They fill the little kiosk and the area around it. It's unclear whether you're supposed to just buy them and leave or if you can eat them there.

I'm not a durian fanatic, but I'm also not a durian hater. Something in this riles Nadezhda. She accused me once of being abnormal. "A person can't be neutral when it comes to durians, Aruna," she said in an admonishing voice. But it's clear to me that with regard to fruit, people like Nadezhda are no different from, say, Suharto or Bush. Either you're with us or you're against us. That's how they see the world.

"Or we could stop here on the way back from the hospital," the driver suggests, confused by our lack of response. "If you don't know how to choose a good one, the staff can help you. Just tell them if you like your durians sweet-sweet or bittersweet. They have all kinds."

Now why is Bono suddenly so quiet? Isn't this place also on his sacred list?

Just imagine. What justice there would be in the world if we discovered a secret shed behind this hospital filled with actors who've been paid by this company or that to pretend they were on their deathbeds infected with avian flu! What sweet revenge if I could interview them one by one and upload the videos to YouTube!

And with that, the web of collusion that surrounds the politics of vaccine production would be swept away, all thanks to me—that's right, *me*—a tiny cog in the larger system that they failed to take into account.

But no chance of that. Instead, the hospital is exemplary for a medical institution outside the capital. It's almost sickeningly well organized and well run. When I arrive at the isolation room dedicated to infectious diseases, I'm both annoyed and relieved to see that it's locked tight and that the security guard pacing back and forth in front of it asks us what we're doing there.

Somehow, I feel like something's been salvaged from this world of mine as it falls apart.

20

Selat Panjang

In my dream I see a young woman behind a bar. The bar is inside an exclusive club for rich men. The woman is pretty, but not too pretty; sexy, but not too sexy; and in her eyes there is sadness, or terror—sometimes it's hard to tell where one begins and the other ends.

From her brief conversation with the bartender, I learn a number of things about her. She's from Yogyakarta. She's the oldest daughter of five siblings. She's come to Jakarta to earn money and help her family support her younger siblings, three of them still in school. And she's just come down from one of the club's rooms—"Mr. R. F.'s," she says, her cheeks suddenly a bright red—carrying dirty dishes and glasses.

The bartender appears to be interested in the woman without really paying any attention to her. Perhaps, like many men, he's too used to looking without ever really seeing. "Oh, Mr. R. F.," he says lightly. "He's been coming here for a long time. He's a bit of a mystery—not like the others. But he's polite. And not stingy."

The woman looks down at the ground, yet her eyes are shining. Then she hurries away and heads toward the kitchen. But before she gets there, she stops at a deserted, partially enclosed spot where there used to be a cash register. After glancing to the right and to the left to make sure that she hasn't been followed, she slowly puts down the tray. Then, with trembling hands, she picks up one of the dirty glasses and raises it to her lips. There are still one or two drops left, whiskey by the look of it, but she doesn't seem to care what it is—she sucks it down. I see her eyes narrow, her tongue slowly dancing on the rim of the glass. Sometimes it moves; sometimes it stops. Sometimes she kisses, licks, and sucks on it as she would a lover's lips. Every now and then, I see her moan.

I'm so stunned that I almost don't see the bartender appear behind her. Unexpectedly, he puts his arms around her waist.

"So . . . ," says the bartender. "You're imagining you're kissing him, are you?"

The woman tries to free herself. But he's too strong.

"It's a secret, eh? This unrequited love?"

Again, she gives no answer.

"Let me guess. He's never asked you to sleep with him, but you know he sleeps with other women. Meanwhile, here you are, lusting after him. So you're devouring that glass of his instead."

Her face is pale.

"How about this? I'll help you keep your secret. But you have to sleep with me. I guarantee you'll be hooked."

He tightens his hold around her waist. His hands begin to grope at her firm, full breasts.

Suddenly the glass comes down and puts a hole in the bartender's forehead. Blood sprays all over every surface, including the woman's face and clothes, before he finally topples to the floor.

Ten seconds pass, then twenty, before the woman calmly stoops down over the pool of blood and picks up what's left of the glass.

❦

On the way back from the hospital, we stop at Jalan Selat Panjang. Night has fallen, the streets are bathed in light. Old buildings stand at the road's entrance, shadowy and marvelous in the great auto repair garage of the present. The entire street, from start to end, is made up entirely of eateries—rows and rows of them.

For a while, walking is akin to dreaming: the plumes of smoke and steam from barbecues and simmering vats of broth that penetrate the luminescent shophouse lights; the mad rush of customers and food vendors calling out to one another; the booths crammed with hot-water thermoses and canned and bottled beverages; a lively assortment of vegetables, herbs, meats, and eggs, of dumplings, buns, and noodles, of sweets of every kind. Magazine and pirated DVD hawkers scurry in and out of restaurants; they are joined by swarms of small children selling durian pancakes. In the street, the motorcycles and motorized becaks jostle for space with vendors and pedestrians, leaving them in constellations of dust.

Nadezhda speaks, a dazed look on her face. "Joseph Conrad once wrote about 'inhabited desolation.' But this is more like inhabited chaos."

For a while we just walk, not yet willing or able to decide where we want to eat. All smells, sounds, and colors offer themselves up for contemplation and consideration.

Bono stops at a *bakpau* stand a little farther away from the activity. "All right, cik! Give me five jumbo meat buns, five red-bean buns, six lotus-paste buns, and six pork buns."

Nadezhda snaps dozens of photos: the *langsat* yellow of the buildings in the lamplight; the faces that peep out from behind room windows on the upper floors of the shophouses; details of a restaurant's wooden frame and antique doors. We stare at eels and fish, still thrashing around in their bowls, and live frogs in buckets on the floor, eyes bulging in terror.

Farish. Where is he? Ah, over there, busy chatting on his phone and every once in a while drawing near a glass display case of food to study its contents, half amazed, half bewildered.

We end up eating at two places in succession: a restaurant specializing in Hainanese chicken rice, even though it's Bono's and Nadezhda's second time there, and a restaurant that serves Hokkien noodles. As with the curry paradise of that morning, we agree unanimously that the sensations we experience in both places transcend language.

"If it goes on like this," says Bono, gazing deep into the fishballs, prawns, wontons, and ground-meat mixture garnishing his Hokkien noodles, "wouldn't it all become boring? Even perfection gets dull after a while, doesn't it?"

"Not everyone is as excitable as we are," says Nadezhda. "We're like this because we think about what to eat. To us it's not just food. Whereas most of the people here—I mean, just look at them. They love what they're eating, sure. But it's not an . . . oh, I don't know. It's not an experience to them."

Nadezhda's right. In Jakarta it's not like a good *Ketoprak* here or *Asinan* there leaves us breathless anymore. For us, they've become the norm. And with the formation of a norm, the subject becomes hardened. Today we are at once happy and shaken, because experience has just demonstrated that we have yet to attain the furthest limits of knowledge. Or more precisely, experience has shown us such limits don't exist.

Feeling the uncomfortable ache of my belt digging into my waist, I lean back in my chair and stare at the ceiling fan. Irma's betrayal still plagues my mind. *When will she stop playing this game of hide-and-seek?*

Faintly, I hear Bono urging us to go to a place that allegedly serves the city's best *Tiong Sim* noodles. "If we don't eat there, we haven't been to Medan," he tells us with a sense of ownership that is rather touching.

"Seems like everything around here is 'the best,' Bon," Nadezhda chuckles.

Wordlessly, Bono turns and leads the way along Jalan Selat Panjang.

There are rare moments when the most unimaginable things happen and we stop to think, *Wait. I've seen this before.* In a dream, maybe. Or in a past life. And for a fleeting second, we let ourselves believe that these moments, encased in a sense of familiarity, are pregnant with meaning.

When I stumble across Leon Basri seated at a restaurant along Jalan Selat Panjang, I slow to a halt. My mind flickers to my dream of him at the strange bar named Dominica, ordering the cocktail that convinced me he was my true intended. It seemed nothing but a screwed up idea at the time—just me willing myself to find meaning in a frivolous dream. But now, I'm seeing the man himself right before my eyes. But he's not sitting with a woman, not downing his preferred alcoholic beverage. He's digging into a bowl of noodles.

The first thing I feel isn't sadness, or anger, or even heartache. What I'm thinking is: *So this is the face of my executioner. So this is the face of death.*

It turns out my downfall has long since been planned. The logic is clear: to make sure that people at the Ministry—including the consultants—don't get suspicious. I've been sent here on an investigation, under close surveillance. They made sure not to send me into the field with just anyone. They sent me with a colleague from the same consulting firm, a colleague who has an excellent relationship with the NGO we've been working for, so that when the time came to kick me off the project, people wouldn't chalk it up to bad blood between SoWeFit and OneWorld—wouldn't start asking, "So what's the deal there?" Once they saw how many questions my reports from the field were raising and how negative they were, Leon was dispatched into the field to replace me. As would happen in a military operation.

But then I hear Farish's voice in my ear. "Don't worry. We'll face this together."

In my mind, I experience three more revelations: (1) Only someone stupid would go to a marquee destination like Jalan Selat Panjang while on a secret mission, (2) it turns out Farish really is on my side, whatever his personal motives may be, and (3) Leon isn't that fabulous-looking after all—and he's scrawny and graceless, like someone who needs to eat more. And shifty-eyed. Like a rat. And look at the way he grips his fork and spoon—as if he were trying to scale a rope.

Still, my heart is pounding.

21

The Animal-Lover

I often see myself in that room—black, rectangular, with arctic air-conditioning. In the middle of the room are a chair and table illuminated by a single light bulb. So far, in my dreams, my fate is always decided at that table: with a high school math exam, with an exam from my final year at university, with a qualifying exam for a scholarship.

It always ends in failure. (Also from these dreams: After I screw up my high school exam and fail to get into university, I see myself selling siomay *dumplings by the side of the road. After failing to graduate from university, I receive a reminder every morning when I wake up that I haven't completed my studies and could go to jail for it. After I'm denied a scholarship, I flee to Thailand and become a plaything for white tourists in Phuket.)*

But today, something's different. A middle-aged woman enters the room five minutes after I sit down. There are several sheets of paper in her hands, and she arranges them next to each other on the table in front of me. Without any pleasantries, much less a good morning, she says, "Today you will be taking the Life Values Examination. This exam consists entirely of one question. Eighty percent or above and you pass. Anything below eighty percent constitutes a fail."

I nod.

"*The main criterion: honesty. The second your brain tries to shy away from its first instinct, our sensors will pick it up. The answer will be considered a forfeit, and you will lose points. Understood?*"

I nod.

"*Because this is a new kind of exam, I've brought four examples of possible responses to the question you'll be given so you can have some idea of what's being asked of you. Please take a moment to study them.*"

1. List the first seven things that come to mind when you hear the word "poison."

Sample Response 1: arsenic, cyanide, belladonna, puffer fish, snake venom, Snow White's poisoned apple, poison-tipped arrow.

(Score awarded: 6/7)

Sample Response 2: mercury, arsenic, cyanide, insecticide/pesticide, tetrodotoxin, polonium, botulinum.

(Score awarded: 6/7)

Sample Response 3: sweet potato, apple, asparagus, cherry, tomato, nutmeg, Tropicana orange juice.

(Score awarded: 7/7)

Sample Response 4: anthrax, cyanide, arsenic, tetrodotoxin, formaldehyde, puffer fish, poisonous snake.

(Score awarded: 6/7)

My heart nearly stops beating when I realize two things: (1) I don't understand the logic behind the scoring system, and (2) there is a good chance that I can't use any of the answers printed in the examples.

"Honesty?" I squeak.

"Correct," my examiner replies, her face devoid of expression. "And of course we expect you not to give any of the answers provided in the examples. Understood?"

"Yes," I say with some difficulty. "But I have one condition. You have to tell me my score right away."

To my surprise, the woman nods. "All right."

I'm given ten minutes to write my answer.

Here are the results:

Jealousy, slander, low self-esteem, obesity, betrayal, paranoia, cowardly men.

After examining my answer for two minutes, the woman looks up from my paper with a big smile on her face. "Congratulations!" she says, shaking my hand. "A perfect score!"

For the first time on this trip, Bono is ticked off with me, even though the day has just begun. The drops of morning dew have yet to fall from the leaves. Even the roosters are too tired to crow.

And this is why I'm not too enthused about the "Crack of Dawn" Medan-style kwetiau goreng and bihun bebek he's been raving about for days, as if these two dishes comprise a vital, hitherto omitted part of our education.

Actually, there are a few other reasons for my attitude: (1) My heart and mind are still wrapped up in thinking about that cursed DOCIR project, (2) I'm not a breakfast person, and (3) see my dream from last night.

The Medan-style kwetiau goreng and bihun bebek—flat rice noo-dles and duck vermicelli—are particularly famous because of how clean and unadorned they taste. If the long, thin sheets of the kwetiau in question are best enjoyed with nothing more than sliced green chili and a dash of soy sauce, then the bihun bebek, which is also the most expensive duck vermicelli in the entire archipelago, requires nothing in addition to what comes in the bowl. That is, a mound of plain boiled noodles, plump slivers of poached duck, and a sprinkling of fried garlic chips that lend the dish an extra radiance. Usually, I don't have any problems with such simplicity.

But this morning both dishes taste bland to me. Even the relaxed atmosphere of the café—the Chinese "auntie" busy at the wok; the Chinese "uncle" going back and forth, greeting his neighbors, mostly middle-aged men there to sip coffee and enjoy breakfast after a morning run—fails to rouse my inner sociologist, who under normal circum-stances would readily come to life.

"Guess your sense of taste has been ruined, Run," Nadezhda says with some sadness. "We're all at fault. We ate too much yesterday. Too much heavily seasoned food."

We? Who is this "we"? I may have eaten a lot, but I'd never lose my palate, thank you very much.

"I bet it's poultry. Maybe your body's rejecting anything to do with it," says Farish, trying to lighten the mood.

"Your taste buds are getting too pampered," Nadezhda adds.

I say nothing. If Bono is allowed to be critical, why can't I? Sometimes I feel the wisdom we hear repeated constantly about food or wine should never be taken to heart. For example, that the most con-sistent quality is found in traditional dishes or food served by vendors. (Not always true!) Or that the more subtle the seasoning, the more the meat/fish/main ingredient will stand out. (But what about rendang, or Thai curry, or fish pepes?) Here's another one: heavy wine must be preceded by lighter wine, and fish goes better with white wine while red meat goes better with red. (This isn't always the case, as demonstrated by German Riesling, which almost always goes well with lamb or Cantonese cuisine. And a German Gewürztraminer is almost always a success when paired with Thai food.)

To me, standard wisdom ought not dictate our feelings or opinions. Our enchantment with things ultra-expensive, such as caviar and well-known wines, or things ultra-unique, such as a Serbian pule cheese or a fleck of *bhut jolokia*, the spiciest chili in the world, can be just as irritating as being overly smitten with things ultra-simple, such as popsicles, or toast, or popcorn, or with rare local ingredients such as the *kenikir* herb, or the *popohan* leaf, or the *pegagan* plant.

Which is why I can't understand my sense of taste being seen as faulty when I don't sing the praises of a kwetiau so straightforward in its paleness—a paleness so honest it's almost touching. Or a bihun bebek that doesn't send us reeling because it's not as rich as other versions of the same dish.

Still. I'm human. I'm not that strong. I can't always bear all that is unfair or makes no sense. No sooner do I think this than I feel queasy. I want to leave Medan. Yet I don't want to go back to Jakarta. I'm turning into a drama queen.

But wait. I see something. I see Farish, with that glance that I've come to rely on these past days, seeing me.

❦

The café is bizarre. It's not clear what they specialize in. Various coffee drinks and unhealthy snacks (doughnuts, cronuts, bananas, fermented cassava, and fried ice cream), Chinese food (various noodle dishes, *Cap Cay* stir-fry, and butter-fried chicken), or "Portuguese" food ("Portuguese soup," "Portuguese salad," "Portuguese *rica* chicken" [Isn't rica chicken from Manado?], "Portuguese pudding," etc.) But maybe that's what happens to your identity when you're located smack-dab in the middle of the bustle of Sun Plaza. It is clear that when it comes to buildings, this mall is this city's crowning achievement. The locals' love for it is beyond me.

"People here are really proud of this mall," Farish says with a chuckle. "It's Sun Plaza this, Sun Plaza that."

"Why bring me here at all?" I ask bitterly. "To remind me of Jakarta?"

But Farish has made his choice, and he hasn't had one so far.

What he does have, though, is an agenda. He wants me to meet his friend. And his friend wanted to meet us here.

"A friend?"

"Yes, a friend," says Farish. "We go way back."

There's a big grin on Farish's face when he stands up to greet his friend. They shake hands, then hug. They're close; anyone can see it.

Toba comes from Lake Toba. Where else? He's an environmental activist, but he works mainly in wildlife conservation. He has an interesting face. His jaw and cheekbones are like firm Cubist brushstrokes on a canvas, but his ebony-colored eyes are soft, round, trusting, like the eyes of a coddled puppy. He seems eager to talk about his experiences with his friend, but is a bit hesitant because I'm there. He's unlike the activists I know, all too impatient to share their stories from the field with anyone who'll listen.

Farish realizes what's going on.

"Aruna's an animal-lover, too," he says. He puts his arm around my shoulders. *Don't worry, bro. This gal's one of us.* How quickly my identity has been pulled out from under my feet.

Then Toba begins to talk. He's an animal-lover, but of all the animals whose rights to life and well-being he has fought for, it's the elephant he loves most. He laments that since 2004 more and more elephants have been slaughtered by poachers, especially in the provinces of Riau and Aceh—even though the total number of elephants has gone down by half within a mere twenty years. Just last year, he tells us, dozens of elephants were poisoned or shot.

"After losing their habitat to deforestation, they end up losing their lives as well," he adds. "No one thinks of these elephants as big-eared Dumbos anymore—all sweet and cute—or the great and sacred animals who deliver kings to their palaces. People see them as pests, as bearers of misfortune, as enemies, even.

"I saw with my own eyes, last May, the body of an elephant whose tusks had been lopped off," he says. "My friend—the vet who happened to be tasked with doing the autopsy—found a plastic bag of poison in the elephant's stomach."

He shows Farish and me several photos on his iPhone. Among them are a dozen pygmy elephants who'd been massacred in Sabah less than a week ago. I can't bear looking at them. Animals may be fierce. They may be hungry. They may kill. But they never do so with unnecessary cruelty, beyond the urges that arise in them as a matter of instinct. What is it that causes human beings to be so cruel?

"Toba," says Farish hoarsely, "how far has your organization gotten in your talks with the government?" He explains quickly to me that Toba's organization engages in conserving four keystone species in Sumatra—the elephant, the tiger, the rhinoceros, and the orangutan.

"It's been tough. You just can't talk to those guys—the provincial authorities in Riau and Aceh. The second we approach them, they feel like we're blaming them. They get all defensive and even hostile. 'Only *real* cases, Toba. You know we've already submitted eight cases to the relevant people, right? But have they done anything about them? Did they even read our recommendations?' That's what one of the provincial representatives tried to tell me the other day—till he was blue in the face. 'What can we do if people are afraid to report anything?' he asked. 'Or if they themselves were the ones who poisoned the elephants by coating fruit in cyanide?' Or maybe they've just had it with us. Or they're not scared of me anymore.

"I've been told that the big palm-oil companies have put my name down on a list of activists they're going to kill. Naturally, these companies have their own network of thugs. And let's not even talk about the ivory-trade mafia at large in Aceh. They tell me, 'Your days are numbered, Toba. Just you wait.'"

"And you're not scared?"

Toba's gaze becomes unfocused. But then his deep voice—deep as his namesake—fills the space around us. The background noise fades. I can no longer hear the hum of electronic music from the toy stalls or the banal chitchat around us.

"My father worked the land," he says, "and it was he who introduced me to mangroves and reefs, coves and capes. It was he who taught me to appreciate the dawn, to name the colors of the rainbow, and distinguish this moth from that. It was he who taught me to love the sea and fog and how to tell the difference between the *duku* fruit and the *kokosan*, between the different kinds of rice and different kinds of bananas. It was he who taught me to respect what springs from the earth and what sinks to the ocean floor. In the end we all must return to the earth, so is there any greater act of devotion than surrendering your entire life to it? And is there anyone more shameless than someone who kills innocent creatures?"

22

IVORY AND STRIPES

Bono and Nadezhda are instantly mesmerized by Toba. It isn't entirely unexpected. When the three of us enter the restaurant, which happens to be located smack-dab in Pancasila Youth territory (in name, defenders of our national ideology; in reality, government-sanctioned thugs), the Lake Man brings his own aura—and amazing stories as long as a giraffe's neck. Including ones about food.

My two friends, who before our arrival were racing with each other to analyze every inch of the barbecued pork that has become the pride of this restaurant, seem to stop in their tracks, at a loss for words. For half an hour they say practically nothing, just listen. The slices of crimson succulence that started out as their main objective are still sitting on their plates—as if they've found something more valuable.

I notice Farish doesn't touch the meat. He even sits at a little distance from the table. But, like the others, he is under Toba's spell.

In keeping with what it says on the banner above the door, the lard-lover's paradise begins closing up at 2:45 p.m., fifteen minutes before closing time. Six hours is a civilized amount of time to spend feeding so many people.

For a moment, we stand transfixed outside the restaurant. As far as the eye can see, the road looks desolate and gray, as if filtered by a camera lens into wintery shades—a cloudiness almost intentional and unintentional all at once. We're surrounded by old and new buildings covered in wounds and burns, with broken-down corrugated zinc roofs. Rows of electrical poles lean as if they've just been hit by a cyclone. The roads are dotted with potholes and flank crumbling sidewalks. We stand amidst it all, a handful of people positioned mise-en-scène to complete this dark portrait of a post-apocalyptic world.

The darkness takes on an ominous form when the eye comes to rest on the black and orange stripes screaming for attention at several points along the road: the Pancasila Youth minibus parked in front of the dilapidated colonial structure; a stretch of iron railing painted black and orange; and the security guardhouse in the middle of the road, the front of its exterior plastered with the face of their leader, Yapto S.—a face the whole world has now seen, most likely without his knowledge, thanks to *The Act of Killing*. The signboard reads: "Pancasila Youth Headquarters, Branch: Sei Rengas, Medan District, Jalan Sun Yat Sen."

I shudder. And yet here they are. Chinese-hating goons milling about on a road named after a Chinese national hero across from a Chinese culinary mainstay . . .

Never before have I been confronted with such starkness—a fount of both amusement and terror.

⚜

What do you call the restlessness that never disappears, that lurks and roams through the body like a virus? Whatever it's called, this disquiet compels me to call Priya that afternoon to find out the name and address of Leon's hotel in Medan.

"You want to see him?"

"No."

"Really?"

"I don't. I swear. I just want to know whether his hotel is way better than mine."

And from the tone of her voice, I know Priya suspects that I'm going to do something stupid.

She's right. I *am* going to do something stupid. I show up at the hotel, without makeup, without changing my clothes, under the pretext that I'm Mr. Leon Basri's colleague—"I have to speak with him. His phone's died. I'm his boss, Irma Shihab." I succeed in getting the receptionist to put me through to Leon's room.

When his voice comes through the receiver, I immediately whisper, "Leon, it's Aruna. I'm downstairs. I need to talk to you."

Unexpectedly, he's down from his mountaintop in a flash. He looks like he just woke up. His collared shirt is a little wrinkled.

He's not smiling.

Damn it. He *is* good-looking. What was I thinking the other day?

"Aruna," he says, sounding uneasy. "I know—"

"Traitor," I hiss, drawing my courage from who knows where.

"Let's sit down. I'll explain everything."

"I just want you to admit it," I say in a trembling voice. "You've known for a long time that they were going to kick me out."

"That's not true," says Leon.

In his panic he tries to invite me to sit on a polka-dot sofa in the hotel lobby as he remains standing, watchful, as if measuring the distance between us. What's he thinking? That I'm going to hit him? With my backpack? Or my fist, which prolonged contact with tapioca flour has made meaty and tough?

"Irma just gave me the assignment late yesterday evening. I swear. She said I shouldn't ask any questions, just show up at the airport early the next morning. My ticket had already been e-mailed to me. I was to go to Medan and Aceh, back through Jakarta to Pontianak, then last of all, Mataram. That's all she told me."

"What files did you bring with you?"

He looks at me as if I've asked him something inappropriate.

"Hey, don't blame me," he says. "I'm not here by choice."

What a jerk. Look at him: standing there, keeping his distance, absurd in his conviction that he's the one being persecuted, being judged before he's proven guilty. I want to punch him in his cowardly face.

A voice is calling to me from a corner of the lobby. "Aruna, enough already. Let's go. Enough." For a split second I seem to see my father standing there, but no. The one who *is* standing there, who is now half walking, half running toward me and my sworn enemy is . . . Farish.

❦

And thus we each play our parts, falling into each other's lives. And not a single person knows why or for how long—not that feeble excuse for a foe, or the staff of that luxurious hotel, or the receptionist who murmurs, "Have a good night, Ms. Irma" when I leave with Farish. Not the darkness that begins to enshroud the city like some great, maternal mosquito net, and not me—especially not me—who always thinks I know not everything but something, when in reality I know nothing at all.

❦

Farish doesn't seem particularly interested in discussing all of Leon's faults. Unlike me, still consumed by bile, he wants to talk about other matters—lighter ones, simpler ones. Our childhood foods, our favorite fruits, the names of the trees he had to memorize as a boy. His fierce, unstable uncle who showed up at their house one day after drifting around for some time and then stayed with them for years. Alma, the good-hearted German shepherd—his faithful companion for fourteen years until she dropped dead one day, frothing at the mouth, poison in her belly.

"I'm positive my uncle poisoned Alma," says Farish. "Rumor had it he was a hardened criminal on the run from the police. My mother was the one who forced him to stay with us so he'd be safe and learn how to abide by the norms of decent society. 'Who knows?' Mom would say. 'Environment has an influence, too.'"

Nature versus nurture.

"I didn't say anything at the time, though I already knew—there are people who can change and people who can't. In that respect, humans are like animals. Not all lions are like Elsa in *Born Free*. Imperceptibly, life with my uncle left an imprint on me. Frankly, I spent years feeling oppressed. His cruelty to animals, which I think was his way of compensating for suddenly having to be nice to people, made me want to protect all of them. And I mean *all* of them. Every animal on the face of this earth. Even the big, strong ones who sometimes did harm or killed. I wanted to protect them, too. Because they never did it for fun or on purpose. They didn't know how.

"My hatred of animal abuse left such a lasting impression that at one point in my life, I refused to eat meat. It wasn't easy, that's for sure. Imagine having to explain this at family gatherings, or at workplace functions, or to the mothers of women I was interested in. They couldn't fathom it. A man like me, balking at the sight of meat! They thought it was a bit precious, an unnecessary affectation. Might as well have been trying to explain that I was an atheist.

"At first my approach was more empirical. I'd focus on the facts. Everyone knows that a vegetarian diet is good for your health. Low in saturated fat, richer in fiber. It makes sense, right? That's what I'd tell people, anyway. That my aversion to meat had nothing to do with my morals. It was merely a healthy change.

"Then one day I went with an investigative team of NGO workers to Puan Cepak. It's a small village in the Kutai region of Kalimantan.

You might know it. Anyway, they'd just cleared the area to make room for a huge palm-oil plantation. And there I saw it. I saw the bodies of *dozens* of orangutans, just left there to rot. Of course the government denies any responsibility. Fucking bureaucrats. They just turn a blind eye and say that the orangutans were the victims of forest fires. More like victims of a mass slaughter. Some of my friends who were vets performed autopsies, but of course they just confirmed what we already knew.

"And the most infuriating thing of all? How proud those butchers were. A group of them even casually admitted that they'd gotten tens of millions of rupiah from the palm-oil companies for doing their bidding. We asked them if they knew that killing government-protected wildlife was a federal offense. 'Sure!' they bragged. 'What do you take us for? Morons?' Then we asked them what the government did. And again, they shirked their responsibility without blinking. They said that thanks to regional autonomy and the incompetence of local authorities, forest monitoring has gone to hell.

"So I stayed on in Kutai to interview these savage poachers. The law hadn't laid one finger on them. Not one. They were allowed to come and go as they pleased—in and out of the police station, the Directorate General whatsit, something for the Improvement of the Environment and Nature blah blah, and the local branch of the Ministry of Forestry— like they owned the place. I've lost count of how many surveys we conducted, my colleagues and I, during our time there. Can you believe that 750 orangutans were slaughtered in Kalimantan per year? More than 50 percent for meat and the rest for use in traditional medicine and illegal trade?

"Look. So I haven't been a strict vegetarian these past few years. The older I get, the more my childhood habits rise to the surface. Turns out, I do like eating meat. Sometimes I even relish it, like when we were at the duck place in Bangkalan last week. But as my discipline waned, my morals alone could not stop meat from creeping back into my diet. I tried to justify it at first. For many people, eating meat is completely normal, essential even—it's practically a law of nature. For these people, eating meat isn't an issue of morality. But then I remind myself, crossly, that the laws of nature shouldn't dictate my moral standards either.

"I feel the dilemma of it often: eating meat, yet being bothered by stories about cruelty to animals—from sterilizations performed without anesthetic to birds being boiled alive. And I ask: What kind of a person am I? How can I think one way and act another?

"Once, I read the work of a philosopher who likened species bias to racist theories of the most extreme variety. To him animal rights are social justice advocacy in its purest form, precisely because animals are the most vulnerable of all oppressed groups. We human beings selfishly sacrifice the most fundamental of their interests—the right to live—in order to fulfill the most fleeting of our needs. And in doing so we perceive the pain that animals feel to be irrelevant, unimportant.

"We dull our minds to the calf whose throat is slit for the tenderness of its meat, the duck whose liver is fattened before it's slaughtered and made into foie gras, the goat whose penis is chopped off so it can be eaten by macho men. We talk about the pleasure of eating as if it were a heavenly pleasure—as if heaven itself approves of the fleshly appetites of humanity. We talk about the pleasure of eating in the same way you yourself talk, with a sincerity that every now and then touches the heart. And I know you feeling that way doesn't automatically make you immoral, just as those who slaughter buffaloes for traditional ceremonies or French people who eat rabbits aren't automatically barbaric either.

"So . . . Aruna. Why don't you tell me a bit about yourself?"

Then it dawns on me. Farish wants me to start from scratch. *That was me. Now it's your turn.* He wants us to get to know each other, the way civilized people do.

He also wants me to forget about Leon, for Leon isn't just a traitor and a coward, he's a person who doesn't give a damn about anyone or anything—not even food.

"You really didn't see what he was eating at that tiong sim noodle restaurant?" asks Farish. He's making a funny face. "All he had were coffee and durian pancakes."

I find it quite enchanting, his being seemingly oblivious to the fact that he's just told me about a side of himself that's completely different from who I am, and that the assessment he's just given of Leon comes from another Farish—a Farish who doesn't give a fuck that he's contradicting himself, a Farish who's decided he likes Aruna, who even wants to be a bit more like Aruna, because he sympathizes with Aruna and maybe even . . .

Ah.

23

THE MELODY OF TASTE

I once had a dream where a kindhearted resi—a wise ascetic, straight out of the old tales—was trying to teach me the meaning of gratitude. Here's the story he told.

One morning, a man wakes up and can't see anything. He calls his doctor, who asks him to undergo a number of tests and examinations. Next thing, the doctor sits him down in his office.

"Sorry," says the doctor, "but I don't know how else to tell you this. For the time being, you won't be able to see. Though you may be able to glimpse something every now and then, your vision has diminished by about ninety percent."

The man merely nods, for he is a man of faith.

A year passes, and we come across our man again. He's still 90 percent blind. But he's not unhappy. "I've learned so many new things about the world," he says. "Things that I'd never have found out if I still had perfect vision.

"Only now do I know that watermelon tastes like the morning, weight-less and radiant. That the taste of guava juice sometimes reminds you of body odor—something about it smells like an armpit and produces a bit-terness that makes you itch. I can tell which people are in a room from their

respective scents; I can even tell what kind of mood my wife is in when she opts for Perfume X, not Perfume Y. A flower is more than just a flower to me now—I've learned all their names: the champac, the bromeliad, the frangipani.

"When my wife is cooking eggs in the kitchen, I can tell how she's preparing them from the aroma alone. Every time I smell sulfur, I know she's boiling them. And when she adds a little vinegar to the boiling water to neutralize the sharp smell, I know for sure.

"I love the fragrance of eggs sunny-side up, especially when they're fried in butter and they give off that wonderful, incomparable brown-butter aroma. I can tell from this aroma if the egg is overdone, and whether the yolk is fully cooked or still runny. Even when it's being cooked over too high a flame and releases into the air a smell that resembles burning tires, I still like the fragrance of eggs cooked this way. It reminds me of the simplicity of my childhood, when such eggs only appeared on the dining table on special occasions and were fought over like they were the last things on earth of real value.

"I can tell what kind of omelet my wife is making—a thick, home-style omelet with the texture of a plump potato fritter or a French-style omelet, full of milk and cheese, its lumps daintier, more refined, redolent with the perfume of celery and scallion.

"I can distinguish between all the oils my wife uses for cooking, including different types of olive and corn oil. And I can do the same with various kinds of banana and chocolate. My ability to do the latter brings me joy and sorrow at the same time. I equate chocolate with my grandchildren; they never visit without bringing me some, and they don't understand that my greatest sorrow as a blind man is that I can no longer see the little ways they're growing and changing: if they're getting skinnier or getting fatter, how long their hair is, whether they're looking more like their mother or father, their grandma or grandpa.

"Oh yes, I've also become more discriminating with my sugar. My wife often complains whenever our servant comes back from the market because

she keeps buying cheap coconut-palm sugar—the stuff that's mostly just raw cane sugar mixed with caster sugar, not the real thing. But Nature never lies, and I've learned to read her well.

"I've also learned how to listen with an intensity and focus once monopolized by my eyes. I know from the tone of their voices if my wife is or my children are contented or depressed. I've grown more appreciative of music that can transport you but also makes you feel safe. I find myself listening to more Baroque and choral pieces, more Bach and Beethoven.

"I've also learned how to move, how to touch things with reverence. When I squeeze lime juice over a piece of fish or drizzle sweet soy sauce over a cluster of siomay dumplings, I do so with great care, for only then can I feel that I'm enhancing the flavors of these dishes, rather than detracting from them.

"And, most importantly, I've learned to love my wife more fully, with all my soul, because it is in her that all the colors of life are found. And the same holds true for all the family and friends around me, because I know the ones who love you are the only ones who'll never leave."

✺

In the hotel bar we find Nadezhda, Bono, and their new friend, Toba, doubled over with laughter. The table is strewn with cigarette butts, peanut shells, playing cards, and beer cans. They seem so intimate. It's like they've known each other for years.

When we join them, Nadezhda immediately points a finger in my direction. She's all afire.

"Name," she blurts without prelude, "the ten staple ingredients most important to you. They can be spices, fruits, vegetables, anything. Ten of them."

I've just started putting together a list in my mind when Bono interjects, "Do over! Do over! I forgot to include noodles. I'll tell you my list again: garlic, lemon, red chilies, olive oil, cheese, wine, tomatoes, bread, potatoes, and noodles!"

"Actually, my list isn't too different from Bono's," I say. "Garlic, red chilies, sesame oil, sweet soy sauce, palm sugar, noodles . . . what else? Oh. Chocolate, bananas, corn, sweet potatoes."

"Garlic, lemon, red chilies, olive oil, wine, eggplant, peas, cauliflower, Japanese melon, and peaches," says Nadezhda, who has assembled her list in her usual elegant, civilized way—three kinds of vegetable, three kinds of fruit, two essential spices, one vegetable derivative, and of course, the drink of the gods.

"Ten is too few," I protest as I order a beer. Should I add beer, too? "I still want to add wine. And breadfruit. And cloves and coriander and pandan leaves, tempeh, bird's eye chilies, oranges, mangoes, green coconut—"

"Does 'coconut' include 'coconut milk'?" pipes Farish, probably secretly hurt that no one's asked him.

Nadezhda points a finger at him, saying, "Oh! Sweetheart. Sorry! We forgot to ask you! But to answer your question, coconut milk is coconut milk, and coconut is coconut—"

"Some additions, if I may," says Bono, cutting her off. "Mushrooms, tempeh, bird's eye chilies, fresh mint, fresh basil, all meats except snake meat, prawns, chocolate, cream"—he grabs a fistful of peanuts and crams them into his mouth—"oh, and Thai peanuts!"

"Why do they call them Thai peanuts?" asks Nadezhda. "Roasting them with kaffir lime leaves doesn't make them Thai."

"Well, why do they call the melon you like Japanese melon?"

"I bet my list is more unique than all of yours," Farish booms, probably because he feels he's being ignored again. "Red chilies, green chilies, lime, curry leaves, tempeh, sweet potatoes, bananas, anchovies, noodles, and of course, coffee."

Everyone starts speaking at the same time.

"How could coffee make it onto Farish's list and none of ours? We all love drinking it."

"Hey, it seems everybody likes red chilies. It's on everyone's list."

"Garlic's in second place."

"Noodles, too."

"Pretty much everyone likes noodles. Except Nadezhda."

"Nadz, how come mushrooms and tomatoes aren't on your list?"

"You just want to be different from everyone else . . . you're such a . . ."

"Oh! I forgot to add tofu and eggs."

"Combine tofu with eggs to make *Tahu Telor*."

"That's funny. Eggs aren't on anyone's list."

"I forgot to add cabbage and lettuce, too."

"Seriously? You can't live without cabbage and lettuce? Who are you, Peter Rabbit?"

"Is 'can't live without it' really the only criteria for a top ten?"

"Uh, *yes*. It is. If not, the list will be too inclusive, and what's the point in that? The whole reason for making the list so restricted is to make us think hard about what the ten most important staples in our lives are."

"And you *really* can't live without peaches?"

"Is ice cream a staple?"

"No. That's like trying to sneak coconut milk in under coconut, or foie gras under duck."

"So we can't say yogurt, then?"

"Hmm . . . hold on. Let me think. Actually, it's a good point. How could I forget to put yogurt on my list?"

"Butter! I'm switching out lemon for butter!"

"Bon, this isn't a test, you know."

"I feel like I'm being tested."

"On what?"

"Your insight as a chef."

"Hey, wait a sec . . . if olive oil's on my list, it wouldn't be fair to leave out butter."

Suddenly, a peal of laughter splits the air. I've almost forgotten that Toba is among us. That likeable stranger. Might he have a list?

But he doesn't give us one—and it isn't because we're too shy to ask. Nor is it because we don't want him to think we're imposing a dynamic on him that we've built up among ourselves, with all its jokes and references, meaningless to anyone else. He probably just wants to keep his distance because he's used to being alone.

In our room that night, Nadezhda and I talk until morning. She's writing a bunch of articles about food for a magazine and her blog. Just frivolous ones, she says. The important thing is that they're fun.

The first will compare two kinds of menus—a traditional one and a super-modern one. This could be very fun indeed if it uses hyperbole. The second will be on Indonesian sayings that refer to food. There are tons of them, aren't there? The third is about popular drinks that contain poisonous ingredients. Because, *really*, who isn't secretly interested in poison?

Then, all of a sudden, I'm telling her about my strange dream from the other night and its numerical logic, which I still don't get. I also tell her about the different samples of response I was shown before giving my own. As she listens, she is writing furiously in her notebook.

"I know why response number one only got a six out of seven," she exclaims, as if she's just discovered a magic formula for miracle milk.

"Why? Was it Snow White's poisoned apple?"

"No, there's an argument to be made for that. Fairy tales shape our perceptions, after all. The problem was that two of the things on the list were the same thing: the belladonna and the poison-tipped arrow.

Poison-tipped arrows were often made using belladonna, at least if we're talking about medieval Europe."

"Yes, but not all poison-tipped arrows—"

"It's called a dream, darling. Let me take a stab at interpreting. Now look, it's the same problem with lists two and four. Insecticide/pesticide and cyanide were on the second list, and both insecticide and pesticide contain hydrogen cyanide, a gaseous form of cyanide. Puffer fish and tetrodotoxin were on the fourth list: that's another duplicate!"

"What I don't get is why all the answers on list three were given points."

"That's because you don't understand the toxin content of the foods we eat every day. Sure, they're not a problem in normal doses, but they can be dangerous in excess. Cherry leaves and seeds contain cyanogenic glycosides, and I think apple seeds do, too. Sweet potatoes have a higher cyanogenic glycoside content, especially in their roots. One of the enzymes I know it contains even helps in the production of hydrogen cyanide. Cooked sweet potatoes are actually the safest because the heat gets rid of all its toxicity. Nutmeg contains myristicin—who knows where I learned that. It can make people hallucinate for hours, sometimes days. Tomatoes . . . hmm . . . if I remember correctly, they contain solanine. It's not dangerous to humans, though there have been cases of people being poisoned to death by tisanes—ones containing tomato leaves. Asparagus . . . now this is really tragic. They contain phosphorus and mercaptan. They can't be taken with wine. Nothing could be sadder, if you ask me."

"All right, Madam Professor. What about the final item? Tropicana orange juice?"

It seems Nadezhda's knowledge about poison has reached its limits. After we Google it, we discover that Tropicana-brand orange juice had come under scrutiny from America's highest authority regarding foodstuffs and chemicals because it was flagged as containing fungicide, an unauthorized chemical ingredient. The research results indicated that the fungicide levels were within normal limits, and Tropicana orange juice was allowed to remain in circulation. So where's the problem?

But wait. Not so fast. Take a gander at the footnote: "This fungicide causes testicles to melt."

"Melt?"

"Melt," she says.

From solid to liquid. From present to absent. We muse on this awhile.

Meanwhile, outside, the night has flown by. One thing is clear—the person who came up with sample response three is (or must be?) a fruit expert who enjoys having sex. He must have been so sad when he and his partner couldn't "do it" anymore that he claimed orange juice was behind it all.

24

TOBA

Finally, the time comes for something spontaneous that doesn't involve going to a restaurant.

We arrive in the city of Parapat just before midday. The area is beautiful, albeit quiet—many of the places to stay in the small lakeside town are open only on certain days, and the tourists who weren't too keen on spending the night sleeping in the car or on the beach have chosen to go to other places that offer more food and accommodation.

We've come in search of Naniura, of course. From Toba, we know naniura generally has to be ordered the week before, and is usually available only on Sunday. But a relative of Toba's who's skilled at making naniura is willing to have us over to her house so she can demonstrate. Once in a while she sells her naniura on the main road stretching along Ajibata Beach, outside the terminal for ferries crossing Lake Toba to Tomok on Samosir Island. The road has a lot of restaurants—ones specializing in Bataknese cuisine and ones that sell roast pork, ones offering halal food for Muslims and ones that trade only in fruit and souvenirs.

Ajibata Beach is very beautiful indeed. The sand is white and the water clear. There are rocky stretches, rolling hills, and leafy trees. *I could be happy living here,* I think to myself. Just me, and Farish.

Toba's cousin lives nearby. "She's of Boru Sinaga descent," says Toba, as if it should affect how we behave toward her. "Don't ask about her husband. He ran away recently and married someone else."

When we arrive, we engage in pleasantries with the mistress of the house for a little while before she offers us something to eat. She's a woman of few words. Her jaw is firm, her eyes are sharp, her voice is deep. We don't ask about her husband, though there are photos of him everywhere. When it's lunchtime she asks us to gather in the kitchen.

Naniura, the middle-aged woman tells us, is fish that isn't cooked. The best fish to use in the dish is black carp. If possible, it's best not to use a fleshy fish or one with too much fat.

"It's both easy and hard to make." As she says this, she glares at Nadezhda. Maybe beautiful women remind her of wayward ones—the kinds who steal other people's husbands.

We watch as this woman slices the carp into fillets before immersing them in water to which she has added salt and juice squeezed from dubious-looking kaffir limes whose skins border on black. Then she boils a stalk of red torch ginger, slices it up, and pounds it into a fine paste. After this she grates a knob of turmeric—already peeled—and dissolves it with a bit of boiling water. Then she peels and slivers young galangal, ginger, *kencur* root, shallots, and garlic before dry-frying them all together in a wok with candlenuts, peanuts, and lemongrass, until fragrant.

We look on as she boils bird's eye chilies and squeezes juices from five fresh kaffir limes. After this, she pounds the dry-fried spice mixture into a fine paste along with some *andaliman* peppercorns, the red torch ginger paste, and the boiled chilies. She adds the freshly squeezed lime juice before mixing it evenly until it blends with the spices. And then she pours the spice mixture into the bowl where the fish is soaking as she adds the dissolved turmeric to the fish.

"Stir it like this," she says. "Then put it in the fridge. Let it sit for twenty-four hours."

"The lime . . . ," Bono interjects. His chef's brain seems to be hard at work. His cheeks are flushed—a sign that he's excited. "To ferment it and make it more fragrant?"

"It has a more important function as well," the woman says. "The lime cooks it naturally. It gets rid of the fish blood, also the sliminess and the smell."

"Does . . . does naniura play a role in local traditions?" asks Nadezhda. For the first time, I hear a tremble in her voice, as if she's unsure about what she knows. Not only that, the woman is still glaring at her.

"Some say naniura is the food of kings," the woman says as she looks in Farish's direction, as if he, a nonbeautiful male, is the one who should rightfully be asking Nadezhda's question. "Only the palace chef was allowed to make it. Time passed, and naniura underwent a shift in status and became common fare. I still see this dish served often, at birthday parties or at *parumaen*—that's the local term for the ceremony where the groom feeds the bride. It's considered the most sacred part of the wedding ritual. At least among the Toba Bataknese. Even though I'm a small, one-woman business, I get a lot of requests to make naniura for such occasions."

"So it forms a sort of connection, a bond, between two families?" asks Farish, finally feeling obliged to respond.

"Yes, exactly! But there are also beliefs about how naniura can be made. The fish used to make a batch of naniura can never amount to an odd number. Don't ask me why."

It's a shame we can't stay the night so that we can sample the dish as it's meant to be eaten. We don't have twenty-four hours.

For a moment, I wonder if any of the eateries behind the National Parliament building in the Senayan district of Jakarta serve naniura.

But the truly miraculous thing is how easily enchanted my two friends are. As am I—enchanted by life, all because a guy I'm interested in has touched me lightly a few times on the shoulder and arm.

25

STONE BANANA RUJAK AND *SATE MATANG*

Tuna pasta. Tuna pasta = My mother.

This is a recurring dream.

After she inspects the shabby room I've rented on Jalan Hang Lekiu, who knows how many dozens of years ago now, my mother walks to the kitchen (if it can be called that) and calmly, wordlessly, produces a few items from her shopping bag. A packet of fusilli pasta, a bottle of olive oil, a can of tuna, a can of tomato puree, a carton of cream, three scallion stalks, a few garlic cloves, two Bombay onions, and a few small packets of dried spices.

She begins heating a saucepan of water on the stovetop and minces the garlic, Bombay onions, and scallions before sautéing them in olive oil on medium heat. A little salt is thrown in as well. Then she pours the entire contents of the can of tuna into the wok, along with two tablespoons of the canned tomato puree (not tomato sauce), followed by a quarter of the carton of cream, then another quarter, until the color of the mixture in the wok turns a brownish pink. Two pinches of sugar. A pat of butter. Oregano, sprinkled across the surface like stars. Then she turns to the water in the saucepan, which is now boiling. Oil on water. Half the packet of pasta.

And I, so green, so orphaned, just sit there and weep. I can't stir. I'm too weak to move. I feel small, stunted.

Without drawing near to me, without putting her arms around me or trying to soothe me, my mother says just one thing as she points to her head. "This is where it is—the best database humankind has to offer. Our minds. Our memories."

My sobs grow more violent. "How am I supposed to live having to remember so much?"

"Someday you'll have a thousand recipes stored in your brain," she says. "Trust me. You'll be happy—because you'll never be hungry."

A near-perfect afternoon. A gentle breeze, the scent of forest and sea. A proud, open sky, not too bright or too dark. A sort of pale silvery gray and orange-red refracted from the horizon.

In the garden behind the little restaurant, four young Acehnese women are enjoying their plates of fruit rujak. They're seated around a square box of a table. The garden is very spacious, and the fence enclosing it is almost completely covered by leafy trees. For a moment the sight stops us dead in our tracks—it's been a long time since we've seen such greenness. Never mind that there's a garbage-filled ditch just a stone's throw away.

One of the young women raises her head in our direction and smiles. I smile back.

We've just arrived in Banda Aceh but haven't seen much of the city since touching down at the airport, now sleek and modern thanks to the post-tsunami renovations. But it all happened so fast, without a moment to waste. From the baggage claim area, we jumped straight into our hired car and sped directly to Warung Rujak Blang Bintang, not far from where the old entrance to the airport used to be.

This is all a gift from Rania, an old friend of Farish's who works at a local NGO. It was she who arranged everything.

"Can't think of better timing: this place only opens in the late afternoon, around three o'clock," she says, her pallid, thin-armed, almost Schielean frame in stern contrast with her face, which is bright, expressive, a work of constant improvisation.

When she introduces me to Mr. Maryadi Agam Muda, who's busy assembling the ingredients for his famous dish, *Rujak Aceh*, she tells him I'm a food aficionado from Jakarta. As much as I love how it sounds, I can't quite grasp what being a "food aficionado" means and am somewhat embarrassed that she hasn't mentioned my two friends who, if anything, are the group's true aficionados.

"You've never tasted rujak as good as this," says Rania. "Not in your whole life. I guarantee it."

Their secret?

"Stone bananas," says Mr. Agam, naming the special variety of banana with the nonchalance of someone who's been in the rujak business almost all his life. "Without them, I wouldn't be in business."

I stand there, watching him play cool without even trying, quietly mesmerized by his suavity as he slices so evenly, almost without effort, various fruits and vegetables—jicama, sweet potato, *kuini*, pineapple, *kedondong*, papaya, mango, cucumber—into a large basin. Then, with a mortar and pestle, he grinds together palm sugar, red chilies, shallots, roasted peanuts, several large-seeded slices of the stone bananas, and two other types of fruit that positively elude me: something that resembles a *kawista*—a wood apple—and another fruit that looks like a *salak*, a snakeskin fruit.

"People often call the one that looks like a snakeskin fruit an Acehnese snakeskin fruit—a *salak Aceh*," Rania explains. "But the locals call it a *rumbia*. The one that looks like a wood apple they call a *batok* fruit. Mr. Agam says that the stone bananas make his fruit rujak so distinctive. But for me, it's the batok fruit that does it. That's what gives it a kick."

I notice Mr. Agam doesn't speak much. I look at his biceps. The muscle near the dimple of his elbow; his forearms. I look at his hands, at his long fingers—sunbrowned, strong, a worker's ware. And what hands. How many plates of fruit salad have they produced since 1975? How many gallons of that remarkable rujak sauce? How many stone bananas and batok fruit have they sliced and mashed? And yet, from the quiet, unassuming way the man speaks, when he speaks at all, he probably doesn't think too much about rujak in relation to himself or the passage of time.

Then there's the small matter of Nadezhda. I've never seen her take so many photos of one kind of food. She fixes her lens on the plate of rujak from every conceivable angle and distance, as if worried that the contact she's made with her father's heritage will slip through her fingers. Acehnese blood does flow through her veins, after all.

"How is it?" asks Rania.

"Well. You've said it yourself," answers Nadezhda, with a wide grin. "The best rujak in the world."

"Nadezhda's father is half Acehnese," I say, as if that fact gives her appraisal more validity somehow. I want to add that her mother is part French, part Sundanese, and part who knows what. But then again, what's the point? Her beauty is so unusual and so disabling, it speaks for itself.

And it's not like her to be so readily agreeable, this woman, always ready to doubt others, never plagued by it herself.

She's not the only one.

"I've never come across rujak with sauce of this texture," Bono says. We've been given several plates of roasted peanuts, and he goes through them as if each one is a separate treasure. "I can't describe it. It's almost creamy."

"I usually prefer my rujak sauce without peanuts," I say, having decided I need to act according to my credentials. "A good sauce, I think, should be simple, something like palm sugar, tamarind, chili, and shrimp paste. That's it. Oh, and a dash of salt. But this sauce is . . . I don't know. It's just . . ." I want to say "wow," but refrain.

No one says anything.

"You're absolutely right," I go on, nodding at Rania. "This batok fruit is something else; it adds this . . . this inexplicable tang. And these roasted peanuts—they really . . ." Words fail me. So before I get too embarrassed, I follow Bono's example and pop a peanut into my mouth.

Across from me, Nadezhda the Beautiful is smiling away as if some happy memory has come to mind. I dare not imagine what. Or whom.

Later, something seems to boil up and disgorge—a fragrance, a substance. The air seems to expand, as if a kind of secret pact has been made between Man and Time. We feel all the more reluctant to go. Once again, I retreat into my own thoughts.

Before this, on the flight over, I was incredibly anxious—more anxious than I'd been on the way to the other cities, as if some greater force in the cosmos were demanding I pay my dues, that I take responsibility. For not once since the tsunami have I stepped foot in Aceh. Unlike my more proactive and compassionate friends, who immediately dropped what they were doing and headed to Aceh to help the survivors—in *any* way they could—I chose to bury my head in the problems of my own daily life, with all its petty dramas and obsessions. The closer our plane got to Banda Aceh, the more certain I was: I'd never be able to take it all in. I'd come too late.

So, how very strange I feel at this moment. For at this point, I already feel I've taken in so much. And yet my journey hasn't even started.

It would be impossible not to remember our chance encounter with Leon and his team earlier that morning at Polonia Airport in Medan or the panic that overtook me once I realized we were all going to be on the same flight to Banda Aceh. After that mortifying confrontation in Medan, can anyone blame me? Of course, he was the one traveling on official business, while I had been reduced to an infiltrator, a trouble-maker. It would be impossible not to remember his tall, lanky frame standing with his back to us at the Garuda Airlines check-in counter, and how my heart still races whenever I catch sight of him or even someone who reminds me of him. It would be impossible not to realize that, in many ways, I'm still that same naïve Aruna who's never grown up—who still doesn't understand, after all these years, how to turn her heartbreak into strength.

For some reason, Toba's presence among us fails to make me feel more secure, even though I can see his positive effect on our group dynamic, which until now has tended to center on the culinary. Even Rania's presence is like a breath of fresh air, especially to Farish because now they can shoot the breeze about nonprofit sector politics and wax nostalgic about the old days when they both worked for the same NGO.

By the time our car leaves Mr. Agam Muda's establishment, darkness has begun to descend. When we reach the city center, we drive around the Peunayong district first. We take in the rows of food-vendor carts and their plastic chairs in the empty clearing where the Rex Cinema once stood. We take in the rows of barbershops in Pasar Kaget. We take in the hawkers selling *Martabak Aceh*—an Acehnese version of the ubiquitous egg-and-meat-filled pancake found all over Indonesia, but with the egg on the exterior rather than inside.

Rania isn't a huge fan—thinks it too starchy. Something else clearly excites her though, and she points to the part of the clearing directly opposite the Hotel Medan. "But there, you'll find a place that does an excellent duck curry. The local name is *Kare Sie Itek*. The sauce is red, they use potatoes, and the meat is very tender."

I see Bono and Nadezhda desperately exchange glances—*Should we try some now or later?*—despite how stuffed they look after polishing off two plates of rujak each.

Peunayong. So much of it reminds me of Jakarta's Chinatown. Located in the area known as the Old City, Peunayong was designated Banda Aceh's Chinese district back in the colonial days under the Dutch government. It's situated only about a mile away from the Baiturrahman Grand Mosque, and this was probably done intentionally, to make it easier for the Dutch to keep an eye on activity in the city center. West of Peunayong, not too far away, is the Aceh River, and about two miles to the north is the Strait of Malacca.

"This area used to be called Peunayong Port. The Chinese have inhabited this area since the seventeenth century," says Rania. "You all know your history, I guess. The Dutch politics of segregation. Anyway, the Dutch did this here, too, using race as the basis for maintaining district boundaries until the end of the nineteenth century. The marketplace, ostensibly, was where different groups could interact. But it only strengthened the divide."

We're standing in front of Peunayong Market. After the devastation wrought by the tsunami, the buildings in this area were rebuilt by the city government and a few foreign NGOs. From outside the market area, I see three multistory buildings: the first for stalls selling fresh fish and vegetables; the second for selling chicken, duck, and various spices; and the third for beef and goat meat.

All along the road, trucks are loading and unloading goods, jostling for space with cars and becaks. Ancient monasteries, convenience stores, fabric shops, auto parts sellers, pharmacies, and cafés are interspersed between rows of old buildings.

At a glance, there is nothing to distinguish these rows of shop-houses from those found in Chinatowns the world over: saddle-shaped roofs covered in sheets of zinc, floors laid with tile, doors and windows flanked by hinged wooden boards. Entryways with decorated arches, and an arcade in the front courtyard composed of a row of concrete pillars bearing motifs of dragons and rolling clouds pieced together from ceramic fragments. Among the pillars, vendors and visitors mingle. And in the cafés, old men and women sit at the end of the day to chat, to watch television while smoking and sipping their coffee, or to simply *be*. You can hear the *khek* dialect interspersed with snatches of Mandarin. We know all this: the nooks and crannies where the stories that make up human existence fuse and become one.

Rania is telling us one of those stories now. "I was born in 1965 in Banda Aceh, but was raised in Medan. We used to live in this area, before the market was built. I don't remember anything about those days. I was just a baby. When I was in elementary school, my father told me about how the shophouses at the intersection outside the fish market were looted when I was just one year old. That was when anti-Chinese and anti-Communist sentiment was at its peak. We weren't Chinese, but since we lived in the vicinity, we were sent packing, too, and forced to flee to Medan.

"Many of my father's friends got rich in Medan and didn't want to come back here. But my father had sentimental ties to Aceh—this city especially. And so, twenty years later, we returned. Now my father is dead. My mother, too. I live by the sea on Weh Island, off the coast from here, with my dogs. They're my loyal companions and protectors. But almost every year some of them are poisoned by neighbors, and we say nothing. I'm not sure if it's because we don't love and value our dogs enough or it's because we're more afraid of violence and conflict. It gives you pause, though. Sometimes it breaks my heart."

Meanwhile, the car continues toward the Grand Mosque, and, once we're on Jalan Diponegoro, Rania speaks again. "See that row of shops there? Last year four of them were set on fire. Three were stores owned by the Ramai group, and one a store owned by another conglomerate called Sejahtera. They're both local stalwarts. Anyway, nobody knows who did it or why, but it caused quite the commotion." She's pointing now to a Pante Pirak convenience store by the side of the road. "The group that owns *that* chain practically runs Banda Aceh—and we're not just talking about convenience stores. They own waterparks, restaurants, bakeries, salons, modern cafés, you name it. They started out as a single clothing store, not far from the Rex, and pretty much dominated the landscape. But now that the national convenience store chain Indomaret has reached Aceh, Pante Pirak just went totally berserk."

On the main street behind the Grand Mosque, we pass stores selling cloth and gold. Nearby, a Buddhist monastery and three churches stand miraculously undamaged, and in apparent harmony. A Catholic church called Our Lady of the Sacred Heart, a church of some Protestant affiliation, and a Methodist church. Expensive luxury cars jam the road, as if they, the cars and the road, belong to an entirely different history—one that's still being written, unfolding in accordance with a logic that has nothing to do with destruction or tears.

That night, we eat at a restaurant famous for its *Sate Matang*. It seems like everyone is anxious to vent.

To my right, Farish, Rania, and Toba:

> "People hate me because they think I'm in over my head.
> I even manage all my supervisor's schedules and accounts.
> But I don't mind—I asked for that responsibility. 'Sir,' I
> said, 'let me handle your schedule. That way, your office
> won't always be crowded with people waiting around to
> talk to you.'"

"Mighty noble of you. And his secretary didn't protest?"

"Nah, she couldn't handle the responsibility, and she knew it, too. If it were all up to me, I'd try to schedule meetings for him only on Fridays or Mondays. That way, if he has to head out of town during the weekend, he can come and go straight from the office, no time wasted."

"If you ask me, it's imperative that a meeting starts on time and keeps to a strict agenda—who will be talking and what about. And if it'll last from nine to eleven, then say so. Don't just say from nine to whenever."

"That's what I think, too."

"And of course people just hate you more because you say the first fucking thing on your mind. But what can you do? There's always hierarchy in bureaucracy."

"You know what I find really annoying? When Mr. Second-Tier Civil Servant doesn't have the guts to speak to the secretary general and Mr. First-Tier Civil Servant doesn't have the guts to speak to the minister. Then everyone ends up waiting on everyone else and nothing gets done."

"Not to mention the fact that we live with our decisions—the ones we make and don't make today . . . and the consequences can be long-term. Get this: once I was part of a team of consultants that was asked to put forward ideas for an anti-corruption strategy to be implemented nationwide. That was in 2003. In 2006 we'd just entered the drafting stage for the strategy. Now you take a wild guess how long it took. The law only fucking came out in 2011."

"See? That's why consultants should be bolder in asking for more money. If we don't, they'll treat us like cows, constantly milking us for ideas. Consultants should be highly paid. Hell, we should get fucking top dollar; we're the ones who bring in our contacts and networks to get projects rolling."

"I agree. Actually, there are lots of promising kids working in the Department of Foreign Affairs. A lot of new blood. And they know their stuff when it comes to recruitment. No wonder the National Investment Coordination Board is poaching them. Still, they'd be hopeless if they had to clean up the ministry bureaucracy from the inside."

Nadezhda and Bono:

"What's up? Why the long face?"

"I'm fucking depressed."

"Um. That's not news."

"No, seriously. I just read an article about that marvelous chef in Modena . . ."

"Massimo Bottura?"

"That's him. The one whose restaurant was ranked third on 'San Pellegrino's World's 100 Best Restaurants' list."

"Really? You're still obsessed with those lists? When are you going to get over them?"

"What do you mean? I'll always be obsessed with them. Those lists are important. People these days don't have the patience to do thorough research. They go for the bottom line."

"But ultimately, all lists are subjective—it all depends on who puts them together."

"Yes, but they still set a certain standard. After all, the people who put them together have experience. They're considered experts in their field."

"But those lists can't set the standard forever. They're seasonal, subject to change."

"They're still important, no matter the establishment: a restaurant can't be okay all the time or on top forever. Every restaurant has its moments."

"Okay, so what's the problem exactly? You want to get on that list? 'Siria: Third-Best Restaurant in the World'?"

"You're such a bitch."

"And that's why you love me. So tell me, what's so special about Bottura? What makes him better than everyone else?"

"I've never tried his food. I imagine it must be out of this world. But this article was talking about the way he thinks, his approach to food."

"Which is . . ."

"He sees food as a metaphor. Each dish he creates, according to the article, tells a story. His most famous dish, for example, is called 'camouflage.' It is a combination of foie gras custard, dark chocolate, and espresso foam—the inspiration came from a conversation between Picasso and Gertrude Stein in Paris at the beginning of World War One. They saw a camouflaged truck across the street—"

"Hmph."

"What do you mean by 'hmph'? As a Parisian you should appreciate—"

"*Naturellement.* But I don't see the connection."

"According to the article, Picasso, who'd never in the whole of his life encountered camouflage, much less that of the kind used in war, said something along the lines of, 'Ah, we're the ones who created that—that's Cubism!'"

"Ha ha."

"Funny, right?"

"Uh . . ."

"C'mon. Funny, right?"

"Okay, okay. It's funny."

"So picture this: I see you and Aruna covered in mud, riding a motorized becak in Medan, and this inspires me to create a dessert that looks like pempek. So instead of being vinegary and spicy, the sauce is sweet, made from, say, palm sugar or chocolate, to represent the muddiness of things. As for the part of the dish meant to resemble the pempek—let's make the ingredients something rather unexpected. Potatoes, for example, to symbolize transportation. Something that rolls . . ."

"Hmm . . ."

"Same thing, right?"

"All right. I get your point. But potatoes and palm sugar?"

"Why not? I can put my own spin on 'black on black' if I want. That's another Bottura creation."

"Oh right. The dish that was inspired by Thelonious Monk."

"What don't you know? Anyway, what's stopping me from whipping up any old dish, throwing in some spherical ingredient, then claiming, oh yeah, I was inspired to create this dish after listening to Bonita's cover of 'A Pair of Eyes'?"

"Well, no one's stopping you."

"My point is who'd be able to say, 'Bono's such a liar,' or 'Bono just made that up so he can sound artsy-fartsy.'"

"True. Nobody would dare accuse you of being a liar. But everyone would be entitled to think it."

"Hmph."

"Oh, come on, you. Cheer up."

"So I'm right. That's the key to success: get famous and people will believe anything you say."

"Yep. Life just isn't fair."

Meanwhile, the sate matang is certainly robust, and its meat well done, in keeping with the dictionary definition of what "matang" is: "well done, cooked through." But the "matang" of its name actually refers to the name of a village in Bireun, where the dish originated.

The beef has been cut into large cubes—all lean, without a trace of fat. Before being skewered and grilled, each piece has been simmered in a coconut milk sauce until thoroughly saturated in sweetness and spice. The skewers of satay come with a plate of peanut dipping sauce. But this isn't a satay for sauce lovers. No. This satay demands a more sophisticated and discerning palate. Bono makes comparisons to *Sate Klathak* and *Sate Maranggi*. Nadezhda makes reference to Sate Bali or Balinese satay. As if they want to prove that good satay, true satay, doesn't need to be dipped in anything at all, they push their plates of peanut sauce toward me, making a huge production of devouring skewer after skewer.

And as for me, do I protest? Do I proceed to immediately drench all my satay in sauce to show them I, too, have my own opinions? No. Why? Because I'm still floating in the ocean of voices not my own. I feel attenuated. So much for being the designated "food aficionado." All I have on my mind and palate is Leon's voice, which I keep hearing in my ears. It seems to permeate the restaurant.

26

COFFEE, MEN, AND PRIZEWINNING SONGBIRDS

Nadezhda often speaks about feminine cities and masculine countries, the woman that is Paris and the man that is Spain; London, the city of men, and Vienna the coquette; transsexual Moscow, homosexual Bangkok, and asexual Japan.

To me, Aceh is the Land of a Thousand Coffee Warungs, and Banda Aceh is the City of a Thousand Coffee Warungs. And it is almost 100 percent male. All along the road I see men everywhere, mainly in the small traditional coffeehouses. Everywhere—from the insides of buildings to the courtyards outdoors, in the nooks and crannies fragrant with coffee. Coffee strained through a socklike sieve before it's poured from one long-spouted stainless steel pot into another, or stirred straight into boiling water before it's poured into a glass, sans grounds. I see men everywhere. Watching. Sipping. Filling the air with their aromas and appetites.

In the Ulee Kareng district, at the famous Warung Kopi Solong, men are scattered throughout like coffee beans of the celebrated Gayo variety.

This morning the six of us are sitting in the back near the bean-grinding station, having coffee.

The barista is friendly. "Can you guess what I put into my Robusta beans?"

"How should we know?" we reply.

He grins. "Butter," he says breezily. "You really can't tell?"

Then, just like that, in keeping with convention, the men opt for black coffee while the women order *sanger*, milky coffee with sugar. And thus Nature lays bare a collection of correspondences: men = dark; women = light; men = bitter; women = sweet.

Out of idle interest I center my attention on Toba. Whenever he smiles or stretches his arms, he transforms, turning into the contours that shape his cheeks and his jaw, his this and his that. *How male can you get?*

So then, why is it that, despite being in He-Man Land, my gaze keeps shifting to the one man beside me, who gives me a nudge with his wiry arm whenever I'm in need of human touch? This man, who doesn't seem to care too much for human beings, yet waxes so eloquent about fauna and flora? Who'll occasionally sit alone, brooding in the darkest corner and waving away all offers of a stiff drink yet other times gulps it down seriously, earnestly, as if he were conducting his own case study for the push and pull between discipline and punishment? This man—capable of netting and containing my rage with the precision of an avid butterfly collector.

I don't tell Nadezhda how I sometimes catch a whiff of other scents he gives off—sharper, more intimate ones. The smell of his fatigue when he took off his shoe at one point to adjust his sock. The old-man smell of long-accumulated sweat tinged with the smell of popcorn (I should know—I'm popcorn, after all). That distinctively male smell that rushes out every now and then from his crotch when he shifts in his seat.

I don't tell Nadezhda because I'm used to thinking of men as her domain.

There really and truly are, it would seem, certain women—like champagne—to whom the whole world belongs.

The food at the restaurant isn't memorable. One might even say it's not that good. But Amir, our driver, can't stop smacking his lips as he provides commentary on this dish and that—the *Keumamah* and *Gule Pliek Ue*; the *Sie Reuboh*, *Lepat*, and *Eungkoh Bilih Paih*; the *Eungkoh Tumeh Asam Keueung* and *Pacrie Nanas*.

Meanwhile, I become more and more convinced that really good Acehnese food is probably found only in local households, not restaurants. A lot of my Acehnese friends in Jakarta have said the same thing. I whisper as much to Rania.

She seems pleased. "And not only that!" she says. "Guests are never *not* served food in an Acehnese house. I'm not just talking about snacks. It has to be a complete meal. Rice, meat, vegetables—the works."

But it looks like she doesn't want to hurt the driver's feelings. They've known each other for a while.

"Oh, I almost forgot," says Rania. "There's one more thing. In general, Acehnese men know how to cook. Don't ask me why; they just do. Even their knowledge of spices is above average."

Coincidentally, Amir is blathering on to Bono and Nadezhda along similar lines, pointing to the scraps on his empty plate.

"Take this curry, for example," he booms. "A man's dish—Adam's domain. Now picture this: We're at one of last year's *kenduri*. It's a community-wide feast to mark the harvest. It's March. There are four thousand people! Now guess. Who do you think made the beef

Beulangong curry? Who do you think sliced up the jackfruit and seasoned the meat? Us menfolk! Us Adams, of course, working together. And all the while, all the Eves did at most was stay inside and make the easy dishes: rujak, pickles, *Bubur Kanji Rumbi* . . ."

I exchange glances with Rania, who, despite Amir's affirmation of her theory, seems undecided whether to openly acknowledge the sexism. "It's true, though. A beulangong is a large clay pot, so obviously a lot of people need to pitch in."

But then, in the background, I hear Amir's voice grow gentle. Through the crevices between his teeth, stained yellow with bits of *boh itek masen*—salted duck egg—I hear "shamas, lovebirds, mynas." I prick up my ears.

"The birds who win that competition are fantastic! And pricey! Last year's champion, a white-rumped shama, sold for 130 million rupiah!"

"So which birds make the best singers and which ones usually compete?" asks Toba.

"There's a bunch of them. There's the orange-headed thrush—we like to call it the *teler-teler*. It's exactly the same size as a collared dove. There's also the crested jay, a type of myna with a crest like a candle. And the beard bird, also known as the grey-cheeked bulbul, which is akin to a pied starling but smaller and usually a light-brown and cream color, with a beard like an old man." He laughs. "There are lots of different beard birds, too—more than one kind: *tembak* beards and *besek* beards, and who knows what beards besides. But none of them can compare to the white-rumped shama—that is, when it comes to sound quality, stamina, and how many songs it can memorize."

"What about lovebirds?" asks Toba. "Isn't that a bird one sees a lot at these competitions?"

"That's right. But the better ones are all imports. The local ones— their eyes are usually of average size and shape—aren't all that special. The ones that are imported, though, have large, round eyes and a wonderful sound, high and clear. I mean, really unique. I like canaries and oriental magpie-robins, too. That last one I mentioned is black and white, and their voices are kind of like the white-rumped shama's, which is actually red and has a tail—"

"You said you keep birds, too, Amir?" asks Farish. "And enter all the competitions?"

"Sure do," says Amir with a grin. "And I'll tell you, what I don't do for those birds! Preparing them is serious business. Two to three months before the contest, I start giving them vitamins and Scott's Emulsion every day. I feed them crickets, caterpillars, and ant eggs. Once in a while, during the monsoon season, they get *Timphan* dumplings—a local sweet snack made of glutinous rice, banana, and coconut milk—to improve their stamina. Then, when it gets hot, I give them bamboo worms to keep their body temperatures down. Sometimes I even give them carrots and apples to keep them in good shape."

"Wow," says Toba, with a ripple of laughter. "Their diet's healthier than mine."

"So, Amir," I cut in. "You're not worried about catching avian flu?"

Amir looks at me like he doesn't understand the question.

27

FAITH AND GOD

Dear God:

Even emeralds can't compare to the glorious greenness of the sea You've reserved especially for these shores, for this beach called Lampu'uk, ravaged almost eight years ago now by nature's wrath. These days, tourists may rave about the great surfing, the refreshing coconut water, and the bargain-priced seafood. But believe me when I say I see the signs of Your marvels—even if I don't always believe. These vast piles of boulders lining the shore. This ocean, so green. This sand, marble-white and shimmering. The mosque that refused to be swept away. And those seven hundred new houses from the Turkish Red Crescent. Good deeds, I know, are part of Your wonders.

So then, answer me: why tear away the women of Lampu'uk— nine-tenths of them—from their children, their husbands, their parents?

⋎

It's a long time before I realize there's a cut on my hand, right on my middle finger, that won't stop bleeding. From the rooftop of the Tsunami Research and Disaster Mitigation Center, we can see the ocean and the line separating it from land. A line that vanished overnight that fateful day, obliterated by the rolling waves.

The red stain from the blood dripping onto the asphalt looks like gift-wrapping ribbon. It makes me shudder, reminding me of the bodies that were flung ashore like bits of burned paper, scattered and set adrift throughout the city. It's hard not to be reminded of a certain tasty, though visually riotous, dish—*Ayam Tangkap*, also called Tsunami Chicken, because the crisp, fried curry leaves in it really do look like scraps of paper, scraps of blighted life.

Not far from where we stand, looking out, are brand-new houses with zinc roofs of red and gray scattered across a grassy field. From the midst of all this juts a two-storied structure, fractured, proud, like a wartime relic: both witness and survivor of a great tragedy.

I hear Nadezhda's voice in my ear: "I feel like I'm watching a scene straight out of *The Walking Dead*. Any moment now a bunch of zombies are going to come lurching out of that building." She's trying to lighten the mood, and she's not entirely wrong. But my head is full of other images.

Not too far away, in that same grassy field, a helicopter—that icon of rescue—is parked by a riverbank. Behind it, across the river, red-roofed houses and leafy trees stand in rows. They are equally sapped and remorseful, as if silently weeping over what they miraculously, unfairly, escaped that December.

A ferric, metallic smell assails my nostrils—the smell of blood. Then another voice approaches. The voice I've been waiting for.

"You're bleeding," it says.

"Yes," I say, and all of a sudden my eyes fill with tears. And just like that, the voice transforms into the hand that I've longed for. In the blink of an eye, with astonishing speed, it is on my reddening finger.

"Paper cut?" he asks.

"Uh-huh."

"When?"

"Beats me."

And there we are: two people on the roof of a desolate building, casting our far-flung gaze at the row of mountains and valleys in the distance. They look almost as if they wish to entrap the sea, to lay siege and bring it to justice in a vicious circle of their making. What did you know, oh you mountains and valleys, of the waves that would come tumbling in?

I'm aware that I'm looking at all this with half my vision directed at the man beside me—the man who is stealing glances at me, trying to read my mind. All along the main road, about a third of a mile from shore, even the warungs and cafés look quiet.

"See that minaret?"

I cast my gaze to the right. A tall, slender minaret with a color composition resembling that of a birthday cake—pink, cream, roasted-candlenut brown, and something else, something like bitter-gourd green—stands just a few steps apart from the beach, among houses whose residents clearly desire more color in their lives: Mediterranean blue, ivory yellow, violet. Forest green, lime-green, terra-cotta orange.

"It can't be," I whisper. "Is it possible? Did that minaret dodge destruction as well?"

"It's very possible," says Rania, suddenly standing nearby. "In these parts, people believe in God's miracles."

The Lampisang health clinic on the city's outskirts isn't on our list of activities—not since the termination of our mission. But we visit anyway. Something about the place makes me depressed. From the outside, the building looks like it's sustained heavy damage. It's a good thing that the signage is still legible: both the health clinic's name above the front door and the sign carved in stone by the roadside. The latter reads in gold letters without any punctuation: "Great Aceh

Regional Government Inpatient Health Clinic Lampisang District of Pekanbada." All around, black dust etches itself into the surrounding area like a burn wound on white paint. The local government clearly doesn't have the funding to repair the health facility, on which so many people rely. I have no expectation there'll be anyone inside. The building looks deserted.

So, naturally, I'm surprised to catch another tiny miracle. Just inside the entrance, two young nurses—women wearing head scarves—faithfully pore over a sheaf of documents at a small, flimsy table. Upon further examination, one leg is wobbly. The ceiling is studded with holes. The floor tiles are cracked. The stairs are coated in dust. The air-conditioning doesn't work. A lot of the patients' beds—most of them have mattresses covered in leather—are torn.

The nurses are very pretty. One of them has alabaster skin, naturally rosy cheeks, the most perfect straight nose. Eyes of the bluest topaz. What's more, she's nice. Her colleague is equally pleasant and just as easy on the eyes. Trusting, too. They don't ask many questions, give us free rein to look around—at every room, ward, storeroom, and bathroom, bar none.

I don't have the heart to ask whether they want to keep working, with no patients, with no doctors, with no real roof, with no sign that further help is on the way. But surely I should ask *something*. So I inquire, a little stupidly, about the tsunami—where they were at the time, what they were doing, what they were thinking after they realized what had happened. I instantly regret it.

As much as I can understand it, they don't believe, as most of their friends and relatives do, that the tsunami was ordained by God for the sole purpose of testing and strengthening their faith. Yet they don't seem shaken by any of it, the loss of family and friends. It seems that they're genuinely grateful—for everything. This isn't resignation to fate or Allah's will. This is something different.

"And more importantly," says the woman who looks like a Persian film star, "all the enmity and strife were forgotten. I'm talking thirty years of conflict."

"You mean the civil war?"

"Yes. Because all of us, including the Free Aceh Movement and the Indonesian government, had to work hand-in-hand in order to rebuild Aceh."

If a politician on TV said the same thing, I'd probably puke. I hate hollow sloganism. Besides, a lot of my Acehnese friends in Jakarta are of the opinion that the Free Aceh Movement didn't have much choice but to sign the peace treaty—years of war with the federal government had weakened them. But when the same words come from the lips of someone like her, a woman who has to submit morning, noon, and night to the inane specifics of Sharia laws that don't make any sense (at least not to me) and who could be hauled off anytime by the Wilayatul Hisbah for breaking rules that (again, to me) are subject to such wide interpretation—why do they sound so bracing?

"I don't mean to make light of the concrete improvements we've had," she adds. "The paved roads, fancy cars, and four-star hotels. But it's peace I'm most grateful for. No more curfews, military checkpoints, relentless terror. Peace."

I feel my eyes welling up. It doesn't feel like a corny moment. I look at Farish. He gets it, but *Hey*, his eyes seem to say, *what can one do? We're humbled, and that's that.*

We listen on to her. All along, I wonder what makes for a certain kind of rancor. What makes us so untrusting, so open to disappointments and failure? Is it because we don't know how to give thanks? A grateful heart, they say, invites miracles, so why can't we be more like this woman, see the things in our lives that for their apparent smallness can change so much: patience, consideration for others, a generous and liberating mind?

After listening to their stories for a while, about the ebb-and-flow involvement of this NGO and that in repairing the clinic, about the punishments for the latest violations of Sharia law, I ask the obligatory question.

"Cases of avian flu?" says the Persian film star. "No—not yet."

"Word is that a patient in Banda Aceh recently came down with it," I say.

"Really? Where, exactly? They must have been referred to the other hospital, then." She hesitates. "The new one."

I fall silent. I don't remember the patient's background. Or where the patient is from or which hospital he or she is in. Nor have I brought the relevant file, because after all, this is none of my business, right? I mumble a name, then by degrees take my leave.

For a second I worry that this wonder of the world will leave Farish breathless, too—the woman's a thousand times more beautiful than that fucking what's-her-name Inda. But I genuinely see no sign that he's interested in any woman besides me. Not even Nadezhda.

Before we leave the clinic, I ask the woman whether I can take a picture of her and her colleague. Sure, she says. I observe how the sun strikes the green of her gown, making her eyes look even bluer.

When Farish and I are back in the car and I show the photo to the others, I realize that printed on the front wall, among other things, is a logo, "Secours Islamique and Islamic Relief Worldwide," and in slightly ungrammatical English beneath, "Disasters Committee Working Together."

From the look on Rania's face and how pursed her lips are, I prepare myself for a lengthy speech about the post-rehabilitation "effectiveness" of NGOs.

28

LUST VERSUS LOVE

"Ever since I discovered sex, I've always played the role of teacher. My lovers are my students."

"What?"

Nadezhda nods, as if to confirm what she just said. She's just ordered room service: a platter of *Asam Keueng* and a plate of ayam tangkap—the same two dishes she took only one or two bites of back at the restaurant. But it's no use criticizing Nadezhda, no use in saying, "What a waste of money."

She has money. I don't. And I'm not her mother, so I have no right.

As she lies faceup on her bed, she repeats what she just said, her two legs floating upward occasionally and swimming in the air. In Jakarta she does Pilates with a private instructor at least three times a week. "Pilates is like a new religion for me," she told me once. "Through Pilates I've learned how to better understand my body."

"Women are always quicker when it comes to understanding their bodies," she drones on. "If they're willing, that is. Once they know which parts are sensitive to touch, they'll never put up with awful sex again."

Where's all this coming from? I think.

The pair of perfect legs is now at a ninety-degree angle, and with ease, with grace, she brings her whole upper body—head, neck, chest, stomach—up toward her legs. Her arms make downward motions like the wings of a butterfly, as if she needs to support her weight so she can maintain her position. "This is called 'the hundred,'" she says lightly. "You do this a hundred times. You must try it. It's fantastic for tightening the abs."

"Nadz," I say cautiously, "not all women are like you. I don't even have a boyfriend. How am I supposed to think about who's the teacher and who's the student? Or the difference been awful sex and non-awful sex?"

Despite myself, I'm getting wet.

I know she knows I'm horny and that I need to overcome my lack of sexual self-confidence by whatever means necessary. And she's right about the two dishes she's ordered on an instinctive whim. While it may be true that I tend to lack confidence and motivation around Nadezhda, I do know the difference between good food and bad. And this asam keueng, made fragrant by the addition of bilimbi juice, not lime juice like in the restaurant, is definitely delicious.

The WhatsApp message startles me, not just because it's from Farish but because it's seven fifteen in the morning.

Hey. You up?

I reply three minutes later because I'm attracted to him, and be that as it may, he can't know how I feel. At least not now. *Wassup?*

Wanna visit the Zainoel Abidin Public Hospital?

Sure. Why?

Apparently your boy was just there. And apparently they weren't cooperative.

Who wasn't cooperative? The hospital?

Yup, the hospital.
Hmm.
Leave at 8?
Hmm.
Is that a yes or no?
Okie dokie.
C U.
C U.

Once a consultant, always a consultant. I almost kiss Nadezhda, I'm so happy.

At the last minute, Toba and Rania want to come, too—only then do I ask myself why Rania's always at the hotel so early in the morning.

"On the way back from the hospital, we can stop at the Tjut Nyak Dien Museum for a bit," says Rania. "If you want to. There are a lot of local snack vendors by the main road. It's better to buy them there than somewhere else. Afterward we could also go to the Tsunami Museum. It costs a fortune—a colossal waste of money if you ask me. Again, only if you want to."

All along the way, Toba, Rania, and Farish engage in fairly intense discussion about NGO politics, local politics, and how the tsunami changed—and yet didn't change—a lot of things.

At a lull I ask, "So how safe are we, really? Me and Nadezhda, I mean. Walking around Banda Aceh without wearing head scarves?"

Something stops Rania from answering. It's a question that has weighed heavy on my mind, though.

Two years after the tsunami, so I've read, at least one hundred and thirty or so people were sentenced to floggings for supposedly violating local religious laws. A friend of mine in Jakarta was incredibly stressed because after losing both parents in the tsunami, her younger sister was caught red-handed with her boyfriend in an Internet café, guilty of "heavy petting and kissing," reported one local radio station. They received sixty lashes each.

I recall again the two nurses at the health clinic. How does it feel living life every day with such attractive faces in a place where women are forced to take responsibility even for the worst outcomes that spring from other people's lusts?

I suddenly understand what Rania is unable to utter.

Being blown away isn't something that happens to you every day—or ever, for that matter. But the new wing of this hospital isn't just mind-blowing because of its hyper-modern appearance. Rather, behind its appearance I can feel the mechanical workings of a new system—one that is sound, solid, and *genuinely* modern. Astounding how the system has changed the behavior of the patients and their relationship to the hospital.

I decide to sit down in the lobby and take it all in. The clean floor and gleaming surfaces, the trash receptacles in every corner. The efficient service counters, the bathrooms that don't make one shudder in disgust. I watch visitors move around the space, how they seem to think twice about littering or sitting on the floor, about eating and drinking wherever they like. I watch patients sit down and line up in an orderly fashion. There's German money behind it, I heard, big government money. Even the demeanor of the place follows suit.

I nudge Farish.

"What if they report us to DOCIR?"

"Who cares?"

"Who told you they weren't cooperative?"

"Someone."

"Come on," I say, wringing the hem of Farish's shirt. Why is he being so juvenile? "Who?"

"Okay, okay. Diva told me."

"I see. And who told her?"

"Who else? Enough already. Let's check if Team Leon asked the hospital to say they had an avian flu patient in critical condition, even though it's not true."

Team Leon. It sounds so animalistic. And how about us—what's our team name? Team Farun? Or Team Fara? How about Team Firaun ("Firaun" as in pharaoh or tyrant? Hmm. Maybe not.) How about Team Arish? Or Team Holyfucking Stupid?

But I continue to let myself follow Farish from counter to counter (so orderly, so clean, with clear, legible signs and icons) until we arrive at the Swine Flu and Avian Flu division in the Leuser Annex in the old wing of the hospital.

The inpatient rooms are spacious, clean, and empty, as in not a single patient. Each room has been named for a bird—the Spotted Dove Room, the Kingfisher Room, the Cockatoo Room—complete with accompanying pictures on the walls.

"This used to be the children's annex," says the Leuser Annex coordinator with a smile, as if she has fond memories of the place. Her name is Farida. She's in her midfifties, perhaps closer to sixty. She's friendly and receives us with open arms once we successfully convince the head nurse of the infectious diseases division in the new wing that we aren't reporters or just poking around for fun. (Farish told them we're from the Ministry of Livestock.)

She spends fifteen minutes showing us around. So far, this annex is the most equipped and well-organized facility we've visited. When we express our amazement, Farida sighs, though her smile doesn't falter.

"To be honest," she says, stroking the sophisticated pieces of equipment in the observation unit as if they're her children, including a special fridge for storing cultures from patients before they're sent to R&D. "I'm constantly worrying all this billion-dollar equipment will rust because it's never been used. I keep asking the higher-ups why we don't put it to use in other parts of the hospital. It's a shame, don't you think? It cost so much money. But they never listen to me. So there you have it—all because they had so much money, they didn't know how else to spend it."

"Ma'am, you said the equipment is rarely used. So there aren't many patients being treated here?"

"'Aren't many'? More like practically none."

"Really? How many patients have there been this year?"

"This year, none. Last year there were only two cases, and they were only suspected ones. Both of them were treated in the inpatient area, and their conditions were monitored. Once they were stable, they were free to go. They were here for four days at most."

Secretly, I've already made note of this information—it was written down on the whiteboard in the corridor:

1. Date of admittance: 17 July 2011.
Date of discharge: 21 July 2011.
Status: Susp. H5N1.

2. Date of admittance: 1 September 2011.
Date of discharge: 4 September 2011.
Status: Susp. H5N1.

"Sometimes I get *so* bored supervising this annex. Especially since everything has to be kept confidential and doing anything requires permission and strict procedure. It feels like we're wasting away here."

"But I heard there was a new case."

For a moment the woman looks confused. Then something seems to spring to mind. "I remember now. Yesterday two people from Jakarta came to visit, saying they were from the central branch of SoWeFit. They looked around, but only briefly. However, they did speak with the head of the hospital in the new wing for a long time. When they were gone, he called me into his office.

"He began talking about how all the people who worked in this hospital were honest and professional and that there was no higher calling than to provide the best possible care for the sick. Everything else, especially anything to do with politics and business, we should avoid as much as possible, and that should be the case in all matters, no matter how tempted we might be to do otherwise. Integrity is more rare than knowledge, he said.

"Then he got up from his seat and thanked me. But before I left his office, he whispered, 'We don't have any avian flu patients, right?' 'No, sir,' I answered, and he shook his head again. 'That's what I thought,' he said with a smile."

Amazing. Massive fail for Team Leon this time around.

Because I've just obtained evidence of Leon's rottenness, I almost forget that Farida is still with us when we leave the Leuser Annex and head down the corridor of the old hospital wing to the parking lot. She seems thrilled at being able to leave her post for a while.

"This part of the hospital is actually very susceptible to flooding. When the tsunami happened, the water was almost seven feet high." As she speaks, she points toward a grassy area that's been turned into a cluster of pleasant public gardens.

Before we go out to meet our car, which is picking us up outside the lobby, I turn and shake Farida's hand again. She's like an older version of the two nurses in the Lampisang health clinic: sweet-natured, generous, without any pretentions. She squeezes my hand in return. For a very long time.

"Are you married, my dear?"

For some reason I laugh. Everyone I know has stopped asking me that question or is tired of asking it.

"Not yet, ma'am."

But Farida isn't willing to let go of my hand just yet. Her expression turns serious. "Loving someone isn't easy, dear," she says. "Because loving someone means you have to be prepared to lose them. But it's better to have loved than to never have loved at all."

I feel like I've heard someone else say those words. My mother, maybe, or a character in a film. But before I can recall whom, Farida says, "Today is my husband's birthday. When the tsunami hit, he was on the beach with our youngest grandchild. If he were alive today, he would be sixty-five years old. I loved him very much."

29

CREAM, OYSTERS, AND THAT FISH SCENT OF MINE

*In my dream I see Nadezhda at a very upscale restaurant in some European
city. With her is a man of unlimited funds and means. Each dish is placed
before them with great flourish and respect, with a different wine each time,
accompanied by long, drawn-out oohs and aahs from Nadezhda and her
dining companion, as if they're being surprised every twenty minutes by some
new, soul-stirring work of art.*

*I don't find it strange at all that Nadezhda looks a lot like Julia Roberts
from* My Best Friend's Wedding. *Long, disheveled locks; hands constantly
in motion; an ample laugh bursting from her lips every now and then.
Even her dining companion—who calls her Jules, Julia's character in the
movie—looks a lot like Rupert Everett.*

*Suddenly Rupert tells Nadezhda—"Jules"—that there's something
she must do. He acts as if she's committed some sin and wants her to
repent.*

*Indeed, Nadezhda-Jules has sinned: by being an inspector for that noto-
riously elitist restaurant handbook, the Michelin Guide.*

"What do you want me to do?" asks Nadezhda, half in tears.

"I know how much pain it'll cause you," says Rupert, bringing his super-handsome face close to Nadezhda-Jules's super-lovely one. *"But I think it would be best for you to join Le Fooding."*

"All right," says Nadezhda-Jules, looking like she's trying to be brave despite the spasms she feels in her chest. *"But on one condition."*

Rupert waits expectantly, eyes gleaming.

"Help me steal Dermot from Cameron."

Dermot Mulroney, as we all know, is the actor who plays Jules's friend in the film, and Cameron Diaz plays his fiancée, of whom Jules is crazy jealous.

Rupert smiles. Then he kisses Nadezhda-Jules's hand and immediately orders the most celebrated wine on the menu to mark the momentous occasion.

When Nadezhda-Jules reports to the Le Fooding office the next day, she is immediately given an assignment. Her first task is to slip into a small village in the south of France. It doesn't appear on Google Maps. There, she must look for any and all restaurants worthy of being included in the annual Le Fooding guide.

"Remember, we are the antithesis of the Michelin Guide," says the man briefing her. *"We're different, independent, down to earth."*

When he says this, Nadezhda-Jules looks like she wants to protest: How can you be down to earth if you have a private plane? But she remembers, perhaps, that appearances aren't always an accurate reflection of reality. Anyway, with that famous face—and wide mouth—of hers, she has to try extra hard not to seem like she's used to being pampered and fussed over.

After she lands safe and sound (that is, with limbs and head intact), Nadezhda-Jules wastes no time. With the help of the GPS on her wrist-watch, which also functions as a camera and a knife, she immediately sets to work. So deeply in character is she that I'm positive she's secretly regretting having such a well-known face. Though Nadezhda-Jules herself, *as an observer of culinary affairs, doesn't seem overly concerned that the inhabitants of Pezenas, Languedoc-Roussillon—with its total population of less than 2,600 people—will recognize her, I think of what Julia Roberts's friend, Hugh Grant, might say at that very moment. Something like: "Remember, you're the most famous woman in the world."*

Yet, I know how Nadezhda-Jules thinks. To her, men are always wrong for some reason when it comes to assessing reality—especially when that reality involves rescuing famous women. Just look at how much effort Hugh put into protecting Julia from being targeted by the paparazzi in Notting Hill those many years ago. So I understand completely when Nadezhda-Jules decides to follow the example of the very wise Ruth Reichl, who, when she first started her career as the restaurant critic for the New York Times, protected herself and her integrity by donning disguises.

She's just about to take a bite of dessert, a modest pear tart, when she's suddenly set upon by a group of people and forced into a truck. I examine them closely. It turns out that they're all internationally renowned restaurant critics—five men, one woman. The woman looks a bit sorry for Nadezhda-Jules, but she's the only other woman in that truck; she'd be outnumbered from the get-go. I can't imagine that any female restaurant critic would have any sympathy for someone who looks like Nadezhda-Jules.

"You write for Le Fooding," says one of them. He spits on the ground: pah! "Do you know what this means? You have deliberately spit on the foundation so laboriously laid down by the gods and goddesses of all that is civilized. You have deliberately mocked the standards they have put in place regarding how to weigh a dish's good and bad points. Therefore, as punishment, you shall be exiled to a deserted island."

"Don't you know who I am?" says Nadezhda-Jules piteously. "What am I supposed to do on a deserted island?"

They don't give a damn. The American food-critic legend is impatient to get to a famous seafood restaurant in Montpellier about forty-five minutes away. The female critic refuses to eat any bread except that of the Pôilane bakery in Paris and immediately gets slammed for snobbery by the other American critic—a popular one—who's boasting about his latest list, The Top Twenty Pizzas in America. The two critics from Asia are squabbling about the origins of satay and Nasi Padang—*or to put it another way, dishes that come from Indonesia but are claimed by other countries as theirs.*

Suddenly a voice speaks in a soothing British accent.

"Well, what about a tropical island? You'd have an abundance of food to eat there." The owner of the British accent, as it happens, is also a famous novelist. "Not only that, you'll have plenty of time to devote to godly submission and prayer. And with that face, who knows? You might even meet a hot Latin lover in a paddy field and live happily ever after in sexual and spiritual bliss. And wouldn't that just be perfect?"

❦

"Pengkang!" exclaims Nadezhda, repeating the same word she's been exclaiming all day—at the airport in Jakarta, on the plane heading to Pontianak, at the airport in Pontianak, on the car ride to the hotel. Her manner is that of a child hankering after some new toy, pestering her parents to purchase it.

Every time I hear the word, I can't tell whether I'm tickled or annoyed. Tickled because it really is quite a funny-sounding word and annoyed because "pengkang" sounds akin to *pekak* or *kak*—"grandfather" in Balinese—though I was taught by my mother to call my grandfather *pak mem* or *kaki*, the latter being the source of some debate during my childhood since it was also the Indonesian word for "foot." It was confusing enough whenever his feet (*kaki kaki*) got involved (e.g., "There's an ant on my grandfather's/foot's foot/grandfather"). Imagine when "kaki" began springing up in other contexts: "A ceremony will be held at the foot/grandfather of Mount Agung." Or, "I lay my fate at the feet/grandfather of the God of Love." Or, "I offer up my prayers at the foot/grandfather of that banyan tree."

"Pengkang," however, doesn't have the same wealth of meaning. It's the Pontianak term for lemper. That's right: those now ubiquitous glutinous rice rectangles of Javanese origin stuffed with shredded chicken and wrapped in banana leaves, aka lemper. But with a twist. Pengkang is stuffed with dried shrimp and shaped like a cone.

"It's a local specialty of Chinese extraction," says Nadezhda, as if this fact enhances its culinary value. "The interesting thing is that pengkang should always be eaten with a dish called *Sambal Kepah*, though the sauce the clams are served with is more like a sweet-and-sour sauce than a spicy sambal one. Also, pengkang always come in pairs—they're tied together before they're grilled. Cute, huh?"

"And where must we go to get this extraordinary dish?"

"To a restaurant called Pondok Pengkang, outside Pontianak," Nadezhda says with that enthralling nonchalance of hers, as if giving us the address of the nearest convenience store.

"*Outside* Pontianak? How far?"

"A street called Jalan Peniti, in Siantan. In the Regency of Mempawah."

"That's like an hour away, Nadz," says Bono, staring at Google Maps.

"We could just go on to Singkawang from there," says Nadezhda. "Since we only have one night."

"But Singkawang's too far away," I protest, even as I realize how tragic it would be to come all the way to West Kalimantan, unfunded and out of wounded pride, and not go to the city of Singkawang. "It's ninety-three miles from here, give or take. It's practically on the Malaysian border!"

With her usual brazenness Nadezhda turns to Farish—*my* Farish—and bats her eyes. "Can we go to Singkawang? Pleeeaaase?"

Not long after I give in (when have I ever said no to Nadezhda?), it occurs to me: there was a time when we used to say, before setting out on trips, that we wanted to "discover new things"—"be surprised" by unexpected experiences. And that's exactly what would happen. In those days, we didn't have any assumptions, or even expectations. We'd discover and celebrate all of it: the wonderful and captivating, yes, but also that which wasn't. And for a while there would be something sacred about the relationship we had with those experiences, as if they belonged to us and us only—for that which was new to us was that which was new to the world.

Now in this age of technology, of information galore, we may say the same things, when in fact we are no longer talking about discovering something new. Rather, we are talking about something already discovered, already widely known and shared, so all that remains for us to do is sharpen our personal perceptions. If we think pengkang is really nothing special and there's no art in it, or that it's a culinary gem worthy of esteem, more interesting than Javanese-style lemper, say, only then do we make it our own.

But these are complicated thoughts I'd rather avoid, and there are too many of them running through my head. I especially want to avoid those involving a certain someone who's trying not to stare at me from behind Nadezhda's dense thicket of hair that she didn't have time to blow dry this morning. The same someone who, yesterday, on that strangest of nights, surrendered himself to me for some reason—let me breathe him in. Not all of him, mind you. Just his notes of coffee and wood. And the aroma of cheese that has long been giving him away (though he was embarrassed about it, and faintly melancholy). And in return I surrendered myself to him, though not all of me either: the cream, oyster, and fish scent of my body.

❦

Nadezhda's probably right about a lot of things. But she's not entirely right in this particular matter.

She's telling me about women who flare up like a candle the second a man parts their vulva—who instantly lap up and devour, with the flames of their new knowledge, the pastures of manhood. Women who, after sleeping with their first man, start asking their men to touch this spot or that jot, this comma or that semicolon, for how long, yes, longer, yes, longer, don't stop!

She's probably talking about herself. But how many people in the world are like Nadezhda?

I deeply suspect that there are different levels of readiness. Young women aren't like men—they don't immediately start out thinking about their bodies being with those of other people, of two bodies becoming one. Thoughts of sex will come, of course, but those thoughts usually come later. Still, it doesn't mean that there's nothing there.

Young women touch themselves once in a while, yes, but the pleasure they feel, unlike older, more experienced women, is akin to that of eating alone. It's a singular pleasure—one that wouldn't be as pleasing, I'm pretty sure, if the experience was shared. And yet in other respects, women share so much with other women—the boys they like, the pervs and creeps who try to woo them, that first kiss . . .

Maybe this is why so many young women tend to idolize certain men, otherworldly men. They fall for them precisely because they are unattainable and belong to another world. They aren't sinful because they're not real.

They're not the man lurking by the tree outside your house at certain hours of the night who whips out his penis whenever you pass by. They're not that friend of your uncle's who likes to make eyes at other women, including you, even (or perhaps only) when his wife is in the same room, and who offers to buy you a drink at the bar after running into you and your friends at a nightclub.

Nor are they the men you revere, who inhabit the same world but are much older—my high school PE and English teachers, in my case—those you consider safe and beyond reach because of those demarcations: teacher versus student, old versus young, those who are married versus those who've never had sex.

So when I bare every inch of myself to someone, I know he's the one and want him to be the one. Of all the men in the world, I've picked Farish because I just know he'll never leave me. Even when he already knows how I smell and taste down there.

As I hear Nadezhda blathering on about the "madwoman" who sat next to her on the flight to Pontianak, I see what are starting to become very familiar sights: an enormous house that belongs to the governor of the province ("Mr. Cornelis has served two nonconsecutive terms, seven years total," our driver boasts); the regent's office, of similar size; the district head's office, enormous as well and resplendent in bright candy hues; the local headquarters for the national organization for civil servants' wives unwilling to be bested by the others. In short, shows of government grandeur that provide points of contrast with their surroundings: the little bridges that cross the streams, connecting the main roads with citizens' houses; the channels of water flowing parallel to the streets; the Duri River in all its beauty; the houses that remind me of those in Banda Aceh, sans the zinc roofs.

"So I thought the woman was a typical *ibu-ibu*. You know the type. The wife of some rich regional government official who makes trips to Jakarta to throw money around and who feels superior to her ibu-ibu friends because she's 'part of the metropolis.'" Nadezhda speaks with some vehemence. "But also the kind who'll immediately revert to narrow-minded parochialism when her part of the country is criticized or misunderstood by those in the capital."

"So what's wrong with that?" asks Farish.

It suddenly occurs to me that he may not feel part of the metropolis himself. I've noticed that he's happy to talk about being from Padang, especially when we were with Toba and Rania, or about certain worlds in Jakarta that he knows much about. But he keeps his own counsel when our conversation meanders to the Paris and Melbourne and Cambridge of Nadezhda's universe. Suddenly I'm assailed by anxiety. After last night—and the nights before when my feelings were building up, layer by layer—I've developed another feeling for him: loyalty.

"Nothing," says Nadezhda. "What was wrong was that she dared to talk big—to me. *Me*. Can you imagine? Shameless about it, too."

As Bono listens, he titters, like a horse out of a Disney movie. He seems to be enjoying all this immensely. They really are perfect for each other.

"At first she went on and on about her life and how different it used to be when her husband was still alive and her children were living at home. Now they're scattered all over the place. Now if she wants to go anywhere, she has to go solo.

"At the time, I'm still thinking, 'Oh, she's probably worried that people think she's searching for a new husband, or maybe she even feels guilty about it, so now she's trying to justify traveling around alone.' And up to this point, I'm still fine . . .'"

Outside, by the side of the road: an Aladdin Optical outlet, coffeehouses and reflexology parlors, a restaurant called Oizumi Ramen, a Padang cuisine restaurant called Siti Nurbaya, little alleys forging paths into the very belly of the city, eateries with no names. They all flash by, one after another.

". . . until suddenly this woman says that tomorrow she's going to Singapore to spend time with her youngest, who's at Cambridge. At first, I'm thinking, 'Cambridge? Really?' But before I can even react, the woman adds for emphasis, 'Cambridge University. In England.' So I immediately say, 'Oh, wow. That's wonderful. Which college?'

"'Cambridge University, in England,' she repeats a little tentatively. 'Yes, I know—I'm familiar with both the university and the city,' I say, trying not to sound like an asshole. 'But Cambridge University is made up of thirty different colleges. So which college is your youngest attending?' The woman looks confused. 'My youngest is at Cambridge University in England,' she repeats, so inanely that now I'm the one who feels stupid. I think maybe this woman genuinely doesn't know which college her son is attending. It's entirely possible. A lot of parents of foreign students don't understand, don't care about such details. To them, the main thing is 'my child has been accepted by a prestigious university.'"

"So you didn't say that you went to Cambridge?" asks Bono.

"Nah," says Nadezhda.

I have to admit, in this respect, Nadezhda really is pretty cool: at least she doesn't show off in front of people she doesn't know well.

"But for some reason, I remembered my own days at Cambridge, and how hard it was to get in, much less stay on without overdosing or becoming a lesbian. I was also reminded of how momentous it was when we found out which college had accepted us—Newnham or Murray Edwards, Lucy Cavendish or Clare—because it meant different professors, different dorms, not to mention different traditions. And for some reason I felt so bloody irritated. Anyway, I worked terribly hard to control myself."

The Kapuas River, the longest river in the archipelago, stretches before us, fanning out left and right, lush with coconut palms, perfect as a postcard.

"So, just when I've managed to shrug it all off, the woman then says that her super-genius kid is studying medicine, and because he's so smart, he's just been asked to be director of the World Health Organization. 'The World Health Organization?' I say, my eyes popping out of my head. 'The director of the World Health Organization,' she repeats, beaming with pride. 'He's still at university, and he's been asked to be director of the World Health Organization?' I ask, and the woman simpers once more. 'Yes. He's getting a master's and a PhD degree at the same time.' At that point I'm so amazed, I'm not sure if

I should blow up at her or laugh. And before I can even say anything, the woman says, proudly, 'He's just like my late husband. He used to be director of the World Health Organization, too. And he was from Pontianak, like myself.'"

I laugh along. It *is* a hilarious story. So hilarious that, for one brief moment, barriers are bypassed, and I see Farish turn back from the passenger seat and cast a gleaming, almost loving grin my way.

30

PENGKANG COUNTRY

Me, twenty-four years old: I burst into tears when the waiter tells me that the restaurant I'm seeking has closed down. "Signorina," says the waiter, "this is Venice. Here, everything changes so fast."

"That's not true," I say between sobs. "Nothing ever changes here. You always end up back in the same place no matter where you start out on this island. And I've circled the city three times."

"But almost all the restaurants in Venice serve linguine alla vongole."

"Yes, but I want their version of it."

"Signorina, why don't you try eating here? I'll bring you a linguine alla vongole a hundred times more delicious."

"Grazie. You're very kind. But I should just go back to my home country. I came to this city for the specific purpose of eating at that restaurant. Many years ago, in my previous life, I ate there with my parents. Their names were Giancarlo and Aurelia. From then on, they never ate at any other restaurant."

The waiter stares at me for a very long time.

"Bene," he says at last. "If that's the case, safe travels, signorina. See you in a hundred years."

For the first time on this journey, we're taken hostage by our driver. Shortly after we cross the Kapuas River, he suddenly stops the car. Then he requests that we all get out and pay our respects to Tugu Khatulistiwa—the Equator Monument—as if without doing so we won't truly internalize the significance of being on the equatorial line, equidistant from both poles.

But travel requires that we be respectful and considerate to others, so we acquiesce to the wishes of our good driver. He is, after all, the owner of the place where we're staying in Pontianak (800,000 rupiah round-trip from Pontianak to Singkawang and back, gas not included—a cheap package courtesy of his hotel). And though he keeps repeating that he's a devout Muslim originally from Palembang with a wife of Dayak descent who's converted to Islam, and that he's uncomfortable about being in the vicinity of any food with pork in it, he's willing to drive us to Singkawang.

The monument is bizarre. The original structure, a sort of gyroscopic tower built in 1928 by the Dutch and not particularly well designed, has been overshadowed by an enormous structure resembling a mausoleum. From the roof of this second structure, a humongous replica of the old tower protrudes. I'd love to be able to say something nice to our driver, like, "Wow! It's great!" But I simply can't. We just circle the structure for a while, unwilling to enter despite our driver's goading. Fifteen, twenty minutes pass before we finally feel brave enough to get back into the car, nodding enthusiastically, if a little inanely, and showing each other the photos we've taken.

The restaurant—a traditional-style building with a raised floor and located by the main road—is large and empty. The walls at the front of the house resemble large, open windows with latticework carved in traditional patterns. On the inside, on sections of wall covered in yellow paper overhead, drawings of the restaurant's specialties are displayed in rows, interspersed with photos of a young President Sukarno: Sukarno sitting, Sukarno giving a speech, Sukarno laughing.

When our food comes out, it's served on the standard red dishware of Chinese restaurants—patterned with flowers, shells, Chinese characters, and a yellow border with a blue gatelike motif. Nadezhda was right: the two portions of pengkang we order come in pairs so we each get one dumpling. They resemble the *Ketupat* dumplings that are often served with satay.

The sambal-based dish it comes with—Nadezhda was right again—looks more like Chinese-style sweet-and-sour clams, the sauce thick with cornstarch. The Pengkang themselves are a cross between two more familiar versions of glutinous rice dumpling: the Javanese lemper and the Chinese *bacang*. When I break mine in half and examine its contents, the still-intact shells of the dried shrimp seem to be imprinted into the rice itself. For a moment I'm startled, because in a certain light it's like looking at gold foil. I can almost hear it crackle, like a copper rod slapping against water.

Even the taste is far more complex than that of your average bacang. Its savory deliciousness is due to all the oil—that much is obvious—but the combination of sour, spicy, and sweet flavors is almost beyond all conceiving. And this also holds true for the freshwater prawn satays, six enormous pieces to each skewer.

Another thing I notice: in West Kalimantan cuisine, tomatoes, chilies, and Bombay onions aren't just used as seasonings to be minced, pounded, or ground into a paste. They're also used for decoration. Resting on the platter of stir-fried water spinach are Bombay onions sliced into elegant curves reminiscent of the intricate gold pattern of an embroidered *songket*. The red chilies are lovably chunky.

It's a curious palette. The *Sambal Teri*—anchovies in a sweet and sourish sambal sauce—has exactly that boldness of form and color. I even hold a tomato or two to the light to give them a good look over, and they are interestingly protuberant—fat and long, like potato wedges. As with the onions and chilies, there's a peculiar charge to the color of said tomatoes that makes them brighter, clearer, more neon than average.

Then I remember: I've had this same impression before, when I ate at a restaurant in South Jakarta specializing in the Samarinda cuisine of East Kalimantan. For reasons unknown to me, it vanished almost overnight, right when they were starting to gain a reputation for themselves. How extraordinary the dishes were—the green, silver, and scarlet! You could practically taste the crispness, the freshness, from the colors alone.

But this evening, the dish that most pampers my vision and palate is a platter of clam satay. In appearance they resemble your usual Malaysian satays made of chicken, beef, or lamb. They're slathered in muddy-brown peanut sauce and beautified with a garnish of tiny green scallion rounds, and I'm at pains to find the right words to describe their flavor. *It's so . . . so . . .*

"Cosmic!" says Bono, leaping to his feet, face aglow. It's as if he's just discovered a new law of physics.

We linger in the restaurant for some time, for the afternoon has brought with it a relaxing breeze. It's also an opportunity for Farish's fingers and mine to entwine themselves beneath the table every now and then. We watch and giggle as Nadezhda terrorizes the waiters for this recipe and that. We follow Bono with our gaze as he wanders around the restaurant, taking photos at the satay grill and chatting with the family who owns the restaurant before finally ordering an entire box of pengkang—which we'll eat who knows when—to be delivered to our hotel the following day. There is a new complicity between us, delicious and subversive.

31

THE CIK WITH THE PINK ROLLERS

I kind of regret leaving for Singkawang so late in the day. Getting there from the restaurant in Siantan takes about three hours, and when we reach Singkawang, in the pouring rain, night begins to fall, turning all into shadows and ash.

But it doesn't take long for us to see what's before our eyes: a city that appears to be frozen in time. Old shophouses and coffeehouses unfaded by rainwater; Buddhist monasteries of cotton-candy hues that seem to assert themselves despite the menacing shadows cast over them. Alabaster-pale faces that come from a faraway land, seemingly unweathered by heat or rain.

After circling around on Jalan Diponegoro, which is as quiet as a ghost town, I finally tell the driver to park in front of a small general store that also sells various *manisan*—fruits pickled, dried, or preserved in syrup. Bono looks anxious because there's no trace of a single restaurant from his sacred list.

"Damn it, don't they have a sign? The noodle place is supposed to be on this road, near that temple over there." Bono shakes his head, half panicked, half starving.

"So tell me," says Nadezhda with an irritated expression. "Where'd you find this list?"

"The Internet."

"From someone's blog?"

"Yes. But all the information is incomplete. Sometimes it just gives the name. Sometimes there's a note—a hundred yards from this store or fifty-five yards from that temple—but none of it's accurate!"

Nadezhda looks as if she wants to make some stinging remark, but for some reason doesn't. Instead she hurries after me, and we enter the manisan store, as if hoping that it will help her behave. It's impossible that anyone could have the energy to bicker after our food orgy only a few hours ago.

As if trying to remain faithful to his convictions, Bono chooses to roam outside, sniffing the air while he's at it, with his iPad, Internet, and sacred list. He's quite a sight. But who knows? Maybe these spectral restaurants will materialize, emerging from behind a curtain of rain. As a gesture of brotherly solidarity, Farish chooses to get drenched with him, though I know he couldn't care less about the food he might miss. Men.

The store, meanwhile, is delightful. All kinds of manisan, in glass jars, are lined up on the wooden tables at the front of the store, and there's a special section devoted to dried fruits. A middle-aged man sits in the doorway, a little to the side, his features a combination of Malay, Chinese, and Dayak. Spontaneously, he introduces himself. We ask if he's the owner. He says no with a friendly smile and nods in the direction of an ethnic Chinese woman, also middle-aged, sitting behind the cash register inside.

The cik, pale as marble, rises from her seat and invites Nadezhda and me to sample various manisan—"Those are peaches. That's kedondong. That's snakefruit in spicy syrup."—and half an hour later we've each purchased around eleven pounds of this and that. How wonderful to become two children again! To be surrounded by all that sweetness and light!

Moments later Farish approaches us. He immediately sits down next to me and holds out his hand. I place a single *ceremai* on his palm. I long to taste the sweetness of the tongue caressing the pale berrylike fruit. But life is about delayed gratification. In return for my patience, he offers his sweet and sticky fingers. We watch our fingers interlace for one second, two.

Not too long afterward, Bono shows up. His face and hair are soaked.

"Did you find it?" I ask.

He shakes his head. He looks dejected.

"Enough already. Let's not look for noodles now. We'll try again tonight. How about looking for something lighter first?"

"Like rujak?"

"Yeah, what's that rujak place called? Thai Phui? The one you said was famous."

The cik's face lights up. "I know the place you're talking about," she says with an accent difficult to place. "It's near the market."

A quarter of an hour later, after circling the downtown several times, where we pass warungs selling grass-jelly cappuccinos and a bunch of others specializing in "smashed" chicken or *Ayam Penyet* (fried, then beaten with a mortar and pestle to make it more tender; "A culinary colonizer if there ever was one," Bono grumbles), we finally find the rujak cart. For a while we just stand there, staring at the modest cart and the tarpaulin behind it, mud-spattered and at a seventy-five-degree tilt, as if it's just been hit by a hurricane. It's wedged in among houses in a tiny alley that I'm not sure I'll ever be able to find again.

Two simple tables and long wooden benches stand in a covered area behind the rujak cart. The space shares a wall with the house next door, which, once I take a peek, turns out to be very picturesque indeed—an old house on stilts like the ones they use as film sets for Indonesian horror films, with walls of ivory yellow, windows painted a salted-duck-egg blue, and maroon tiles. A woman in her sixties sashays onto the veranda in a housedress and a head full of rollers. She leans on the low wall that separates the eating area and the terrace of her house and chats animatedly with the rujak seller in a language we don't recognize.

The woman seems intrigued by us. How could she not be? Among the members of our company are the Beauty Queen and the Marvelous Chef, two rare specimens you don't see every day. Then, in a halting Indonesian, she asks, "Where are you from? What are you looking for?"

With a surge of hope Bono immediately asks about the location of his noodle eatery. "Cik, would you happen to know where . . ."

Meanwhile, Nadezhda and I are busy choosing from the menu that's been painted on the tarp: Fruit rujak? Rujak with peanut sauce? *Lim Mui* prawn crackers? Lim Mui pineapple? Vermicelli soup with anchovies? Rice porridge with anchovies?

"What the hell is Lim Mui?" whispers Nadezhda.

But it's beginning to get dark, and I'm worried we'll run out of time before we can sample the special dishes Singkawang is known for—kwetiau goreng and *Bubur Babi*. And they're two dishes I don't want to miss. It'll take four hours to get back to Pontianak, and once we arrive at the provincial capital, we still have to try its dinner specialties.

Finally, Nadezhda and I agree to get two orders of fruit rujak to go and bring them wherever we end up eating next. As it happens we don't need to go far. The friendly but slightly vain cik tells us that there's a place right next door that's famous for its kwetiau goreng. "Just take the rujak with you," she says, as if sending her grandchildren off to play at a neighbor's house.

Our company walks through the drizzling rain to the building next door. Sure enough, in the courtyard out front is a signless cart selling various kinds of noodles, including kwetiau, with half a dozen seats, almost all of which are taken. Relieved and convinced that in a little while we will be dining on wok-fried flat rice noodles, I want to go back to the car to get my pen, which I've left behind. But Farish stops me.

"It can wait," he says. "The car won't be parked here, remember? Our driver's a man of strong faith. I bet he doesn't even allow his car to be in the vicinity of pork lard."

Unconsciously, for one second, I stroke his hand. I still don't believe he's decided to stay with us on this expedition, which has nothing to do with sick poultry. And I still can't believe that his reason is me.

We sit at tables close to the cart. An old *koh* and his son, in his thirties, take turns preparing the food. My heart races in excitement, as if this is the first time I've ever seen anyone make noodles, rice, or kwetiau goreng as the Chinese do—swiftly, deftly, hyperkinetically, accompanied by a fire dance that begins with a roaring blaze before the flames begin lapping at the contents of the wok. I'm so mesmerized that I don't even realize that we're being *totally ignored*. Instead of being served, we're not even being seen.

"Your conclusion?" says Nadezhda.

"They're suspicious of outsiders," says Bono.

"Oh, come on. Let's not be so sensitive." Even as Farish says this, he sounds uncertain.

Nadezhda suggests offering herself to the koh and his son.

"Both of them?" asks Bono.

"Yes, both of them," says Nadezhda, sashaying toward the cart. "Father and son. My specialty, really."

Her charms don't work; our order still doesn't come. Bono is getting restless, as are Farish and I. But then I remember my fruit rujak, still sitting in its brown paper bundle. Like an elementary school student who's just remembered the lunch her mother packed, I quickly give it a try: one spoonful, two. Fruit rujak with cuttlefish is a Singkawang specialty. So why am I not impressed?

"Let me try," says Nadezhda. She hasn't taken two spoonfuls before she pushes it aside. "No good!" she says a second later.

"No good in what way?" Bono asks, though we already know he's not a rujak fan in general.

"Atonal," says my other friend, as lightly as if she were saying, "No kick," or "Blech." But this time my planet and Nadezhda's are in alignment.

It's 5:45 p.m. There's no other choice—we have to return to Pontianak. Farish has just called the driver, who's laying low who knows where in order to escape the fires of hell. Suddenly the friendly but slightly vain cik from next door shows up and walks our way. Her head is still covered in pink rollers, but she's abandoned her floral-print housedress in favor of a blouse and orange pants. Without waiting for an invitation, she sits at our table so that Bono and Farish, already on their feet, looking out for our car, are forced to sit back down. When she hears that our food still hasn't come, she immediately heads over to the koh and his son and begins stamping her foot until the entire courtyard is quaking in fear.

"We're going to my place," the woman says firmly. "They'll deliver your food there."

Not one of us dares to protest. And so we troop back to the intriguing-looking house and spread ourselves out on the veranda. In less than five minutes two young men blushing bright red ("The koh's grandkids!" our host whispers gleefully) are hurrying over with three plates of our kwetiau goreng and two bowls of bubur babi. When Bono gets out his wallet, they shake their heads and bow repeatedly. "On the house," they insist. Then they dash back next door like a pair of chicken poachers.

The mistress of the house grins. "Come on," she says. "Hurry up and eat, before it gets cold."

The sight of my kwetiau goreng makes me so happy. I make note of its color—a glossy dark brown—and also its texture and the thickness of the gravy, which sets it apart from kwetiau goreng as it's often done. Plus they haven't been stingy with the fishballs I so love. These are densely packed, like *keket* fishcakes, but more springy and petite.

Bono and Farish seem more interested in the bubur babi—Farish because he's trying to avoid "the forbidden meat" (the kwetiau goreng contains pork) and Bono because he's always interested in trying new things. The rice porridge is brimming with vitamin K . . . kind of: *kecambah* (sprouts), kencur (a type of galangal), *kangkung* (water spinach), *kunyit* (turmeric), *kacang panjang* (snake beans), *kacang tanah* (peanuts), kerupuk (prawn crackers), and, most importantly of all, finely minced *kesum* (Vietnamese mint). It is the spiciness of the kesum leaves that puts the "pedas" in variants of bubur babi called bubur pedas. *Pakis* (fiddleheads), *serai* (lemongrass), and *daun salam* (bay leaves) play a role, too, though they don't start with *k*. And as accents: crisp-fried anchovies and juice from a fresh lime, drizzled on top. Superb.

Once we've polished off everything on our plates, we realize we haven't said a word to our gracious host. We haven't even asked her to join us. How can we take our leave without seeming rude now? *Thanks so much for all your help, ma'am, but we really should be heading back to Pontianak . . .*

It turns out she has a lot of stories to tell. At first we listen halfheartedly, but we're gradually sucked in and lose track of time. We listen as she tells of the history of Singkawang: how the majority of the city's residents, about 70 percent, are Chinese, and how Chinese settlement here has been going on since the eighteenth century—a byproduct of a flourishing gold-mining industry that was responsible at one point for producing a seventh of the world's gold. Of that 70 percent, the majority of the local Chinese are of Hakka, and the rest are Teochew.

"My father is Hakka, but my mother is part Dayak and part Malay. My kids are gorgeous. They have fair skin from their Chinese side, but they also have big, round eyes." She widens her own eyes, which are pretty big themselves.

"Now two of my kids have settled in Singapore. Both of them are working, but one of them *still* has no interest in getting hitched! At least they're not here anymore. I mean, don't get me wrong, it's not that I wouldn't be happy if my daughters lived in Singkawang. But how are they supposed to find good husbands here? They're too smart, too self-sufficient. Meanwhile, a lot of families here sell their girls to the foreigners who come from all over, businessmen from Taiwan, China, Malaysia, Singapore. All so they can be someone's—anyone's—wife! Can you imagine? I'd rather kill myself than sell my own daughter. Granted, a lot of businessmen are willing to pay more than the amount set by those son-of-a-bitch marriage brokers. Sometimes a broker will only ask for five million rupiah, and the businessman will pay up to thirty million. Actually, most of these contract marriages aren't legal either. Or, they are, but only for a certain length of time—usually, up to five years. But it still doesn't mean this city's ideal for my daughters."

"When was the last time you saw them, cik?"

"Oh, I'll see them in a bit at Yuan Xiao Jie."

We hear the words, but we don't understand.

"You know. The fifteenth night of Chinese New Year."

More silence.

"It's the Cap Go Meh Festival," says the woman with a smile, as if recalling some pleasant memory. "It means my husband and I will get to see our grandchildren again. They come to see us in Singkawang almost every year and watch the festivities at the same time. We usually go as a family to offer prayers at Tua Pek Kong temple along with the *tatung*. They pray for protection—to be impervious to harm."

"Tatung?"

"You know, the spirit mediums who can't be hurt by sharp weapons. They run themselves through with knives and swords during the procession, but it doesn't leave any wounds."

"Does Cap Go Meh involve any food?"

"But of course!"

Then the woman tells us all about the Bacang Festival, also known as Duan Wu Jie. To honor the memory of Qu Yuan, a poet who drowned himself in a river, people scatter uncooked grains of glutinous rice over the water to prevent the fish from eating Qu Yuan's body, which, mysteriously, was never found. Then people gather to eat the rice dumplings the Bacang Festival is named for before jumping into the river together.

Similar rituals, though not as specific, are observed throughout the lunar year. In addition to the rites performed in the temples as part of Sembahyang Rampas, known among other Chinese communities as the Hungry Ghost Festival, people prepare offerings for ancestors whose spirits are restless because their bodies were never found or because their descendants neglect them. On the same day, people also distribute rice to the poor and the needy.

The woman continues. "If I'm not wrong, the Mooncake Festival next year will be sometime in late September. The next Onde-Onde Festival will be late December this year."

"How cool is that," I say, thinking of all the people in Jakarta who fly en masse to Singapore every year to shop their hearts out—under the pretext of celebrating Chinese New Year.

"Singaporeans come here to watch the festival, too," the woman says, as if reading my mind. "Especially those with family in Singkawang. This is where a lot of them come from—the ones of Hakka descent, anyway. Back in the day, when their ancestors lost the Kongsi Wars with the Dutch, they fled from Singkawang and went to other islands and cities to start new lives. If not in Sumatra, then Kuala Lumpur or Singapore."

"Wasn't Singkawang originally part of the regency of Sambas?" asks Farish.

"It was the capital! But around thirteen years ago, Sambas was split into two regencies, Sambas and Bengkayang. At the time, Singkawang was made part of Bengkayang. Now Singkawang has become a proper city—it's classed as a level two region, separate from Bengkayang."

"But the population's still not that big," says Farish. "A little less than five hundred thousand, isn't it?"

"Far less. Two hundred thousandish, most likely. That's why people get excited about the Cap Go Meh festival. The city feels more lively."

"How are relations between ethnic and religious groups?" asks Farish, suddenly switching modes from NGO activist to TV talk-show host.

He keeps grimacing when no one else is looking. Maybe he has a stomachache. Or maybe he's stressed out by watching our car enter and exit the alley multiple times before disappearing yet again, to somewhere uncontaminated by "forbidden" things.

"It's been pretty peaceful so far," says the woman, plucking a piece of rose-apple from my unfinished rujak and popping it in her mouth. "But the Islamic Defenders Front has a branch here. And you know what they're like. They always fret when they see anything Chinese that sticks out too much. Like, oh, I don't know, those dragon statues, for example. Such upstanding citizens they are otherwise! Sometimes they stage protests or make trouble. Now Hasan Karman, who used to be our mayor—*he* was a decent guy. Strong. Firm. He was the first ethnic Chinese mayor to be elected in Indonesia. He's not in office anymore. The pair who won the last regional election was Awang Ishak and his running mate, Abdul Muthalib. There were even accusations from Hasan Karman's side about the election results. He said they'd been fixed. But he was overturned when he took it to the federal level."

Farish asks, "Wasn't there the sense that ethnic Chinese voters were being discriminated against around the same time Hasan Karman announced his candidacy?"

I'm pretty impressed that he knows so much about it.

"Yes, in 2007. The thing was, many of us—our people, I mean—didn't get our voting ballots. Whether it was intentional or not, who knows? So we protested. People took to the street. The Regional General Elections Committee finally gave in, and we were allowed to vote."

It's 6:45 p.m. That's it. It's time. Slowly, I get to my feet.

"I'm sorry, cik, but we should go," I say carefully. "Thanks so much for your company and your incredible stories."

The woman looks at the others, as if wanting to see what they think.

I try again. "We hate to go . . . but we do have to go back to Pontianak. We only have tonight and part of tomorrow to sample the cuisine there. We return to Jakarta tomorrow afternoon."

"Before you leave for Pontianak," she says, as if not really listening, "you have to stop by this rice porridge place." She hands Bono a business card with the name of a restaurant on it. "It's on Jalan Diponegoro. There's a big sign. You'll see it from the car. Don't bother with the Pasar Hong Kong district here. *Bubur Gunting, Kembang Tahu, Sotong Pangkong*—you can find all that in Pontianak. But this porridge place has no equal. It's the most delicious porridge in the world. Or, as we say here, *nyaman inyan!*"

The restaurant is spotless: shiny white-tiled floors and walls, a light-green-painted door, and round white tables with red plastic stools. The owners are a couple and their two daughters. The four of them look like they come from another world. Their fair-skinned faces beam as if smiling is just what they do, and they look back at us—shyly, surreptitiously—in all of our own otherness as well. If the husband, who doesn't say much, is obviously in charge of the kitchen, then the wife is the restaurant PR manager. Her Indonesian is more fluent, and she's more communicative.

But it's their children who really make an impression. Both of them are still in elementary school, one in her final year, the other in third grade. When the youngest isn't bringing us tea or water, she sits at a table in the corner and diligently does homework. I notice Bono can't stop taking photos of the child. He does so secretly, without her knowing. He really does have a soft side, this sweet, funny tornado.

There are certain things that transcend barriers and language. It's as if we don't need to tell the amiable koh we're in a hurry. Swiftly and expertly, he prepares two bowls of *Bubur Babi*, pork porridge, for the three of us to share. Farish declines; this is where he draws the line.

Everything seems to shimmer. And then he cracks an egg over the porridge while it's hot. The egg white billows like a cloud; the yolk spreads like a ray of light. The result? One of the universe's tastiest dishes. Though out of solidarity with Farish, I only try a bite.

Religion makes us poor judges of art.

᭦

It's exactly eleven o'clock at night when we reach Pontianak. Not wanting to waste time, we ask our driver to stop on Jalan Gajah Mada, near our hotel. I pay him the fare. One should see the look on his face. How is such a relief even possible? Farish says he didn't dare eat anything the whole time we were in Singkawang.

We start walking down the street. Contrary to our expectations, there aren't that many street vendors left or places to hang out by the side of the road. Jalan Gajah Mada at night in Pontianak isn't like Jakarta's Jalan Gajah Mada, which is eternally bathed in light.

After walking for twenty minutes, we finally stop at a tent warung selling panfried *Ko Kue* and *Chai Kue*. Ko kue is a kind of steamed rice cake made from rice flour or taro flour, mixed with chives, then stir-fried with chili peppers in a large, shallow wok. Unlike its panfried dumpling cousin, *kuo tie*, which is usually served dry, ko kue is served with the oil and a reduction of the sauce it was fried in so that it's a bit moist, without affecting the crispiness of the dumplings. Chai kue is a filled dumpling with a definite shape, like a sunny-side-up egg or a round *serabi* pancake. It's starchier, yet packs more flavor because it has a charred, smoky taste to it.

Because it's late, the warung appears to be getting ready to close. Several low benches and stools are already being put away. But Koh Awe, the old koh who owns the warung, just sits there in the corner of the tent without making a sound. He has a sour expression on his face. The cheerful face of a gubernatorial candidate with a Pepsodent-white smile peeks out from the campaign poster behind him.

His assistant, a boy, begins to fidget when he sees how intensely we survey the premises and facilities, from the enormous woks to the molds for the batter, from the metal pans filled with cooking oil and fried garlic chips to the assorted sambals and ingredients for red-bean shaved ice on a low wooden table an inch from the exhaust pipe of a parked motorcycle near the road.

"How many?" the boy asks, with an impatient expression. "All we have left are chai kue."

"What's inside them?"

"All sorts of things. But right now the only fillings are chives, taro, shelled mung bean, and jicama. Which ones do you want?"

We order a dozen pieces of each. Farish orders a shaved ice, and so do I.

Once we realize the chive and taro ones taste the best, we order more: twenty pieces total. And once those are gone, we ask for eight more.

The boy raises a hand. "Sorry, sold out! We're closed!"

With heavy hearts—even heavier now that we know that a single chai kue from paradise costs a mere two thousand rupiah—we move on and keep heading down the ruler-straight road, going farther and farther from the hotel. The distance we cover doesn't feel long, and we're not tired.

Ten minutes later we see a vendor selling sotong pangkong—"beaten squid." In the covered area behind him, a group of men are playing dominoes. Out of curiosity, and also some strange doggedness that comes with the length of our journey, we order a portion to go.

For five minutes we stare at the skinny man as he squats on the floor, barbecuing a sheet of dried squid over a charcoal grill, then beating it to make it tender.

"How much?"

"Twenty thousand rupiah, my friends!"

The squid immediately leaves a bad taste in our mouths—it's expensive, there's no culinary skill involved, and it's tough, to boot!

Bono can't stop fuming. "A bicycle tire would taste better than this!"

He only ceases when we arrive at a long-established restaurant famous for its "100 percent halal" beef kwetiau.

Maybe by this time the fatigue has set in, but we don't know it. For some reason we keep finding faults—the noodles are too dry; it tastes too bland; there are too many bean sprouts. We're so disappointed that we don't even have the appetite to go in search of the Pontianak specialty *Lek Tau Suan*, a sweet yellow soup made of shelled mung beans served with slices of deep-fried dough fritters. And this, despite our seeing lek tau suan vendors spread out all along the length of Jalan Gajah Mada a mere hour ago.

"This must be what they call fatigue," says Nadezhda, ever the philosopher. "There are times when one has to concede that one has reached the limits of pleasure and that one's senses have shut themselves down."

"Nadz, *please*," I say.

"Let's go home," says Bono, sounding like a routed soldier. "Tomorrow's another day."

32

WET

Tomorrow's another day. But what will happen to me the day after? And the day after that? After returning from Banda Aceh to Jakarta for a single night following that failed expedition? After not reporting to Irma or my boss at OneWorld, only to leave again the next day with a ticket already in my possession (paid for by the project I've abandoned without reporting to) with a band of big-city mischief-makers, for Pontianak, where I was no longer needed? After deliberately not responding to Irma's texts? *Aruna, let's talk when you get back. Aruna, are you back? Aruna, are you okay?*

Not Run. A-RU-NA. How can Irma address me so formally after all this time?

And let's not think about Farish. How can I face the rest of my tomorrows without him? Take now, for example, as I try to figure out how to sneak out of my room—to leave Nadezhda by herself with her sharp senses and powerful radarlike intuition—in order to sleep with him. Yes, sleep with him. Like we did last night in that hotel room near the Jakarta airport, after returning from Banda Aceh and before this morning's flight to Pontianak, my shrieks and moans shaking the heavens.

It's amazing how quickly two become one, a man and a woman, one cavity, one warmth, fluids mingling, loins melding. I imagine that only a mother who's given birth to a son knows what it feels like to live in that circle—birth, destruction, resurrection—she who prepares her womb to be torn apart so that her child, her love, can detach himself from her in order to live. No wonder, then, if no love can surpass a mother's love for her son or that a son pays his mother the greatest respect when he chooses for his mate the woman who most reminds him of her.

But the man who entered me last night, incubating in my wetness, calling me his darling and saying I was beautiful, the man who parsed the scents of my body, all one million of them, with his nose and his ravenous tongue—won't he detach himself from me, and detach himself for good? Since I don't know how to ask someone to stay? Since I don't know how to claim ownership of anyone?

Last night, he said I was beautiful. Why on earth would he whisper such a lie?

"I'm fat," I said, hiding my flabby stomach under the covers.

But he pulled them away. "Let me look at you," he said. "You're not fat. You're beautiful."

Suddenly I burst into tears.

I'm back in the present, back in Pontianak. Nadezhda mumbles next to me as she sits on her bed, like she always does when typing on her laptop. "Behind a stone, there lurks a prawn . . . like water on a taro leaf . . ."

"Those are easy ones," I say in an effort to redirect my thoughts. She really is writing an article about popular sayings and food.

Nadezhda looks up from the screen. "You really know what they mean?"

"Of course. The first means that someone has a hidden motive. The second means someone keeps changing his opinion."

I always feel ridiculously pleased when I see Nadezhda's amazement at something I've said.

"Oh, come on," I say. "Find a harder one. Or one that hardly gets used. Those two are so cliché. You might as well ask me what it means to 'eat one's share of salt.' Or to 'find a fallen durian.'"

"Not bad, Run," she says, genuinely impressed. But she wouldn't be Nadezhda if she didn't try to best me. "All right. Tell me what this one means. I bet even you won't know: 'The rhinoceros eats its child.'"

"Huh?"

"The rhinoceros—"

"Okay, okay," I say quickly. *Damn it.* "Does it have something to do with a person who isn't right in the head?"

"Nope. Nowhere close."

"Okay, I give up."

"It means that a parent has disowned a child to protect his or her reputation."

I burst into laughter. "What the . . . *you're* the rhinoceros!"

Nadezhda laughs. "Talk about analogies that miss the mark. Does a rhinoceros really have a reputation to protect? I mean, it lives in mud."

We giggle maniacally for a while as we continue to talk about the contents of Nadezhda's column. We also talk about sayings that involve chickens ("Like a chicken eating grass" for someone who's barely making ends meet), geese ("You don't need to teach a goose to swim," which means you don't have to teach a smart person what to do), and other birds ("Like a bird is he; the body is caged, but the eyes soar free"—such is the fate of a cooped-up child). For a few brief moments I can forget about tomorrow.

Then, all of a sudden, I hear myself blurt, "If you ever come across a saying that means a thin man could never love a fat woman, let me know."

Even I'm astonished when those words tumble out of my mouth.

In Jakarta, after Farish and I did it several times (and I started to be brave enough to open my eyes while he was having his way with me), I realized it was morning. The sun penetrated the curtains, sprinkling our bare legs with flecks of light. Seized by the embarrassment of us being so together, so naked, in that strange bed, I pulled the covers over my exposed breasts.

He stretched. And when his eyes opened, he smiled. "What is it?"

"It's almost six thirty," I said. "We have to be at the airport in a little while."

"Okay," he said, reaching for me.

Brushing his hand away, I grabbed a glass of water from the bedside table, desperate to go to the bathroom and brush my teeth.

"Hey. C'mere."

"We have to get ready," I said.

I couldn't even bear to let him look at me. Not in my disheveled state. A single second of clarity was all it would take for him to realize that what had happened between us was madness, that it should be aborted as quickly as possible. Besides I was frightened, sure that my words—my sworn morning-time foes, and the foes of all solitary souls—would betray me the moment I was forced to return to earth.

"Okay," he said.

And for a split second, I worried he would think I was rejecting him.

"Are you sure you still want to come along? To Pontianak?" I asked.

"Of course!"

"Any word from Darius and Diva?"

I had my back to him, but I could still feel his smile. The night before, a few minutes before he kissed me in the cab—those critical minutes that caused me not to go back to my apartment after all, that brought us to that hotel instead—we had been laughing together over those two names: Darius and Diva. "Like a pair of failed Broadway musical producers," he'd said. "Like two twins who do low-grade stand-up comedy," I'd said. I guess it's true. Great minds think alike.

"Don't worry, darling. If they want to contact me, fine. If not, that's fine, too. I'm a free man after all."

Did he have to call me 'darling'?

"The culinary tour we're doing isn't . . ."

But it wasn't the time to explain. Or demand explanations. What was the point of always feeling, at every moment, that people were saying anything but the truth? What was the point in disbelieving the tangible and real? What was the point in making one's self miserable?

All right, I thought, willing myself to stop. With difficulty, I turned to face him. We locked eyes. Bowing his head, he kissed my hand. And my eyes grew wet once more.

"Aruna," he said. "I'm not a jerk."

Now, in Pontianak, in this room I'm sharing with Nadezhda, that scene plays again and again in my mind. Including the moment when he pulled me on top of him and kept me there for a long time. But what if he isn't really in love? But what if it's just temporary? *But, but, but.*

Then I recall what my grandmother once told my father, whose own favorite word was "but": "If you start out by being dissatisfied with what you have, imagine what will happen when you lose it."

33

The Conference of the Birds

When I was ten I wrote a short story about an old woman who was very lonely and had no husband or children.

One day she went to the market and bought a sheep. Days passed, then weeks, then years, and that sheep was her only friend. Every time she finished knitting something from the sheep's wool, she would daydream—of a field, of a house, of the children she wished she had. And whenever she began to do this, the sheep would shake its head and say: "It's just a dream." And that's what the sheep continued to say until the old woman died.

The story was inspired by a French children's book that my mother once read to me. The sheep was called Patapon.

∿

Several days ago, before we left Aceh for Jakarta, and long before we left Jakarta for Pontianak, Farish and I made a pact to forget about avian flu politics until the completion of our trip as set out by our ticketed itinerary. But opening a laptop sets oneself up for failure. And I just can't resist Google.

In the past week, two out of three patients in England have been confirmed as suffering from a new virus similar to SARS. The most recent case, which involves two siblings, proves that the deadly virus spreads through human-to-human contact. Of the eleven confirmed cases of novel coronavirus (nCoV) infection worldwide, five have resulted in death. The majority of the infected victims were residents of or visitors to the Middle East. The public has known about nCoV since September 2012, when the World Health Organization released a statement concerning a Qatarese man who contracted the virus during a visit to Saudi Arabia.

Interestingly enough, the following statistics had been added as a footnote to the article above:

Of the eleven nCoV cases, which were confirmed by laboratory results, five have occurred in Saudi Arabia, with three deaths; two in Jordan, where both patients have died; three in England, where all three are undergoing treatment; and one—the Qatarese man—in Germany, who has recovered and needs no further treatment.

Truly, the world is never just "the world." And victims are never just "victims." And so here is a disease that knows no boundaries, treats everyone in the world as equals, and yet people are still trying to emphasize that this is "Me" and that is "You."

"Run?" says Nadezhda presently, just as I've slipped under the covers and switched off my bedside lamp.

"Yes?"

"A lot of people don't pay attention to physical appearance if they feel like they're compatible with someone." Her tone is serious. "To them, the person they feel compatible with is the person they think is attractive."

My heart races.

"So?" I say, still trying to play dumb.

"So that's the answer to your question."

"Oh. Right."

"And by the way," she says, "it's not a problem for me if you want to sleep with him tonight."

⋎

I've overslept. On the desk there's a note from Nadezhda: *I'm in the lobby with all my bags. If you don't come down and check out in the next thirty minutes, Bono and I are going out to get some* Kwee Cap.

Starting last night, kwee cap has become Nadezhda's new peng-kang. It's kwee cap, do or die. To be honest, though, once I do some Internet research on the dish I previously assumed was a portmanteau of kwetiau and kecap (aka noodles and sweet soy sauce, or HEAVEN ON EARTH!), I'm not particularly enthusiastic about tracking it down. Like Bono, I've always liked my noodles on the skinny side, and my pasta the same—spaghetti, spaghettini, vermicelli, capellini, the thin strands you find in bowls of chicken noodles in Jakarta's Chinatown. As such, I'm much more interested in *Bakmi Kepiting*, the crabmeat noodles Pontianak is so famous for, even if one can find it easily enough in Jakarta. The flatter varieties of noodles and pasta, such as fettuccine, bucatini, or kwetiau, I enjoy only when the sauce is sufficiently flavorful and bold and has been absorbed into the noodles themselves. In this dubious-looking kwee cap dish, though, bloated sheets of kwetiau languish in a heavy broth-based soup. I feel full just looking at it.

I do manage to get to the lobby in less than half an hour. My opinion immediately gets skewered, like the apple William Tell shot off his son's head.

"Isn't it obvious?" snaps Nadezhda. "The kwetiau's function is to neutralize the incredibly greasy broth! And the soybeans in the soup add some crunch, don't they, not to mention the crispy prawn crackers. You seriously don't want to give it a chance?"

I don't blame her for being mad. It's almost 10:00 a.m., and kwee cap, like kwetiau and bihun bebek in Medan, is a breakfast dish, often sold out by now. But in her own words: incredibly greasy. She knows this, so why the need to defend the culinary merits of a dish so obviously unhealthy? Isn't it enough that we've spent days accumulating belly fat without exercising at all? (Though I don't see the slightest hint of any on Nadezhda.)

Farish seems to be sending me a coded message from where he's sitting: *Eednay elphay?*

I grin. Bless him. I'm well aware that my solidarity with him and his eating preferences grows stronger every day. I know that, as a Muslim, he's trying as hard as possible to avoid eating pork. Yet he always joins us when we eat dishes he knows contain pork lard—those more subtle about it, like the chai kue we ate last night and the "chicken" noodles in Medan, but also the more straightforward ones, like the food at that killer porridge place in Singkawang and the restaurant opposite the thugs' lair in Medan.

However, there must be something about lovemaking—something that sparks a sense of solidarity and lays bare one's deepest secrets, yes, but that also demands certain sacrifices be made as a result of that alliance. Does Nadezhda feel like I should bend to her wishes? Because she's being so gracious about a situation I myself feel ambiguous about?

In the end, after we check out and leave our bags with the concierge, we circle the Chinatown area in our car, slowing down whenever we see a restaurant or cart that looks like it might sell kwee cap. But no luck.

All along the way I search for signs of swallows. My bird-watching friends say they're one of Pontianak's distinctive features. "A lot of ethnic

Chinese in the city center breed swallows in their homes," said one of these friends. "They eat the nests and sell them as well. Check the roofs of the shophouses—there are sure to be lots of swallow 'apartments' there. A lot of the birds are free to come and go as they please since they always return."

However, like my deranged friends, who are searching for kwee cap like ants searching for sugar (that last expression, another gift from Nadezhda, the Queen of Popular Sayings!), I don't see a single swallow. Then I remember my friend also saying the best times to look are when the sun is about to rise and just before sunset.

Our driver takes us to a tiny street. He's positive there are kwee cap sellers there who stay open until eleven. "'Cause they're no good, I bet," Nadezhda grumbles ungratefully. Finally we decide to get out of the car and walk down the street. Ten minutes pass, then fifteen—and still no kwee cap. Guess kwee cap and we just weren't meant to be. Clever creature, that kwee cap, knowing it should stay away. If only everyone could be as smart.

And yet, the cold war between Nadezhda and me continues.

Our hunger and the blazing sun leave us washed up in front of a store that sells . . . it's not entirely clear. But above the door are the words "Sheelook Aquarium." Next to it is an unnamed restaurant with a darkened interior—as if the lights haven't been turned on yet. Or maybe this area's experiencing a partial blackout. What does catch our eye is this: "Mi Kepiting" in big letters on the window of a small stall outside the aquarium store. Crab noodles.

"Well, we did want to try that mi kepiting restaurant on Jalan Gajah Mada," says Bono, ever the slave to his sacred lists. "It's the most famous one. And it's pretty close by."

"Enough, already," says Nadezhda, in a tone of defeat. "Let's just eat here. We can see how these compare with those incredible noodles of yours later."

A teacher of mine once said, "It's when we don't expect anything that we receive."

So is it really possible for someone who doesn't take words all that seriously, who's guilty of proclaiming at least nine different foods to be "the best in the world" even as she genuinely values sage advice about how we can't, and shouldn't, compare apples with oranges, tea with coffee, sugar with salt—to mean it when she says this is it, the best of the best?

Sure, it's possible. And I'm not the only one feeling that way when our bowls of mi kepiting are set on the table. It's a humble dish, modest at a glance and unburdened by reputation—a dish which, upon close scrutiny, you know will be delicious, with its yellow noodles coated in brown sauce and all its other droolworthy attributes (the *keket* fishcakes, some boiled, some fried; the fishballs, prawns, and crab claws; the three to four chunks of meat; the two crunchy sheets of deep-fried wonton). It's a dish that sweeps all speech from our mouths the second it makes contact with our tongues.

And with these small undercurrents of happiness, I'm reminded again of something my grandmother said once—a Minangkabau woman who spent her whole life steeped in the pictographic Arabic and Minangkabau writing of her culture—"There's a poem called 'Manteq at-Tair,' or 'The Conference of the Birds,' written in the twelfth century by the Persian Sufi poet Farid ud-Din Attar. I first read it as a girl, but only now do I realize what the last stanza of that long poem means, that there are things so beautiful and so impossible to fathom that no human being, not even a poet, can penetrate them."

This is the last stanza: "They knew that state of which no man can speak; this pearl cannot be pierced; we are too weak."

Maybe it's times like these when we really don't need language. What's the use of language if we already have this conference, this gathering—four people who are, for one brief moment, happy?

34

Super-Expensive Wine and the *Kitab Adab Al-Akl*

WORK PERFORMANCE EVALUATION

Aruna Padmarani Rai

December 2011–December 2012

Aruna is intelligent and hardworking but daydreams a lot, as if her mind is somewhere else.

She is quiet and sometimes comes across as passive. She also isn't very fond of socializing.

The few times she has displayed enthusiasm are when she has been given field assignments.

She appears to be virulently anti-family and anti-marriage.

Chances are, she hates men.

Clearly, she thinks to herself, this is just a bad dream.

Work-free days. Is this my life now?

◈

"Do you have a secret life?" Nadezhda asked me.

I thought about my other friends. Those who probably did have secret lives would never confess to them; those who didn't, like myself, would probably say yes.

So I said yes.

That was after we returned to Jakarta from Pontianak—ten days after I met with Irma and tendered my resignation from the avian flu project, and eight days after OneWorld called me in and told me to take some time to think things over before deciding whether I wanted to continue working for them or not.

I was overwhelmed by shame. I stopped calling my friends. I stopped hanging out at Siria. I stopped reading anything that had to do with avian flu. For some reason I even began to feel lukewarm about Farish, who was still working at OneWorld. Or maybe because I was disappointed that he didn't—or rather, didn't need to—do something radical like I did.

Twelve days after I resigned from OneWorld, I attempted to get myself a secret life.

I began jogging three times a day. But on the days I didn't go on morning runs, I ate french fries from the Burger King on the ground floor of my apartment building. I started a small indoor organic garden. I borrowed ten million rupiah from my mother and invested all of it in a stock recommended by a friend. I replaced Gulali's dry cat food with the steamed salmon I would eat for dinner and nearly bankrupted myself. I had a flirtatious online chat session with three men at once, two of whom I'd just met through Facebook. I watched free porn on the web until a virus crashed my computer and I was forced to promise God that I'd never do such filthy things again.

I wasn't consistent, though.

I wouldn't always refuse when Farish asked if he could come over and spend the night. And I wouldn't refuse when he asked me if I would suck his dick. But each time he left, I trained myself to think, *This is the last time. Don't feel like you owe him anything.*

Nadezhda laughed. "But he's your secret," she said. "Because of him, you have a secret life."

Then one day I experience something surprising. I'm swimming in a pool at a five-star hotel, having used Nadezhda's membership card, when I fall in love with a little girl. She's in the kiddie pool, learning to swim. Her mother is from the Philippines, and judging by his speech and accent, her father appears to be Italian.

I watch as the girl skirts the edge of the pool, pausing every time she reaches one of the corners to peer into the pool's depths as if assessing the danger of the situation. Every time she gets splashed with water, she shrieks—out of fright, but also out of joy. She's adorable. I can't turn away.

The following week I attend a party with Nadezhda at her behest. "It's a birthday party for a close friend of mine," she says. "She's turning forty. Come with me. We won't stay long."

I try not to think about how I'll fall into that category soon: a woman in her early forties.

On the lawn outside the enormous house, a boy is sitting on a swing. He's around four years old. The swing creaks and squeaks as it rises and falls, rises and falls. His shadow sweeps across the grass and bounces toward some banana trees at the foot of a concrete wall that juts into the sky, overshadowing the trees. He's so cute. He has rosy cheeks, and his eyes are big and round. When his mother comes out and carries him back into the house, I think how lucky I'd be if I were his mother.

Bono is worried because he thinks I'm clinically depressed.

"I'm not clinically depressed."

"Nadezhda told me all about it. She says you feed Gulali fresh salmon every day and that you read trashy novels and never change your clothes."

"The woman's a liar. Of course I change my clothes."

"Come to Siria tonight. I've invited some good friends of mine. They're all excellent wine drinkers and have some of the most refined palates in the country. We'll be at a special table in the back, in a private room. Come on, it'll be fun."

The other women—two socialites—and I watch as the four men swirl the wine in their glasses. They raise the glasses to their noses and breathe in the aroma before each taking a generous sip. Bono is in his chef's uniform, but the other three are wearing expensive-looking jackets with silk handkerchiefs protruding from their breast pockets. They converse consistently and fluently in English. Four empty wine glasses have been placed before them.

Man Number One, a banker who used to work for a well-known investment firm in New York, has just raised the stakes to five hundred dollars. *Five hundred dollars!* That's how confident he is about being able to guess the provenance and vintage of the three wines that Bono has specially procured for the evening.

They sniff the wine in their glasses again. Then they take another swig, a bigger one than before, fully savoring the flavors before letting some of the liquid flow down their throats. Without swallowing the rest of it, they breathe in through their lips and allow themselves to become one with the fragrance permeating their mouths. I watch them hold their breaths before releasing the air through their nostrils. Only then do they allow the wine to glide beneath their tongues before they gulp it down. They nod their heads and roll their eyes thoughtfully. They smack their lips.

Silence.

About six minutes later Man Number Two, a businessman in the mining sector, squints and says, "Definitely a Bordeaux."

The others nod.

"The dominant grape is clearly Cabernet Sauvignon," he continues. "And there's definitely some Merlot and Cabernet Franc in there as well."

"Given its vitality and boldness," declares Man Number One, "I bet it's a superior second growth—as good as a first growth in terms of quality. And it's an excellent vintage. That goes without saying."

Impatient to have his say, Man Number Three, the handsomest, squirms in his seat. According to the socialite on my right, he owns several boutique hotels in Bali, Jakarta, and, soon, Raja Ampat.

He speaks. "The color is on the lighter side, the tannins are firm but not too forward, and the aroma is intense. This must be an old Bordeaux."

"I detect spices and a hint of tobacco," says Number One, glancing at Bono, who just sits there and smiles.

"I bet it's a Medoc," says Number Two. "It's not that full-bodied, so it can't be from Saint-Emilion, or Graves, or Pomerol. So which estate is it from?"

"Can't be Margaux," says Number Three, taking another swig. "Pauillac, perhaps?"

"Definitely not a Margaux," affirms Number One. "The bouquet's not bold enough."

"But it can't be a Pauillac either," Number Two snaps. "A Pauillac is entirely different in character. This wine is smoother, more elegant, a little bashful, even."

"I agree," says Number One. "It's very feminine."

"But it's so fragrant," says Number Two. "Like fall. Dry leaves . . . earth . . . ripening apples . . ."

"I'm positive it's a Pauillac," says Number Three.

"Maybe it *is* a Margaux," says Number One, uncertainty creeping into his expression. "A Margaux would have the same elements. Strong notes of earth and wet leaves after a rainfall. Notes of chocolate, clove, and nutmeg, with hints of sweet fruit, like cherry or plum."

Suddenly, Bono cuts in. "All right, so what's the verdict?"

After a few more minutes of intense concentration, they each have their answer.

Number One: Margaux. Chateau Pierre Lichine. Vintage: unknown.

Number Two: Saint-Julien. A 2000 Chateau Talbot, because 2000 was a good year for Bordeaux.

Number Three: Pauillac. Chateau Mouton Rothschild, more than twenty-five years old. It could also be from Napa, more specifically, an Opus One—a joint venture between Robert Mondavi and Baron Philippe de Rothschild.

With pride, Bono produces the bottle in question. "Gentlemen," he says theatrically. "May I present to you a 1989 Chateau Gruaud Larose from Saint-Julien."

There's a collective gasp from the three men. They race for the bottle.

"No way!" says Number One. "How long have you had this, Bon? It's from 1989? Oh my God!"

"No. Way," says Number Two, stroking the bottle like I might stroke Gulali. "Isn't this a 'super second'? One of the best second-growth Bordeaux in the world?"

Because none of them have guessed correctly, the bets are canceled. They all smile in relief.

Before they finish the bottle, Bono begins pouring the second wine into glasses, where the three men can't see him. And the process begins again and is repeated for the third wine.

I've always been jealous of people like this—people whose jobs involve gathering in fine-dining establishments enjoying hellishly expensive wine, while most people have to sell flip-flops to have enough to eat. But this time, for the first time, I'm impressed by these upper-class palates. Life isn't fair, but I have to admit that all the luxury they live in hasn't been in vain.

When I'm offered some wine from one of the super-expensive bottles—the second, a Burgundy, and the third, a Brunello di Montalcino—I feel as if my feet have been rooted to the earth. It's flavor is so deep, so grounded. I swoon.

Of this I'm sure: only lovemaking, or things analogous to it, could make me feel this way.

I wasn't the least bit drunk last night. This morning I even feel refreshed. Then, inexplicably, I miss Farish. But he has to go to work. So I have to make do with Gulali, the stockpile of salmon in my fridge, and a bunch of pirated DVDs.

In the evening I call him. "Let's go to Mataram," I say. "After all, it *was* supposed to be our last stop on that project."

Farish says nothing.

"I promise not to do any avian flu investigating while we're there," I say.

After almost a minute of silence, he replies, "I can only take two days off from work."

That night, after we make love multiple times, I fall in love with him again.

Who does Lombok belong to? Lombok—the island of the *Babad Lombok* and *Nagarakertagama*, the island of Muslims and Hindus, of Christians

317

and animists. It's the island of the Sasaknese and Balinese peoples, of Peranakan Chinese and of Indonesian Arabs. The island of the Sumbanese and the Javanese, too. The island of the religions Wetu Telu and Boda.

Lombok is an island of cassava and corn, of cloves and cinnamon. Of coconut and tobacco, banana and vanilla. But it's also an island of tofu- and tempeh-makers and of dried shrimp and salted shark-meat producers. Of jackfruit dodol and salted-egg eaters and of *Ayam Taliwang* and suckling pig aficionados. It's an island of *turi* trees, so profuse and loved you see them everywhere alongside the rice paddies to prevent soil erosion.

That said, the driver who takes us from the airport to our hotel in Mataram doesn't seem too taken with any of it.

"Everyone knows water is scarce in Lombok," he says. "It's most dire in the south and central parts of the island, but actually, all of West Nusa Tenggara is experiencing a water crisis. Deforestation's to blame, and illegal logging, not to mention the unusually long dry season. It's affecting agriculture. And everyday life, too. The wells in my village are beginning to run dry."

Around two hours later we're at a restaurant highly praised by a friend. The food is served buffet-style. Behind the glass window are enormous tureens brimming with meat and vegetable dishes of all kinds; almost all of them look unhealthy. Not a single person there seems friendly—not the restaurant owner, not the waitstaff, not the customers. They all eye us with suspicion.

On my plate are some slices of tempeh in sambal sauce, sautéed green beans smothered in coconut milk, grilled chicken, sautéed mustard greens, and a dry, fluffy heap of *serundeng*—grated coconut seasoned and toasted in a wok. Someone sets a bowl of chicken curry in the center of the table for all of us to share. I look up. It's Bono, of course, eyes always bigger than his stomach, attempting to make it all better. I still don't touch it.

I'm happy he agreed to come along with Farish and me, but this food! Oh son of a bitch, what a disappointment. It tastes like the blandest of home cooking—nothing to justify a special trip. The worrying thought crosses my mind that Lombok's reputation for food has been exaggerated.

I feel trapped. And whatever others may say about ayam Taliwang, Lombok's signature chicken dish, I don't love it. The spice mixture the chicken is coated in is tempting, no doubt, made of dried red chilies, tomatoes, Bombay onions, garlic, palm sugar, salt, shrimp paste, and kencur. But with all the versions of ayam Taliwang I've tried, in Jakarta at least, all that lingers is the spiciness. The same goes for *Kangkung Plecing*, which is often so hot I can't even taste what should be a refreshing combination of water spinach, grated coconut, and peanut. Oh, and that stupid *Beberuk*. Don't even get me started. It's crazy how spicy the stuff is. But I banish these thoughts. Anything that allows me to spend time with Farish shouldn't be refused. And now that my two closest friends know about us, I feel much more relaxed.

Then, just for the hell of it, we ask the guy at the table next to ours where we can find the tastiest ayam Taliwang in Lombok. Without even lifting his head, he gives us the name of a restaurant specializing in Taliwang cuisine. According to Farish it's not too far away.

"Let's go there later," says Bono. "Or tomorrow."

No one protests because we really don't have that much time, and the idea is to pig out.

Even Nadezhda doesn't say much. She's been looking a bit glum since we met up at the airport in Jakarta. Sometimes I forget that she's never wanting for things to do. Maybe she's beginning to get bored with these trips.

Outside, the streets are dark and desolate. Like Banda Aceh, Mataram goes to bed early. To get to this restaurant, we traveled down dark roads practically devoid of any illumination. It's a far cry from our ride from the airport to the hotel, which spoiled us with endless stretches of picturesque rice paddies and fields, the landscape looking like something out of a child's drawing: sun, clouds, birds, houses, fields. That's the part of this story I'll remember and take home with me.

I receive a WhatsApp message from Priya: *How backwater is it? Worse than Banda Aceh?*

She used to work for two people on the Aceh-Nias Rehabilitation and Reconstruction Board. She feels like she knows Aceh well.

Almost.

Oh dear. Anyway, did you eat anything yet?

Yup. Meh.

Are you still following up on the avian flu stuff?

What's with Priya? Why is she asking something she already knows the answer to? I don't respond for a while, a bit ashamed about having to say no. Then I think, *Why should I feel ashamed to admit my failure to someone whose job seems to involve constantly changing jobs? And why shouldn't I tell another food lover that I'm here on a culinary expedition?* So I tell it like it is, and just like that, as if we're talking about the weather, she changes the subject and begins to discuss all the places she ate at when she was in Banda Aceh. Places that slipped under my radar when I was doing research. Silly girl.

I suddenly lose my appetite and become anxious again because Priya's touched on the subject of avian flu. I stop texting.

The night is still young, and Bono asks our driver to head to an area with lots of restaurants.

The driver looks at Bono like he's a creature from outer space, and says, "There aren't any areas with lots of restaurants. They're scattered all over town."

Suddenly Bono asks him to stop the car. Startled, the driver hits the brakes, and the car behind us almost rear-ends us.

"Are you crazy?" shrieks Nadezhda. "What is it?"

Bono points to a restaurant by the side of the road. "Look at the name!" he says frantically.

We all look up. On a bright-red signboard in bright-yellow letters: "Nasi Tempong. Super-Spicy Sambal. Duck, Braised Beef, Catfish, Chicken, Fish."

"*Nasi Tempong*! *Tempong* rice!" Bono shrieks excitedly, looking almost deranged. "How crazy funny is that? Come on, we have to try it."

"What's crazy funny?" asks Nadezhda, whose knowledge of street slang is fairly minimal. I quickly whisper in her ear what "tempong" means—a portmanteau of *tembak* or "shoot" and *bokong* or "ass" (i.e., anal intercourse). Instead of being shocked, she giggles. Of course.

I giggle, too. "Slut," I say teasingly.

Farish, who sometimes still tries to act holier than thou, attempts to provide some balance. "'Tempong' is just a variation of *tempeleng*," he says. "It means 'to slap.' Eating nasi tempong feels like being slapped because its sambal packs a punch."

We all ignore him.

We get out of the car and march toward the restaurant. The driver watches in bemusement—"Who are these people," he's probably asking himself, "hopping from one restaurant to another? Who does that?"

The intriguingly named nasi tempong—or rather, this restaurant's version of it—is advertised as rice served with tofu, tempeh, fried chicken, fried battered *jambal* fish, raw vegetables, fresh Thai basil, and a spicy shrimp-paste sambal. Bono's a bit sore because when the dish arrives, the jambal fish is missing. Also, the sambal isn't at all peanut-based, and though it's spicy, it's not enough to make us feel we've been slapped. As usual, Farish doesn't care. Good, bad, it's all the same to him. Nadezhda's still snickering.

My eyes search the restaurant. There's nothing special about it. The waiter looks a little stressed at how earnest Bono and I seem about analyzing their dishes. Then I see him: a man in his sixties smoking in the corner. There's a strange charisma about him. His posture is ramrod-straight, almost regal. He moves like a wise man. My heart is beating slightly faster. To clinch matters, he catches sight of me. There's a spark of recognition. Stubbing out his cigarette, he approaches our table. He asks where we're from, what we're doing in Lombok, which hotel we're staying at. We invite him to sit with us.

My instincts are proven correct: he's intelligent and his manners are warm. His sentences flow easily, though we're a bit startled that he immediately begins talking about the teachings of Islam.

"Now, I'm not an Islamic scholar," he says, "and have no intention of becoming one. Islam doesn't actually glorify religious scholarship that much. It's not about the laws that are set by certain authorities, but rather that which is dictated by the human heart."

He orders another cup of coffee, most likely his umpteenth.

"What's more," he adds, "societal values are always changing, and it's inevitable that interpretation of how to apply such laws will change over time."

Then he asks if we've heard of Al-Ghazali and his book on the manners of eating—the *Kitab Adab Al-Akl*. We shake our heads.

"The book," he says, "talks almost entirely about the etiquette of receiving guests. Serving others food provides an opportunity to express friendship. Etymologically, the English word 'companionship' means 'to share food with others.' Did you know that?"

No, we didn't.

It is Nadezhda who speaks first. "My father's half Acehnese, and as far as I know our etiquette demands that we serve guests food. Not just tidbits either, but a whole meal, like something one would sit at a table to eat. If we don't have anything suitable on hand, we'll do our best anyway."

I remember Rania saying something similar.

The man smiles. "Islam says the very same thing. To quote a well-known hadith: 'He who sleeps with a full stomach while his neighbor goes hungry is not a believer. It is only proper that he invite his neighbor to eat with him.'

"And there's another hadith," he continues, "that lists seven rules when it comes to eating. Rule number one: if you're eating with your elders or people in positions of authority, you shouldn't start eating first. Rule number two: in keeping with Persian tradition, you're not allowed to eat with others in silence; you must make conversation. Rule number three: you're not allowed to eat more than other people. Rule number four: you're not allowed to force others to eat. Rule number five: there's nothing wrong if someone washes his hands in a basin—if he's just finished eating alone, he's allowed to spit in it. Rule number six: you shouldn't embarrass someone by watching them eat. Rule number seven: if a guest has something in his hands that is considered *haram*, you shouldn't do anything about it.

"However"—and here he breaks into a smile—"times have changed, and we only heed those we consider relevant."

He stands.

"Oh," he adds before heading off to his motorcycle, which is parked outside. His gaze falls on Bono. "If the less-than-halal is the fare that you seek, try the street near your hotel. The taxi drivers will know the place. My Christian friends say what they serve there is every bit as good as the famous version you'll get at Bu Oka's in Bali."

35

CROCODILE

A crocodile is chasing me. I run through the swamps, swim across a river, dodge trees and tall grass, crouch behind large rocks, and hide in an abandoned warehouse. And just when I think the crocodile has given up, I feel something slithering over my feet and am bitten by a snake!

Nadezhda finally tells me her woes.

"I've fallen in love with someone."

I can feel my heart pounding. Suddenly I feel guilty for reading her diary.

"Who?"

She's quiet for a moment. My imagination goes wild. Is it Chrysander the Greek? Or Aravind the Indian?

"Just . . . someone," she says with some effort, for I know she really wants to say it—the name of the man she loves.

"Just tell me," I say. "It's me. You can tell me anything."

"He's Irish," she says. "He's a writer and art critic."

"Hmm," I say, though it makes perfect sense. "Where'd you meet him?"

"At an art festival in Berlin. I watched him in an onstage discussion with a famous historian. In fact, I attended the event specifically because he's someone I worship. I've been reading his writing for years and was always taken with the beauty of his language. He was always sharp, witty, elegant. After it was over I introduced myself and gave him my card. Before long, he e-mailed me. After e-mailing back and forth for a while, we agreed to meet in Vienna. And that's how it all started."

"Does he love you?"

"Very much." Her eyes fill with tears.

"So why aren't you two together?"

Nadezhda raises her head and looks at me as if I'm stupid and know nothing about the world.

"You really don't know?"

Suddenly I do know. I reach for her arm and pull her close.

"I'm so sorry," I say softly. "So . . . what are you guys going to do? Do you have a plan?"

"He has three kids," she says. Now she's really crying.

Though I don't know what it's like to sleep with someone who's married and has kids, it still disturbs me deeply to hear about it. He's had sex with his wife multiple times—often enough to produce three children. He must be reasonably happy and attracted to her. So why does he still feel something's missing in his life? Why fuck other women?

"He must have slept with other women before," I say. "You can't be the first, or the only one. He's probably been sleeping with a bunch of other women while he's been seeing you. I mean, you live far away, on a completely different continent, fourteen hours away by plane."

Nadezhda's sobs grow louder. "If you met him, you'd know he isn't a creep," she says haltingly. "He's so—oh, how do I put it in words? So . . . soulful."

"That's the most dangerous kind of man."

"What do you mean?"

"Men like that fall in love too easily."

"Why do you think that?"

I can't explain what I'm thinking at the moment. Something I read once in a very wise novel that brought me to tears.

I let Nadezhda lie on her bed, face buried in a pillow.

Half an hour later, realizing that she wants to be alone in her anguish, I leave the room and knock on Farish's door. When he opens it I immediately put my arms around him.

The next morning, when Nadezhda is already showered and dressed, I decide that the moment has come.

"You know," I say cautiously, "a guy like that will always be restless. And he'll always have doubts about life. He'll search and he'll search. He's easily moved. He's melancholy. Who knows whether he's searching for sadness, or beauty, or both. He wants to fall in love. Or he's fallen in love with the concept of falling in love. If the source of his inspiration starts to lose its luster, he'll search for someone he thinks understands him, someone else who's searching for what he's searching for, someone who loves ideas, who lives for the journey, who's captivated by words. I feel like that's what's happened between you and . . . what's his name?"

"Gabriel."

"How long has this been going on?"

"Two and a half years."

"How many times have you seen each other?"

"Eleven times. Maybe twelve."

"Where?"

"Lots of places. All over Europe."

"So . . . he's never come to Jakarta?"

"Not yet. He needs a good excuse to come to Asia, let alone Jakarta. He's a columnist for a magazine, and he has to get permission from his editor. And his wife."

I take a deep breath. "I know it'll be hard for you, but you have to break off this relationship. The sooner the better."

"But I always go to Europe."

"You don't realize it, but you're the one who's doing all the work, buying plane tickets, taking long flights, paying for hotels—unless he's helping with the costs. Meanwhile, all he has to do is fly in from . . . where does he live?"

"London."

"There, see? He has it good, using his family as an excuse—the same family he's abusing."

"I always refuse when he offers to pay. I don't want to feel like a mistress."

"Don't you see? You're already a mistress. Come on. You deserve better than this."

I let our conversation sink in. Suddenly she takes my hand in hers and holds it very tightly.

"Yesterday, Bono told me he's in love with me," she says.

This time my heart almost falls out of my chest. "He's probably just kidding around. You know him. You can never tell whether he's being serious."

Nadezhda says nothing, and I know immediately that she's not joking.

"That's the problem, honey," she says at last. "People I'm not in love with are always falling in love with me, and everyone I fall in love with belongs to someone else."

I'm reminded of what I read in Nadezhda's diary. It's the same story: her and Aravind, her and Gabriel. Both are writers she admires. Both send her letters and set her adrift with words—elegant words, achingly true words, words that turn you to jelly.

But there's another heartbreak involved here; and it grieves me, too. It's the broken heart of someone I equally cherish whose love has been spurned.

Then I think of my relationship with Farish and how he's changed. How I've changed.

Could it be that I'm the lucky one?

For the first time ever, Bono goes out to eat alone.

"He's going to the 'secret' restaurant that guy was raving about," says Farish. "The one that's supposed to be way better than Bu Oka's restaurant in Ubud."

"Impossible," declares Nadezhda. "No one can compete with Bu Oka."

"There's no sign, apparently," Farish continues. "And the location's unclear. Tucked away in some alley. It'll take some maneuvering in order to get there."

When Bono returns he acts as if nothing has happened. He shows us photos on his iPad. It's a tiny, cramped eatery with a shady tree out in front. There are four long tables with six benches each, a specially allocated area for displaying the restaurant's wares, and an open-air kitchen in the back. I see a few motorcycles parked outside the restaurant and a dog chilling out on the terrace.

Even more odd are the photos of the food. They show skewers of satay with pork chunks so red they look like they've been painted, and pork that's being cooked in the same manner as *Ayam Singgang*. There's a jumbled heap of fried pig skins and satay of a more civilized color—akin to sate buntel—made of ground meat. There's beef curry, spicy shredded chicken, tempeh in sambal sauce. I see no evidence of a suckling pig that rivals poor, besmirched Bu Oka's.

"Was it good?" I ask.

Bono is quiet for a moment before he replies. "How do I explain? It doesn't taste like what you get at Bu Oka's. That's all."

I smile. Then I remember Nadezhda's dilemma and I'm sad again.

⁂

About an hour later we stop at a restaurant specializing in Central Javanese cuisine. Definitely Javanese. Just look at the menu: *Nasi Semur Daging, Nasi Rawon, Nasi Pecel, Mi Bakso, Es Dawet, Wedang Jahe*, and so on. We place our orders.

"What are we doing here?" asks Nadezhda when our dishes arrive. Her mood has changed.

"People say the food is good," says Bono.

It's the first time he's spoken directly to Nadezhda since she rejected his love.

It's the first time Nadezhda doesn't respond to Bono with a bunch of rhetoric. She looks down and begins tucking into her *Soto Ayam*.

⁂

We're outside a small store, waiting for the tofu vendor to fry up our order, when my phone vibrates. It's a text message.

It's Irma. I'm taken by surprise.

Aruna, are you in Lombok?

How did she find out? Then I remember: I told Priya I was going to Lombok to eat myself to death. Shit. I have to respond.

Yes, I am. How are you?

When are you coming back?

Tomorrow.

Did you see?

See what?

In the newspaper? Or on TV in the news?

Haven't picked up a newspaper in the past two days. Haven't watched TV either.

I wait. She doesn't text again.

Should I be nervous? One thing I know for sure: I want nothing more to do with an organization that's screwed me over so royally.

❦

Tahu Lombok—literally, "Lombok tofu"—is as soft as silk and melts in one's mouth, like the smoothest of custards. The tofu squares are put into a box, and we share, using toothpicks as forks. The store behind the tofu vendor sells more food: *abon*, honey, and salted duck eggs, both baked and boiled. There are various kinds of dodol, too: pineapple, jackfruit, and durian.

So intrigued are we with the tofu that our driver takes us to a modest house nearby where people make the stuff. When we peer into a small, dark room in the back, we find a young woman working there. She is keeping watch over tofu slices lined up in rows on tall shelves constructed from seven wooden stakes fastened crosswise to each other.

In front of the shelves are two baskets filled with fresh tofu. The pieces are put into plastic bags, and in two more days they'll be ready to be sold at Cakranegara Market.

Shortly afterward, we're brought to another house belonging to a family of tempeh-makers. From the way the couple and their teenage children welcome us, you'd think we were old friends. On the veranda, they point out with some pride, the fruits of their labor spread out on straw mats.

"It's the same process they use everywhere to make tempeh," says the man of the house as he serves us tea.

The soybeans are rinsed, soaked, shelled, and steamed until tender, then poured into a large, shallow basket and fanned until cool. Next, they are molded and placed inside plastic wrappers, after which the plastic is pierced with a long, pointy straw or a fork to make small holes. So the tempeh can breathe, like a living creature.

Afterward we head to the district of Ampenan, where we come across a part of the old city that strikes a pang to the marrow. Buildings whose beauty, like other Dutch colonial buildings we've seen, remains undimmed by the layers of mildew and dust. Windows and doors of pale blue and salad green. Streets shaded by palm trees.

It's midday and the roads are deserted, as if they've never seen cars or people. This part of the city seems to stand alone, untouched by modernity.

"There are a lot of Peranakan Chinese on this street," our driver says. "And there are lots of Arabs on the others. They're all store owners. There's the Bodhi Dharma Monastery, which is two hundred years old, on that side, over there. Then there's the coastal Buginese district—the fishermen's district. And there's also a Malay district with places that sell grilled fish and instant noodles—warung-type food."

But just about a hundred yards from where our car has stopped is an arched gateway, decisively cutting off the older district from the rest of the city, with an enormous intersection connecting five roads. A five-way intersection: hence the name, Simpang Lima. Aglow with the present.

Something in Nadezhda seems to give way. She asks if we can go back to the hotel.

Once we're back in our room, I turn on the TV. Nadezhda immediately flops down on her bed and busies herself on her phone. God knows what she's doing. Maybe she's chatting with the married jerk she's in love with, who won't shell out a single cent to see her in Jakarta, who isn't interested in where she lives or her culture or her family, and who probably secretly doesn't care.

I ignore her, this friend of mine who falls in love at the drop of a hat. I've already told her what I think.

It takes about fifteen minutes before the Metro TV channel begins showing the latest news. A corruption scandal involving a member of parliament. The murder of an army general's son. A plane crash near Makassar that's killed 216 people, including the pilot, copilot, and crew. I watch until the program is over, all the while paying close attention to the news ticker at the bottom of the screen. Nothing at all about avian flu.

Two hours later we head to the place specializing in Taliwang cuisine. It's the one the guy at that first restaurant mumbled at us. The layout reminds me of a Sundanese restaurant, with tables in low bamboo shelters strewn around a garden. I don't pay too much attention to my surroundings because I feel like something's not quite right. What was Irma talking about? But I'm too proud to text her. I ask Bono and Farish to scan news sites on their phones. Still nothing related to avian flu.

When we get back to the room, I decide to text Irma after all.

Irma, what news were you talking about?

Twenty minutes pass before Irma replies.

Can I call you?

Sure.

Three minutes later Irma calls.

"Aruna," she says, her voice trembling, "Leon was on that plane."

Ten seconds. Twenty seconds. Maybe a full minute that feels like an eternity passes before I'm able to speak.

"But . . . surely, Leon's still . . ."

"No, Aruna. Leon's gone."

I feel something shatter inside me, breaking into a million pieces.

Amazingly, Farish permits me to mourn for the man I once worshipped. When I run to the hotel lobby and slip into his arms with another man's name on my lips, he pulls me close, strokes my hair, and whispers, "It's okay, it's okay. He didn't feel anything. It all must have happened so fast." There is not the faintest sign of resentment or jealousy.

But there's always a disparity between news and fact, history and story. That night, I cry until my tears run dry.

In the morning, the details of Leon's last days start to come to light.

After Lombok, which he visited after Pontianak, he went back to Jakarta. Because Farish and I had backed out of the project, he had to take on the workload we'd left behind.

Five weeks after that he was asked to go to Makassar. Which is fishy from the start, I think. The cases of avian flu in Makassar were reported at least two weeks before Farish and I started our own investigation. What was the point of him going to Makassar so belatedly? But this is no time to trouble myself with unproductive thoughts about conspiracies and the like.

We already know the rest. Fate picked that ill-fated plane out for him, and he was cast into the depths of the open sea with 215 other people. And that, most likely, only after the flames and the impact of the crash had completely incinerated his body.

From late morning to midday, I walk around in a daze, like a motherless chick. Bono and Nadezhda seem unsure of how to behave toward me. True, the situation's a strange one—Leon wasn't anything to me, strictly speaking, and as such, expressing condolences seems both too much and inappropriate. Yet they all know he had a special place in my heart.

In the midst of it all stands Farish, steadfast and kind. Not once does he make me feel guilty, or even a little ridiculous, for weeping over another man who never made an effort to know me when he could have.

At half past eleven Bono and Nadezhda go out for lunch.

The two of us are left alone in the lobby—Farish and me. He holds my hand tightly in his. He knows food is the last thing on my mind.

"How about we visit the hospital nearby?" he suggests out of nowhere. "Just for fun. There's a public hospital down the road, not even a mile away. It looks pretty big."

The thought crosses my mind that he's crazy, taking me to a hospital when Leon's just died; when his body's been smashed to pieces, never to be found; when he can't even be laid out in a mortuary, bathed, anointed, and given a proper burial.

But it gradually dawns on me that I miss going to hospitals, that I miss the sense that I may be of use, that I miss the responsibility of being someone trained to wipe out disease. Maybe this is one way of paying my respects to Leon, whom I had no power to save.

Unexpectedly, I nod. We still have time. Our flight doesn't leave until five.

⚜

The sight that greets us at the hospital can't be described in words. Order lies in ruins everywhere I look. The stairs are broken in places and covered from top to bottom in moss. The walls and floors are filthy and coated in dust. The ICU unit has "Staff Only" printed above the entrance yet is wide open and packed with visitors, as is the elevator, despite the "Only For Patients, Oxygen, and Food Trolleys" sign above it. The leftover food from patients' trays lie rotting outside their rooms. There's a sea of patients' relatives sleeping in hordes in the corridors, with their straw mats, prayer rugs, and clothes. Food and drink spill all over the floor. Empty plastic food containers are strewn across the lawn.

But two things make me especially queasy. The first is a six-bed inpatient room with at least fifteen people surrounding one of the beds as they pray over a patient in critical condition. They're scandalously noisy. And they're everywhere: congregating at the patient's bedside, sitting in front of or next to the other patients' beds, spreading out mats and sitting on the floor and leaning against the wall. Several of them have brought drink cartons and bottled water with them.

And this is all happening in the presence of a large sign on the wall that clearly states:

WE REQUEST THE COOPERATION
OF PATIENT FAMILY MEMBERS & VISITORS

1. OUR PATIENTS NEED REST IN ORDER TO RECOVER. PLEASE BE QUIET.
2. TO KEEP THE ROOMS ORDERLY, PLEASE DO NOT BRING IN CARPETS OR MATS.
3. ONE VISITOR PER PERSON.

POLICY OF NURSING MANAGEMENT DIII KLP1 & III
THE YARSI MATARAM NURSING SCHOOL
2013

The state of the Infectious Diseases Unit is just as nauseating. I deduce from the whiteboard in the hall that there are no avian flu patients, only hepatitis patients. A little before this, at the unit entrance, I felt my energy level rising when I saw the nurse's station, which looked reasonably neat and clean, and the first nurse I'd seen since arriving at the hospital.

Farish and I request permission to look around a bit. As usual I explain that we're from the Ministry of Livestock.

"Any recent cases of avian flu, nurse?" I ask once we're done looking around and are walking away from the area where the confirmed hepatitis cases are being treated.

"No, none," she answers.

But then her colleague, who's just emerged from behind a curtain, whispers something to her.

The nurse changes her story. "Oh, right. Actually, there were."

"When? About seven weeks ago?"

"Oh, way before that. About six months ago."

"How long were they treated here?"

"They weren't. By the time they were brought here, they'd passed away."

And this she says in an even voice, without the slightest hint of empathy, eyes still glued to her records book.

"But the room was quarantined, wasn't it?"

"Not really," says the nurse.

Not really? My hands tremble. I almost can't believe it. Even before my anger subsides, I see—and this almost makes me faint—a mangy cat saunter into the unit past the nurse's station and head right into patient treatment area.

I point a panicked finger at the cat's footprints. "Nurse, nurse! There's a cat in the patient treatment area!"

The nurse doesn't budge. "Oh, that must be Miss Yeller," she says calmly. "She often comes by. We all know her."

❦

I feel like I've taken part in a pilgrimage, thanks to Bono and Nadezhda, who go on and on about this dish and that: how this luffa squash was more tender than that luffa squash; how this fried pigeon was crispier than that fried pigeon; how this oyster sauce tasted fishier than that oyster sauce. It turns out they went back to Ampenan, to Jalan Pabean, and ate at a Peranakan restaurant there.

Meanwhile, my hands are still trembling so much I can't hold my water glass. I feel weak and nauseous. I scold myself. *You aren't fit to eat. Not with that excessive appetite of yours and a brain that thinks of nothing but food 24/7. You aren't fit to be blessed with good digestion and an educated palate. You aren't fit to live—not when others are being ambushed by stray cats on their deathbeds or soaring through the air to their graves.*

That evening, as we're once again waiting for a flight at an airport, all I want to do is return home to the things that give me peace: the warmth of Gulali's body, my father's grave, and maybe even my mother's house.

36

Doing and Dreaming

This is my favorite dream.

One day my grandmother is telling me about certain months in her childhood, when the twilight hours would last for ages and be drenched in violet. "At times," she says, "when you walked toward the horizon, away from the call to prayer summoning men and beasts homeward, it was as if you were drowning in the orange of the setting sun. It was as if you were in another world—one that made you believe that you had to befriend spirits if you wanted to prosper in this earthly life. The twilight and the spirits themselves were friends, as all shape-shifting creatures are. And you'd see for yourself how a tranquil afternoon would bring a glorious morning the next day. And this is why people always pair pagi *with* sore, *siang* with malam—morning with evening, noon with night. Aruna, I bet someday restaurants will be naming themselves after these pairs." (And of course, she's right: Pagi Sores and Siang Malams—you'll find them all over the country.)*

Then the dream starts all over again. Sometimes a few details change. But whenever I reach that point—when I behold my grandmother's face, surrounded by her beloved turkeys—I realize just how much I know. I know things that have never been uttered or acknowledged, things never even written down in secret to be discovered later, things that have nothing to do with how much my grandmother loves me.

I know she loved my father—not because he was her youngest or most like her in appearance but because he was the only one of her children to give her a grandchild. She also loved my father because he was willing to yield to his wife and became a quiet man in order to do so. I know my mother didn't like my grandmother, and I also know my mother loved another man and thought my father wasn't smart or ambitious enough for her. I know my father didn't really like my mother, mainly because he knew she looked down on him and that she was her father's daughter (and Pekak I Wayan Gede, her father, certainly wasn't the most sincere person in the world; everything he did was for his image, for prestige, for everything but love). But what prevented my father from leaving my mother was how much she wanted a child, even if he wasn't sure he was ready to become a father. My mother really was the wiser one in this matter.

And I know that only when I was born did my father understand what love meant.

A year has passed since that trip to Lombok. I don't believe in celebrations, whether they're for birthdays or wedding anniversaries, religious holidays or holidays in memory of specific individuals.

But exactly one year after that harrowing day, the day of Leon's death, I revisit a few things: hospital reports (I kept some files for myself), the bills from hotels and restaurants we visited, the photos I've downloaded onto my computer, the notebooks I was keeping at the time.

In one of the notebooks, I find incomplete rosters of curiosities: recipes, the composition of various spice mixtures, restaurant names, street names, names of acronyms for this organization or that, names of chefs and restaurant owners, names of actors and actresses I liked, names of television dramas I was addicted to, snatches of conversation, a few stanzas of poetry about solitude, some vague charts, an unfinished short story, a few swear words I won't mention here, three mentions of Leon and at least a dozen of Farish.

Naturally, a few things have changed in my life. Farish and I have agreed that at our age we don't need to announce that we're officially a couple—we're not in middle school or high school anymore. After much consideration we've decided to live together, unmarried, with all the social ramifications thereof. We don't want to get married for a while. We have so many friends who had kids, then got divorced because they never experienced what it was like to live as a couple.

It turns out that forgetting Leon isn't a hard thing to do because, really, nothing ever happened between us—except for me stupidly letting myself become "an owl pining for the moon." But my outlook on death is still the same. I've visited his grave twice because, however you look at it, he did die young, and so tragically, and that seems a great injustice to me. Especially since he once made my heart race and my head spin, and such things still deserve gratitude.

My outlook on work, however, has changed a bit. At the beginning of 2014, Indonesia officially became a producer and exporter of vaccines, and of the seven vaccines being developed nationwide—for tuberculosis, hepatitis B and C, rotavirus, HIV, hemorrhagic dengue fever, and avian influenza—the most advances have been made when it comes to avian influenza. Yet I'm no longer caught up in every new move the virus decides to make. The most important thing for me was finding an opportunity to "set things right" with Irma, whom I'm still fond of, though she's decided to remain at DOCIR despite the hot mess that it is. We met at a Turkish restaurant, ordered various *mezze* and grilled lamb, and drank glass after glass of apple tea. She asked me to come back and work for her, as my own agent, not OneWorld's. But I refused.

"Let's just be eating buddies," I said. "It's more fun that way."

My relationship with my mother is improving as well. I see her once every two weeks. Even though our opinions frequently clash, and she expresses hers harshly more often than not, she's never once commented on my unorthodox lifestyle. Gradually, my love for her has turned into what it wasn't before—now, there's a certain equality between us that puts me at rest. Sometimes we cook together and exchange recipes.

Two times a week I swim. Once a week I have a meal with Nadezhda, who I know is still secretly seeing that cretin, Gabriel, and Bono, who is busy starting up Siria II. I've invested in Siria II. Not a lot, but enough to make my opinions heard. Sometimes, the three of us conduct kitchen experiments based on our travels. Appetizers reminiscent of ko kue and chai kue, but with slightly different fillings and sauces; a soup reminiscent of pindang patin, but with a Western touch; a French-style salad with a pinch of Thai basil.

Based on my observations, as well as Nadezhda's, it appears Bono's gotten quite close with a woman who's apparently a foodie as well. But he's also gotten close with a middle-aged Caucasian woman who visits the bar at Siria almost three times a week. Some people think he's going out with both of them. Some people also say he's dating someone who lives overseas. We're not interested in speculating. We're just relieved he's finally made friends outside of our triangle.

I no longer wear a size large or extra-large. My jeans are even a size small. Like Nadezhda, my new religion is Pilates. Farish and I have set up a small consulting firm. Sometimes SoWeFit asks for our help on health-related projects. In keeping with my promise to myself, I agree only to projects that don't involve Irma.

And even though Farish and I never talk about children, much less plan to have any, I remain open to the possibility of becoming a mother.

There really are, it would seem, things we do and things we dream. I want to live both.

NOTES

I am indebted to several texts on food and wine for information and inspiration:

- Jean Anthelme Brillat-Savarin's *The Physiology of Taste: Or Meditations on Transcendental Gastronomy* (translated by M. F. K. Fisher with an introduction by Bill Buford; New York: Vintage, 2011)
- Felipe Fernández-Armesto's *Food: A History* (London: Pan Books, 2002)
- D. Johnson-Davies's translation of *Al-Ghazali on the Manners Relating to Eating (Kitab adab al-akl)* (Cambridge: the Islamic Texts Society, 2000)
- Muriel Barbery's *The Gourmet: A Novel* (London: Gallic Books, 2009)
- Daniel Boulud's *Letters to a Young Chef* (New York: Basic Books, 2006)
- Jonathan Safran Foer's *Eating Animals* (London: Penguin Books, 2011)
- Michael Pollan's *In Defense of Food: An Eater's Manifesto* (New York: Penguin Press, 2008)
- Peter Kaminsky's *Culinary Intelligence: The Art of Eating Healthy (and Really Well)* (New York: Vintage, 2013)

☐ Steven Poole's *You Aren't What You Eat: Fed Up with Gastroculture* (London: Union Books, 2012)

☐ Jane Kramer's "The Reporter's Kitchen" in *Secret Ingredients: The New Yorker Book of Food and Drink* (edited by David Remnick; New York: Modern Library, 2009)

☐ Jay McInerney's *Bacchus and Me: Adventures in the Wine Cellar* (New York: Vintage, 2002)

☐ Kevin Zraly's *Windows on the World: Complete Wine Course, 2008 Edition* (New York: Sterling Publishing, 2007).

Additional information was gleaned from mailing lists and articles online.

The stanza of poetry in chapter 33 is excerpted from Farid ud-Din Attar's *The Conference of the Birds* (translated by Afkham Darbandi and Dick Davis; London: Penguin Classics, 1984).

I-tsing's description of Palembang is excerpted from Paul Michel Munoz's *Early Kingdoms of the Indonesian Archipelago and the Malay Peninsula* (Singapore: Editions Didier Millet, 2006), which in turn was adapted from a passage in I-tsing's *A Record of the Buddhist Religion as Practiced in India and the Malay Archipelago (AD 671–695)* (translated by J. Takakusu; Oxford: Clarendon Press, 1896).

Nadezhda's analysis of group sports and the concept of kitsch was inspired by "Sports Chatter" and "Travels in Hyperreality" in Umberto Eco's *Travels in Hyperreality* (London: Picador, 1987).

Nadezhda's quote about grief is excerpted from Joan Didion's *The Year of Magical Thinking* (New York: Vintage, 2007).

The first course on Bono's menu at Aditya Bari's abode was inspired by Jason Atherton's signature dish from Pollen Street Social in London.

The parts about kulat mushrooms and naniura were inspired by my talks with leading Indonesian food activist Lisa Virgiano.

The idea for foie gras noodles, Wagyu-beef-fried rice, and spicy stir-fried bitter beans atop a sliver of fried tuna belly sprang from the creations of Adhika Maxi, chef of the Union Brasserie, Bakery, & Bar in Jakarta. I am greatly indebted to him and his wife, Karen Carlotta (K. C.), one of the finest pastry chefs in Indonesia.

The tips for serving Indonesian dishes with a Western touch were inspired by an episode of *Kulinaria*, which I co-hosted with William Wongso and which aired in 2003 on Kompas TV.

Information about the 1918 Pandemic spreading to Java and Kalimantan was drawn from the abstract of a study entitled "Menguji Ketahanan Bangsa: Sejarah Pandemi Influenza 1918 di Hindia Belanda," sent to me by Pandu Riono.

ACKNOWLEDGMENTS

My gratitude to Pandu Riono, for his valuable contributions on epidemiology and avian flu; to culinary maestro William Wongso, whose knowledge of flavors and spices is second to none; and to Lisa Virgiano, whose dedication to this country's cuisine never fails to inspire me.

To Wahyu Muryadi, for his contributions on Madura and places to eat in Bangkalan and Pamekasan; to Geumala Yatim, who took Maggy and me to some of the best restaurants in Banda Aceh; and to Nezar Patria, for telling me much about the culinary history of his ancestors.

To Zinnia Nizar-Sompie, that most gifted pastry chef, who's done a beautiful job of designing my website and who has always been a great help to me; to Ara Nizar, who has also been very generous with her time and energy; and to Cecil Mariani, my loyal eating companion, for being her amazing self and for her ceaseless good spirits.

To Katarina Monika, Christa Linggar, and Michael Chrisyanto at SOSJ for giving me such a gorgeous first book cover; to Nic Schaeffer for his invaluable artistic touch; and to Barata Dwiputra for the eye-catching illustration of the iconic chicken noodle (*mi ayam*) bowl.

To Siti Gretiani, my awe-inspiring Indonesian publisher, for her support, guidance, and acuity; to Hetih Rusli, who has graciously helped perfect this novel; and to my friends at Gramedia Pustaka Utama, especially Dionisius Wisnu, for all their support and help.

To my translator, Tiffany Tsao, for her grace, meticulousness, and all in all brilliance. For breathing new life into this novel. And for her patience and friendship, which mean a lot to me.

To the soulful Gabriella Page-Fort of AmazonCrossing, for her friendship, support, and continued faith in me. And, as ever, to Kirby Kim, my agent at Janklow and Nesbit, for finding my books a place in this world.

To Winny Roesad, for her friendship and generosity, and to various friends for love and companionship and food, at home and abroad, especially Nesya and Marvin Suwarso, Peter Milne, Winfred Hutabarat, Yenni Kwok, Amrih Widodo, Inez Nimpuno, Maya Kono, Monica Tanuhandaru, Lauren Hardie, Avi Mahaningtyas, Poppy Barkah, Dael Allison, Wim Manuhutu, Maya Liem, Willemijn Lamp, Sylvia Dornseiffer, Irfan Kortschak, Kadek Krishna Adidharma, Sarita Newson, Tash Aw, Aamer Hussein, Margaret Scott, Katrin Sohns, Amit Khanna, and Ken Chen. To Anthony, especially, for supplying me with books, films, and music and for making me smile.

To my parents, who taught me how to eat; and to Sachiroh, for twenty-two years of love, support, and protection. To Isabella "Belly" Queen of Spain, my loyal writing companion for thirteen years and the world's most beautiful cat. My deepest love and thanks to Nadia Larasati Djohan, precious daughter, best friend, and ultimate dining companion—and recently, a frighteningly competent literary advisor to her mother.

Last and foremost, to the two incredible women who have accompanied me on my travels, Ening Nurjanah and Maggy Horhoruw. I love you gals.

ABOUT THE AUTHOR

Laksmi Pamuntjak is an award-winning Indonesian novelist, poet, food writer, and journalist. Her debut novel, *Amba*, won Germany's LiBeraturpreis, was short-listed for the 2012 Khatulistiwa Literary Award, and appeared on the *Frankfurter Allgemeine Zeitung*'s Top 8 list of the best books of the Frankfurt Book Fair in 2015. She is also the author of two collections of poetry and five editions of the bestselling and award-winning *Jakarta Good Food Guide*, and she has served as translator for Indonesian poet and essayist Goenawan Mohamad.

Cofounder of Jakarta's Aksara Bookstore, Pamuntjak was selected as the Indonesian representative for Poetry Parnassus at the 2012 London Olympics. She currently divides her time between Berlin and Jakarta. Visit the author at www.laksmipamuntjak.com.

ABOUT THE TRANSLATOR

Photo © 2015 Leah Diprose

Tiffany Tsao is a writer, translator, and literary critic. She spent her formative years in Singapore and Indonesia before moving to the United States, where she received a PhD in English from the University of California, Berkeley. She currently resides in Sydney, Australia. Her translations of Indonesian short stories, poetry, and essays have been featured in *Asymptote, LONTAR, Cordite Poetry Review, Asia Literary Review,* and the anthology *BooksActually's Gold Standard 2016.* Her translation of Dee Lestari's novel *Paper Boats* was published in 2017 by AmazonCrossing, and her translation of Eka Kurniawan's short story "Caronang" was nominated for the Pushcart Prize. Her debut novel, *The Oddfits,* was published in 2016.